KISS ME TWICE

Thank the good Lord, she was no lady. That didn't help her think of anything to say. She should probably be nonchalant about the kiss. After all, she approved of free love, and that included kissing, didn't it?

The problem was that Loretta didn't feel the least bit nonchalant. She felt spectacular, actually, and that sort of precluded nonchalance.

Malachai mumbled something.

After clearing her throat, Loretta said, "I beg your pardon?" Then she wished she hadn't used the word *beg*. It came too close to what she wanted to do, which was to beg Malachai to kiss her again. She retained enough pride to know that begging the man for *anything* would violate every female human principle she held dear.

But he had just perpetrated a kiss from which Loretta's senses still reeled. And she had rather hoped the delicious pleasure she'd felt from the kiss had been shared by him. . .

BOOK YOUR PLACE ON OUR WEBSITE AND MAKE THE READING CONNECTION!

We've created a customized website just for our very special readers, where you can get the inside scoop on everything that's going on with Zebra, Pinnacle and Kensington books.

When you come online, you'll have the exciting opportunity to:

- View covers of upcoming books
- Read sample chapters
- Learn about our future publishing schedule (listed by publication month *and author*)
- Find out when your favorite authors will be visiting a city near you
- Search for and order backlist books from our online catalog
- Check out author bios and background information
- Send e-mail to your favorite authors
- Meet the Kensington staff online
- Join us in weekly chats with authors, readers and other guests
- Get writing guidelines
- AND MUCH MORE!

Visit our website at http://www.kensingtonbooks.com

A PERFECT ROMANCE

ANNE ROBINS

ZEBRA BOOKS
Kensington Publishing Corp.
http://www.kensingtonbooks.com

This book is dedicated to my daughter Anni Oshita, who over-heard the conversation between the Moor man and the other guy in a doughnut shop across the street from Pasadena City College about ten years ago. I knew I'd be able to use it in a book someday!

ZEBRA BOOKS are published by

Kensington Publishing Corp.
850 Third Avenue
New York, NY 10022

All Kensington titles, imprints and distributed lines are available at special quantity discounts for bulk purchases for sales promotion, premiums, fund-raising, educational or institutional use.

Special book excerpts or customized printings can also be created to fit specific needs. For details, write or phone the office of the Kensington Special Sales Manager: Kensington Publishing Corp., 850 Third Avenue, New York, NY 10022. Attn. Special Sales Department. Phone: 1-800-221-2647.

Zebra and the Z logo Reg. U.S. Pat. & TM Off.

First Printing: November 2004
10 9 8 7 6 5 4 3 2 1

Printed in the United States of America

ONE

April 14, 1912

Even after the ship left Southampton, Loretta Linden firmly believed she'd been put on this earth to save it from itself.

Once the enormous liner, the largest ship the world had ever seen, had been sailing through Atlantic waters for a couple of days, her beliefs suffered a dramatic change. It became depressingly clear to her that she wouldn't be able to save even herself, much less the rest of the world.

When the unsinkable *Titanic* scraped against the legendary iceberg shortly before midnight on April 14, gashing a 300-foot hole in its side, Loretta's only reaction was gratitude that the ship's rolling and rocking had ceased. She actually prayed the cursed ship *would* sink; at least she'd be out of her misery. Later, this reaction would shock her, as she'd been in the habit of considering herself an optimistic, unselfish sort of person, and not one to wish disaster on anyone.

"Miss Linden!"

Loretta turned over in her berth and attempted to focus on the door, an action that made her head hurt and her stomach lurch. Miss Marjorie Mac-

Tavish, the stewardess who had been seeing to all of Loretta's wants and needs, in spite of Loretta's best efforts to resist her, stuck her head in the room, looking considerably less serene than usual. Loretta recalled the crunching noise, lurch, and overall ship-shudderings of a few minutes previous, and deduced that Miss MacTavish had come to reassure her that things were peachy with the vessel.

She intended to say something like "Yes?" or "What is it?" but could only manage a groan that lifted slightly at the end.

To Loretta's surprise, Miss MacTavish rushed up to the berth and commenced shaking her shoulder. The sensation was most unpleasant and Loretta frowned at the intruder. If she'd been stronger, she might have struck her.

"Ye mun rise, Miss Linden! The ship has duffed agang an iceberg. She's foundering and ye mun get to a lifeboat."

Loretta's eyelids hurt when she blinked at the woman. The ship had duffed agang an iceberg? She'd never heard Miss MacTavish in so Scottish a mode. "You mean we bumped into something?" She croaked the words, but the stewardess understood.

"Aye! That's what I'm tellin' ye! Get up and gang aboon!"

Aha. So that's why her stomach had quit heaving. How gratifying—although Loretta wasn't sure what ganging aboon entailed.

With a great effort of will, she said, "Don't mind me. I'll just rest here for a little while." Rather she die now and get it over with than attempt to make it to a lifeboat and resume her dreadful seasickness. Anyhow, the *Titanic* was unsinkable. All the advertisements had said so.

Miss MacTavish's lips pressed together. Loretta was amazed to note that the stewardess could express anger—and to a first-class passenger, at that. She might have been pleased with this demonstration of humanity on Miss MacTavish's part had the latter not then grabbed her by the arm and begun tugging.

"No, please," Loretta whimpered, fearing for her stomach.

"Stop your fittering and get out of bed this instant, Miss Linden! Quit daidling! You mun come immediately! The ship is foundering!"

"Nonsense. The newspapers all call the *R.M.S. Titanic* unsinkable." While Loretta knew better than to believe everything she read in the newspapers, she'd yet become accustomed to regarding the ship as perfectly sound.

Another yank, this one so hard Loretta's upper body slid off the berth. In order to prevent herself from crashing to the floor, Loretta swung her legs around and braced herself with her feet. "What are you doing?" The question was more of a whine than she'd intended it to be.

"Saving your bluidy life! Rise up and get ye to a lifeboat *now!*"

Loretta blinked at Miss MacTavish, whom she had never heard use bad language before. She noticed that the other woman's cheeks were flushed, her hazel-green eyes blazed with some passionate emotion, and her hair, usually impeccably dressed, was falling out of its bun and making her look younger than she generally did.

"Where's your cap?" Loretta had become well acquainted with Miss MacTavish in the four days the ship had been on the water. She knew full well that the stewardess never went anywhere unless she was scrupulously groomed, complete with starched white apron and chaste white cap.

Miss MacTavish's hand flew to her head and she patted wildly at her fiery red hair for a moment before she shouted, "Och, what does my bluidy cap matter? Scutter up now or ye'll croak in your berth, and *then* who'll carry Mrs. Pankhurst's torch?"

When she and the stewardess had first met, Loretta had come away with the impression that she had rather annoyed Miss MacTavish by endeavoring to enlist her in the cause of women's suffrage. Miss MacTavish, although irked, had not overtly demonstrated the least indication of her feelings. Until this minute, Loretta had not understood that Miss MacTavish could succumb to sarcasm. Mrs. Emmeline Pankhurst was one of Loretta's heroines.

The stewardess's words stung, but they also served to jar Loretta into an understanding of the present crisis. If Miss MacTavish could lose her temper, something was definitely amiss. Loretta couldn't make herself care.

"Here!" Miss MacTavish snapped, sounding much less Scots now that Loretta had obeyed her at last. "Don your spectacles. Ye'll be of no use to anyone if you canna see."

Be of use. The words sank into Loretta's fuzzy head and ignited the process of waking up. *Be of use.* Yes. That's what was important now, not her seasickness. She might be of use to someone else. Loretta's primary aim in life, and not merely because it annoyed her parents and her other stuffy relations, was to be of use to her fellow human beings on this earth . . . at least the female half thereof. The males could cursed well take care of themselves.

Hooking the gold eyepieces over her ears, she

bucked up minimally. "Thank you." Her cabin came into such clear focus that she had to close her eyes for a moment and allow her stomach to settle and her head to stop swirling. To her amazement, both cooperated for the first time in two days.

"Here. Don your shoon. It's frightfu' bluthrie up there." Miss MacTavish hurled Loretta's shoes at her.

"Where are Mrs. Golightly and Eunice?"

Before she had become so very ill, Loretta had decided to make a special project of the poor Yorkshire woman, Isabel Golightly, and her six-year-old daughter Eunice, whom she'd met on the dock at Southampton when Eunice had stumbled and scraped her knee in Loretta's vicinity. Eunice was a charming girl and an intelligent one, and Loretta judged Isabel to be among the more downtrodden women of the world. She had figuratively rubbed her hands in delight at having such a worthy cause to occupy her thoughts and actions during the voyage to America.

That was before she'd succumbed to *mal de mer*, a malady Loretta had assumed she'd be above, since it hadn't plagued her on the crossing from New York to Southampton several months earlier. Showed how much she knew about ocean travel.

"I dinna know. They're probably doon aboot in third class." Miss MacTavish's voice was hard and she added a sniff to the end of her sentence. She didn't approve of Loretta's having deliberately descended into steerage and consorting with the poor immigrant families crammed in down there. She more particularly didn't approve of Loretta's interest in Mrs. Golightly and her daughter.

She'd told Loretta—politely, of course—that a woman of her high social standing, even if she was an

American, had no business mingling with the hoi polloi. Loretta had set her straight, or tried to, in no uncertain terms.

Miss MacTavish, being a tough nut and firmly attached to her native British class distinctions, had remained unconvinced by Loretta's impassioned lectures and her forward-thinking egalitarian principles.

Feeling minutely stronger, Loretta stood. She did so cautiously and braced herself with her fingers on her night table. Her stomach didn't rebel, which she considered a positive sign. After taking two deep breaths, she ventured another question. "Did the ship really hit something?"

"An iceberg." Miss MacTavish had gone to Loretta's small closet. She reached in and grabbed a woolen coat. Turning, she tossed it to Loretta, along with a life preserver. "Put those on and come wi' me. Get ye some gloves, too. Everything's tap-salteerie up there, and it fleeful caud."

"Yes. Of course." Loretta stuck her arms in the coat and wished ladies were permitted to wear trousers, which *must* be more serviceable in an emergency than the skirts fashionable in 1912 that bloomed around the hips and narrowed toward the ankles. She had long believed that Mrs. Bloomer had the right idea. She only wished now that she'd acted on her beliefs regarding rational dress and brought some split skirts with her aboard the ship.

If Miss MacTavish was correct, and Loretta saw no reason to doubt her . . . yet . . . the passengers on the "unsinkable" *Titanic* were in deep trouble. And, while Loretta sincerely doubted that anything truly bad could happen to the *Titanic,* which was brand new and built according to the latest views on safety and sound construction techniques and was equipped with some sort of special hull that could resist anything, she saw it as her duty to assist others, even if that only meant soothing rattled nerves or helping youngsters and the elderly to lifeboats.

"Are ye able to walk?" Miss MacTavish eyed Loretta doubtfully.

Loretta was a trifle doubtful herself, and not merely because of her narrow skirt that made her feel more like a duck waddling than a woman striding purposefully toward her future. "Yes. I believe so."

"Good. Then come aboon a' me."

Miss MacTavish hurried out the door. Picking up her skirt, Loretta followed her and was appalled to see a small trickle of water slithering down the hallway. "Good heavens! We really *are* in trouble."

"We're sinking."

The words had been uttered as a flat statement that struck Loretta as horrifying. She stared at Miss MacTavish's back for only a second. Sinking. *Titanic? Sinking?* Impossible.

She glanced again at the trickle of water. Perhaps it wasn't impossible. "Are you sure you don't know where Mrs. Golightly and Eunice are?"

Miss MacTavish had already knocked on the door of the cabin next to Loretta's. "I have'na idea." She didn't wait for anyone to answer her knock, but jerked the door open and leaned inside. "Everyone out! The ship is in trouble. Grab your life preservers and get aboon—er, above, on deck!"

A rustle and a couple of squeaks greeted this peremptory message. Loretta had met her next-cabin neighbors, two elderly sisters, a couple of times before confining herself to her own cabin.

"Is anyone helping those below in third class?" she called to Miss MacTavish, who had hurried along the hallway to the next cabin door.

Before knocking at that cabin, she turned and cast an exasperated glance at Loretta. "I dinna know. Probably the stewardess and steward. For mercy's sake, just get yoursel' aboon and into a lifeboat!"

But Loretta knew she couldn't do that. Not until she had determined that dear Eunice and her mother were safe.

"I'll find Mrs. Golightly first!" she called back to Miss MacTavish.

"*No!*" the stewardess shrieked, staring at Loretta in alarm.

Loretta paid her no heed. She waved a wool-clad arm in Miss MacTavish's direction. "Go back to warning the passengers."

Then, because she'd made it her business to discover how a first-class passenger could descend into steerage, in spite of the White Star Line's prohibition against intermingling of passengers, she dashed to the service door at the other end of the hall.

"*No!*" Miss MacTavish screamed at her back once more. "Save yoursel'! For the love of God, Miss Linden, ye canna—"

But Loretta, who had never believed she couldn't do anything, ever, didn't wait to hear what Miss MacTavish believed she couldn't do. She knew she could. And she did.

TWO

October 1914

Fog slithered under the doorjamb, adding a dampness to the room and mingling with the odors of thin soup, stale sandwiches, unwashed male bodies, and the vague Ecclesiastical scent of incense that Loretta Linden would forever associate with the Ladies' Benevolence League's soup kitchen and the nuns who helped run it.

The subdued murmur of voices provided a counterpoint to the far-off, melancholy warning of the foghorn sounding from its island in the Bay. In short, the room fairly pulsed with charity and benevolence, and even though Loretta was far from popish herself, she loved it. She counted the hours she spent here as some of the most fulfilling in her life. She dipped her ladle into the big iron soup pot, and her heart brimmed with love.

"It was the Moors done it."

The ladle in Loretta's hand checked in its forward progress for only a second. She focused more closely on the man holding out his bowl to her. He was a scruffy object, and he looked as if he'd been in a brawl recently. Unfortunately, his appearance wasn't unusual in the soup kitchen.

"The Moors," the man insisted. "They was the ones. They come in and took over." He shook his dirty gray head. "Poor damned Spaniards didn't have a chance."

Deducing that the man's comments were not directed specifically at her and that she didn't need to respond, Loretta finished filling his bowl and again dipped her ladle into the huge pot of bubbling soup.

The Moor man moved down the line toward another woman who was handing out sandwiches; and the man behind him, who had seemed to be listening intently, nodded as he held his bowl out for Loretta to fill.

Working in the soup kitchen was often dispiriting, sometimes discouraging, and always interesting. Loretta knew in her heart that it was also vital. These men would have no food at all, unless they stole it, if not for the good ladies of the San Francisco Ladies' Benevolence League and the nuns from the Sisters of Charity. If the ladies and the nuns left it to the men of San Francisco to feed the poor, the poor would starve.

"The Moors," repeated the first man. "They was the ones."

"Yeah," said the man behind the Moor man as Loretta filled his bowl. "But they don't serve soup as good as this."

"It was the Moors." The Moor man nodded at the man behind him, as if pleased to find someone who shared his opinion.

"This place has good sandwiches, too. Them ladies at the Salvation Army place don't make good sandwiches." With filthy fingers, he lifted the piece of dark bread covering the insides of his sandwich. "It's got meat." His voice was filled with wonder.

"Damn Moors."

"Real meat. And cheese."

Loretta watched the two men shuffle off and sit together at one of the splintery tables against the far wall of the soup kitchen's dining room. They continued talking around and past each other between bites.

As she filled more bowls held out to her by more dirty, ragged, impoverished men, she wondered what caused some people's minds to wander so far from reality as the minds of those two men seemed to have done. Had they been touched in the head at birth? Had their brains been ravaged by accident or alcohol? Were the alienists correct, and could miserable childhoods and poverty and violence induce insanity?

Some of the men served by this soup kitchen, she knew, had been laid low by drink, but many more of them, especially those of color, only needed an opportunity. And an education. Loretta deplored San Francisco's educational deficiencies, even for white children, which sent her mind reeling in another direction.

Her blood boiled when she considered her yellow sisters and their offspring. The Chinese Exclusion Act was a product of the devil, in Loretta's humble opinion, and fostered terrible abuses and inhumanity, especially, as ever, to female Chinese. If women ever got to take their rightful places in the polling booths, the fat politicians who passed such monstrous legislative acts would be voted out of office in no time at all.

Her indignation caused her ladle to tremble, and

she spilled soup on her next customer, who jumped backward. "Jeez, lady, I didn't do nothing."

Embarrassed, Loretta murmured, "I beg your pardon," and refilled the man's bowl, vowing to keep her mind on what she was doing. She almost succeeded. She only wished there were more people in her great city who recognized the need to rectify society's wrongs—and who would do so according to Loretta's school of thought.

"It gets dark earlier and earlier these days," Loretta muttered as she struggled to lock the door.

"It is autumn," Marjorie MacTavish replied in her even, musical Scots burr. "The days are always shorter in autumn."

Loretta slanted a glance at her secretary. She sometimes suspected Marjorie of veiled sarcasm. "Of course. Help me here. Push against the door, if you will. The recent rains have made the wood swell."

A pause ensued. When Loretta turned to glance at her companion, she saw Marjorie eyeing her tan gloves in dismay. "Take 'em off if you're afraid they'll get dirty." Because Loretta truly esteemed her secretary and believed that the woman was not beyond redemption, she attempted always to keep her temper, even when Marjorie tried her patience. What did gloves matter, when compared to human lives?

With a sigh, Marjorie sacrificed her gloves and pushed at the door, and Loretta finally managed to get it locked. "Did you bring the Runabout?" Loretta stuffed the door key into her handbag and pushed her spectacles, which had slid down her nose during her struggle with the door, back into place.

"Yes."

Loretta heard the edge to her secretary's voice and eyed her slantwise. "I know you don't care to drive the automobile, Marjorie, but it's good to do things that frighten you occasionally. Otherwise, you'll become a mass of nerves and neuroses and you'll never get better."

"I know." Marjorie compressed her lips as if she were holding back a sharp retort.

"I think," Loretta mused, "that it might be good if I were to make you an appointment with Dr. Hagendorf. He's an excellent alienist."

"I dinna need to see an alienist," Marjorie averred. "I'm'na crazy."

Eyeing her secretary with reproach, Loretta said, "Alienists aren't just for crazy people. Dr. Hagendorf can help with your phobias."

"They aren't phobias, Loretta. I dinna even *believe* in phobias!"

"I can't see that it matters whether you believe in them or not. You seem to have at least one."

Marjorie huffed.

With a sigh, Loretta wondered if the woman would ever overcome her inhibitions. Two years had passed since that awful, horrid night when the *Titanic* had sunk to the bottom of the Atlantic, taking over fifteen hundred people with it. But Marjorie was as steeped in her terror of the ocean deeps as ever. Her anxiety about driving the Runabout was minor compared to her complete and absolute dread of the ocean.

Marjorie's case was a sad one, and one that had entailed a complete life change for the poor woman.

But Loretta wasn't giving up on her. She honestly believed that Marjorie would benefit from seeing Dr. Hagendorf, a friend of Loretta's, and an alienist devoted to the methods of Dr. Sigmund Freud.

Naturally, when Loretta had first brought up the subject, Marjorie had been shocked and had rebelled against doing anything so contrary to her conformist ways. Loretta trusted in her powers of persuasion, however, and she expected Marjorie to cave in to her stronger will one of these days.

The two women had reached Loretta's Runabout. "Hop in," she said cheerily, and thought wryly that it would be a cold day in hell before poor Marjorie MacTavish *hopped* anywhere.

Marjorie got into the machine, however, and Loretta cranked the engine to life. Then, since Marjorie couldn't be made to hop, Loretta did so, leaping into her automobile as agilely as if she were a child instead of a twenty-eight-year-old spinster lady past her last hopes. Not, of course, that *she* considered herself thus. That was only society's opinion. Loretta knew better.

She swerved into traffic, and Marjorie let out a yelp. "There's no need to scream, Marjorie. I know what I'm doing."

Marjorie's only reply was a whimper. Glancing at her, Loretta wondered how a person could accumulate so many disabling terrors during a relatively short lifetime. Granted, poor Marjorie had lost many friends and co-workers, not to mention her career as a stewardess, when that ship had hit the iceberg and sunk, but she still seemed awfully poor-spirited to Loretta.

Another friend of theirs, Isabel FitzRoy, née Golightly, claimed it was because Marjorie had grown up in Scotland, where class distinctions and strict rules of behavior had been instilled in her from birth, and that Loretta should stop hounding poor Marjorie. Loretta resented that. She didn't consider her hints and lectures *hounding*. She was only trying to help.

Isabel had said with a laugh that one person's meat is another person's poison, but Loretta couldn't see what that had to do with anything. She vowed to keep trying with Marjorie. Perhaps one day the woman would emerge from her shell.

They managed to arrive at Loretta's mammoth Russian Hill abode without hitting anything extraneous on the way. As usual when she traveled with Loretta, Marjorie muttered a brief, whispered prayer of thanks before exiting the automobile. Shaking her head, Loretta entertained a rare uncertainty about her ability to help Marjorie ever loosen up.

It wasn't until her housekeeper, Mrs. Brandeis, opened the door to them that Loretta remembered the parcel she'd meant to bring home. "Drat!" she cried, stopping short so that Marjorie bumped into her. She turned. "I beg your pardon, Marjorie. I left Eunice's birthday present at the soup kitchen. I'll have to run back and fetch it."

Marjorie said stiffly, "I should fetch it for you, Loretta. I'm your secretary, after all."

"Fiddlesticks! It was my mistake. I'll get it." And that was another thing: She couldn't seem to convince Marjorie that she was Loretta's *secretary*, not her slave. She clattered down the front porch steps and turned to wave at her secretary and housekeeper. "I'll be back before dinnertime. If the

FitzRoys arrive early, tell them I'm sorry and I'll be home soon!"

She wasn't certain, but she thought she heard Marjorie mumble something. Fortunately, Loretta couldn't hear what it was.

"Blasted lock," Loretta's eyeglasses slid down her nose as she set her shoulder against the door, pushed as hard as she could, and tried to turn the key. It didn't turn. It was as stuck as stuck could be.

It came, therefore, as a shock to her when the door burst open, a hand like a ham grabbed her and slammed her against the wall, her spectacles flew across the room and clattered to the floor, and an arm as big around as a tree trunk pinioned her by means of her throat. She would have screamed, had she been able, but she was being quite effectively throttled by the arm, and she couldn't. In lieu of other options, she kicked like a mule.

"Damnation! Ow! Stop that!"

She gurgled back, furious, and kicked again.

"Will you stop that?"

The arm withdrew from her throat, and Loretta managed to shriek "*Help!*" before she was spun around and hugged against a body like a giant redwood tree, this time by *two* arms like tree trunks. She presumed the second arm belonged to the same man who'd pinioned her against the wall. One of the hands attached to one of the arms covered her mouth. It was so big, it also covered her nose and chin. Scarcely able to maneuver her lips apart, but fighting for her life, she bit into a part of the hand. She didn't know which part it was, but her action produced another bellow of rage and another spate of swear words.

"*Damn* it!"

The arms loosened and the hands grabbed her shoulders, uncovering her mouth, which she'd have used to scream some more, except that whoever belonged to the ham-like hands, the redwood-tree body, and the tree-trunk arms started shaking her. Her teeth clanked together and she feared her neck would snap. So she kicked out again, this time a little higher, and her captor might have lost something of value to him if he hadn't jumped aside. Loretta was very disappointed.

"You damned little cat!" the beast shouted. "Stop that!"

All at once, the room flooded with light, the shaking ceased, and Loretta finally saw the man belonging to the arms, hands, and body. Out of breath and pulsating with terror and rage, she balled her right hand into a fist, and aimed a punch at the monster's stomach. He caught her fist in the hand with which he'd pulled the light cord and held it. Hard. Loretta now feared for her fingers.

"Who the devil are you?"

Panting, she glared up into two of the fiercest brown eyes she'd ever encountered, including even her own, which could be extremely fierce when she was roused. She was roused now. She wanted to kill this person, whoever he was. "Who are *you*?" she snarled back. "*I* belong here! *You* don't."

"Huh."

Whoever he was, and even without her eyeglasses, Loretta could see that he was brown as the proverbial berry, as big as a house, strong as Hercules, and wore one gold earring that glinted in the light shining down upon them from the single bare bulb on the ceiling. Loretta saw that he also had on a black cape and a cap with gold braid on it. She'd never seen anyone dressed exactly that way before.

She also realized that, although he'd brutally manhandled her, her fear was vanishing fast, perhaps because he was staring at her in so puzzled a fashion. She doubted that a man truly lost to all morality would bother to register confusion before dispatching his victim. He released her hand at last and she stepped away from him, tugging at her shirtwaist and skirt, which had become disarranged in the row.

"Well?" she demanded. "Who are you, and what are you doing here?"

He, too, straightened. "Quarles," he said in a voice like rolling thunder. "Captain Malachai Quarles." He gave her a tight grin. "Your turn."

Loretta, who possessed a literal mind, wondered only for a second what he meant by that. Understanding struck, and she said, "My name is Miss Loretta Linden. What are you doing here, Captain Quarles? I presume you aren't a mere cat burglar." She sniffed. "If you are, you're a stupid one. There's nothing in the soup kitchen worth stealing. We serve the poor."

"Huh." Captain Quarles turned away from Loretta and stooped to glance under a table. "I got a tip that one of my crewmen might be here."

"We *are* near the dock," Loretta said. With another sniff, she added, "Don't you feed your crewmen, Captain Quarles?"

He didn't deign to reply, but continued searching. Loretta was unused to being ignored. While her height was unimpressive, being a mere five feet and a bit, she had a powerful personality and was accustomed to people recognizing her as a force to be reckoned with. Yet Captain Quarles was doing an excellent job of pretending she wasn't even there. He looked under another table.

"Are you expecting your crewman to have expired from drink? Is that why you're searching under the tables?" She'd aimed for sarcasm, and was proud of the result.

Obviously unimpressed, Captain Quarles said, "Huh," again.

Irked, Loretta spotted two gleaming circles lying on the floor not far off, went over and picked up her eyeglasses, and hooked the earpieces over her ears. Now that she could see him clearly, she decided that he bore no resemblance whatsoever, in the least little degree, to her notion of a sea captain, perhaps because of her experience on-board—and off—the *Titanic*. Captain John Edward Smith would forever be engraved in her memory as the epitome of a ship's captain.

On the other hand, Captain Smith had allowed his ship to smash up against an iceberg and had died for his mistake, along with most of his crew and the passengers, so perhaps her notion needed revision.

Tabling the captain issue for the moment, she stamped up to Quarles, grabbed one of his massive arms, and tried to turn him around to face her. The tactic didn't work, as Captain Quarles was approximately as malleable as a granite statue.

Since she couldn't budge him, she decided to pester him instead. "If you'll condescend to tell me who your crewman is and why you think he's here, perhaps I can help you locate him." It sounded reasonable to her. She wondered if the captain would agree with her.

He seemed to. Straightening, he squinted down at her. He was a tall man, although not exceptionally so. Loretta judged him to be about six feet tall. But he was built like a monument. He also had curly dark hair that was longer than need be, eyebrows that didn't arch but tilted slightly upward at the outer edges, giving him the look of a pagan idol, and full lips. And then there was that earring. Loretta swallowed, thinking it would be easier to stand up to the man if he were a shade less alarming.

"What do you have to do with this place?" he asked. His voice rumbled like thunder even when, as now, he wasn't speaking loudly. He'd nearly deafened her when he'd roared at her to stop kicking him.

"I am a volunteer." Loretta said it proudly. The irrelevant thought that she might look better if she hadn't replaced her eyeglasses flitted through her mind, and she swatted it away as if it were a pesky fly.

"Huh. I figured you for a do-gooder."

"That's a disparaging term and one I do not allow to—"

He interrupted her, waving her explanation away with a powerful hand, as if he didn't care what she allowed or didn't allow. "I'm looking for Derrick Peavey. You know him?"

"The men who avail themselves of our services don't normally give us their names," she said, outraged at having been thwarted while delivering a lecture.

"Yeah? Can't say as I blame them. What's that room there?" He pointed.

Irate, but unable to think of a reason to deny him the information, especially since she didn't expect he'd be deterred by her silence, Loretta growled, "The kitchen."

"Huh." Captain Malachai Quarles strode toward the kitchen door, his cape swirling around his booted feet, and bringing to Loretta's mind tales of swashbuckling pirates and adventurers and so forth. She hated when her mind did that. She tried so hard to keep it under control, too. Peeved that he wasn't deferring to her, she rushed after him.

He didn't seem to notice. Opening the door, he looked right and left, found what he was seeking, and pulled the chain. Another bare bulb, this one illuminating the kitchen, flared to life. Loretta heard the captain grunt, and then he vanished into the room. She hurried inside. Unlike the captain, Loretta, who prided herself on her nerves of iron but was tenderhearted in spite of herself, uttered a gasp of consternation.

Captain Quarles knelt beside a man huddled on the floor behind the kitchen counter. The man's head rested in a small pool of blood, and several small, shiny yellow disks lay scattered around him. Ignoring the disks, Loretta ran over to Captain Quarles and gazed down at the victim, aghast. Then she recognized him. "Why, it's the Moor man!"

The captain glanced up at her, and she detected antipathy on his hard face. "Peavey isn't a Mormon, for God's sake. He's a sailor!"

Vexed, Loretta knelt beside the captain. "I didn't mean that he's a Mormon, although I don't know why a Mormon can't be a sailor. What I meant was that he was talking about the Moors this afternoon when he came in for his soup and sandwich."

"Ah." Captain Quarles nodded as if this information came as no surprise to him.

He didn't enlighten Loretta, who took his silence amiss. "Well?" she demanded. "Why was he talking about the Moors? He wasn't making any sense."

The captain had opened Peavey's coat and shirt and was pressing his ear to the man's chest. He scowled at Loretta, who correctly interpreted this as a signal for her to keep still so he could verify that his crew member still lived. Loretta was beginning to seriously dislike the brusque captain. It came as a surprise to her when his harsh features softened, and he heaved a huge sigh.

"He's alive."

"Thank God."

"I doubt that God had much to do with it. More likely it's Peavey's hard head." The captain reached for the mentioned head, and made as if to lift him.

Concerned, Loretta leaned over to grab his arm. "Don't raise his head! He might have a concussion." Her bosom pressed against the captain's arm, and she felt heat flow through her body from the point of contact to her nether limbs. She'd never had such a reaction to a man's touch before, and it embarrassed her. She tried to pretend nothing was wrong.

"What do you suggest I do?" the captain asked with sarcasm that, unlike that of her secretary, was unconcealed. He didn't seem one bit interested in Loretta's bosom, either, which was perhaps more mortifying than the fact that her bosom pressed against his arm in the first place. Abruptly she released him and sat back on her heels. Her breasts felt as if they had been branded.

Sucking in a deep breath and telling herself not to shout at the boorish man because she didn't want to be one bit like him, Loretta said, "I shall call a physician friend of mine. He can tell if it's safe to move him and what should be done for him. This man might have to be hospitalized."

"Huh. Peavey won't like that." The captain frowned at his fallen employee.

"Nevertheless, if he has a concussion, great care must be taken before moving him." It irked Loretta that she sounded so prim and stuffy. She was accustomed to numbering among her friends all of the most liberated and forward-thinking individuals in San Francisco. Neither she nor they were stuffy. The captain brought out her very worst characteristics, and she disliked him for it.

She wondered if he'd be nicer to her if she wasn't wearing her spectacles. Then she swore at herself for so much as thinking about so trivial a matter under the circumstances.

"All right. Call the damned doctor."

With a huff, Loretta stood and patted her skirt down. "There's no need to swear."

He rolled his eyes, and Loretta stomped to the telephone, which was in the back room of the soup kitchen. First she dialed her friend, Dr. Jason Abernathy, who ran a clinic for the poor in San Francisco's Chinatown district. Dr. Abernathy said he'd be right over.

Then she called the police. Anticipating indifference at best and refusal to assist at worst, she wasn't surprised when the person who answered the telephone at the police station didn't seem interested in a brutal attack upon an individual the policeman considered a derelict.

"I demand that you send a team to investigate this matter," Loretta told the policeman in her sternest voice. "This man, whatever his position in life, was attacked inside the Ladies' Benevolence League's soup kitchen on Powell Street. He's still alive, but that may change, in which case your department will be investigating a case of murder!"

The policeman remained unmoved. In fact, he sounded a trifle bored. Loretta's brow creased when she heard his next words.

"My name," she responded stiffly—she generally didn't approve of trading on her name, although it was an old and honorable one in the city by the bay—"is Loretta Linden. That's L-i-n-d-e-n." She listened to the man's next question with a wry expression on her face. "Yes. He's my father."

Suddenly the telephone receiver was snatched from her hand, and she jumped back with a startled cry. Naturally, the person who had perpetrated the uncivil deed was Captain Malachai Quarles. She pushed her eyeglasses up her nose and scowled at him. He didn't seem to notice.

"Get someone over here now. This is Captain Malachai Quarles, and the injured man is one of my crew."

Loretta gaped, infuriated, as the captain listened for a very few seconds, then said, "Good. Right," and slammed the receiver into the cradle.

He turned and glared down at her again. His face seemed able to exhibit only two expressions: sarcasm and anger. "The police will be here shortly."

Loretta expelled a large breath. "Do you mean to

tell me they responded to your command, and they were going to ignore my civil request?"

The captain shrugged. "Didn't sound like a civil request to me. Sounded more like a demand." He went back to his fallen employee and again knelt at Peavey's side.

Frustrated and wishing she could batter the captain, Loretta decided she'd be shirking her duty as a woman and a Christian if she gave vent to her own feelings when a creature in distress lay nearby. Even if he was a man.

Because she'd been friends with Dr. Abernathy for years and had seen him at work more than once, Loretta decided that the best thing she could do for Mr. Peavey was to wash the blood off his face and cover him with a blanket or something. The floor was cold, and she'd learned from Dr. Abernathy that people who had been felled by a blow sometimes went into shock and needed to be kept warm. Therefore, she shrugged out of her woolen coat—Loretta didn't suffer from her secretary's delicacy of feelings—and gently tucked it around Mr. Peavey. The captain grunted. Loretta didn't know if it was a grunt expressing approval or what, but she opted not to pay attention to it.

Fetching a clean dish towel from the drawer where they were kept, she wetted the cloth at the sink and trotted back to Peavey, trying her best to ignore the captain's piercing eyes, which seemed to follow her every movement. They made her nervous. Unaccustomed to being nervous, Loretta took this, as she so far took everything about the captain, amiss. "Stop staring at me!"

"You're cold."

She gave him a withering glance. "I am not."

He gestured at her bared arm. "You've got gooseflesh."

Blast and hell. Loretta glanced at her rebellious arms. Sure enough, they had gooseflesh. "It's nothing," she said curtly.

"Huh." Standing abruptly, Captain Quarles unfastened his cape and threw it over Loretta's shoulders. It puddled at her feet.

Huffy as well as embarrassed, as well as stimulated strangely by the warmth of the wrap and the faint scent of the sea and of the captain it carried with it, Loretta snapped, "There's no need for that."

"Nuts." Captain Quarles sneered at her. "Little Miss Ministering Angel. Here, give me that." He snatched the wet towel from her hands and started carefully wiping blood from Peavey's face.

"How dare you?" Loretta demanded, trying to keep her voice at a whisper in deference to the injured man, but so affronted that she wanted to scream at the captain. She reached for the towel, but Captain Quarles held tight.

"Will you stop that! I'll clean him up."

He gave her another sneer and his gaze raked her from tip to toe, making her blush and, thereby, enraging her further. Loretta didn't take kindly to being made to blush.

"I thought ladies were supposed to faint at the sight of blood."

"*I,*" said Loretta, thoroughly offended, "do not faint at the sight of *anything.*"

"I'm not surprised. Go look for the doctor, will you, and quit getting in my way."

Because the captain was so very large, and because she felt it would be more humiliating to fight

and be defeated than to submit gracefully to his ob-
noxious command, she turned on her heel and
headed for the door. She had to bunch his cape up
in her fist because it tended to drag, being very
much too big for her.

Her joy when she beheld Dr. Jason Abernathy exiting the automobile he'd parked on the other side
of Powell Street, while not boundless, was nevertheless sincere. The doctor, who shared Loretta's
interest in numberless causes, would be a pleasant
change from the captain, with whom she shared
absolutely, positively nothing.

THREE

"Jason!" The fall evening was crisp, but thanks to the captain's cape—curse the man—and her gratitude at seeing her friend, she rushed out the door and over to his automobile, holding the cape up so that she wouldn't trip on it and go sprawling. "Thank God you're here. I'm afraid the poor man has a concussion."

Giving her a friendly hug, Jason said, "I'll check on him. What happened, for heaven's sake? People don't often get bashed in the Ladies' soup kitchen."

"I know. And I haven't an idea in the world what happened. All I know is that I returned to the soup kitchen to fetch—Oh, my!" Loretta slapped her hands to her cheeks, recalling the evening's dinner engagement, and almost losing her cloak. She grabbed it and held on.

"Don't worry," Jason said. "I was on my way out the door to go to your house for the party when you rang me. I called Miss MacTavish and told her you'd be delayed. I'm sure Miss Eunice will understand. Fetching cloak, by the way."

Deciding to ignore his comment about the captain's cloak, Loretta chuckled as she pictured little Miss Eunice Golightly, soon to be Eunice FitzRoy, since her stepfather was in the process of legally adopting her. "I'm sure she will. Thank you very much, Jason. I forgot all about the party until right this minute."

He patted her on the back. "Think nothing of it. I know your mind is generally on loftier matters than mere dinner engagements."

With a frown, Loretta tried to decide if he was ribbing her, and if she should be offended. Ultimately concluding that she was better off not becoming riled with a friend, and that Captain Quarles was enough of a problem for one evening, she continued to frown. "I'm sorry Eunice won't get her present until later, though."

"If anyone in the universe will understand that disappointment is a part of life, it's Eunice, Loretta. Don't fret."

While Jason was absolutely correct, Eunice being something of a genius who already understood more about life than most adults, Loretta still shook her head, feeling not merely sorry for Eunice, but also feeling as if this whole problem was somehow her fault. But that was utter nonsense, and she knew it in her brain. Her heart, which occasionally behaved irrationally, was another matter. However, she chose not to fret, as Jason had suggested.

"As I already mentioned, that's a fetching cape, Loretta, but it seems a trifle large for you."

Unconsciously borrowing vocabulary from the despicable captain, Loretta said, "Huh." Feeling emotionally unequipped to explain Malachai Quarles to Jason, she added, "They're in the kitchen."

"They?" Jason snapped his black bag open as Loretta led him kitchenward.

"Yes." She couldn't repress a sniff of disapproval. "The man is a sailor, apparently, and his captain came looking for him."

"Ah. Wonder why the man came here if he's gainfully employed."

Loretta thought that if she worked for Captain Quarles, she'd do anything within her power to keep away from him, but she didn't say so. "I have no idea, although his mind seemed to be wandering when he was in here earlier today, and he seems to have a fixation on the Moors' invasion of Spain."

Jason's eyes opened wide. "How remarkable."

"Indeed. I can't imagine how he got back in after the door was locked. Or maybe he never left." She pondered that possibility. Had the man been hiding out in the soup kitchen all day? Why?

As they approached Captain Quarles and his crewman, Loretta noticed that the small yellow disks had vanished from the floor. She frowned at Captain Quarles, but didn't mention the matter.

The captain rose to his feet and held out a large, rough, and very tanned hand for Jason to shake, which he did without even registering distaste. Loretta considered this faintly disloyal, although she knew she was being irrational. She allowed herself another significant frown, however.

"Captain Malachai Quarles," said the captain in his rumbling bass voice.

"Aha!" Jason sounded delighted. Loretta glanced at him sharply. "I'm Dr. Jason Abernathy. I thought you looked familiar. I've seen your picture in the newspapers. Delighted to meet you, Captain Quarles."

Loretta's mouth dropped open and her bosom

swelled with indignation. How *dare* Jason express delight in this wretched man's company!

"Thank you, Dr. Abernathy. Likewise." The captain's gaze sought his stricken employee. "Peavey's awake, and he seems to be coherent. I didn't want to move him."

Again, Loretta felt indignant. "You *would* have moved him, if I hadn't stopped you."

Both men glanced at her and away again, as if she were nothing more than a nettlesome insect whose presence had made itself felt only slightly and, having been judged insignificant, could be ignored.

Jason withdrew his stethoscope from his black bag and knelt beside Peavey. "How do you feel, Mr. Peavey?"

"Got a headache." Peavey's voice was rough around the edges, as if he'd had to force it through a space too small to hold it. "Feel like hell." His gaze, which had been taking in the kitchen and the captain and the doctor, picked up on Loretta's presence, and he swallowed. "Sorry, ma'am."

"For God's sake, don't mind *her*," the captain said. Loretta wanted to bop him one.

As if sensing Loretta's mood, Jason spoke before anyone else could. "Let's just see what's going on here." After unbuttoning the man's shirt and shoving his undershirt up, he pressed the stethoscope to Peavey's chest in several places. "Sounds all right so far." He folded the scope and stuffed it into his bag. "I'm going to have to palpate your head. I'll try not to hurt you."

"Uh-huh." Peavey braced himself, and the doctor started probing.

As she watched, Loretta winced in sympathy, then sought the captain. He was, naturally, looking at her and had caught her expression, which might be—and undoubtedly was, by him—interpreted as an example of womanly weakness. Drat him. She scowled at him. His sneer altered not. Beastly man. *Wretched* man.

She was saved by the sound of people at the door. Hurrying out of the kitchen, Loretta saw that the police had arrived. Had they done so at her bidding, she would have greeted them gladly. As it was, she resented them almost as much as she resented Captain Malachai Quarles.

A sergeant of police spotted her and came forward. "Good evening, ma'am. I understand there's trouble here."

"Yes. A man named—"

"Excuse me, ma'am, but I understand Captain Quarles is here."

Loretta felt herself swelling, rather like a hot-air balloon she'd seen recently in Golden Gate Park. Only it wasn't hot air inflating her; it was pure, unadulterated rage. "Captain Quarles has nothing to do with this!" she said, rather more loudly than she had intended.

"This way," a voice rumbled at her back.

Loretta shut her eyes and counted to fifteen, ten seeming insufficient to the purpose.

"Sergeant Bowes, Captain Quarles." The policemen, all with broad smiles on their faces, walked right past Loretta and up to the captain. The sergeant held out his hand, and the captain shook it. "It's good to meet you. I've read all about your treasure ship in the *Chronicle*."

As she glowered after them, Loretta's brain commenced to whirl. The captain had been in the *Chronicle*? With his treasure ship? What treasure

ship? Both the policeman and Jason had mentioned seeing the horrid captain in the newspaper.
Had the man done something noteworthy? Loretta
read the newspapers, but her interests were political and social. She didn't pay much attention to
other news, most of which she deemed frivolous.

Perceiving no alternative unless she wanted to be
left out of the action entirely, she walked after the
new arrivals and the captain and into the kitchen.
Inspecting the captain from behind, she decided
he still didn't look like any self-respecting sea captain she'd ever seen. He looked more like a pirate.
She hated to admit it, but he had quite the swashbuckling air about him.

Jason was still in the process of examining Mr.
Peavey, so she stood back, leaned against a counter,
and watched. Loretta Linden wasn't accustomed to
being out of the limelight. Nor was she accustomed
to feeling left out and ignored. The sensations
didn't sit well with her.

While Jason continued to prod and probe
Peavey's body, the police sergeant began his interrogation of Mr. Peavey. The sergeant's minions
started inspecting the premises, for all the good
that would do them, Loretta thought bitterly. She
was intimately acquainted with the Ladies' Benevolence League's soup kitchen and, except for the
body and blood on the floor, she hadn't detected
a single thing out of place.

She remembered those shiny yellow disks and
her gaze sought the captain. He was no longer
there. Damn the man to perdition, he'd probably
escaped with the loot!

A deep voice behind her made her jump, and
she whirled around. There he was, all right. He'd

sneaked up behind her on the other side of the counter, the repellent, skulking brute. Giving him one of her more magnificent frowns, she hissed, "Who *are* you?"

His dark eyes gleamed maliciously. "I told you who I am. Captain Malachai Quarles."

She knew he was toying with her. She hated him for it. "You know very well what I mean," she said, giving a broad gesture that almost cost her the warmth of his cloak. She clutched it to her bosom, still frowning. "All these men seem to know you from the newspaper. What did you do? Murder someone?"

"You'd like that, wouldn't you?" the captain said snidely. "I'm sorry to disappoint you, Miss Linden. These gentlemen have read about me in the newspapers because I am captain of the ship *The Moor's Revenge*, and my crew and I have recently discovered a sunken Moorish ship off the coast of a small, unnamed island in the Canaries, along with a king's ransom in old Moorish and Spanish coins and other ancient treasure and historical artifacts."

Merciful heavens. "Oh." Her mind raced. "Is that why Mr. Peavey was raving about Moors earlier in the day, when he was taking luncheon with us?"

"I suppose. His mind goes off on tangents sometimes." The captain shrugged his mammoth shoulders.

Loretta wished she hadn't noticed his shoulders. They were at present straining the fabric of his fine lawn shirt as well as her feminist principles. She rather wished she could inspect those shoulders more closely. She also wished she hadn't noticed the fineness of the cloth out of which his shirt was made, since she believed she ought to be above such things.

Curse her eyeglasses! She was sure that if she weren't wearing them, she wouldn't be so keenly aware of the captain's manly charms. She also suspected the captain wouldn't be treating her in this offhand, not to say ungentlemanly, way, if she weren't wearing them. Captain Smith, of the doomed *Titanic*, had been the soul of courtesy. Then again, Captain Smith was dead.

Mentally smacking herself, Loretta brought her brain back to important issues. "Yes. I suppose that explains it, then." She recalled the shiny yellow disks. "Is that what you picked up from the floor? Those golden coins? Were they part of the Moorish treasure?" She sniffed to let the captain know what she thought of people who stole from the incapacitated.

His eyes narrowed. "You saw the coins?"

"Of course, I saw the coins! I'm not blind, even if you *did* knock my spectacles off."

"Huh." One of his big brown hands lifted, and he stroked his chin. Loretta had a mad impulse to take over the operation from him.

Whatever was the matter with her? She'd never had these impulses before, not even with men whom she liked. She abominated the captain. "Well? Were they Moorish coins? Or Spanish coins? And did you steal them from Mr. Peavey?"

With a glower that was ever so much more magnificent than any she could produce, curse the man, Captain Quarles snarled, "I don't steal. Yes, they were Moorish coins. Now will you be quiet about them? I don't want the whole world to know about this!"

Loretta considered the possibility of a person exploding from an excess of built-up bile. "Well, you can jolly well tell *me* about them, *Captain* Quarles, because your employee was blackjacked in *my* soup kitchen! I'll not let the matter rest," she warned him.

"Why doesn't that surprise me?" the captain muttered under his breath. "All right. If it'll keep your mouth shut, I'll tell you about it." And with that, he reached across the counter, snagged Loretta's arm in a grip like iron, and dragged her toward the kitchen door.

Only out of deference to the ill man, Loretta didn't shriek with rage. "Stop that!" she whispered furiously.

"Huh." He didn't alter his path or lighten his grip on her arm, but led her relentlessly from the kitchen. After he'd shut the door behind them, Captain Quarles released Loretta's arm. She had to command herself not to rub the bruised place—but she wouldn't give the unmitigated *animal* the satisfaction of knowing he'd hurt her. "Sit down."

"I prefer to stand."

He eyed her evilly. "Suit yourself. And don't go blabbing about this, Miss Linden. It's not for public knowledge. If the press gets hold of it, God alone knows what will happen."

"I," said Loretta through tightly clenched teeth, "do not *blab*."

With a look of utter disdain, the captain said, "All women blab. But you'd better not this time."

"Why, you insufferable lout! I'll have you know—"

"Do you want to hear this or not?" demanded the captain. "If you do, quit blabbing."

Irate that the captain should consider her legitimate concerns *blabbing*, Loretta perceived no way to alter his opinion without confirming it. In spite of herself, she obeyed him, shutting her mouth with a clack of teeth and wishing for the first time in her life that she carried a gun. Even a small one would result in satisfying pain to the overbearing captain. She said through her teeth, "Tell me."

"I'm in partnership with William Frederick Tillinghurst." One black eyebrow lifted over a devilishly dark eye. "You've heard of him, I suppose?"

"I know him. He's a business associate of my father's," Loretta conceded, wondering as she spoke if she was unconsciously attempting to impress the captain with her social status, damn her ego to perdition.

If her ego had been seeking to undermine her egalitarian principles with snob appeal, the attempt failed. The captain said, "Tillinghurst is my partner in the treasure hunt. He provided the funding, along with Stanford University and the Museum of Natural History, and I provided the ship, the crew, and the expertise. We found the galleon, and my divers raised most of it. It was an incredible find, and of tremendous historical and monetary value."

"You," Loretta said in a scathing tone, "are primarily interested in the historical properties of the find, no doubt." She gave him a sneer of her own. Not having had much practice, she feared her effort paled in comparison to any one of his sneers.

She was right, as she noticed immediately when he sneered back at her. "As surprising as I'm sure you find it, yes, that is my primary interest. I don't need the money."

How fascinating! Again borrowing from him, she said, "Huh."

He went on, "The ship docked in San Francisco a week and a half ago. I'm surprised you haven't read about it in the newspapers, because there was a lot of publicity. Tillinghurst likes that sort of thing."

He frowned, leaving Loretta to deduce that Tillinghurst's partner was not, unlike Tillinghurst himself, a publicity hound. She almost wished he were, because it would give her one more good reason, not that she needed another one, to hate him.

"About three days ago, some of the treasure disappeared, along with two of my crewmen, including Peavey." He gestured at the closed kitchen door. "I don't want it to get out that we've had any trouble of this nature, because it will reflect badly on my operation."

Loretta sniffed. "Perhaps it will reflect the truth," she said, taking venomous glee from the fact that her words made the captain wince.

"I've worked with Peavey and Jones for years. They're both good men. I can't believe they had anything to do with the missing artifacts."

"There were those coins on the floor," Loretta reminded the captain.

He didn't appreciate the reminder. "Yes. I saw them."

"Yet you still exonerate Mr. Peavey?"

A pause followed her question. Loretta thought at first that he didn't intend to answer it, and she began to swell up again.

She deflated when he said suddenly, "Peavey's not smart enough to plan a successful theft and disappearance. Jones is smart enough, but I can't feature him doing it. He's a good man, and an honest one, and he has a lot to lose if he were to be caught perpetrating a felony. Besides, if Peavey's a crook, why was he sandbagged?"

"I have no idea. Why don't you ask him?"

The captain's alarming eyebrows dipped ominously over his eyes. "I intend to as soon as your friend the doctor is through with him."

"Hmm." In the silence following the captain's remark, Loretta pondered Peavey's case, which, she hated to admit, held a good deal of interest. After thinking hard for a moment, she said, "I suspect Mr. Tillinghurst."

"You suspect him of what?"

"Of stealing the treasure and kidnaping your crewmen."

The captain's eyes opened wide and he stared at Loretta as if she were some species of pernicious and hitherto-unknown-to-him beetle or worm. "Don't be any more of a fool than you can help, Miss Linden, please. And I beg that you won't spread *that* absurd lie around."

"I do not spread lies," Loretta stated in a measured voice in which even she could detect the outrage. "And I am not a fool." She also disliked Mr. Tillinghurst a good deal.

The captain waved a hand in a gesture of dismissal. "Anyhow, I told you the story. Now I'm going to go back to Peavey. Stay out of the way, will you?" He turned around and would have left her there if she hadn't hurried after him.

"Well?" she said, irate. "Why don't you suspect Mr. Tillinghurst? If you know him, you must know he's a money-grubbing, conscienceless, self-serving oppressor of the masses."

The captain stopped walking so abruptly, Loretta bumped into his back and bounced off. She was prevented from falling on an indelicate part of her anatomy by one of the captain's huge hands when it whipped out and grabbed onto the front of his own cloak. Roughly, he drew her upright, stood her on her two feet, and released her. With a couple of quick dance steps, Loretta managed to remain upright.

"Oppressor of the masses?" Quarles said, his voice ripe with sardonic amusement. "Are you a communist, Miss Linden?"

"No, I am not! And Mr. Tillinghurst is an awful man. He treats his employees like dirt."

"Huh. That may or may not be so, but I doubt that he'd risk his reputation as a sound businessman"—he gave the two words a good deal of emphasis—"by stealing his own treasure."

"Aha," said Loretta triumphantly, choosing to ignore their difference of opinion on the oppression issue. "But *is* he? Is the treasure his? Or yours? Aren't there regulations governing the disposal of sunken treasure—after it's been . . . unsunk? Retrieved? Especially if the expedition was carried out in conjunction with a museum or an educational institution? You said it was, with Stanford."

"Recovered," the captain said sourly. "And I know the regulations. So does Tillinghurst. Neither he nor I were responsible for the lost treasure. And I won't believe Peavey or Jones are guilty, either, unless it's established to me beyond doubt."

"Hmm." Deciding she'd better shut up now, since they'd entered the kitchen, she saw that Mr. Peavey now sat in a chair. She rushed over to Jason, who was just shutting his black bag. "Then he doesn't have a concussion?"

"Doesn't seem to," Jason said, smiling at her. She valued him greatly in that instant, since he was a man who cared about her unconditionally and who, moreover, with very few lapses, recognized her as the intelligent, capable, and upstanding woman she was. "He was primarily only stunned, although there was quite a cut on his forehead. Head wounds tend to bleed copiously." Lowering his voice, he told Loretta, "I don't think Mr. Peavey is playing with a full deck."

Recalling Mr. Peavey's earlier remarks about Moors and what the captain had called Peavey's "tangents," she said, "I think you're right."

"How are you feeling now, Peavey?"

Loretta was astonished that the captain's voice could carry such regard and genuine concern. It also didn't rumble as it did when he spoke to her. Although she hated to give him credit for anything, she wondered if he might actually care about the men under his command. She decided to withhold judgment on the issue.

Peavey was a ghastly sight. Dr. Abernathy had cleaned his wound, stitched it, and the poor man's head was now wrapped round with a white bandage. Blood had trickled down his neck and onto his shirt, and his trousers were dirty and ripped. He pressed a hand to his bandaged head and said with a moan, "Head hurts."

"I can imagine." Grinning, Captain Quarles added, "Although that's probably the best place they could have hit you if they wanted to spare your life."

Loretta huffed in sympathetic indignation.

Peavey grinned at his captain, "You're right there, Cap'n Quarles."

Loretta decided to save her indignation for someone who deserved it.

Quarles sat himself on a chair and drew it close to his injured crewman. Putting a large brown hand on Peavey's shoulder, he said gently, "Can you remember what happened?"

The captain lifted his head and frowned at Loretta, who had drawn closer. She frowned back and didn't budge. This was *her* soup kitchen, after all. Or . . . well . . . if it wasn't hers exactly, she probably gave more to it by way of financial and physical support than any other charitable lady in San Francisco. Therefore, she didn't move when the policeman frowned at her, either. He could jolly well stand there and take notes and ignore her. She wasn't going anywhere.

Peavey had been thinking about the captain's question, an activity that seemed to cause him a good deal of pain. "Uh-uh. I can't remember nothing. There was this dungeon, and there was these gold coins. Moorish coins, Cap'n Quarles. I remember that much. But I don't remember nothing more."

"A dungeon?" Loretta repeated.

The captain scowled at her.

Peavey, glancing up at her, said, "Yeah. A dungeon. In a castle or something."

"Was Jones with you?" the captain asked.

"Jones. Jones." Peavey strained to think some more. "I don't rightly recollect. I recollect Jones." He smiled, as if proud of this feat of intelligence.

"You recollect Jones being with you in the dungeon with the treasure?"

The captain's attempt at clarification met with a blank stare from Peavey. The captain sighed. Loretta decided to take a more active role in this interrogation. Kneeling before Mr. Peavey, whose eyes grew big and who shrank away from her as if from a goblin, she took his hand and held it in a comforting manner. "I'm so sorry you were hurt, Mr. Peavey." She pitched her voice to a musical purr. To the devil with the captain and his black scowl. And that of the Sergeant Bowes, too. Jason, she saw out of the corner of her eye, was grinning like a sly cat. "Do you remember me? I was the one who served you soup this noontime."

Peavey's expression held a shade less terror. "Uh . . . yeah. I guess. Good soup."

"Yes, it is good soup," Loretta agreed tenderly. "And we serve good sandwiches."

With more animation, Peavey said, "Yeah. With meat and cheese."

"With meat and cheese. Do you remember where you were before you came to the soup kitchen, Mr. Peavey? The policemen would like to know that. It might help them in finding out who hurt you."

Peavey's brow furrowed in his effort to concentrate. "It wasn't the Moors," he said at last. With a glance at his captain, he added, "Must've been them Spaniards." He nodded. "Must've been. They wanted their treasure back. But I didn't take it. It were in the dungeon. I only took a couple coins to show the cap'n, so's he could get it back again."

"Do you remember where the dungeon was, Mr. Peavey?" Loretta, who feared the *men* on the case would discount this poor man's words as mere rambling, hoped Peavey could give her a clue. She'd

love to be able to solve Mr. Peavey's case, especially
if the police and Captain Quarles were baffled.

Peavey thought some more. He sighed heartily.
"It were in town. I think. Or right out of town. A
castle in town—or beyond the town limits. Full of
treasure, it were, too. In Toledo?" He glanced a
question at Loretta and then his captain. "Were it
in Toledo?"

"Perhaps," Loretta said, standing because her
knees were aching. She offered the captain a cold
glance. "I tell you, Captain Quarles, it's Tillinghurst."

Peavey nodded. "Toledo."

To Loretta, Quarles said, "Don't be an ass."

Loretta was still seething when she parked her
Runabout in front of her massive marble porch
later that evening. Captain Quarles—and what a
splendid name for him—had not only called her an
ass to her face, but had scoffed at her suggestion
that Mr. Peavey be brought to her house so that she
could nurse him.

"I'd sooner leave him to the tender mercies of a
school of piranha fishes," were his exact words.
"He's coming back with me to the hotel."

"What hotel?" she'd demanded, aiming to over-
rule him if he mentioned some dive on the Barbary
Coast.

"The Fairfield," he said, putting her arguments
to an end before she'd presented them. The Fairfield was the most exclusive hotel in San Francisco.
Perhaps the entire United States.

Jason pulled his automobile up behind hers. He
quickly got out of it and hurried to escort her to

the party going on inside her mansion. "I get the feeling you and the captain didn't exactly hit it off." As usual, he was amused. He was always amused by the human condition.

Loretta didn't know how he maintained his sense of humor in the most trying of situations. She'd certainly lost hers, and she didn't expect it to come back soon. "No," she said crisply. "We did not. The man is an unmitigated bully and a beast."

"My, my."

The front door opened, and Marjorie MacTavish, standing in a pool of light and looking very pretty, which was moderately surprising, said, "Thank goodness you've come. Poor Eunice has been very worried about you." She gave Jason a frigid look. "Dr. Abernathy didn't explain what had happened."

"I told you somebody'd been coshed," said Jason, grinning like an imp.

Loretta squinted at her two friends, but decided not to intervene. They were always at daggers drawn with each other. The important thing now was that Eunice needed her. Shaking off Jason's hand, Loretta trotted up the porch steps.

This was more like it. Loretta needed to feel useful, and now she could be of cheer to her friends. Casting aside her fury at the men of the world, she bustled past Marjorie and hurried to the dining room, where the guests were in the middle of Eunice's birthday dinner.

Bursting into the room, she cried out, "Happy birthday, Eunice! I have *such* a tale to tell you!"

FOUR

"Take it easy, Peavey. Let me hold your arm." Captain Malachai Quarles did more than take Peavey's arm. With one arm encircling his back and the other gripping his arm, he supported the man's entire weight. That was all right. Peavey didn't weigh much, and the captain was as strong as an ox.

"Pretty lady," Peavey mumbled as he allowed the captain to help him into the elevator. "That were a pretty lady. Cooks good, too."

Malachai Quarles glowered at the uniformed elevator operator, who had glanced askance at Mr. Peavey and his blood and dirt. As it did with everyone—except Miss Loretta Linden, damn the woman—the captain's glower snapped the operator to silent attention. He even trembled slightly.

"Sixth floor," Malachai growled.

"Yes, sir!" The operator pulled the lever, and the elevator started to rise.

"I don't think she cooks the food herself," Malachai said under his breath, pushing the words through seriously gritted teeth.

The woman was a meddling busybody and a shrew. A shapely meddling busybody and shrew. Rather a toothsome bundle, in fact, if it weren't for her mouth. It was perfectly kissable when she wasn't blabbing, but she was a blabber and no mistake. He didn't offer these opinions to Peavey, who seemed to have taken a shine to the Linden female, which might be considered one more indication of Peavey's weak wits, if another one were needed.

"She don't cook it? But she serves it up." Peavey sounded disappointed.

"Don't worry about Miss Linden, Peavey," the captain advised. "You need to think about what happened to you so we can find the man who hit you."

"Oh."

"Sixth floor," the elevator operator said.

"Huh." Malachai felt the operator's gaze on himself and Peavey as they left the elevator and walked down the hallway, Malachai again bearing Peavey's entire weight. "Got your key, Peavey?"

Because he was a kindly superior to his men, whatever Miss Busybody Linden thought of him, he had arranged for Peavey to have a room to himself, right next to the captain's own room. Now he wondered if that hadn't been a mistake, and that he oughtn't to have given Peavey a roommate.

None of the evening's disasters would have happened if Percival Jones had roomed with Peavey, but Percival Jones was a black man, and the Fairfield didn't cotton to Negroes rooming with white men within their hallowed walls. Malachai would have gone to a different hotel, had not Mr. Tillinghurst talked him out of it.

"Can't have my people staying in dumps, Quarles," Tillinghurst had said. "It's either the Fairfield or you and your men stay on my estate. I'm not going to have the press telling the world I'm a damned miser."

Although Malachai thought his partner's argument ridiculous—Malachai had never given a rap what the world thought of him—he bowed to Tillinghurst's wishes. And look what had happened because of it. Peavey and Jones both—what? Kidnaped? Mutinied?

No. Malachai wouldn't allow that anyone on his crew would do such a thing. He hired only the best men, and they'd all been with him for years. He'd hand-selected the crew who'd gone on his most recent adventure aboard *The Moor's Revenge*.

Then what had happened? Where was Jones? Where were the missing artifacts?

Recalling Loretta's suggestion that Tillinghurst was behind the loss of both man and treasure, he snorted.

"You okay, Cap'n?" Peavey sounded worried.

"I'm fine," Malachai said with a heartiness he didn't feel. "It's you we're worried about. You and Jones." He balanced Peavey on his feet, holding him with an arm around his waist, and fished in his pocket for his room key. He'd go through Peavey's pockets himself to see if he could discover Peavey's own room key. Tonight, however, Malachai aimed to keep Peavey with him. He didn't altogether trust Peavey's addled brains not to take him wandering off again.

"Jones? What's the matter with Jones?"

Turning the key in the lock and pushing the door open, Malachai said, "He disappeared the same time you did."

"Did I disappear?" Peavey's tone was one of mild inquiry.

"You sure did."

"I didn't know that." He sounded faintly pleased. "And you went lookin' for me?"

"I did." Carefully, Malachai guided Peavey into the room and across to a fancy overstuffed chair, depositing him on the crushed velvet fabric without a thought to dirt or bloodstains. To hell with the Fairfield's furniture. With the money they charged, they ought to be able to clean any number of over-stuffed chairs.

For some reason, his mind returned to Loretta Linden telling him that Tillinghurst was a self-serving oppressor of the masses, and he grinned in spite of himself. Damn, he hated rabble-rousing women. Even shapely ones with big brown eyes that sparkled at him from behind the lenses of their eyeglasses. *Especially* those. They were dangerous, those ones.

"Thankee, Cap'n. That were right nice of you." Peavey sniffled and wiped away a stray tear with the back of a filthy hand.

"Hell, Peavey, you're my best man. Can't let you disappear, now can I?"

With a smile full of teeth that, while yellow, were still straight and, wonder of wonders, all there, Peavey said, "Reckon not, sir."

"You're going to stay here tonight, Peavey, in this room. Tomorrow, we'll go out looking, and you can tell me if you spot the castle you were held in."

Even as he spoke the words, he knew them to be futile. There was no castle, and there was no dungeon, and Derrick Peavey was a mental case. Malachai probably should stop using him. But he was a damned fine seaman, and he knew his job. It was only while on land that Peavey faltered.

Yet he didn't know what else to do, except talk to Peavey some more. That would probably be futile, too, damn it.

"Look in your pockets and see if you can find your room key, Peavey. If you can find it, I'll go next door and fetch you some clean clothes."

Without answering in words, Peavey began turning out his pockets. Two gold coins spilled out onto the Fairfield's thick woolen carpeting. Peavey stared at them stupidly. "Moors," he said. "It was the Moors done it."

"Yes," Malachai said, "It was the Moors."

"But I don't know how they got in my pocket. Them coins, I mean. Ain't no Moors in there."

Malachai shook his head. "No. There aren't any Moors in your pocket. But I don't know how the coins got there, either." He feared it would be hard going to discover the answer to that one.

A key fell out of Peavey's other pocket and clanked against the coins. "Damn. Is that the key, Cap'n?" He bent to pick it up, groaned, and sat up straight again, his hand pressing his bandage. "Head hurts," he explained simply. "'Cause of the dungeon." He squinted into space for a second, thinking hard. "Nor it weren't the dungeon. It were the place where the pretty lady fed me the soup."

Malachai picked up the key and the coins. After giving the matter some thought, he decided to follow up on this thread, however feeble. At least Peavey seemed to be making connections. "Why were you still there, Peavey? In the lunch place with the pretty lady."

He made an effort and didn't snort over this description of Miss Linden. However apt it was, it failed to take into consideration all of her other, less endearing qualities. The trouble with women was that a man couldn't tape their mouths shut while accomplishing the only act in the world women were good for.

"I weren't *with* her, Cap'n!"

Malachai regretted having shocked his crew member. "I meant, where the lady served you the soup. Why were you still there?"

"Still there?" Peavey looked blankly at his captain.

"Didn't you go outside again after you ate your lunch?"

"Uh . . ." Peavey scratched his bandage.

"Did you stay in the soup kitchen? After you ate your lunch?" Malachai cursed himself for straying from the dungeon. He didn't really care why Peavey had ended up getting himself coshed in the soup kitchen. He needed to know where the stolen artifacts were.

"Oh." Slowly, Peavey nodded. "It was 'cause them Moors was after me. I think." His brow furrowed as he pondered his last statement. Poor Peavey. Thought didn't come easy to the fellow. "Nor it weren't the Moors. It must've been them Spaniards. They was the ones after me. To get the treasure back." He nodded, as if proud of having acquitted himself well during the past painfully contemplative minutes.

Suppressing his frustration, Malachai asked gently, "Is that why you stayed in the soup kitchen after lunch? Because you were afraid the Spaniards were after you?"

A grin split Peavey's face. "That's right! I hid out behind the counter in the kitchen. Them Spaniards, they was chasing me 'cause I took some of the coins to show you."

"Ah. I see." He saw absolutely nothing, except that Peavey had evidently been followed from his fictitious dungeon where he'd discovered the stolen artifacts to the soup kitchen where he'd had lunch, hidden behind a counter, and been knocked unconscious.

But who had followed him? And where had he been? Figuring it was probably useless but worth one last shot, he said, "And you don't remember where the dungeon was? The dungeon where you found the coins?"

"Uh . . ."

Malachai watched the man closely and knew he was thinking as hard as he could. Poor Peavey. Thought wasn't exactly his best friend.

Because he hated watching a man suffer, especially one whom he knew to be a good, if dim, bulb, Malachai finally said, "Go in the bathroom and take a bath, Peavey. I'll get you some clean clothes." Remembering an admonition from Dr. Abernathy, who, Malachai conceded, seemed competent in spite of his overt fondness for Loretta Linden, he added, "Don't get your bandage wet."

"Aye-aye, Cap'n." Gingerly, Peavey levered himself out of the chair. He glanced a question at his captain, who pointed the way, and Peavey slowly and carefully took himself to the bathroom.

As Malachai studied Peavey's unsteady progress, his mind unwillingly returned to Loretta Linden. As much as he hated to admit it, he'd rather enjoyed crossing verbal swords with her. It was just as well that he'd never see her again. If there was anything he didn't need to get entangled with, it was a respectable female. They were dangerous, respectable females, because if a fellow allowed himself to get carried away and have fun with them, they were likely to anchor him for life.

He shuddered eloquently, thinking he should thank his lucky stars he'd escaped that fate. He'd avoided it for nearly forty years now. It would be a shame to let his guard drop now.

Nearly forty years.

The captain frowned and shrugged off his cape, the same cape he'd wrapped around Loretta Linden earlier in the evening. He sniffed, but caught no traces of her scent lingering on the garment. It was just as well. Catching a glimpse of himself in the mirror as he went to hang the cape up in one of the Fairfield's abundant closets, he decided he still looked pretty good for an old salt.

True, he had a couple of silver threads intermingling with the dark brown on his head. And his face had been battered by the weather for so many years, it was lined. But he remained good-looking, in a rugged sort of way. Malachai had heard that many women favored rugged men over those soft specimens who toiled in banks and offices.

He couldn't help but wonder if Loretta Linden did.

Loretta stamped her foot, and then felt silly. She wasn't generally given to childish displays of temper. "Leave me be, Marjorie! I *shall* wear my eyeglasses. There will be *no one* at this stupid party whom I should wish to impress with my loveliness." She sniffed. "Besides, if a gentleman doesn't find me attractive merely because I need spectacles in order to see properly, he's not the gentleman for me."

She didn't bother to say that she was nearing

thirty, far past her prime and on the shelf, as it were, and that no man would want her anyway, eyeglasses or no eyeglasses. Loretta seldom felt sorry for herself, deeming self-pity unworthy of a true woman of the modern age, and it galled her that she'd been feeling the least little bit blue-deviled since her encounter with the detestable Captain Malachai Quarles. She told herself it was because she wanted to set him straight on a number of issues and would now be unable to do so. She was honest enough to admit, if only to herself and only occasionally, that there were other reasons she'd like to see the captain again.

Marjorie MacTavish, elegant this evening in a green ball gown that Loretta had given her and that brought out the green in her eyes, frowned at her employer. "Codswallop. I dinna understand why you canna lower your standards for one wee tiny evening. After all, it's your parents' ball. Don't you owe them the respect of looking your best?"

Marjorie's sensible speech only served to infuriate Loretta. She whirled on her secretary. "It is from my parents that I inherited these eyes, Marjorie MacTavish! If they don't like the fact that I can't see clearly without my spectacles, they should blame themselves, not me!"

"Piffle."

But Marjorie knew when to back down, thank God, or Loretta might have had to chastise her severely, and Loretta hated doing that. Poor Marjorie carried enough burdens already, with her death grip on conformity and her various and sundry neuroses and phobias. Loretta knew that she tried her secretary daily with her outré notions and free-thinking ways.

Nevertheless, Marjorie seemed to feel compelled to complain about another of her millions of grievances against her employer. "I dinna know why you're making *me* attend the ball. I'm a secretary, not a social equal."

Ah, good. A chance to lecture. Loretta always felt better when she was imparting her philosophy of social parity unto a fellow woman. "That's utter nonsense, Marjorie, and you know it! It was an accident of birth that decreed I be born into a family with money and you into one without wealth. Wealth has nothing to do with worth! And furthermore—"

"Tell that to the king," Marjorie muttered under her breath. "And I hate going to grand balls. I feel completely out of place."

Wagging a finger at her secretary, Loretta said, "That's because you've fallen victim to the prevailing attitude that social position is a state of affairs bestowed upon us by God, instead of a system of social injustice cooked up by *men*. *Men* are never happy unless they're grinding others beneath their boot heels. Now if *women* ruled the world—"

But she didn't get to finish her lecture because she and Marjorie were interrupted by a knock on her door.

"Loretta, darling, are you ready?"

Lorretta's mother's sweet voice made Marjorie smile. It made Loretta stick her tongue out and roll her eyes. Oh, she loved her mother, all right, but Mama was so utterly conventional. The poor woman should have given birth to Marjorie. The two were exactly alike.

She found that notion so amusing, it cheered her up, and she didn't regret too much having her lesson to Marjorie interrupted. "I'm ready, Mama." She added, perhaps because she knew it would vaguely irritate both her mother and Marjorie, "and so is Marjorie."

A soft sound came from Marjorie, although Loretta couldn't exactly describe it. A huff of annoyance, perhaps?

"Let me see you, dear," said her mother, wisely overlooking the secretarial issue. "Are you wearing the rose silk?"

"Yes, Mother." Loretta heard the note of resignation in her voice and bucked up. It wouldn't do to allow her mother to believe she'd won a point, so she aimed to pretend it was her own idea to wear the lovely ball gown, rather than one of her less conventional creations. "I'm also wearing my spectacles."

Silence met this declaration. Marjorie made a face. Loretta marched to the door and flung it open. Her mother, a small, vague, pretty woman from whom Loretta had inherited her abundant brown hair and myopic brown eyes, smiled at her anxiously. "Well," said that lady, "I wish you wouldn't wear them, but you still look lovely, darling."

Deciding a graceful acknowledgment of her mother's praise would not compromise her position as an independent, free-thinking woman in this oppressive man's world, Loretta said, "Thank you, Mama," and kissed the older woman on the cheek.

Giving up on the eyeglasses issue as well as the secretarial one—she had long since given up attempting to change her daughter's political attitudes—Mrs. Linden said, "Will you stand in the reception line with your father and me, darling? For a little while, at least?"

Loretta submitted to this request, too, with only a long-suffering sigh to let her mother know how silly she considered reception lines. *Her* friends, the actors, poets, communists, authors, columnists, artists, activists, and other Bohemian souls dear to Loretta's heart, had long since abandoned reception lines as the relic of a bygone era.

She turned toward her secretary. "Come along, Marjorie. The guests are arriving." She took Marjorie's arm and dragged her out into the hallway. If she hadn't done so, Marjorie might well have remained in Loretta's childhood bedroom for the rest of the evening. Loretta called this sort of behavior on her secretary's part "skulking out of sight like a subservient lackey without a brain to call her own." Marjorie called it sensible secretarial behavior.

With a sigh of her own, Marjorie said, "Yes, Loretta." She and Mrs. Linden exchanged a glance of commiseration.

The evening was cool and breezy. No fog polluted the air, which was crisp and smelled vaguely of the sea. Malachai breathed in a lungful of it and wished he were elsewhere in San Francisco, a city he had come to like a lot.

"I hate these damned society parties," he grumbled as he and William Frederick Tillinghurst mounted the stairs leading up to a grand mansion's front porch. He stared up at the imposing structure with disfavor mixed with interest.

After years at sea, he was now in a position to settle down. Thanks to his own efforts in the line of treasure-hunting, as well as a number of shrewd business investments, he could retire from his hard life and relax a bit. What's more, he wouldn't have to skimp if he decided to build a home of his own. He'd almost decided San Francisco was the city to do it in, and, thanks in part to Derrick Peavey's supposed dungeon, he'd been inspecting the various mansions in and around San Francisco for several days. This place was a little old-fashioned and Baroque for his taste.

"We've got to civilize you, Quarles." William Tillinghurst, a small, pinch-faced man who reminded Malachai of a weasel, gave him a sour smile. "You're society's darling at the moment. Act like it, will you?"

"Hell." The thought of being anyone's darling gave Malachai the willies and the creeps.

"Anyhow, we need these people, so act like a gentleman for once, if you can't actually *be* one, will you? If it weren't for investors like these, where would our expedition be?"

"It wouldn't be," conceded Malachai grumpily.

"Then behave yourself. It won't kill you to act agreeable for a few hours."

Malachai wasn't sure about that. "Who'd you say these people are?" He stuck a finger between his neck and the starched collar of his starched shirt and wished he hadn't knotted his cravat so damned tightly. He'd have a rash by morning.

"Linden. Albert and Dorothea Linden. They're nice people, and Albert is the man whose bank lent us the money to proceed with the expedition."

Malachai stopped short. "Linden?"

Tillinghurst glanced over his shoulder. "Yes. Why? Do you know him?"

Could it be? Could the annoying Loretta Linden be the daughter of all this . . . this . . .

Malachai took another gander at the Linden's mansion . . . opulence? Pomposity, rather.

He grinned and hoped so. "Never heard of him."

With a grunt, Tillinghurst yanked on the bell pull. Instantly, a liveried footman opened the door. He told the minion, "Tillinghurst and Quarles. Captain Quarles." The servant bowed and ushered them inside.

They were late, or they'd undoubtedly have been greeted by an open door, blazing lights, and even more liveried servants. Malachai allowed his hat and cape to be taken by yet another servant, and glanced around. Nice place. If Miss Linden did belong to this house, she wasn't hurting for money. That made sense, since she obviously volunteered at that soup kitchen, and only women with money could make pests of themselves in that way.

"If you please, sirs." The door-opening servant— was he a butler? Malachai had never seen a real live butler until he'd partnered up with Tillinghurst— bowed. "Come this way."

The two men followed the butler, who looked ever so much more comfortable in his uniform than Malachai felt in his. Music and chatter grew louder as they approached the ballroom of the mansion. The butler—if he was a butler—opened the massive double doors and announced, "Mr. William Tillinghurst and Captain Malachai Quarles."

The reception line had long been abandoned, and nobody heard him, which was fine with Malachai. He didn't like it that Tillinghurst was right about him. He *was* society's current darling, and he was sick to death of being fawned over by flirtatious females who wanted a fling with the dashing captain, and stuffy males who only wanted the captain to know they were above him socially. Malachai didn't give a tinker's damn about social position. He only went to these functions because Tillinghurst said it was good for their project and, while he didn't much care about Tillinghurst, he cared passionately about his work.

He followed Tillinghurst into the room, then stood at the top of the short staircase and scanned the crowd for a small, brown-haired woman with abundant curves and a hellish disposition.

FIVE

Even Loretta had to admit that her parents' ball-room looked rather like her idea of a fairy kingdom, thanks to all the tiny electrical lights twinkling everywhere. There was a lot to be said for electricity, she thought, although candles were probably more romantic. Then again, Loretta, as an aging spinster with no men lurking on the horizon, had no use for romantic trappings. She told herself it was just as well, and knew in her heart she lied.

The guests, too, looked glorious, as if they might be royalty, or as close to royalty as America's elite society could get. The women were dressed to the teeth, and their diamonds, emeralds and rubies flashed and twinkled as brightly as the electrical lights themselves.

Her mother would be thrilled because everyone who wasn't laid up with a legitimate illness or injury had accepted her invitation. It was because the fools wanted to meet Captain Malachai Quarles and William Frederick Tillinghurst. Loretta's nerves crackled at the mere thought of the captain. She was sure it was aversion to him that had her so on edge. In her heart of hearts, she didn't believe *that*, either.

She stood now with Dr. Jason Abernathy, whom her parents always invited to their parties because his parents were part of "Old San Francisco" society. In other words, they were socially prominent and rich. The fact that their son had, so to speak, let his side down, was a sad disappointment to everyone in the rarefied atmosphere of San Francisco's upper echelon, but it was one that could be overlooked on social occasions, especially since his Chinese wife had died. Were she still alive, matters might have been different.

Marjorie MacTavish stood nearby, still lovely but even more nervous than she'd been while in Loretta's room. Jason Abernathy had that effect on her, probably because he teased her a lot. Loretta suspected they were both sweet on each other, but for some reason they both chose not to let the other in on the secret. She considered them both sillies.

"Loretta," Marjorie pleaded, her voice quiet in an attempt to influence Loretta into lowering her own voice. She did this often. It never worked, but she continued to make the effort. "That isna true, and well you know it. And please try to keep your voice down. People are staring."

"Let them stare," Loretta declaimed, her bespectacled eyes daring anyone to dispute her words, even those not directly involved in the conversation.

"Oh, dear," whispered Marjorie, despairing.

"Besides, it *is* true, Marjorie. Those men are sick. They aren't depraved. Or," she amended graciously, "if they *are* depraved, their depravity is a result of their poverty and not the other way around."

Jason, grinning like a fiend, said, "I think there are points to be made on both sides, Loretta. You know as well as I do that some of the people who perpetrate crimes in our fair city aren't doing so merely because they're poor and need whatever it is they steal. Some of them are flat evil."

Loretta hated it when her friends turned against her. Nevertheless, she had to concede that Jason was, in part, right. "Perhaps. But not very many of them come my way." She sniffed. "In the soup kitchen, we see derelicts, but most of them are either driven low by poverty or drink, or were born with weak wits to begin with."

"And you dinna consider drinking a fault?" Marjorie demanded.

"It's a weakness," Loretta conceded, "but so many of the men we see at the soup kitchen have been driven to drink out of sheer hopelessness."

"How can you possibly know that?" asked Jason, still grinning.

"I've seen the poverty in which they live," Loretta said, shuddering slightly at the recollection of her tour of the slum areas of San Francisco. "It's poverty and despair, not any particular birthplace in society, that dictates whether a person lives a wholesome life or turns to sin and degradation."

"Codswallop. And how, pray tell, can you possibly know *that*?" As a rule, Marjorie remembered her position as Loretta's secretary and didn't speak back to her employer, but every once in a while she forgot herself.

Loretta valued those times and tried to advance them. Beaming at her secretary, she said, "Why, I'll tell you. In fact, I'll give you an example. Do you recall the other day when I came home late? It was dear Eunice's ninth birthday, and I had to stay at the soup kitchen because there had been an incident there."

This time it was Marjorie who sniffed. "An incident, you call it. I call it a crime."

Loretta waved this away with an immaculately gloved hand. "Yes, well, the fact is that the man who was injured was feeble-witted."

"His captain wasn't," Jason muttered. "He was sharp as a tack."

"He was a beast," Loretta corrected, the mention of Captain Quarles having brought to her mind a host of grievances she had against him. "But that's not the point. The point is that when the injured man, Mr. Peavey was his name, ate luncheon with us earlier, he was raving about the Moors invading Spain."

Marjorie's eyes grew wide.

Jason, interested, said, "I didn't know that."

Loretta nodded firmly. "Yes, indeed. What's more, he was referring to the historical event as if it were a current development instead of one that occurred a thousand years ago. I found out later from Captain Quarles that his confusion was probably due to the fact that Mr. Peavey had been involved in Captain Quarles' treasure-recovery mission. That, and the fact that Mr. Peavey's wits are weak to begin with."

Captain Quarles' name coming from her own lips made her frown. In her imagination, she'd been calling him *Captain Quarrels*, and she'd inadvertently emphasized the second syllable of the captain's name. Peering at her friends, she deduced they hadn't caught anything amiss in her pronunciation.

"I'm sure you've read about it," she went on. She certainly had, although she hadn't done so until after her meeting with the captain. Since that day, she'd been devouring every article she could find about the captain and his exploits.

"Of course I've read about him. But how does Mr. Peavey's weak wits prove anything?" demanded Marjorie. "According to you, the poor man had been hit a cruel blow on the head. That might addle anyone's wits."

"Yes, but don't you see, he'd been raving *before* the blow fell!" Loretta felt triumphant. "What's more, he was deep into a conversation with another one of our guests, yet they were talking about totally different things. Only neither man recognized the fact. It was quite amusing, really," she admitted.

"I doubt Peavey would think so," a voice like waves crashing against a granite cliff came at her back.

Loretta jumped a foot and spun around. "*You!*" she cried, feeling herself flush.

"I," said Malachai Quarles smugly, towering over her and overtly pleased at having startled her.

Before she could shout at him, Jason stole her thunder. Sticking out his right hand, he said, "A pleasure to see you again, Captain Quarles. How's our patient doing?"

Taking Jason's hand and shaking it heartily, Malachai said with a smile that robbed Loretta of her breath, "Peavey's recovering very well, thank you, Dr. Abernathy. Your competent doctoring has saved him a lot of agony in years to come. If he hadn't had that shoulder tended to, it would have bothered him forever." With a squint at Loretta, he added, "However, I fear his wits are permanently addled. They were before he was coshed. I doubt they've improved any since."

"That," said Loretta, trying to ignore the captain's brilliant white-toothed smile and so furious she could scarcely form coherent sentences, "just made my point! That poor, poor man!"

The captain's right eyebrow lifted over a sardonic and wickedly gleaming dark eye. "Peavey would be the first to tell you he can't think straight, Miss Linden. His prowess lies in deeds, not words. In spite of his mental failings, he's a first-class seaman. That day he took a meal in your soup kitchen was the first time I've ever seen or even heard about Peavey accepting charity." He placed a malevolent emphasis on the word *charity*. "I'm sure it was a momentary lapse brought about by hunger."

"Why, you—"

Breaking into the spat rather loudly as the orchestra struck up a waltz, Jason held his hand out to Marjorie. "Will you waltz with me, Miss Mac-Tavish?"

Shooting a worried glance at Loretta and the captain, and for perhaps the first time since she'd met Dr. Abernathy, Marjorie accepted an offer made by him with alacrity. "Aye. Thank you!"

Loretta took umbrage in the fact that her secretary sounded relieved. She turned on Malachai like a termagant. "You're doing that on purpose!"

"Doing what?" the captain asked, his voice as mild as milk.

Looking him up and down as if he were some odd and malignant life form, she waved her arms in the air in a very broad, unladylike gesture. "That! Lurking and looming! You lurked behind me and now you're looming over me, trying to intimidate me!" Planting her fists on her hips, she snarled, "Well, it won't work, curse you!"

"Good. Let's dance." And with that, Malachai grabbed Loretta around the waist and swept her off into the waltz.

She didn't stand a chance of rebelling, since he was so much larger and heavier than she. Neither her size nor his affected her voice. "Let go of me this instant, you brute! How dare you—"

"Sweep you off your feet?" Malachai suggested. "Carry you away on the wings of music? Entice you out of your humdrum life?"

"No!" she shouted. Fortunately, only those couples dancing closest to them heard her. She was embarrassed when several shocked faces turned her way.

"Tut, tut," said the captain. "You're making a spectacle of yourself, my dear."

"Curse you," Loretta whispered fiercely. Having been recalled to her spectacles, she realized they'd slid down her nose. She wanted to push them back up, but the captain had usurped her hands and she couldn't.

"My, my, such language from so exalted a lady."

"I am not," she muttered.

"You're not a lady? I'm glad to hear it."

She shot him a suspicious glance. "Just what do you mean by that?"

The glance was a mistake, because Loretta got trapped by those gleaming dark eyes of his. She felt herself flush once more, only this time it was fueled by some kind of internal heat with which she was unfamiliar. It wasn't rage, although she was certainly angry, and it wasn't embarrassment, although she was terribly vexed.

Good heavens. Could this be lust?

Loretta, who espoused virtually every modern cause that came her way, had long been an advocate of free love, and not merely because the notion shocked her parents. She honestly believed that an uncommitted relationship was better than a bad marriage. In her slum work, she'd seen too many couples who believed they were shackled together for life even though they were miserable with each other. Of course, the fact that *women* were unable to secure employment that paid them well enough to support themselves and their children was the primary cause of *that* injustice.

But she was straying from the point. She advocated free love. The fact that she'd never had the opportunity to test her conviction as regarded a sexual relationship unencumbered by the bonds of matrimony bothered her some. She told herself that no man had yet come up to her exacting standards, although in her more honest moments, she didn't believe it.

Honestly, Loretta feared the answer was more simple—and more dismaying—than that. She was a high-minded, intellectual, independent woman—and she wore eyeglasses—and men didn't find her desirable.

"I don't generally care for ladies," the captain said in answer to her question. "I'm glad to discover you aren't one."

"That's not what I meant, and you know it." Loretta attempted a brief rebellion, but the captain held her fast. "Do you always make women dance against their will?" She hoped his conscience would be pricked.

Either he didn't possess a conscience, or it was an impenetrable object. "Only occasionally."

He gave her a smile that would have sent her reeling if she hadn't been held so tightly. He had *such* white teeth, and *such* a rich bronze complexion. It didn't seem fair somehow that Captain Malachai Quarles should be so attractive, physically, when he was such a brute.

Unable to do anything more effective to demonstrate her displeasure, Loretta huffed indignantly. Subsiding into the waltz, since she had no other choice, she acknowledged to herself—she'd never say so to the captain—that her partner waltzed rather well for so large a man. Of course, he'd recently become the darling of society, so he'd presumably had lots of practice dancing with all the current debutantes. Not to mention their mothers, some of whom, Loretta was sure, had no doubt offered the captain a good deal more than a waltz or two. She realized she was grinding her teeth and stopped at once.

Because she thought it might annoy him, she said after a lengthy pause, "How do you like being the toast of the town, Captain Quarles? On our first meeting, I got the impression you didn't enjoy publicity. I must have been wrong, since you're in all the newspapers every day." She attempted a smirk, but it didn't work very well because Malachai swung her into a series of turns that robbed her of breath.

"It won't last long," he said blandly.

"Whoo!" Embarrassed by her loud exhalation, Loretta swallowed another breath and managed to pant, "What won't last long?" She was sorry she'd done so as soon as the words were out because she

didn't want the arrogant so-and-so to think she cared.

"My fame." He still spoke casually, as if fame meant nothing to him.

Loretta was loath to believe it. She wanted the captain to be guilty of every sin in the book, including vanity and greed. Fortunately, the music came to an end so they had to stop dancing. She was about to pass out from lack of breath, and she cursed both herself and Marjorie for forcing her into too-tight stays for her parents' party. She was usually more sensible than this.

She and Malachai applauded politely, the captain as serene as a mirror-smooth ocean, Loretta puffing like a steam engine. She refused to look at him, but she felt his gaze upon her. She was about to turn and storm off when he said, "You might think about getting more exercise, Miss Linden. You're out of breath, and we only danced one little waltz."

Goaded beyond endurance, Loretta said through clenched teeth as she shoved her eyeglasses back into place, "I do *not* need more exercise! It's my damned corset!"

As luck would have it, the applause stopped a split-second before the word *damned* popped out of Loretta's mouth. She felt her cheeks flame up like a fiery sunrise as every person in the ballroom turned to stare at her. *Damned*, combined with the word *corset*, and Loretta had stepped far beyond the bounds of polite conversation. Gasps and titters floated up from the assemblage of beautifully clad party guests.

Smiling down upon her as if she were an amusing child, Malachai said, "Did he really say such a thing in your presence, Miss Linden? Tsk, tsk. I'm very sorry. I'll speak to him about using such shocking language in front of a lady."

Loretta had never seen an entire herd of people lose interest in anything so fast. As suddenly as they'd begun staring at her, the company turned away and resumed talking about other things. And she had the captain to thank for saving her from social pariahhood—or, at the very least, a lecture from her father. She'd sooner jump off a high cliff than be indebted to Malachai Quarles for anything at all.

"Curse you!" she whispered at Malachai, who was grinning down upon her like one of the devil's operatives who had caught a human object in a lie and was now going to exact payment.

"What dreadful language. I wonder where you learned it."

"Monster!" She whirled around but didn't get far.

He took her arm. She tried to shake off his hand, but, as ever, couldn't. "My goodness, Miss Linden, you're certainly a fiery young lady. I mean, of course, young *woman*. You've proved yourself to be no lady."

"Let me go," she growled as he started off, taking her with him by the simple expedient of hanging onto her arm and walking away from where they'd been standing.

"Not yet." He glanced down at her, his chiseled features wearing an expression of benign and only vague interest. "I think it would be best if you picked up your feet, Miss Linden. You're likely scratching the polish on this lovely dance floor. I doubt that your father would approve."

Her heels screeched against the highly polished parquet flooring, and Loretta finally gave up and lifted her feet. She was in enough hot water with her parents; she didn't need her father complaining to her about having to resurface the ballroom floor. "What do you know about my father?" she demanded in a hiss like a kettle boiling.

"Not a thing except that he disapproves of his hellion of a daughter." Malachai sighed dramatically. "The trials parents endure for the sake of their children. Fortunately for him, your brother is more conformable than you. Or so I understand."

It was true. Loretta had long since given up trying to raise her brother to a sense of his societal obligations. He was not merely rich as Midas, but stiff as a stick, and he believed anyone not wealthy was somehow undeserving. In other words, he was a prig, and Loretta didn't like him. "Bother my brother! Let me go!"

"After I get you a glass of punch. Isn't that what gentlemen are supposed to do for ladies with whom they've danced?"

"Gentlemen?" Loretta said with awful sarcasm.

"Men, then," the captain amended genially. "You seem a trifle hot under the collar, however. I'm sure a glass of punch will cool you down."

"Oh, Loretta, dear!"

The tittering voice of her mother slapped Loretta's ears like a wet washrag. Loretta, finding herself next to the punch bowl and on her own once more, Malachai having released her arm, turned with resignation. Once again pushing her spectacles up her nose, as they'd slid a trifle as the captain had dragged her to the refreshment table, Loretta said, "Hello, Mother." Loretta loved her mother dearly, but she wasn't happy to see her. Her voice reflected it.

"I'm so glad to see the two of you together, dear," Mrs. Linden said, bestowing a smile of affection first upon her daughter and then upon the captain. Loretta's teeth started grinding again.

The captain executed a perfect bow. Loretta glowered at him. "May I get you a glass of punch, Mrs. Linden? I was just pouring one for your daughter." He gave Loretta the same perfect bow, marred only by the sardonic grin on his face.

Loretta would have loved to throw the punch in his face, but she couldn't humiliate her mother by doing so. Besides, she was thirsty after that energetic waltz. "Thank you." She pushed the words out through her teeth.

"I should love to have some punch," Mrs. Linden said, happily unaware of the tension roiling in waves from her daughter and bouncing off the captain as if it didn't exist.

Loretta didn't like the way her mother's pretty brown eyes were twinkling. She'd seen that look on her mother's face before, generally when Mrs. Linden was about to foist some young man upon her peppery daughter in the hope that Loretta would forget about her causes, get married, start a family, and stop embarrassing the family. If it hadn't worked with any of the other young men in San Francisco, it sure as the devil wouldn't work with Captain Malachai Quarles. Loretta wouldn't disappoint her mother by saying so, at least not right here, right now.

Mrs. Linden took the punch from Malachai with a charming smile and turned to her daughter. "I was going to bring Captain Quarles over to you so that I could introduce you, dear, but he said you two were already acquainted."

Loretta pried her teeth apart. "We weren't exactly

introduced. Captain Quarles tried to strangle me in
the soup kitchen several days ago."

She regretted her sarcastic statement as soon as
she saw the color leave her mother's face and a bewildered expression consume it. In fact, Mrs.
Linden's expression was evolving into one of shock
and horror when Loretta, feeling guilty, decided to
ease her mind. She hated doing it. She wanted the
world to detest Malachai Quarles as much as she
did. "That was only a joke, Mother."

Blinking first at Loretta and then at Malachai,
Mrs. Linden said, "Oh? I . . . uh . . . don't think I understand, dear."

Before Loretta could speak again, Malachai took
over. "Perfectly understandable, Mrs. Linden. Your
daughter is something of a jokesmith, I gather." He
looked reproachfully at Loretta. "You shouldn't
tease your mother, Miss Linden. She might take
you seriously one of these days."

"Indeed," murmured Mrs. Linden, whose expression now evidenced hurt.

Loretta wanted to take a blackjack to the both of
them. "It wasn't really a joke." Her jaw was aching
from having clenched her teeth so tightly, and it
was difficult to speak for the rigidity of her face
muscles. "The captain broke into the soup kitchen
because he thought one of his men was there."
Which reminded her of something. She turned on
Malachai. "Just exactly who told you Mr. Peavey was
there, anyhow?"

"Perhaps we should discuss this at another time,
Miss Linden. It doesn't seem appropriate conversation for so pleasant a party."

"Why, you—"

"Indeed, Captain Quarles," said Mrs. Linden,

lightly stepping on and squashing her daughter's irate retort. She'd become an expert at thwarting Loretta in exactly that way years earlier.

Loretta shut her mouth with a snap and vowed never to speak to Captain Malachai Quarles or her interfering mother again. She sniffed and downed the rest of her punch.

With a worried glance at her daughter, Mrs. Linden said, "It's about time for the buffet to be served. Will you escort Loretta to the buffet, Captain Quarles?"

"But—"

Again Loretta was thwarted, this time by the captain. "I'd be delighted to do so." Taking Loretta's hand and placing it on his arm, he leaned over and spoke in an undertone. "I'll tell you all about how Peavey got to where he was coshed."

"That's lovely, dear." Mrs. Linden smiled brightly on the ill-matched couple and tripped off, Loretta presumed, to find her father.

Having vowed only seconds earlier never to speak to Malachai again in this lifetime, Loretta now broke her vow. Scowling hideously at him, she snapped, "You're a big bully, Captain Quarles. I presume you know that."

His eyebrows lifted so high they nearly got lost in his hairline. "Your mother seems to like me."

"She doesn't know you."

"A shame, that. Here, let me take you in to the buffet. I meant what I said. I'll tell you all about Peavey."

Indignation warred with curiosity for only seconds before it suffered a humiliating defeat. For all her anger at the captain and all her outrage that he should manhandle her and embarrass her and make her feel small and insignificant, she still felt a strange reluctance to part from him.

Although she didn't want to admit it, especially to herself, she wondered if her reluctance stemmed in part from her not caring to see him dance with other ladies, some of whom were younger and more beautiful than she. Of course, they were all idiots who had no conversation, but Loretta had noticed that men generally didn't care if a woman was stupid as long as she was pretty.

Men. She despised most of them. Almost all of them, in fact.

She had a dismal feeling that one of the reasons she so hated men was because no man, as of the current date, had ever attempted to seduce her. The notion was so depressing that she decided to encourage her wrath in an effort to conquer it.

"Have a seat, Miss Linden. I'll fetch you a plate."

She sat and remained mute, her lips pressed so tightly together, her cheeks ached.

"Is there anything in particular you like?" He smiled sweetly at her.

She glared back at him and spake not.

With a knowing grin and a devilish twinkle, the captain then asked, "Is there anything in particular you *don't* like?"

Finally, she couldn't keep silent another second longer. Glaring up at Malachai, she whispered harshly, "I hate you."

He shook his head sadly. "And here I thought we were getting along so well."

If she'd had anything in her hands, Loretta would have thrown it at his insolent back as he strolled away from her to pick up a plate. It was fortunate for her such a satisfying gesture was denied to her. She'd already made a exhibition of herself and would inevitably hear about it from her father in the morning.

What she should probably do was get up and leave the blasted captain with his blasted plate full of food. Loretta glowered at the buffet table, thinking *that would teach him.*

If she did that, however, she'd never learn about Mr. Peavey and why he'd been knocked out in the soup kitchen.

On the other hand, Captain Quarles deserved to be abandoned. Interesting scenarios, most of them involving the captain standing alone in a church and waiting for his bride—Loretta, naturally—who never came to take the wedding vows, entertained her for a few seconds before she told herself not to be an idiot. No woman would ever leave the captain at the altar, for the simple reason that no woman would be fool enough to agree to marry him in the first place.

So the best thing to do would be to get up and leave.

She frowned, recalling the Peavey problem. There was no way to ensure that she'd ever meet Captain Quarles again, much less that he'd talk to her about Mr. Peavey if they did meet. She wanted to hear about Peavey. And that, blast it, meant that she'd have to sit there and wait for him to come back to her.

Curse her curiosity. It was forever getting her into trouble.

Malachai was halfway through the buffet line before he realized he wasn't bored. He frowned when he then realized he wasn't bored because he was having so much fun tormenting Loretta Linden.

He didn't like the notion that a *woman* was entertaining him. On the other hand, Loretta probably wouldn't be so much fun if she weren't such a magnificent target for teasing. If he were, say, to hold a sensible conversation with her—not that such a thing was possible with a woman—she'd undoubtedly turn out to be just as boring as all the other women he'd ever met.

Looking around, he saw that there were a lot of them present, too. Women here and women there. Women, women everywhere, nor any one he wanted. Coleridge had got his poem wrong.

Unfortunately, many of them wanted him. If Malachai had still been a young man—a *younger* man, that is to say—he'd have appreciated the attention. As it was, he'd long ago had his fill of silly, brainless women who only wanted him to spice up their lives while their husbands entertained their mistresses. After you'd done the one thing worth doing with a woman, what did you do then? Malachai always wanted to go home, and they always wanted him to stay and listen to them complain about their husbands. High society wasn't Malachai's cup of tea.

But Loretta Linden . . . well . . . Malachai glanced at her surreptitiously as he plopped crab cakes onto his plate and grinned. She sat there seething like a geyser about to blow, clearly weighing her options. Should she walk off and show him how much she hated him or wait so that she could learn about Peavey?

He wasn't surprised to find her where he'd left her when he returned to her chair, holding a plate heaped high with delectable things to eat. He'd taken a lot because Loretta might be small, but she wasn't skinny, bless her. She had flesh on her. Malachai liked his women with flesh.

Executing another bow, mainly because he knew it would annoy her, he then took the chair next to her. He had to run off a young cub in order to do it, but one glare had been enough. The poor fellow jumped up as if he'd sat on a hot rock and run away with his tails flapping behind him. The younger generation had no grit in them.

"You're a brute," Loretta said in greeting. "That poor fellow did nothing to you."

"I did nothing to him, either," Malachai pointed out. "Besides, he was in my chair."

"You're worse than a brute. You're an arrogant fiend."

He gave one of his standard shrugs. "He could have stayed if he'd wanted to. Fellow has no gumption."

"Honestly!" Loretta ignored the plate he held out for her, turning her head away and glowering at the crowd surrounding the buffet table. Two young ladies, catching her baleful look, started and hurried away from her.

Malachai chuckled and popped an olive into his mouth. "Why'd you wait for me if you hate me so much?"

She transferred her glower to him. "You know very well why I waited. I want to know what happened the other night. How did Mr. Peavey get into the soup kitchen after I'd locked it up? How did the other men get there? *Why* was he there? How did you find him?"

So Malachai told her. He was pleased to note that

she became engrossed in his tale, momentarily forgot she hated him, and began taking things from the plate and nibbling them. She had the brightest eyes. Her eyeglasses—he'd been surprised to see them at first, before he realized she'd worn them to irk her parents—only magnified her beautiful brown eyes, which were plenty large enough to begin with.

When he was through with his tale, she continued to stare at him for a moment, then said, "That's it? He hid behind the counter, some men broke in, and then you broke in, and then I came in, and you tried to throttle me?"

"That's it."

"And you've looked for Mr. Peavey's dungeon since then?"

"I've looked. Every blasted day." Malachai cast his weary gaze at the embossed ceiling, recalling what seemed like a thousand San Francisco houses he and Peavey had investigated during the past week. He was sick to death of climbing up and down hills and ogling rich men's estates. Damn it, he wanted a house of his own; he didn't want merely to stare at those belonging to other people. He was getting too damned old for the adventurer's life.

Or . . . well . . . not too old, exactly, but he was . . . tired of it. Yes, that's what his problem was. It wasn't age. It was a certain fatigue that came with doing the same thing year after year. He felt better after he'd cleared up the age issue in his mind.

"But *why?*"

He shrugged. "I have no idea."

"But it makes no sense! Anyway, how did you know to look in the soup kitchen?"

"I'd been searching for Peavey and Jones, and I asked people as I went along. A Chinaman who'd worked for me once told me somebody sounding like Peavey and talking about Moors had eaten lunch in the soup kitchen."

She frowned, and two tiny lines furrowed her brow right above her nose. They were cute, those lines. Malachai had a sudden and, fortunately, brief urge to kiss them away.

Lord, what was the matter with him? Just because he thought Miss Linden was a spicy dish, there was no reason on earth to want to kiss her. Anywhere. He'd been avoiding respectable females for nearly forty years now, and he wasn't about to be snagged by one at his age.

Damn. There he went again, focusing on his age. And he wasn't old, dammit.

Anyhow, Loretta Linden didn't appear to want to snag him. In actual fact, she seemed rather more inclined to shoot him. And then kick him after he fell down dead. The truth rankled even as it tickled him, although he didn't know why it should.

She shook her head, still frowning. Malachai appreciated the way her pink ball gown left so much of her skin exposed. Her shoulders were soft and white, and he itched to caress them.

Borrowing from Loretta, he shook his head, hard, and decided he was losing his mind.

Loretta smacked a fist against her pink-satin knee. "I tell you, it's Mr. Tillinghurst. He's involved in the villainy somehow."

It was probably the best thing she could have said under the circumstances because it was so absurd, it made Malachai forget all about Loretta's skin and how soft and enticing it looked. "Damnation, will you stop being stupid? That's the most imbecilic accusation I've ever heard!"

SIX

The morning after her parents' party, Loretta was still fuming about having been called an imbecile by Malachai Quarles. "Damn him!"

"Damn whom?" asked Marjorie, who had resigned herself to Loretta's cursing. She held an ankle-length, rust-and-white-striped cotton day dress that Loretta had asked her to fetch from her closet.

"Captain Quarles," Loretta growled, tugging a knee-length, yellow silk chemise over her head and smoothing it over her hips. She squinted at those hips in the mirror, wondering if she ought to lose weight. Perhaps Captain Quarles would like her better if she weren't so—

She didn't allow herself to finish the thought. She also gave herself several hard mental slaps for almost having had it in the first place.

As if she gave a rap what Malachai Quarles thought of her! Why, the thought was not merely idiotic, but was certainly doomed to failure, even if she allowed herself to have it, which she wouldn't. Malachai Quarles was nothing to her but a minor thorn in her side. He wasn't worth the snap of her fingers.

"Hold your arms up," Marjorie told her, opting

not to comment on Loretta's feelings about the captain.

Loretta eyed her narrowly in the instant before Marjorie dropped the dress over her head, but discerned no emotion on her secretary's face. Marjorie was an expert at hiding her feelings, thanks to her years as a White Star Line stewardess. Loretta often suspected her of harboring rebellious thoughts, but so far, Marjorie had remained stoic.

This morning, unlike most mornings, Loretta appreciated her for her forbearance. If Marjorie had said anything nice about Malachai Quarles, Loretta might have been pushed into throwing a temper tantrum.

As Marjorie pulled the dress over Loretta's arms and body, Loretta's voice was muffled by the fabric. "But I'll show him."

"You'll show who what?"

Loretta's head popped through the neck opening of the dress, and she adjusted it around her hips—which were *not* too large—as Marjorie shook out the rust-colored cotton top with a detachable shawl collar that went over the striped dress. Marjorie herself was clad in an olive tailored suit with a collarless jacket and an ankle-length skirt that Loretta had given her for her birthday.

Although Loretta believed that a slavish devotion to fashion was both unseemly and ridiculous, she appreciated nice clothes and made sure her secretary always dressed as well as she herself did. It had taken, literally, months to convince Marjorie to wear the clothes Loretta had made for her. The stubborn woman had some nonsensical notion that it was improper for an employer to supply her secretary with a fashionable wardrobe.

Loretta had finally shut her up by telling her she refused to employ a frumpish secretary because Marjorie's dowdiness would reflect poorly on her as an employer. Although Loretta still had her doubts as to whether or not Marjorie approved of taking clothes as part of her salary, at least she no longer quibbled about wearing them.

Taking the rust-colored top from Marjorie's fingers, dropping it over her head, and tugging it past the various obstacles in its way, Loretta answered, "I'll show Captain Quarles that I'm right."

Marjorie sighed and picked up Loretta's hat, a felt number with an upturned brim that matched the rust of her top and which had a nice plump, brown ostrich feather as trim. Loretta had searched her heart and her conscience for a long time before she'd allowed the ostrich feather to be used as an adornment on her hat, but the milliner had assured her that the ostriches lived on a nice, tidy farm in Pasadena, California, and weren't mistreated when their feathers were being harvested, so Loretta had allowed it. She didn't believe in slaughtering animals for the sake of fashion.

"What are you going to be right about?" Marjorie asked, handing Loretta the hat.

Loretta plopped it on her head, adjusted it—her hair was so thick, this operation sometimes took a bit of maneuvering—and secured it with a long, sharp hat pin. "I'll show him that I'm right about Mr. Tillinghurst."

Holding out Loretta's gloves, Marjorie asked, "What about Mr. Tillinghurst?"

Turning away from the mirror, satisfied with her appearance, Loretta took the gloves. "I'll prove to him that he's a villain, is what."

"Captain Quarles is a villain?" Marjorie sounded startled. "I know you dinna care for him, but—"

"Not Quarles," Loretta interrupted. "Tillinghurst is the villain." She sniffed. "Although it wouldn't surprise me to discover that Captain Quarles is right behind him in the villainy department."

Since she'd brought her own hat to Loretta's room when she came in to help her dress, Marjorie now stood before the mirror and put it on. Loretta envied her secretary that brilliant red hair of hers. Wouldn't she just love to have Marjorie's hair? Captain Quarles wouldn't call her an imbecile if she had hair like that.

Again, Loretta took herself to task for thinking about the captain in that way. She reminded herself that it didn't matter a bean whether or not the captain thought she was attractive or repugnant. The captain was a fiend, and Loretta hated him. "I absolutely love that hat, Marjorie. I'm so glad you're wearing it today."

Marjorie sighed. "You provide me with the best wardrobe any secretary ever had, Loretta. And you shouldna do it."

"Fiddlesticks. I won't have a dowdy secretary. It's bad for my image." She laughed, the absurdity of her remark having restored her humor.

Marjorie shook her head. That head looked wonderful now, topped by the brown felt hat with its turned-down brim, decorated with olive and brown felt cutouts. The two of them were going to appear absolutely modish and perfectly businesslike, not to mention innocent, when they visited the Museum of Natural History to observe the new exhibit of Moorish artifacts on display. All the artifacts had been found by Captain Malachai Quarles in his recent treasure-recovery mission. All the artifacts, that is to say, except those Mr. Tillinghurst had stolen.

Loretta *knew* it was Tillinghurst, mainly because she knew Tillinghurst. And she'd prove it. Somehow. She plunked herself down on her bed and toed a black leather shoe with a small buckle trim toward her. She leaned over with a grunt and slipped it on.

Perhaps she *should* lose a pound or two. Not for the sake of her appearance, but because she was finding it difficult to bend over. Loretta hated dieting.

However, she was quite fond of brisk exercise, and perhaps that might be put to good use and she wouldn't have to cut down on her meals. She'd simply take more walks. That's what she'd do. Instead of driving the Runabout to the soup kitchen and to her other charitable works, she would walk. That would melt the pounds away, she'd enjoy the exercise, and she would no longer grunt when she leaned over.

Or when she danced a vigorous waltz, although that crisis had been occasioned by her too-tight corset. She wore no whalebone today. To the devil with stays!

She grunted again when she reached for the other shoe and her vow to take more long walks solidified. For her health's sake, of course. Not for the sake of any man, and especially not for that of Captain Malachai Quarles. She felt better for having decided to get more exercise and stood up smiling. "Ready?"

"Aye," said Marjorie doubtfully. "Where did you say we were going today?"

"To the Museum of Natural History." Loretta snatched up her black handbag and opened her bedroom door with a flourish. "Onward and upward!"

"Onward, at any rood," muttered Marjorie as she walked out the door.

"Buck up, Marjorie." Loretta, following her, skipped down the stairs of her imposing Russian Hill home with energy.

In spite of last night's ball at her parents' house, and even after going to sleep far past her usual bedtime, she felt very well this morning, perhaps because she'd slept late and missed her father's telephone call. Marjorie had given her the message, and Loretta planned to ignore it. If her father disapproved of her behavior at his parties, he could dashed well stop insisting she attend the stupid things. Loretta felt much more at home with her radical friends than she did in her parents' stuffy mansion on Nob Hill.

She waved a cheery good-bye to her housekeeper, Mrs. Brandeis, and her two housemaids, Molly and Li, took a fashionable woolen coat from the hall closet, threw it on, and exited her grand home. Standing on the porch, she took in a deep, fortifying breath of morning air—well, it was actually almost noonish air—and said to Marjorie, "I believe we shall walk to the museum."

Marjorie, who had also put on her coat, cast a doubtful look at the gray, menacing sky and then at her pretty brown shoes. "Oh?"

"It's not far," Loretta said bracingly. "And the weather is quite nice for walking."

"I think it's going to rain."

"Pooh. If it rains, I shall hail a cab." And Loretta

set off, clacking down the marble porch steps and striding briskly down her long drive to Lombard Street.

"Vurra well." Marjorie followed her employer, not quite as briskly, but resigned to her fate.

Lombard Street itself was eminently walkable, being paved with bricks and with a sidewalk built like a staircase. The beautiful street twisted and turned and let the two ladies out on Leavenworth Street, where Loretta recommenced her striding.

Marjorie, puffing, said, "Please slow down a wee bit, Loretta. I'm'na race horse."

Loretta slowed her steps, critically eyeing her secretary. "Are you wearing a corset?"

Shooting a quick, embarrassed glance around, Marjorie hissed, "Aye! Dinna talk about corsets on a public street, for sweet Jesus' sake!"

"Fiddlesticks. I keep telling you that corsets were designed by vicious male criminals to keep women oppressed. I wish you wouldn't wear them."

"Aye, I know you do." Marjorie sounded the tiniest bit resentful. "However, I, unlike you, amna comfortable appearing in public with next to nothing on!"

"Piffle. I have plenty of clothes on. Only *my* clothes don't cut off my circulation and obstruct my breathing."

"Aye, aye, I know all about that." Marjorie frowned at Loretta, which was the most overt rebellion she ever allowed herself. "However, even you mun admit that you looked vurra bonny last night, *in* a corset and stays." Again, she glanced around, this time embarrassed by her own words. Fortunately for Marjorie, there was no one close enough to overhear the two women's conversation.

"And I also almost dropped dead from lack of oxygen after dancing one little waltz," Loretta said bitterly.

The truth was that Loretta *had* looked almost beautiful the prior evening, and the truth was also that she *had* been coerced into wearing her corset and stays. She'd also nearly passed out after that waltz, although the humiliation of that event didn't quite make up for how wonderful she'd felt, knowing she looked her very best and that gentlemen had paid her some attention.

The combined effects of the last evening's ball rendered Loretta unusually confused this morning, too. While she hated having given in to pressure from her mother and Marjorie on the corset-and-stays issue, she had also found the masculine attention she'd garnered, in spite of her eyeglasses, most gratifying.

She chalked up her mixed feelings to years of forced capitulation to masculine domination and felt a trifle better as she marched along, taking very big, very unladylike strides. Once more realizing she'd lost her secretary, Loretta sighed and slowed down. "Sorry, Marjorie."

"That's quite all right," Marjorie gasped.

Although Loretta wouldn't say so, she felt rather wilted herself by the time the two ladies arrived at the Museum of Natural History. Their first stop, after checking their coats in the cloak room, was the ladies' restroom on the first floor. She was distressed to see that even her ostrich plume drooped slightly.

"It's the damp," said Marjorie, patting the moisture from her own face with a handkerchief, as Loretta tried to fluff the feather up. "It will probably perk up as it dries out."

"Yes. I'm sure you're right." Small comfort. Loretta had been looking forward to appearing her best for this exhibit. Not that she had any expectation of meeting anyone she cared about, of course, but still . . .

Curse it, she was hoping she'd bump into Malachai Quarles! Who was she trying to fool? Herself? Taking a leaf from the captain's log, Loretta called herself an imbecile as she gave up on her feather. She granted Marjorie one of her brightest smiles. "All ready?"

"Aye."

"Do your feet hurt?" Loretta's did. That was another thing she wouldn't confess aloud. However, she began to think they'd catch a cab home.

"A wee bit. Not badly."

"Good."

They each picked up a brochure about the Moorish exhibit at the front desk and meandered through the museum until they got to the room where the display was set up. "I've been looking forward to seeing this ever since that poor man got knocked out in the soup kitchen," Loretta told her secretary.

"Ah," said Marjorie.

"Did I tell you that as he walked through the food line, he talked about the Moors?"

"Aye."

"It was as if the Moors had invaded Spain during the last weekend or something."

"Aye, so you said."

"The way he spoke about the event sounded so current."

"Mmm."

Perceiving that she'd get no help from her secretary as far as conversation went, Loretta shut her mouth. She was unusually nervous today. She couldn't account for her state of agitation except by acknowledging that she anticipated seeing Malachai Quarles at the exhibit. She hated herself for her emotional condition almost as much as she hated the captain.

Pride and self-respect came to her aid, and Loretta was sure she didn't *look* perturbed, however upset her innards were. Because she wasn't wearing a corset and could, she took a deep breath before entering the Moorish Hall.

Her breath left her in a whoosh when she first glimpsed the extent of the treasure Tillinghurst and Quarles had recovered. "Oh, my! Will you look at all this!"

"Och! Mon!" Marjorie stared about her, her mouth open. "It's vurra bonny."

"Isn't it?" Loretta moved into the hall, her disquiet forgotten as her eyes scanned the room. She didn't know about Marjorie, but her imagination was instantly stirred by the exotic display. She knew those rugs hadn't been recovered from the sunken ship, since any rugs aboard the vessel must have long since disintegrated under tons of salty ocean water. However, the museum-display people had managed to secure examples of Moorish rugs from somewhere, and, as wall hangings, they served as a lush background to the splendid furniture, gold fittings, weaponry, armor, jewelry, art objects, and plates gleaming in front of their eyes.

"Where do you suppose they got that gorgeous silk inside the display case? The one with those wonderful cups?" Loretta's voice had sunk to a whisper without her conscious effort.

So had Marjorie's. "I have'na idea. It's so . . . so . . . opulent."

"Good word for it." Loretta aimed toward the first display case on the left.

"I've never seen such craftsmanship," admitted Marjorie. "It's vurra different from the Chinese objects I've seen."

"Yes, it is. Chinese art is more familiar to us here in San Francisco, too. Perhaps that's why this all seems so exotic."

"That," added Marjorie, "and the fact that it's a dunnamany years old."

"Indeed, it says in the brochure that the vessel sank almost a thousand years ago. Oh, look at this, Marjorie!" Loretta had stopped in front of a glass display case in which resided several intricately crafted frogs that were obviously made of some kind of metal. "I wonder what they're made of? Do you suppose they're copper? Look at the verdigris."

"They're brass, coated with copper," a rumbling purr came from behind them.

Loretta closed her eyes for only a second, before turning and frowning at Captain Quarles. "I might have known you'd sneak up on us," she said by way of greeting. "You always do."

Marjorie muttered, "Loretta!" under her breath.

"Nonsense," said the captain, grinning like Lewis Carroll's Cheshire cat. "Your nerves are only a trifle ragged, Miss Linden. It's probably from having rotten eggs and tomatoes thrown at you as you orate on street corners and in parks."

Loretta felt herself get hot. She knew he was only goading her in order to get a reaction, and she wouldn't let him succeed. "Ha," she said, and turned back to the display case. "How funny you are, Captain Quarles. What does that card say, Marjorie? I can't quite see it from here." She was wearing her eyeglasses, too, curse it.

"Um . . ." Marjorie, glancing uneasily from the captain to Loretta and then to the case, opted to ignore the tension fairly snapping in the air. "It says that this frog is a . . . Oh, dear."

Loretta could have kicked herself. She could also have kicked Marjorie for having such delicate sensibilities. The cursed frog was probably a fertility symbol, and Marjorie was embarrassed to say the words out loud. "Move over, and let me take a look." She tried to keep her tone of voice sweet, but it cost her. She wanted to deck Marjorie and then bash the captain over his arrogant head with the damned fertility symbol, if that's what it was.

She scooted Marjorie out of the way and looked for herself. She was right. "It's a fertility symbol," she said, rather too loudly. But she was so annoyed, she couldn't help it. To make up for it, she said more softly, "I understand many cultures use frogs as fertility symbols."

"True, true," said Malachai in a bland voice. "I should think rabbits would be more appropriate."

A stifled squeak came from Marjorie, and she pressed a gloved hand to her mouth, mortified.

"Yes, well I doubt the Moors and rabbits were acquainted back then, Captain Quarles. You probably don't know that rabbits were introduced to Europe not long ago." Loretta spoke sweetly and hoped he'd choke on it.

"Actually, rabbits were discovered in Spain in about 1000 B.C., Miss Linden. I think you're referring to rabbits in England." Malachai's voice rivaled that of Loretta's in the sweetness department.

Curses! Foiled again! "I beg your pardon."

His alarming eyebrows V'd over his eyes. "Please don't. It doesn't suit you."

Puzzled, and knowing she was going to regret asking, she did it anyway. "Don't do what?"

"Beg. It doesn't suit you."

She sniffed.

He went on, "Anyhow, I was speaking of my own culture and a possible fertility symbol, you see."

"Ah," said Loretta. "And exactly what culture is that, Captain Quarles? Merchant seamen? Treasure hunters? Overbearing ocean captains?" She could have bitten her tongue when the last suggestion slipped out. She'd planned on staying cool and serene during any future meetings with the aggravating Malachai Quarles.

"Tut, tut, Miss Linden. I'll begin to think you don't care for me if you keep calling me names."

Marjorie grabbed Loretta's arm. "Look, Loretta, there's another lovely display over there. See? There are several suits of armor. I adore armor." She tried to walk away and take Loretta with her, but Loretta dug in her heels and didn't budge.

"Yes, Marjorie. I'll investigate the armor in a moment. I'm not finished inspecting the frogs yet." She stared into the glass case, although her appreciation of the case's contents was hampered somewhat by her exquisite awareness of the captain's presence.

Letting go of Loretta's arm, Marjorie said firmly, "Well, *I* shall visit the suits of armor."

"Fine," said Loretta. A vague feeling of peril engulfed her when her secretary abandoned her to Malachai's tender mercies. It was absurd, she told herself. It was nonsense. She was in absolutely no danger whatsoever from Captain Malachai Quarles.

Unless, perhaps, she feared she might succumb to the lure of his intense sexuality.

A thrill shot through her, the likes of which Loretta had never experienced before, and an intriguing idea occurred to her. Could Captain Malachai Quarles be the man to whom she would surrender her virtue?

Instantly, Loretta objected to the way she'd phrased the question. It was melodramatic, old-fashioned, and sounded silly to Loretta's modern ears. Surrender had to do with battlefields and wars. It had nothing to do with a free-spirited woman willingly having sexual congress with a gentleman. She meant a man. Loretta also objected to the concept of *ladies* and *gentlemen* as a class.

Also, and perhaps more important, virtue wasn't at issue here. A lady's *virtue* was a concept dreamed up by men in their desire always to keep women subservient and obedient to their whims and fancies. *Men* never worried about *their* cursed virtue. They had burdened *women* with the concept of virtue in their dastardly scheme to keep women from achieving their rightful places in the world.

Well, Loretta was having none of that! If she wanted to ravish the captain, she'd cursed well ravish him!

A glance sideways and upward made her passion cool moderately. He was a very large and intimidating man. The thought that *she*, a tiny woman, might ravish *him* was a trifle implausible. It was also as irritating as anything. She couldn't understand why she should find him attractive, when he was such a devil.

Every time they were in each other's company, he taunted her and crept up behind her back and startled her and so forth. She didn't approve of that aspect of his personality, although she was willing to admit, for the sake of free love and her principles, that he was an attractive man. In actual fact, he was about the only man she'd come across in her adult life with whom she'd consider proving her principles, at least in the area of free love.

The notion of rolling around, naked, on a bed with Malachai Quarles, made Loretta's blood heat up. Not to mention her cheeks.

"Are you interested in fertility symbols, Miss Linden?"

Was there a seductive edge to the captain's voice? Or was her inflamed imagination imbuing his voice with innuendoes that weren't really there? Loretta decided to proceed carefully. It would be totally demoralizing to give the captain the idea that *she* desired *him* before she knew his own feelings on the matter.

"I am interested in all aspects of different cultures, Captain Quarles. The Moors evidently used frogs as fertility symbols, which is interesting as an aspect of their culture." Her voice was matter-of-fact and the sentiment it spoke was valid. That was good. Loretta was proud of herself.

"I see."

Loretta waited for the punch line, but it didn't come. Again, she sneaked a peek at him, but Malachai had turned his head and his attention was focused on another object. When Loretta turned her head slightly to see what had captured his interest, she saw Marjorie, standing as if she'd been turned into a pillar of some hard substance, staring with fixed intensity at the suits of armor on the other side of the room.

Loretta swallowed a gasp of surprise. Was the cursed captain interested in *Marjorie* and not in Loretta at all? Loretta's heart suffered a sharp spasm before she told herself not to act like a sniveling lunatic.

Even if he were interested in Marjorie, Marjorie would put him in his place in no uncertain terms. While Marjorie was the most conformable of women, an aspect of her personality which Loretta found frustrating under normal circumstances, she was equally adept at delivering cutting remarks designed to keep people, and especially men, at bay. She'd demonstrated this ability often enough on Jason Abernathy. Not that Jason didn't deserve it, since he was forever teasing Marjorie.

Besides all that, if the captain favored Marjorie and if, by some remote possibility, Marjorie returned his regard, it was nothing to Loretta. Absolutely nothing. Less than nothing.

"Why are you staring at my secretary?" she demanded imperiously.

Malachai shifted his gaze to Loretta. After a pulsating second, he said, "Why? Are you jealous, Miss Linden?"

Loretta gave the captain a scornful look. "Don't be any more of an egotistical male creature than you can help being, Captain Quarles, please."

"I'll try," murmured Malachai in a parody of submission.

Loretta couldn't suppress her huff of annoyance. "For your information, I'm very protective of my staff. I won't allow my secretary to be . . . to be made sport of."

"Now why," demanded the captain, his good humor fading, "would you suppose I would make sport of your secretary?"

Because he was a fiend and a brute? Although Loretta believed that to be true, she had no real proof. "Because you're staring at her." It was weak, but it was the truth.

"Don't be an utter fool, Miss Linden."

And with that, and with a preoccupied expression on his face, Malachai strode away from Loretta, who was left gaping in his wake. *Damn* him!

When she observed Mr. William Tillinghurst at the other end of the Moorish hall, slightly behind Marjorie, who still stared at the armor as if enthralled, she calmed down considerably. Perhaps it wasn't so much that the captain found her company boring that made him leave her side, or that he was interested in her secretary, as that he wanted to talk to his partner. She watched the two men, trying not to appear as though that was what she was doing, and saw that they didn't appear to be particularly happy to see each other.

What did that mean? Had their partnership suffered a rupture? Had the captain finally, after professing scorn for her suggestion, begun suspecting Tillinghurst of treachery? She wished she could overhear their conversation.

With that desire in mind, she moseyed over to Marjorie and stood next to her. The exhibit of armor was closer to the two men than where Loretta had been at the fertility case.

She wished she hadn't thought of the case in exactly that way.

Under her breath, she spoke to Marjorie. "I'm sure Tillinghurst is the one."

Slowly turning her head so that she could see Loretta's face, Marjorie said, "I beg your pardon?"

Loretta narrowed her eyes at Marjorie. "Don't act the innocent, Marjorie MacTavish. I already told you what I think."

After expelling a big sigh—it sounded like one of resignation—Marjorie said, "Och, aye. You believe it was Mr. Tillinghurst who took some of the treasure. Without any proof, and with absolutely no other reason for thinking so than your intuition."

"It's not intuition," protested Loretta. "It's a knowledge of human nature. And of Tillinghurst. I never did like that man."

"Aye, of course. Well, that means you must be correct about him being a thief."

"Is that sarcasm I hear in your voice, Marjorie MacTavish?"

Marjorie glanced at the ceiling and managed to look martyred. "Perhaps."

"Well, you can stop it, because I'm right, and I'll prove it."

"How?"

Loretta was sure Marjorie believed she'd asked a stunning question, but Loretta had already given the matter some thought, and she wasn't put off. "I'll show you."

And with that, she took her secretary's arm and hauled her toward the two men who were still whispering at each other several feet away.

SEVEN

Hearing the approaching clack-clack of two pairs of female shoes—busybody shoes, damn them—Malachai turned and scowled at the ringleader of the duet. "What?"

Loretta brought herself and her reluctant secretary, whom she was dragging after her, to a halt and scowled back at him. Malachai figured that was fair, since he'd scowled first.

He was still annoyed, however. He had a lot of things to discuss with Tillinghurst, and his partner had been rather elusive of late. Although he still considered Loretta's suggestion that Tillinghurst had stolen the artifacts outrageous and not worth the breath it took to explain it, he wondered if Tillinghurst might know more about the theft of the treasure than he claimed. Malachai himself considered Tillinghurst something of a worm and didn't much like him, although he hadn't thus far believed him to be crooked. Damn Loretta Linden for planting ideas in his head!

Tillinghurst, noticing the women and pasting on a syrupy smile, said in his smooth, high-pitched, tinny voice, "Now, now, Malachai, you need to develop some manners. You're a favorite in society now, you know. Can't be snapping at the ladies." He removed his own expensively detailed derby hat and executed a slick bow. "How do you do, Miss Linden? And Miss . . ." His voice trailed off.

Malachai sneered inwardly. William Tillinghurst didn't acknowledge people's secretaries as a rule. Even if he and Miss MacTavish had been introduced at the Lindens' party, Tillinghurst would have forgotten all about so insignificant a personage.

Smiling sweetly, which sent Malachai's deception-detection instincts on high alert, Loretta returned Tillinghurst's bow with a bob of her head and said, "This is my secretary, Miss Marjorie MacTavish, Mr. Tillinghurst. And I'm fine, thank you."

"Ah, good. And how do you do, Miss MacTavish?"

"I'm well, thank you," Marjorie mumbled.

"I have a question for you, however, Mr. Tillinghurst."

Malachai's suspicious instincts were instantly heightened by the guileless expression on Loretta's face as she spoke to his partner. Malachai knew good and well that Loretta suspected Tillinghurst of dire dealings. She wouldn't be smiling benignly at a man she believed capable of theft unless she had ulterior motives. Would she?

He watched, both fascinated and worried. He didn't trust Tillinghurst. And, damn it, he didn't trust Loretta Linden, either.

"I'll be happy to answer your question, Miss Linden." Tillinghurst's countenance took on the aspect of a grinning ferret. Malachai wouldn't have been too awfully surprised if he'd lunged and sunk his teeth into Loretta's pretty, prying nose.

She pushed her eyeglasses up that nose a little. "I have a knife I'd like you to appraise for me, if you're able to do such things. I believe its origin to be Moorish."

Both Malachai and Tillinghurst were taken aback. Malachai's own attention sharpened significantly, and Tillinghurst's grinning-ferret look vanished and his eyes popped. Almost at once, Malachai's surprise was replaced by profound suspicion. He squinted at Loretta keenly, but her face betrayed nothing of the deep intrigues of which he suspected her.

Had she come here expecting to find Tillinghurst? Had she planned this so-called "Moorish" knife ploy in advance? Completely fascinated, Malachai gazed on as if he were watching a play—perhaps *farce* was a more appropriate word for it.

"A Moorish knife?" Tillinghurst sounded bewildered. "Well, I'm not the world's most knowledgeable collector of Moorish artifacts, Miss Linden, but I'll be happy to take a look at it for you." He and Malachai exchanged a baffled glance. "Er . . . perhaps Captain Quarles would be a better person to ask."

"I don't think so," said Malachai at the same time that Loretta said, "I doubt that." The two of them frowned at each other, then Loretta turned again to Tillinghurst.

"I'd appreciate your help, Mr. Tillinghurst. My father speaks so highly of your collection."

And then, to Malachai's total shock, the woman fluttered her damned eyelashes at Tillinghurst! Malachai could hardly believe that Loretta Linden, of all independent firebrands, had actually done such a thing. The effect was only slightly hampered by the fact that one had to view the astonishing gesture through Loretta's spectacles.

Now he knew for a certified fact that she was up to no good.

"He does?" Tillinghurst looked doubly dumbfounded.

"Yes." Loretta's smile would have turned any man into a puddle of slop, unless he'd had prior experience with her.

Malachai wanted to snatch her up, turn her over his knee, and spank her luscious bottom for being so outrageous. Didn't she know that William Frederick Tillinghurst was a villain when it came to women? Another squint at her told him that she did, and that she didn't give a care.

"I see." A hem and a haw followed this murmured comment from Tillinghurst. Then he seemed to pull himself together, and he smiled back at Loretta. His smile wasn't nearly as sweet as hers had been, but it fell short of a grinning ferret. If Malachai were to put an adjective on it, he'd have called it long-suffering. Odd, that. Tillinghurst didn't normally put up with anything at all, much less idiotic queries from militant young females.

Loretta turned her smile's volume up a notch. Malachai shut his eyes and shook his head.

"Well, I'd be delighted to look at your Moorish treasure, then, Miss Linden. Er . . . do you have the knife with you?"

"No. I didn't know we'd be bumping into you today. May I bring it to your house? Marjorie here is something of a student of Moorish art, and she'd love to see your home. Of course, I've been there with my family, and I've told Marjorie about it. It's filled with interesting artifacts from all over the world, and she'd be so fascinated."

Marjorie uttered a stifled squeak, and Malachai

distinctly saw Loretta's elbow shoot out and poke her, hard, in the side. The secretary's hand came up to rub the sore spot before she could stop herself.

Interesting. Very interesting. What in the world was the little minx up to? But that was a stupid question. Loretta was planning, somehow or other, to search Tillinghurst's estate, although what she expected to find there was anybody's guess. Because of their business association, Malachai had all but lived there for weeks and hadn't found any lost treasure. He hadn't been looking, naturally, but still . . . And how did she expect to accomplish a search if she *did* manage to get Tillinghurst to invite her over? Did she think he'd offer to let her snoop around?

"You want to visit my home?"

If Tillinghurst's look had been directed at him, Malachai thought, he might very well give up an intended visit. Not Loretta Linden. She ignored the pained expression on Tillinghurst's face, gave him a beaming, and highly idiotic, grin, and pretended she'd misunderstood him. "Oh, thank you! That would be wonderful!"

Another noise, not quite a squeak and not quite a moan, escaped from Marjorie's lips. She covered the sore spot on her ribs before Loretta's elbow could connect again.

"When should we visit you?" Loretta asked, as bold as brass. Malachai could only stare at her in amazement.

Making a vague gesture with his bony white hand, Tillinghurst said, "Oh, any time, I suppose."

"This afternoon?" Still, Loretta's face betrayed

only innocent eagerness. A little stupidity, perhaps. Insanity, maybe. Probably insanity, actually.

"This afternoon? Why, I . . . that would be fine, Miss Linden. I should be home by about three-thirty this afternoon. Captain Quarles and I are taking luncheon at the Fairfield."

"Oh, the Fairfield is a wonderful place to dine," exclaimed Loretta with renewed idiocy. Malachai stared at her hard, trying to figure out exactly what game she was playing. "One of my very best friends used to dance there."

"You have a friend who *danced* at the Fairfield?" Malachai broke in. This was too rich. It was too absurd, even for the demented Miss Linden.

She gave him a cool glance. "Yes. Isabel FitzRoy. She had to support her daughter, you see, and dancing was the most profitable way she could find to do it."

Malachai had to hand it to Loretta. She wasn't stupid, no matter how much she pretended. She'd correctly interpreted the expression on Malachai's face. It said that he had a low opinion of women who had to support themselves, mainly because in his experience they were generally strumpets.

Her bosom swelling in outrage, Loretta said, "She, Marjorie, and I were all aboard the *Titanic*, and we all escaped with little more than our lives."

"You were aboard the *Titanic*?" This time Malachai's voice conveyed shock, his amusement having been vaporized at the mention of that greatest of oceanic catastrophes. He even stopped staring at her bosom.

"Yes. We were. And Isabel and Marjorie were good enough to come to San Francisco with me after the tragedy. Isabel was a widow with a young

daughter whom she had to support, and she
needed to secure a job. I was instrumental in getting her employment at the Fairfield, dancing with
customers in the dining saloon." She stood up as
tall as a five-foot-nothing woman could stand, and
lifted her chin proudly. "Isabel is a wonderful, pro-
fessional dancer. It was a *very* good job."

As if she hated to agree but couldn't help herself,
Marjorie said, "Aye, it paid ever so much better
than most jobs, and Isabel was able to save her
money and open a dance academy here in town.
Amazing Graciousness, it's called. All the best people send their children there."

"Exactly," said Loretta, nodding firmly.

"My goodness," said Tillinghurst. Apparently
those were all the words he could think of that were
suitable for polite company, because he stopped
speaking after uttering them.

Malachai, who didn't suffer from delicate sensibilities—not that he believed Tillinghurst did,
either, but Malachai's partner *did* care about
what people thought of him—said, "Good God,
Miss Linden, you continue to astonish me."

She looked up at him with one of the best sneers
Malachai had ever seen on a female face. "Do I?
And why should Mrs. FitzRoy's choice of employment surprise you, Captain Quarles? Or are you
one of those *men* who believe women shouldn't be
allowed to support themselves with well-paying
jobs, even if they're on their own in the big, ugly
world? Perhaps you'd approve if Isabel had
scrubbed floors for a living?"

He shook his head. "Don't put words in my
mouth, Miss Linden. I'm only surprised that a
lady"— he put some emphasis on the word—

"should be consorting with a dancer. Dancers have . . . ah . . . a certain reputation."

"Only because men label them!" Loretta cried, indignant. "Isabel FitzRoy is as fine a woman as I've ever met!"

Another noise issued from Marjorie. Glancing at her, Malachai saw that she had paled considerably and looked as if she'd just as soon be somewhere else. Small wonder. Marjorie MacTavish seemed quite conventional a person to be hobnobbing with Loretta Linden.

Then again, he supposed a secretary didn't have much control over her employer's behavior. If a woman had qualms about an employer's words or actions, she'd either have to put up with them or quit, and Malachai had to acknowledge that Loretta was right about employment. Women's options were limited. For good reason, if you asked him.

Nobody did.

"I'm sure she is," Tillinghurst said soothingly, shooting a black look at Malachai.

Malachai raised his hands, as if giving in to superior forces. "I'm sure of it, too." He made certain he didn't *sound* sure.

Loretta slapped him with another vicious scowl. Malachai was almost glad her manners were too good for her to slap him physically. Not because he feared she'd hurt him, but because they'd probably be kicked out of the Museum of Natural History if they engaged in fisticuffs in the Moorish hall, and he needed to study the collection some more. His initial perusal had persuaded him that even more of the artifacts were missing than he'd originally believed, but he wanted to investigate the exhibit again and question the curator, before doing anything.

It would help if he had a single clue what he *could* do about the theft, but he'd think of something. He always did.

Suddenly a brilliant notion occurred to him. "I say, Tillinghurst, why don't we invite the ladies to take luncheon with us at the Fairfield?"

This time, he was fairly certain the noise escaping Marjorie was a moan.

After the barest hint of hesitation, Tillinghurst said, "What a good idea, Captain." He bowed at the ladies once more. "Would you care to dine with us, Miss Linden? Miss Mac . . . ah . . ." He plainly hadn't bothered to remember Marjorie's name, so he fluffed the final syllables.

"Thank you very much, Mr. Tillinghurst, but I'm afraid we won't be able to join you. Thank you so much for asking."

Loretta didn't once glance at Malachai, who had suggested taking the ladies to luncheon. Malachai wasn't surprised, although he did murmur, "Coward," under his breath.

She heard him. "We," she said pointedly, and this time she looked directly at Malachai, "have many things to do this morning."

He pulled out his pocket watch and squinted at it. "It's not morning any longer."

"Nevertheless, we have things to do." Turning back to Tillinghurst, she said, "Thank you very much, Mr. Tillinghurst. We'll be over to see you at about four this afternoon."

"I'm looking forward to it," said Tillinghurst, sounding a trifle overwhelmed.

Malachai had an urge to applaud. It wasn't just anybody who could put one over on William Frederick Tillinghurst.

* * *

"Come along with me, Marjorie." Loretta took off at a fast clip, her shoes making sharp smacks on the polished parquet tiles of the Moorish hall.

Taken by surprise, Marjorie, who had with great relief turned back to look more closely at the suits of armor, had to hustle to catch up with her. "But . . . wait! Loretta, I thought we were going to view the Moorish artifacts."

"We are. Only we're not going to do it today. We have work to do."

"What work?" Marjorie sounded as skeptical as only Marjorie could when faced with one of Loretta's more outrageous plans.

"You're going to study everything you can find about Moorish artifacts, and I'm going to secure a Moorish knife from somewhere."

Her voice considerably weaker, Marjorie said, "I? Moorish artifacts? Good heavens."

"Buck up," commanded Loretta. "You're going to be a wonderful student. I'm sure of it." She strode briskly into the museum's gift shop and spoke to the gentleman behind the counter. "Do you have a booklet that explains the Moorish exhibit more fully than this?" She flapped her flyer at him.

"Yes, ma'am," the young man said politely. His expression held admiration for the two young women who'd invaded his shop. "We have a pamphlet that gives quite a detailed account of the expedition and the artifacts recovered."

"Thank you." Loretta dug in her handbag and produced a dollar, which she handed over to the young man. Marjorie gasped when Loretta waved a hand at the man, who had cranked his cash register open in search of change. "Keep the change. I'm sure the museum can use it."

Although she had worked for Loretta for two and a half years, Marjorie had yet to get used to the way her employer flung money at every library, museum, or cause that came her way. She scurried after Loretta. "I dinna know how you have any money left, you're so free with it."

"Pshaw. I have more money than I can spend in three lifetimes. The museum needs it."

"That young man will pocket your twenty-five cents, Loretta Linden. You know he will!"

Loretta gave her secretary a pitying look. "Have faith, Marjorie. If he steals my two bits, perhaps it's because he needs it."

Still hurrying, Marjorie rolled her eyes and shut up. It never did any good to argue with Loretta Linden. Loretta didn't know why she persisted in so futile an occupation.

"Anyhow," Marjorie persisted. "I shallna be able to concentrate on your precious booklet, because I'm starving to death."

It was difficult to stop Loretta once she got a notion in her head, but another person's suffering generally did the trick. She stopped walking so abruptly, Marjorie had already sailed past her before she realized it. She turned, frowning, and walked back to her employer.

"You're right," Loretta said. "We should eat lunch before we go to the library."

"We're going to the library?" Marjorie said weakly.

Loretta gave her a stern look. "How else can you learn about Moorish artifacts?"

Since Marjorie had no answer, she didn't reply.

"Let's go to Chinatown. It's not far off, and maybe we can pick up Jason on the way."

Marjorie gave an honest-to-goodness wail of distress. "Och, Loretta, nae! My day is already ruined. Dinna add Dr. Abernathy to torture me along with Moorish artifacts and Chinese food!"

"Fiddlesticks." Loretta laughed, although she knew Marjorie wasn't joking. Jason Abernathy teased Marjorie abominably. But Loretta would just tell him not to, and that should solve the problem. "Come along, Marjorie. I shall hail a cab."

"Thank the good Lord for wee mercies."

Over lunch in a small café near Jason's office on the corner of Sacramento and Grant, Loretta told him about their scheme.

"*Your* scheme," Marjorie corrected her glumly.

"Very well, *my* scheme." Loretta couldn't understand how anyone, and especially a woman in today's society, could be so poor-spirited. Since she'd been pondering the same question as regarded Marjorie for more than two years already, she didn't bother to ask the question aloud at the luncheon table. "What do you think, Jason?"

"Well, as usual, I think you're crazy."

Loretta huffed into her tiny teacup, and some of her fragrant Chinese-blend tea slopped onto her skirt. "Blast! See what you made me do?"

"I didn't make you do anything, Loretta. Don't blame me for calling a spade a spade." Jason peeked at Marjorie, who had been trying to avoid looking at him all during luncheon. "Isn't that right, Miss MacTavish?"

After studying him closely to ascertain whether or not he was serious or intent upon making fun of her—at least that was Loretta's interpretation of her suspicious look—Marjorie said, "Aye. I think you're right, Dr. Abernathy."

"You two!" Loretta had wet a napkin and was dabbing at the tea stain on her rust-colored skirt. "It's a perfectly logical plan. While Marjorie engages Mr. Tillinghurst in conversation, I'll plead some slight indisposition and go outside to take the air. Then I'll look around for any sign of a hiding place."

Jason shook his head. "Loretta, I love you like a sister, but I still think you're crazy. For one thing, do you think Tillinghurst is hiding stolen treasure under a camellia bush in his backyard? He's more likely to have the stuff stashed in his basement or in a separate storage place far, far away. If he has it at all, which is unlikely."

"It is not!" Loretta was always hurt when her friends denounced her schemes.

"Is, too," said Marjorie under her breath.

Loretta chose not to engage with Marjorie, since Jason was plenty all by himself. "Even if you're right, it won't hurt to look. I've been to Mr. Tillinghurst's estate. There are several out buildings that would be perfect for storing stolen art objects. And don't forget that other missing seaman!" She herself had only that second recalled Malachai's second lost sailor. What was his name? Jackson? Johnson? Jones?

After glancing at the ceiling and shaking his head, a gesture Loretta took amiss, Jason said, "And that brings up another point. I seriously doubt that you're going to fool Mr. Tillinghurst into believing that Miss MacTavish is an expert in Moorish artifacts, especially if she's only going to have an hour or so to study up on the subject."

"Aye, my thought exactly," said Marjorie, this

time speaking at full volume. "I dinna think I could make him believe I was an expert even if I were." She furrowed her brow, evidently pondering her sentence and wondering if it made sense.

"Well, you can at least claim to be a student. After browsing books about Moorish art in the library, that will even be the truth."

"I'll be a student under duress," Marjorie pointed out sourly.

Jason laughed. "Every student I've ever met has been under duress, Miss MacTavish." He threw up his hands. "But discussion is fruitless. You know as well as I do that once Loretta gets a bee in her bonnet, there's no dissuading her. I'm sure you'll be safe, at all odds, especially given that Mr. Tillinghurst is the last person on earth whom I'd suspect of stealing from his own expedition."

Loretta shared her frown equally between her two friends. "That's not so. He's an unprincipled, greedy so-and-so, and he might well have wanted more than his fair share of the findings. It was the university who divided the spoils, according to the booklet we picked up."

Jason downed the last of his tea. "Sounds mighty unlikely to me, but I won't argue with you any longer."

Loretta said, "Huh!"

With a laugh, Jason rose from his chair and bowed. "But I need to get back to work. The tongs are acting up again, and I've been stitching up wounds all day."

"Oh, dear. I'm sorry, Jason." Jason's words flung Loretta out of her schemes and plots. She was honestly worried. Warfare between Chinese social clubs, or tongs, in San Francisco was nothing new, but she knew Jason's feelings about the problem, and she knew he suffered deeply. He'd been married to a lovely Chinese woman who had been victimized both by her Chinese kin and by evil white men, and his feelings, however much he masked them with humor, ran deep.

"The tongs?" Marjorie clearly wished she'd not spoken as soon as the words left her lips.

"I'll explain it all to you," Loretta said hastily, not wanting to give Jason the opportunity to embarrass Marjorie. "Thank you for your candid opinion about the stolen artifacts, Jason, even though I know you're wrong."

"I know you do, Loretta." He bent and gave her a brotherly kiss on the cheek, handed the Chinese waiter some money, and waved at the ladies as he left the restaurant.

"Drat him! I had intended to pay for his lunch."

"Aye, I'm sure you did, but he beat you to it," muttered Marjorie. "He knows you too well."

Loretta eyed her keenly. "You don't look very enthusiastic about this venture, Marjorie."

"No. Really?"

"There's no need for sarcasm."

"Och, so you say."

Standing up and smoothing her skirt—she'd managed to blot the tea stain and it didn't look bad at all—Loretta said with a sniff, "I should think you'd be happy to have a chance to rectify a grievous wrong."

Marjorie stood, too, and adjusted her hat. "Aye, and I would be if I believed there *was* a wrong, and dinna feel such a fool. This is a blatherish plan of yours, Loretta. The only reason I'm going along with it is because you're my boss."

This truly wounded Loretta's feelings. She did not consider herself a hard taskmistress. Nor did she believe she was being unreasonable. "It's not my fault you have no spirit, Marjorie MacTavish!"

With a sigh, Marjorie said, "You're right. It'sna your fault."

Feeling misunderstood and put-upon, Loretta didn't speak as they left the restaurant and headed to the public library. She had no idea where to secure a Moorish knife, although she had a friend who owned an art gallery. She would consult Denise about her problem. Denise knew everything about Oriental art and artifacts.

The Moors *were* Oriental, weren't they? Or were they African? Or were they the product of an intermingling between the cultures? Good Lord, she didn't even know that much about them. Perhaps her scheme was a trifle far-fetched.

But that was defeatist thinking. Loretta would have no part of it. Tillinghurst was a villain, and she'd prove it, with Marjorie and Jason's approval or without it. She'd show Captain Malachai Quarles who was an imbecile and who was not.

She realized she'd clenched her teeth when Marjorie, looking worried, said, "I'm sorry, Loretta. I dinna mean to be ugly."

Surprised, Loretta said, "You weren't being unkind, Marjorie. I understand that you can't help how you feel. It's one of the reasons I wish you'd consent to see Dr. Hagendorf. I'm sure he could help you overcome your repressions and neuroses."

After pressing her lips tightly together for only a second or two, Marjorie said, "I dinna believe I want to overcome them. It's my belief some things *should* be repressed."

Loretta sighed heavily. She was beginning to hold out little hope for Marjorie. But Loretta was no quitter. She wouldn't give up on her secretary, and she wouldn't give up on proving that Tillinghurst was a thief and a scoundrel.

At three-thirty that afternoon, Loretta and a very nervous Marjorie got out of the hired cab in front of Mr. William Frederick Tillinghurst's fenced and gated home, which was located just outside of San Francisco on acres and acres of forest land. A small house, much too small to belong to the millionaire Tillinghurst, could scarcely be perceived behind several dozen large trees. While Loretta paid the driver, Marjorie stared at what she could see of the almost-hidden structure. Tillinghurst's entire estate was surrounded by a huge black iron fence.

"Where's Mr. Tillinghurst's house?" she asked. "Surely he doesna live in that wee house over there."

Nodding at the cabbie, who was quite pleased with the tip Loretta had given him in exchange for a promise to wait outside the gates for the ladies' return, Loretta said, "That's the caretaker's house. Mr. Tillinghurst's house is behind the trees."

"How do we get in?"

"There's a gatekeeper." Loretta turned and surveyed the grounds stretching before her. "I'm glad it's not dark yet. I'd rather not snoop around in the dark."

"It's eerie, Loretta. I dinna like the looks of the place. I'll be hag-rid for days."

"Fiddlesticks. It's only a large estate. There's nothing eerie about it." She spoke bravely, but she didn't quite believe herself. The place gave her the willies, even in broad daylight.

Marjorie whimpered. "It's a grand place for to find a gaste or a grapus or two, Loretta."

"What on earth is a grapus?"

Marjorie shivered. "A de'il. A hobgoblin."

"Fiddlesticks," Loretta said again, this time more firmly still.

"Say what you will, Loretta Linden, I'm perishing nervous."

"Nonsense," Loretta said in a bracing tone. "Think of this as an adventure."

"Easy for you to say," Marjorie grumbled. "You dinna have to pretend to be an art student."

Pressing the buzzer on the gate, Loretta said, "Pooh. Students don't know anything or they wouldn't be students. You'll be fine."

As if by magic, the black iron gates—the word *menacing* popped into Loretta's mind, along with the words *hobgoblin, ghost,* and *devil,* and she thrust them away with disgust—began to slide apart. They were well-oiled and made no noise. In fact, they made Loretta, who wouldn't say so to Marjorie, feel a trifle spooked. She didn't approve of mechanical devices that operated silently and without apparent human intervention.

Because she'd sooner die than indicate in any way whatsoever that she was anything other than perfectly at ease, she said, "It's a short hike to his house." She saw Marjorie take a quick peek at her pointy-toed shoes and added, "But don't worry. The path is clear."

"Och, I hate this."

But Marjorie followed her leader up the long, long paved path to William Tillinghurst's mansion.

Loretta felt happier when they saw Tillinghurst awaiting them at his mansion's front door, and with a smile of welcome on his face.

"Ladies, ladies," he said, walking to the end of his porch to meet them. "It's a pleasure to see you again."

"Thank you so much for having us, Mr. Tillinghurst," Loretta gushed. "I've been wanting someone to look at this knife for the longest time."

Marjorie stepped aside so that Loretta's elbow couldn't connect with her ribs after she uttered that brass-faced lie.

EIGHT

Malachai strolled through Tillinghurst's rose garden, chewing on a cigar, his hands clasped behind his back, his head down, pondering the conversation he and Tillinghurst had concluded several minutes earlier. Malachai would have liked to continue it, but Loretta Linden and Marjorie MacTavish had arrived, and he didn't think he could keep a straight face if he had to listen to Loretta chatter to Tillinghurst about Moorish knives.

He grinned around his cigar as he pondered the wonders of Loretta. She was a minx, all right. And a true pain in the neck.

Malachai had never cherished any illusions about women. He respected one or two of them, disliked most of them, and lusted after some of them, but he considered all of them to be manipulative and sly. They were like cats, women were. At least Loretta was an amusing one.

She might also be dangerous to him. Malachai treasured his freedom, and Loretta was the first woman in a long, long time who might, if he didn't keep his guard up, threaten it.

"Freedom," he muttered, wondering as he did so what was so wonderful about it. As a young man, he'd been so damned glad to get shut of the nuns in the orphanage that he'd cut loose with a vengeance. It hadn't taken him long to realize freedom and utter abandon weren't synonymous, and he'd moderated his behavior significantly.

Not for Malachai Quarles the life of a vagabond. He was willing to work for as many years as it would take, and work as hard as he had to, but he aimed to put down roots eventually. He wasn't going to end his life alone and abandoned, as he'd begun it. Even if he only retired to the country to breed hounds, he would *not* be alone.

His background was probably the main reason he was so protective of the men who worked for him. Even nutty old Derrick Peavey. The notion of abandonment gave him a pain way deep down in his soul. Malachai Quarles wouldn't give up on a good man just because he had a delusion or two. He liked the fact that his men were his friends, too. In the absence of family, they kept him from the loneliness he'd experienced as a child.

Of course, a good way to ensure not being alone in his old age was to marry and produce a bunch of brats, but Malachai wasn't sure he was up to that. He'd had no experience with families, after all. And he sure as the devil wasn't going to have any spawn of his growing up as he had: unwanted, unloved, and unsure of anything.

No. He'd be damned good and certain that before he produced heirs, if he ever did, they'd have something to inherit besides money. His partner, Tillinghurst, had confirmed Malachai's belief that money and security were two different things— although money, above all other attributes a man could bestow upon his tribe, meant the most after love.

Love. Everything inside of him winced every time he so much as thought of the word, although he didn't suppose there was anything innately wrong with love. As a concept, love was a grand thing. Hell, the New Testament spewed love everywhere. The Old Testament was another matter, but Malachai was no theologian, so he didn't care much.

Love as modern-day Americans had interpreted it, however, was sappy and mushy and it gave Malachai a stomachache. Hell, what man wanted a woman swooning at him every five seconds? Or, perhaps worse, blackmailing him into doing her bidding by withholding her so-called favors.

Not for Malachai Quarles the role of Sir Galahad or that of that fellow Rudolf Rassendyll from *Prisoner of Zenda*, who was so noble as to be a silly fool. There might, possibly, be a woman in his life somewhere, sometime, but he hadn't found her yet.

The image of Loretta filled his brain, and he grinned in spite of himself. She was a tasty morsel. More salty than sweet. And she was wrapped up in an enticingly curvy bundle. But Malachai had striven always to keep his impulses in check and his anatomy, even the most unruly parts of it, under his own command. He wouldn't get involved with Loretta Linden. No, sir. That would be not merely stupid, but possibly fatal.

He stopped walking abruptly and stared into the distance. Taking the cigar from between his teeth, he leaned forward, narrowed his eyes, and peered fixedly at the form he'd just glimpsed several yards off, bending over and peering under a bush. Had his imagination conjured the woman's image out of whole cloth, or could it be . . . ?

Impossible!

But it was.

By damn, the woman was actually carrying out her scheme! But where was her cohort? Had Loretta left her poor secretary alone with Tillinghurst? Or was Miss MacTavish searching Tillinghurst's grounds elsewhere? How had they managed it? Malachai wouldn't put much of anything past Loretta Linden, but he didn't think even she would poison Tillinghurst just to prove a point. Nor did he truly anticipate finding out that the two women had black-jacked Tillinghurst and tied him to a chair while they snooped around his estate.

There was only one way to find out what they were up to. Throwing his cigar onto the dirt path and grinding it under his boot heel, he set off in Loretta's direction. He walked fast, telling himself his eagerness to see her was only because he was curious about how she was carrying out her design to prove Tillinghurst a thief.

Loretta was still feeling the aftereffects of severe embarrassment as she prowled Mr. Tillinghurst's grounds near his house. Not only did she feel a fool about the knife and slightly guilty about Marjorie, but now, after she'd pleaded a headache and gone outdoors to take the air, she realized she'd set for herself an impossible task.

Tillinghurst's grounds covered acres and acres. She was one small woman. How could she search the whole place in only the half hour or so Marjorie's faltering knowledge of Moorish artifacts would allow her?

She couldn't, was how. She and Marjorie had been unable to find much of anything about the Moors in the library, so most of Marjorie's knowledge was contained in the one small booklet they'd carried away from the museum. And Tillinghurst was already intimately familiar with that booklet. Surely he'd recognize their ruse.

What was worse was that Loretta didn't trust him to be polite about it. He might even demand to know what they were up to. As she stooped over a bush to see if that was really a small door built into the side of the mansion, she worried and thought and fretted and tried her very best to come up with an addendum to her plot. Unfortunately, she was about all plotted out.

"Fiddlesticks," she muttered as she realized she'd discovered the door to the coal bin. A lot of good that would be in finding stolen historical artifacts.

"As I live and breathe," came from behind her.

Startled nearly out of her skin, Loretta let out a sharp cry as she stood up straight, getting her hat and hair caught in the branches of the daphne bush under which she'd been peering. Her voice was far from welcoming when, turning precipitately and espying the captain, she blurted out, *"You!"*

His curly brown hair was so long it kissed the collar of his blue woolen captain's coat, and his earring caught the sunlight and shot sparks of glitter into the air. Loretta got the impression the earring was winking at her. It would.

"Please," said Malachai, reaching for her hair, some of which was tangled in daphne branches. "Allow me."

Her hands had already lifted to fiddle with her hat, and his covered them. Loretta experienced that same electric tingle she'd felt before when they'd touched. She considered it most inconvenient that she had this reaction to the captain's touch. At once she dropped her hands—there was no sense in tempting the fates or her own urges—and engaged her tongue.

"I might have known I'd find you lurking and looming here somewhere!"

"You might have," agreed Malachai. "Although I must object to the word 'lurking.' I'm not lurking. I'm visiting my business partner." Peering down at her in a manner Loretta could only describe as devilish, he added, "I can understand why you might consider me as looming, however that's only because you're so short."

Loretta chose to ignore his explanation and his evaluation of her own personal stature. "I don't know why you insist on sneaking up on me! The least you could do is announce your presence before you frighten me to death."

"I never sneak. I'm too big to sneak."

His assessment of his person should be true. That it wasn't didn't make Loretta feel significantly better. "Fiddle. You sneak, and that's all there is to it."

"This is a lovely hat," the captain said, ignoring Loretta's accusation. "And it's sitting on lovely hair."

Loretta frowned hard, her brow wrinkling up like a raisin. Was he really, honestly and truly, complimenting her, or was there some fell insinuation in his comment somewhere? Being a straightforward woman, she decided to ask. "Are you complimenting me, Captain Quarles?"

"Why, I do believe I am, Miss Linden."

He tucked a lock of hair behind Loretta's ear, and Loretta wondered if her ear glowed visibly. His touch certainly made tingles shoot through her, starting at her ear and radiating throughout her body, until her very toes itched. This was terrible. She didn't know what to do. "Oh."

He chuckled, and the tingles turned into waves. This was worse than terrible.

"Isn't a young lady supposed to thank a gentleman for complimenting her?"

The captain's deep, rumbling voice held a feathering of silk around its edges. Loretta sucked in a breath and held onto it until he left off touching her. Then she said in sort of a gasp, "If you were a gentleman, and if I believed you, I might." Loretta was pleased that she'd managed to produce so fitting a sentence without benefit of her brain, which was at present floundering in a nearby puddle of lust and unable to function properly.

When the captain burst out laughing, she rescinded her approval of her last sentence. The man was absolutely too shocking to be allowed free to roam in society and prey on innocent young women. It wasn't fair.

"I don't need to ask what you're doing here. Obviously you're attempting to discover Tillinghurst's hiding place."

"Don't be sarcastic. I *know* he's responsible for the losses. I'll find where he's hidden the stolen goods, too." Loretta also suspected that Mr. Peavey's dungeon was somewhere on Tillinghurst's property, although she wouldn't risk further ridicule from Malachai by saying so. Tillinghurst's vast estate would be a perfect place for a dungeon, though. Hoping to distract herself from Malachai, whose presence was fuddling her brain, she looked around again, this time into the distance.

"Please," said Malachai, gesturing for her to precede him. "Allow me to help you, as long as I'm here."

"I don't want your help!"

Of all the miserable circumstances! First she'd had to make do with a Chinese knife—and it wasn't even an interesting Chinese knife. It was a Chinese knife that even *she* could identify as such. But it was the best Denise had to offer and Loretta hadn't time to shop around. And then she'd had to abandon Marjorie, whom she knew was a nervous wreck. And now she'd bumped into Malachai Quarles. It was more than a woman should be expected to endure.

"Nevertheless, since I'm too much of a gentleman to allow a lady to wander unsupervised around the grounds of a man whom she suspects of vicious crimes, I shall help you."

"Oh—" Loretta tried to think of a word that would express her soul-deep fury. She couldn't. She vowed to hang out more with her communist friends. They might be a boring and rather silly bunch, but they knew all the bad words. "Bother!" was the best she could come up with on the spur of the moment.

The captain took her arm and began strolling toward the back of the house. "Personally, I shouldn't think you'd find stolen treasure under a bush."

"I didn't think it was under a bush! There was a door there!" She tried to tug her arm away, but couldn't. Damn the man. He was *so* large and *so* strong. If he weren't so infuriating, Loretta would approve of these characteristics. But they only served to make him the most disturbing man she'd ever met, and Loretta, who didn't like feeling discomposed, wished he'd go away.

"A door. I see."

"Oh, leave me alone!" she cried, pushed beyond

endurance. "I know what I'm doing, and I know I'm right. Let *go* of me!" She yanked on her arm hard, and he finally released her, although not until after he'd hung on long enough to make bruises. She rubbed her arm and glowered at him. "Brute!"

"I'm sorry if I hurt you, Miss Linden."

"I don't believe you."

"Somehow that doesn't surprise me."

"Oh, go away. I have work to do."

"Feel free," said Malachai, gesturing for her to continue her search. "I won't tell Tillinghurst."

Loretta felt stupid. She hated the feeling. Nevertheless, because she didn't have much time, she strode up the drive, toward Tillinghurst's garden, where she knew there were sheds and other buildings. Malachai was right behind her. She felt him there, and she wished she could watch him watching her. Was he judging her hips to be too large? Did she think she was fat?

She wasn't fat! She was well-rounded. Jason had said so when she'd asked. She'd asked because for some reason, after she'd met the captain, she'd felt the least little bit insecure about her physical desirability. And it was all Malachai Quarles' fault, curse him.

"That's a fetching costume, Miss Linden. I particularly like the color. It goes well with your complexion."

"Thank you." She kept walking and searching the horizon for hiding places.

"And your hat is cunning. Is that an ostrich feather?"

"Yes." After thinking about it for a second, she gave him another grudging, "Thank you."

"You're welcome."

They walked along in silence, only the crunching of their feet on the pathway announcing to listening birds and squirrels that there were human beings present. After holding out against it for as long as she could, Loretta turned her head to see what Malachai was doing.

He was staring at her hips, was what he was doing. She felt her cheeks get hot. *Curse* the man! She kept walking, trying not to swish her hips. It was impossible, because she was a woman.

"Do you suspect Tillinghurst of hiding Percival Jones, too, somewhere on his property?"

"Ah, that's his name! I couldn't remember." At once, Loretta regretted having given the captain credit for clearing up the confusion in her mind.

"Yes. He's a good man. I'm worried about him."

He sounded genuinely worried, although Loretta wasn't sure. After shooting him another quick, sidelong look, she still wasn't sure. He appeared concerned, but Loretta was loath to give him credit for any tender human emotions.

She said, "I don't know where he might be. Quite frankly, it wouldn't surprise me if he's here somewhere, being held against his will. Mr. Tillinghurst is not a nice man. I don't care if he *is* your partner."

Again, she refrained from pointing out that if a dungeon truly *was* involved in this mess, Tillinghurst's estate was the best place she could think of for it to be. She wished she could find it. And if it contained Mr. Jones, so much the better. Oh, my, wouldn't *that* be a triumph, if she could find Quarles' missing sailor? He couldn't sneer at her then.

"Out of curiosity, what do you have against Tillinghurst, Miss Linden?"

"He's a greedy pig."

"I suppose you could say that about many successful men."

She shot him a mean-tempered glare, and he expounded. "I'm not saying he's not interested in making money. Of course, he is. I am, too, for that matter. What makes Tillinghurst more of a pig than most men?" He smiled a smile that made Loretta's insides quiver. "You can leave me out of the equation, if you wish, since I'm sure I'd skew the results, given your . . . ah . . . opinion of me."

Loretta wouldn't touch her opinion of Malachai Quarles with a barge pole. She didn't have the same qualms about Mr. Tillinghurst, so she let loose.

"He runs three sweatshops in the city of San Francisco, Captain Quarles, in which he oppresses hundreds of women, paying them far less than he should, and far less than similarly employed men would earn. He also keeps them in circumstances that are not merely cruel, but dangerous. Why, what do you think would happen if there was a fire in any of those shabby old buildings?"

"I have no idea."

"Well, I do! The same thing would happen as happened in New York, when all those women were killed in a sweatshop fire several years ago, because the doors were locked and they couldn't escape! It's criminal—or it should be." Loretta pounded her right fist into her left palm. "*That's* why I dislike Mr. Tillinghurst, Captain Quarles. *That's* why I think he's a despicable human being."

"I see."

His frown could have meant anything, Loretta supposed. It was foolish of her to hope she'd made him think about his precious partner in light of Tillinghurst's iniquitous business practices. Still, she couldn't help but add a little fuel to any fire of conscience she might have sparked.

"What's even worse is that he exploits those women who are least able to defend themselves. Most of the women he employs can't speak English, and they're afraid to stand up for themselves. Why, do you know that he actually *fired* a woman who dared ask for a day off to bury her own child? A child who had undoubtedly died because she couldn't afford to buy decent food on the pittance Tillinghurst paid her? Well, he did."

"Er . . . no. I didn't know that."

"You *should* know it. *Everyone* should!" She added bitterly, "Not that it will make any difference to the *men* who govern our city and state. *Men* don't care about how poverty-stricken human beings are forced to live or about women's dead babies. *Men* like to keep women subservient to them. *Men* think it's the *woman's* fault if a woman is deserted by her husband and has to feed her children and herself without assistance from the children's father. *Men* have no compassion for women left alone to rear their children without any help from man or God. Or orphaned children abandoned to wander the streets of San Francisco to live or die according to how much food they can scavenge every day. I have no idea why that is, unless *men* consider such children the result of divine intervention or something. *Men*—"

Loretta didn't get the opportunity to finish her harangue, because Malachai grabbed her by the shoulders, yanked her against his chest, and shut her mouth with his. Had she been able, she would have gasped with shock, but she wasn't. Her paralysis lasted only a second before her body decided to disengage her brain and simply enjoy the sensations of the encounter.

As her body relaxed—against her will, she later decided—so Malachai changed the way he held her. He didn't let her go, and he didn't relax his bearlike embrace. Rather, he shifted slightly, so that he held Loretta more securely, and he started to explore.

First it was his tongue that tentatively pampered her lips apart. Then it slipped into her mouth to play with her own tongue. At the same time, his hands moved over her body. Loretta registered shock when one of his large, warm hands slid to her hips and pressed the lower part of her body into his. For the first time in her life, she felt a man's arousal against her.

And she was responsible for that. A heady awareness of her feminine power flooded her—until she remembered that she couldn't move. The realization made her squirm very slightly, which produced a ragged moan that went straight from Malachai's lips into her mouth. She swallowed it, and it was the sweetest thing she'd ever tasted.

She *was* desirable! She, Loretta Linden, the despair of her family, was a real woman! A woman able to stir the hungers of a man.

And what a man he was. Loretta's thoughts shattered into a million sparkly bits when Malachai's other hand covered her breast. Her breasts had been positively aching for his touch, and she'd not even known it until it happened. Absolutely astonishing.

No wonder her mother had tried to insist that Loretta wear her corset and stays. Corsets and stays prevented men from taking these types of advantages. Loretta chalked up one more positive mark in favor of liberation from confining clothing. Why should women be excluded from savoring such exquisite sensations?

Loretta didn't know how long the kiss lasted. It was far too long—and not nearly long enough. She only realized it was over when her feet landed on William Tillinghurst's drive with such force that her teeth clacked together. Obviously, she'd been dangling from Malachai Quarles' strong arms.

She said, "Ow," rather breathlessly. Then she blinked, and realized she still wore her eyeglasses. Good heavens, the man had kissed her even though she wore spectacles! How utterly fascinating.

Her senses recovered slowly, although it probably didn't take them as long as it felt. Her state of confusion was considerable. After several bewildered seconds, Loretta realized that Malachai had turned his back to her and jammed his hands into his pockets. He had a *very* broad back. She shoved her glasses up her nose with an unsteady finger and didn't know what to say.

If she were the daughter her mother wished she was, she'd slap Malachai's face. She'd have to find it first, of course, but she supposed that's what a lady would do.

Thank the good Lord, she was no lady. That didn't help her think of anything to say. She should probably be nonchalant about the kiss. After all, she approved of free love, and that included kissing, didn't it?

The problem was that Loretta didn't feel the least bit nonchalant. She felt spectacular, actually, and that sort of precluded nonchalance.

Malachai mumbled something.

After clearing her throat, Loretta said, "I beg your pardon?" Then she wished she hadn't used the word *beg*. It came too close to what she wanted to do, which was to beg Malachai to kiss her again. She retained enough pride to know that begging the man for *anything* would violate every female human principle she held dear.

He turned so sharply, Loretta jumped. He looked awfully angry for a man who had just perpetrated a kiss from which Loretta's senses still reeled.

If she felt *this* way, he shouldn't feel *that* way, should he? She had rather hoped the delicious pleasure she'd felt from the kiss had been shared by him.

"I said," said Malachai, "that I'm sorry."

He was sorry? Loretta had the weird feeling that she was tumbling headlong into a whirlpool and that it was going to drown her. She cleared her throat again. "You are?" Her gaze drifted south for a brief instant. He didn't look sorry. He looked ready to perpetrate a ravishment. Mercy, the man was large.

His face took on a thunderous cast. His brow furrowed, his eyes snapped, his heavy eyebrows formed a perfect V over his aquiline nose, and his lips thinned into a forbidding straight line. "I'm sorry, damn it. That was a damned stupid thing to have done."

Loretta could only stare up at him, perplexed. She couldn't understand why he was angry. As far as she was concerned, Malachai Quarles was still a beast—but that kiss had been perfectly splendid.

But everything was coming around and would be all right any second now. She was accustomed to Malachai's frowns. She felt approximately on his level when he frowned, because she could frown right back, even when she was dazed, as she was now.

Being dazed didn't negate her duty as a free-thinking, worldly woman who should not appear to be affected by a mere kiss.

A mere kiss? Loretta, who didn't approve of people lying to themselves, knew it had been more than a mere anything.

That, however, was neither here nor there. Squaring her shoulders, determined not to let him know how much his kiss had dazzled her, she said, "Yes, it was, wasn't it?"

They didn't speak again as they walked back to Tillinghurst's mansion side by side.

Malachai hadn't done such a damned fool thing in his entire adult life. Oh, he'd played around enough in his late adolescence and early twenties, but he'd been smart enough to understand, even then, that it didn't pay to be irresponsible with respectable females. Or any female, really. If a man went too far with a woman, he either got himself shackled for life, or he left tokens of his lust behind to be thrown into orphanages, as he had been.

And orphanages were only for the lucky ones. He hated to admit that Loretta was right about that. There were millions of children who had been abandoned by their parents, either on purpose or as a result of tragedy, and who were forced out onto the streets to live or die according to the whim of a capricious and uncaring God.

As he slumped along beside Loretta, he decided it had been her impassioned rhetoric that had ultimately pushed him over the edge. When she'd begun lecturing him about women forced to care for their children after having been abandoned, he'd snapped.

Damn it all, why should *she* care about widows and orphans? Nobody else did. She was about to drive him insane with her lectures and orations.

Anyhow, what did she know about poverty? She was rich. She didn't know what it felt like to be herded along with a hundred other little kids, as if you were so much cattle, by a bunch of nuns who took care of you because it was their so-called "Christian duty," but who didn't give a hang about you. She didn't know what it was like to wake up in a room full of other kids, all of whom were nearly frozen solid under their thin blankets. She didn't know what it was like to be sick and to have no one to kiss you and make you feel better. She didn't know what it was like to have nothing but thin soup and stale bread for every meal. She didn't *know*, damn it!

Malachai tried never to think about the orphanage. He hadn't been able to help but remember it, though, when Loretta'd started her diatribe. Coupled with his own meditations prior to their meeting today, it had thrown him over the precipice of sanity and into that . . . that kiss.

Good God almighty, that *kiss*.

Would she expect him to marry her now? That's what would have happened even ten years ago. If a man lost his head and kissed a respectable female, she expected him to marry her. Loretta claimed to be an enlightened feminist, but Malachai'd believe it when he saw it. He had yet to meet a woman who meant what she said.

He sneaked a peek at her. Then he frowned. Outwardly at least, she appeared composed. She didn't *look* as if she was about to become hysterical and demand that he make an honest woman of her.

An honest woman. There wasn't any such thing on earth. They were all sly, conniving cats. Malachai snorted, then regretted the lapse when Loretta whipped her head around and narrowed her eyes at him. Her scrutiny didn't last long. Almost as soon as her head turned his way, it turned back to face the walkway again.

She still didn't speak. Malachai began to grow itchy. He told himself it was anticipation. Perhaps dread was a better word. Any second now, she'd lower the boom. He began composing retorts in his head, even though he knew that, as a man of integrity and firm moral standards, he'd probably have to go through with it and marry the wench. It would be his punishment for an act of blatant idiocy. It would be a sacrifice, true. The notion of being shackled to Loretta Linden for all eternity gave him . . . a warm, gooey sensation in his chest.

No! He didn't mean that! What he meant was that it gave him the shivers.

Good God, Loretta Linden really *had* rattled his senses. She was a disaster in human form, was what she was, for God's sake. The mere notion of marrying her was . . . was . . . well, it was awful. Terrible. The worst thing that could possibly happen to him.

Still, that didn't explain why she didn't say *anything*. Loretta wasn't the silent type. Malachai brooded until they reached Tillinghurst's front door. Then he couldn't stand it any longer. He stepped in front of her so that she couldn't move and stood stock-still. "Well?" he demanded, frowning for all he was worth.

She stopped walking, because she couldn't help it, and looked up at him. She was so tiny. Malachai wondered that he hadn't crushed her bones, he'd held her so tightly. The thought made him even angrier. He turned his frown into a glower.

"Well what?"

Her voice was as serene as her expression. It positively infuriated Malachai. He snarled, "Well, aren't you going to demand that I marry you? Isn't that what women do?"

She wrinkled her porcelain brow. It looked to him as if she were considering his question rationally, which nearly sent him into a frenzy.

What the devil was the matter with her? What the devil was the matter with *him*? He wasn't the frenzied sort. He tried to calm himself, but the attempt failed, and he stood there, fulminating like a volcano about to erupt, and she just stared at him. Serenely, damn it to hell.

At last she spoke. "I don't know what you mean, Captain Quarles. If you are suggesting that I should fall into the role men have dictated women should play and, because you lost your head for a moment, force you into a marriage neither of us wants, I believe that, as little as you know me, you should have learned better than that by this time."

And she stepped around him, opened the door, and walked inside, leaving Malachai on the porch, feeling sort of like a salmon might feel if it had been gaffed and thrown onto the deck of a boat to flounder around out of water, gasping for breath— or whatever it was fish gasped for.

NINE

Loretta knew she was walking, because she heard her feet tap-tapping on the tiled entryway of William Frederick Tillinghurst's mansion. Her body felt so buoyant, however, that she needed the confirmation of those clicks on the floor to reassure herself that she wasn't floating on air.

She wasn't sure where the captain was. She'd left him at the door, muttering to himself. That was all right. Let him mutter. She felt simply splendid.

One glance into the parlor assured her that her secretary did not. Marjorie was as pale as a frosty window and her hands were in her lap, gripping her handbag as if she were attempting to strangle it. Worse, she'd begun stuttering.

"B-but, you s-see, I really d-d-dinna know very much a-b-b-bout—"

"Yes," said Tillinghurst dryly. "I gathered as much."

Loretta came down to earth, figuratively speaking, with a thud. She hurried to rescue Marjorie. "Oh, dear, I'm sorry I took so long. My headache is much better now, thanks to my walk around your *marvelous* gardens, Mr. Tillinghurst." She gave Tillinghurst one of the dazzling smiles she'd learned to produce when she was still under her mother's influence. Before she'd become enlightened, so to speak.

Tillinghurst rose to his feet. He didn't look especially dazzled by Loretta's smile. She wasn't surprised. He was such a toad.

"I believe your secretary knows about as little as you do about Moorish artifacts, Miss Linden." His smile could have curdled milk.

Never one to be cowed by men's sour smiles, and especially not the smile of William Tillinghurst, a man she despised and one, moreover, who looked like the rat he was, Loretta laughed gayly. "Oh, my, is that so?" She turned to Marjorie. "I thought you'd studied something about Moorish art, Marjorie dear. But I seem to recall that was a long time ago. In Scotland, wasn't it?"

She saw the relief flood through her secretary and decided a brief lesson in acting techniques would not be amiss. "Oh, aye! That's right. It was in Scotland." Marjorie turned to face Tillinghurst. "It was vurra long ago, you see. When I was a wee lass. In Glasgow."

"I see." He picked up the knife Loretta had left on the table before she'd gone outdoors to spy. "Here's your knife, Miss Linden. I'm sure that if you take it to another expert, you'll learn that my evaluation is correct. It's a simple Chinese ceremonial knife of little worth. They make 'em by the thousands in Canton. Even in various American Chinatowns, one of which is where I suspect yours came from." He held the knife on his palm, its hilt toward her.

She took it and slipped it into her handbag. "Silly me," she said, tittering. She seldom tittered, but she was willing to act like a ninny for the sake of the stolen artifacts. Reaching for Marjorie, she said, "We'd best be going now, Marjorie, dear. Our chariot awaits, and it's quite dark outdoors." Another titter, and Loretta decided enough was enough.

Turning and holding out her hand to Tillinghurst, she said in her usual, no-nonsense voice, "Thank you for your time, Mr. Tillinghurst. I'm sorry we weren't able to offer you a more scintillating artifact."

"Think nothing of it, Miss Linden. Ladies aren't expected to be scholars."

Before Loretta could begin to lecture him, Marjorie gave her a quick—and unseen by Tillinghurst—smack on the back of her arm, and Loretta understood the wisdom of being silent on this occasion, no matter how provocative she'd found Mr. Tillinghurst's comment. It galled her, but she held her tongue. Because she couldn't bear to speak unless it was to set Tillinghurst straight, she merely smiled at him and gave him a nod of her head before turning to leave the room.

Tillinghurst's butler let the two ladies out. Loretta glanced around, but she didn't see Captain Quarles anywhere. She allowed herself to experience a moment of disappointment, but that was all. Not for Loretta Linden the forlorn gestures of helpless womanhood. She would not pine for a man, ever.

Deciding it was far too early in her relationship with Malachai even to think about not pining, she glanced at the door and then the parlor window to make sure Tillinghurst wasn't watching them, and then said excitedly, "I think I found a perfect place for someone to hide a treasure, Marjorie!" She took Marjorie by the arm and started dragging her down Tillinghurst's drive toward the massive black iron gate where, with any luck and Loretta's large tip, their cab would still be waiting for them. "I didn't have a chance to inspect it, because . . ." Her voice trailed off, and she decided to keep Malachai Quarles out of the conversation, at least for now.

"I thought I would die in there," Marjorie said under her breath, stumbling slightly as she tried to keep up with Loretta. "I'll be hag-rid for months."

Understanding that her secretary was not as brisk a walker as she herself was, Loretta slowed down a bit. Her mood was buoyant, and she wanted to run. "I didn't let on, because I didn't want anyone who might be watching to know I'd seen it."

"It was the most horrible experience of my life, Loretta Linden! That crabbity auld man gowking at me with his wee smirk, as if he knew what you were up to. I thought I'd die."

"I'm going to come back again some night when the moon isn't too bright and see if I'm right." Plans started sorting themselves out in her mind. While she and Malachai had been walking, and before their walk had been interrupted by that smashing kiss, she'd seen another building: a strong, brick building, hidden behind a tall hedge. If there was a better place to hide something than in a brick building hidden behind a hedge, Loretta didn't know where it was.

"He knew I was no Moorish scholar. Nor even a Moorish student."

"I can hardly wait to explore more fully. Do you know when the new moon will be, Marjorie?"

"Are you listening to me?"

Loretta jumped. She'd never known Marjorie to shout before. Turning toward her with a hurt frown, she said, "You needn't yell, Marjorie. Of course I'm listening to you."

But she hadn't been, and Marjorie knew it. "Nay. You werena," Marjorie said bitterly. "You ne'er listen to anyone. You only please yourself."

Her secretary's words pricked Loretta, who was in the habit of believing herself to be a considerate, large-hearted woman. Yet she supposed she *had* bullied Marjorie—the least little bit—to perform in a manner antithetical to her closed-in, repressed, neurotic personality today. Not that such practice wasn't good for the poor woman. "That's not true, Marjorie," she said quietly.

"Aye, it is." Marjorie shuddered visibly and her eyes glistened with unshed tears, and Loretta realized she'd been more upset by her experience than Loretta had guessed.

Feeling a teensy bit guilty, she said, "It's good for you to stretch yourself every once in a while, Marjorie. I'm sure you'll benefit from this experience."

"How?"

How? Loretta had to think about it. "Well, it will teach you that even though you're frightened of something, you can overcome your fear." That sounded good.

"But I dinna overcome my fear. My fear was with me the whole time, and it vurra nearly killed me!"

"I'm sure it was still good practice for you. You need to learn that senseless fears like that are . . . well . . . senseless."

"Ye think it's senseless to be adrad in the presence of a man you believe to be the blackest of villains?"

She'd shouted again, and Loretta began to worry a trifle. "Now, Marjorie, I don't believe him to be a murderer or anything. Only a thief." It made sense to Loretta, but it clearly didn't to Marjorie, who started pulling on her lovely red hair. Loretta had never seen her so agitated.

"I think you're mad, Loretta Linden, and I ken you're blathering! I was terrified in there, and all ye can say is that the man's na' a *murderer?*"

Beginning to feel the faintest bit miffy, Loretta said, "Now, now, Marjorie, it wasn't *that* bad."

"*It was, too!*"

"Fiddlesticks. You're overreacting, Marjorie Mac-Tavish. And I still believe that with more practice, you can overcome your silly fears."

Marjorie stopped walking suddenly and whirled to face Loretta. "What if I dinna *want* to overcome my fears, Loretta Linden? Did you ever think about *that?* What if my fears are'na neuroses, as you claim, but normal feelings any normal person would feel when ordered to act mad by a gullion? My ain fault is that I'm a glaikit goff, and I fore'er do what ye tell me to, e'en though I know ye to be a haggis-headed nyaff!"

Loretta's mouth fell open. Any time Marjorie so forgot herself as to spout so many Scottish words in a row, she was really angry. As a rule, the only way a person could tell the woman came from Scotland was from the slight and charming burr when she spoke.

That didn't deter Marjorie, who shook a finger in her employer's face. "*I'm*'na the gudgeon, Loretta! *You* are!" She turned back as abruptly as before, and resumed stomping down Tillinghurst's drive.

Stunned into immobility for a moment, Loretta soon recovered and hurried to catch up with her. "Marjorie! Wait!"

Marjorie didn't wait. She stormed onward, muttering as she did so, "Moorish knives! Millionaire

begowkers! Blather! It's awe blather! What next?
Crockin'? Mayhem? Furiositie? Aye, we're there
a'ready. Mayhap white slavery? Bah!"

Catching up with her, Loretta said, "Marjorie,
wait a moment! I didn't realize how—how—" Oh,
dear. She couldn't think of a diplomatic way to say
it. She blurted out, "I didn't realize what a bundle
of nerves you were. I'm sure you need some sort of
medication. Or at least a chat with Dr. Hagendorf.
It's unnatural—"

Marjorie harshly scraped in approximately six hundred cubic feet of air, and let it out in a screech, and
in English unmarred by her childhood in Glasgow.
"It is *not* unnatural! It's *perfectly* natural to be nervous about perpetrating a fraud on a gentleman!"
She poked Loretta in the chest with her forefin-
ger. "*You're* the unnatural one, Loretta Linden,
with your scandalous ideas and crazy notions, and
you know it!"

Loretta was horrified to see tears streaming down
Marjorie's cheeks. "Oh, Marjorie!" She still believed
her secretary was only a repressed spinster who
needed to face and overcome her fears, but that
didn't negate the honest misery Marjorie was experiencing at the moment. Loretta put an arm around
her. Marjorie stiffened up like a setter on point, but
Loretta remained undeterred.

"I'm so sorry, dear. I didn't realize how very up-
setting you'd find my little ruse."

Allowing Loretta's arm to remain, probably because she had no choice unless she wanted to
engage in a shoving match with her employer, Marjorie unclasped her handbag and dug out a
handkerchief. She engaged it with vigor, mopping
her eyes and cheeks and blowing her nose. "Little

ruse, be damned," she growled. "It was a big, fat lie."

"There, there," Loretta murmured.

"And he *knew* it!" Marjorie said with renewed energy. "Your *little ruse* dinna fool him for a second!"

Regaining her own composure, Loretta withdrew her arm and allowed her secretary to walk unencumbered. Still rather pleased with herself, in spite of Marjorie's not unexpected but exaggeratedly poor-spirited reaction to the day's adventure, Loretta said, "Well, it doesn't matter what he thinks. He couldn't possibly have guessed the real purpose for our visit."

The autumn afternoon had fallen into evening, and the walkway was dark except for a row of dim electrical bulbs lining it at intervals. Loretta wasn't quite sure what she was going to do if the cabbie had given up on them and left, but she'd paid him a lot to wait, so she hoped he'd still be there.

He was. "Oh, good!"

The two women walked up to the gate and stood there, Marjorie gazing up at its solid black ironness, Loretta wondering if she was supposed to push a button to get the gatekeeper to open it.

Nothing happened, so Loretta searched for a button. She couldn't find one, and she searched harder. For only a moment or two, her heart quavered unpleasantly. The tiniest feeling of panic knocked at the door of her composure.

Could Tillinghurst have divined her purpose in coming here today? Could he be planning some dire means of keeping her quiet? Could he—oh, heavens!—could he be planning to kidnap her and Marjorie?

The last thought had just entered her head,

causing her stomach to clench and her hands to curl into fists, when the gate groaned once and slowly started to open.

A voice from behind them said, "Sorry, ladies. I wasn't in the gatehouse when you walked up!" It was a friendly voice, and Loretta's insides un-clenched.

She waved at the unseen gatekeeper. "That's all right. Thank you!" Grabbing Marjorie, she hurried out to the automobile.

The cabbie, with a big smile on his face, jumped out of his machine to open the door for them. Loretta's rattling heart began to slow. Then, because she was suffering from leftover fear and despised her-self for it, she forced herself to step aside and allow Marjorie to enter the cab first. Only after Marjorie was settled and she'd thanked the cabbie for waiting, did Loretta enter the cab, slowly and with dignity.

They arrived at her Russian Hill home in time for dinner, a meal taken in virtual silence, since Mar-jorie was still angry with her.

As for Loretta, she spent the meal thinking. Hard.

She was still thinking when she walked to the soup kitchen the following morning. Although she'd de-cided that she wasn't fat, she had also renewed her vow to get more healthful exercise. It wouldn't do to allow her body to become lax. *Strong body, strong mind* was a sound concept by which to live. Besides, walk-ing assisted her thinking processes.

Because Marjorie had reacted so violently to yes-terday's agenda, Loretta had left her at home this morning. While she missed her company, she worried about Marjorie's overall mental health. She intended to talk to Dr. Hagendorf about the poor woman, with or without Marjorie's blessing.

After reading about it several times over the last few years, Loretta would have liked to undergo analysis herself just to see what the process was like, but she didn't have the time. Also, if her family learned she was seeing an alienist, they'd assume it was because there was something wrong with her. Worse, they'd believe they'd been right about her, and that Loretta had begun espousing radical causes because she was crazy.

Well, she wasn't crazy. She possessed an enlightened attitude and a keen social conscience, two attributes that would help the world a good deal if more people shared them.

The sound of raised voices ahead made Loretta pick up her pace. Curiosity chased indignation from her mind. There had been so much social unrest and political turmoil in recent years. Workers, tired of the oppression under which they'd been laboring for so long, had begun doing something about it. Unfortunately, many of them were choosing anarchy over dignified and legal arbitration for labor unions, and there had been several bombing incidents.

However much Loretta favored unionization as a method of assuring workers their rights as human beings, she didn't believe that violence was ever the answer to any problem. The vision of Malachai Quarles swam into her mind's eye, and she allowed there might be one or two exceptions to her anti-violence stand.

But no. She didn't want to perpetrate violence against the captain. She might be more comfortable if her desires in his regard *were* to physically hurt him. What she wanted to do with Malachai Quarles had nothing to do with damaging his person. Far from it.

Anyhow, that was neither here nor there. As Loretta approached the source of the noise, she turned a corner onto Powell Street and saw that a large crowd had gathered. The fact that she was shorter than most of the people in the mob didn't deter her in the slightest. With loud, "Pardon me's," and shrill, "Step aside, if you will's," she elbowed her way through the assembled masses.

When she got to the inner edge of the circle, her breath caught in her throat when she realized that her very own Moor man, Derrick Peavey, was being beaten by a man who was twice as big as he. Darting forward, she cried, "Mr. Peavey!" With a vicious swing of her handbag, she whacked Peavey's attacker on the back, yelling as she did so, "Stop that, you brute!"

The brute, too caught up in the moment to recognize the sound of a woman's voice, clouted Loretta on the side of her head with a vicious backhanded blow. Loretta flew through the air to the edge of the mob, where she smacked against a body or two and fell to the ground, stunned.

Unable to move due to dizziness and a strange feeling that somehow her consciousness had become detached from her body, she sat there, trying to get her scattered brain cells reassembled. Before she could accomplish this feat, she was plucked up from the ground with a whoosh that scattered her thought processes again, and held tightly in a pair of arms that felt like steel bands encircling her.

She recognized the feel of those arms.

Blinking to clear her clouded vision, she attempted to bring Captain Malachai Quarles' face into focus. "Wh-what're you doing here?"

"Rescuing you, you damned fool!"

Loretta still felt quite fuddled, but she was sure that wasn't an appropriate response to her civil question. Drawing her eyebrows down slightly, she said, "Thass nah true." Then she frowned for real.

Her words hadn't come out right. A brief survey of her mouth with her tongue explained the problem. The inside of her mouth was torn, it was swelling up like a balloon, and she tasted blood. Her tongue hurt, too. She suspected that she'd bitten it either during her flight or her landing.

Wriggling her fingers free from the captain's grip, she felt her cheek and winced. "Wha hap'd?"

"What?"

Speaking slowly, Loretta tried again. "What happened?"

"You ran headfirst into a fight and got yourself knocked cockeyed for it."

The captain had a very curt and unkind way of explaining things. She'd take him to task for it later, since she wasn't up to it at the moment. "Mithter Peavey?" she asked, trying with little success to pronounce her Ss.

"See for yourself."

He didn't release her, for which Loretta was grateful, since she wasn't sure she could stand on her own yet. He turned so that she could view the scene of the former melee.

Mr. Peavey sat on the ground, pressing a rag to his head. A couple of men who looked vaguely like sailors to Loretta's unsophisticated eye were bending over him solicitously. The big man who had been pounding on Mr. Peavey lay unconscious on the ground a few feet off. Loretta blinked, trying to make sense of it all.

"D'I do 'at?"

"What?"

Oh, dear. She wished her tongue and her cheek would behave. Trying again, she enunciated for all she was worth. "Did . . . I . . . do . . . at—that?"

"Do what?"

She realized the captain was carrying her away from the scene of battle. She didn't object, not being up to it. He sat down on some steps of a building a few yards off, and plunked her on his lap. Her head bounced unpleasantly and she reached up to steady it. That awful man lying on the ground had struck her *very* hard.

"That." She pointed for only a second before bringing her hand back so that she could balance her head properly. It felt unpleasantly swimmy and insecure, rather as if it were going to fall off her neck.

"What?" Malachai's voice rumbled dangerously. "Knock that man out? What the devil makes you think you knocked him out?"

Pooh. She was going to have to talk again. She shut her eyes, took a deep breath, tested her tongue against her teeth, tasted blood once more, and wished the captain hadn't asked his question. Nevertheless, unwilling to be perceived as weak by him, she struggled to speak coherently. "I hih-hit"—her *T*s hurt—"him wiff my purth. Purse." So did her *S*s. She checked, and discovered her handbag still hung from her wrist. Good. It was a new one, and Loretta didn't want to lose it. She hoped her spectacles, which were in their case inside the bag, remained undamaged. She'd look later.

"Don't be a fool," Malachai said in his deep, growly voice. "You couldn't swat a fly with that damned thing, much less deck a big fellow like that with it."

"Oh." How disappointing. She'd wanted so much to be of service to Mr. Peavey. "Why'd he hih-hit Mithter Peavey?"

"I don't know. I'll ask Peavey in a minute."

He was holding her quite tightly. While Loretta might have objected had she been in complete possession of her senses and in full health, at the moment his strong arms felt good. With his arms around her, she got the—silly, no doubt, but there anyway—feeling that nothing could hurt her. She realized he was breathing hard, as if he'd been running or doing something else of a strenuously physical nature.

"Were you running?"

"What?"

Why did he persist in misunderstanding her? She was speaking perfectly clearly, if a trifle slowly. She repeated her question. "Were you running? You're patting."

"I'm what?"

Drat. She formed the word carefully. "Panting."

His roar hurt her ear. "Well, of course, I'm panting! When I saw you whaling away at that man with your stupid purse, I damned near fell over! I decked the man and grabbed you up! That's why I'm panting, damn it!"

"Oh." Loretta was rather pleased with his explanation, even if she didn't approve of his profanity. Surreptitiously pressing her palm against his chest, she realized his heart was racing, as well. However, this situation couldn't last. It was inappropriate at the very least, and Mr. Peavey probably needed medical attention. "Puh me dow, pease."

"What?"

Loretta rolled her eyes and discovered that the gesture hurt. She spoke again and with care, "Pwease put me down."

"Are you able to stand?" He sounded worried.

Loretta thought that was sweet. She was not, however, totally sure she knew the answer to his question. "I thick so."

"We'll try it carefully, then."

And he rose from the steps, taking Loretta with him. The view from his arms was interesting. People seemed to be staring at them. She noticed that one of the sailors who had been tending to Mr. Peavey was now in the process of tying up the fallen villain with a rope. "Who is he?" she asked.

"Who is who?"

Loretta didn't understand why the two of them failed to communicate whenever they met. "Tha' man. Th'one who hih Mithter Peavey and me."

"Damned if I know." The captain called to his men. "Johnson! How's Peavey doing?"

"Better, sir," a tall young man with bushy brown hair said. "He's a little shaken up."

"Peavey's always shaken up," muttered Malachai.

"Thath noh nithe," said Loretta.

"Huh."

With more delicacy than Loretta had expected of him, Malachai set her on her feet. She wobbled for only a second, clinging like a barnacle to the captain's hand, before her head stopped swimming and she was able to steady herself on her own.

"Where's your friend's clinic?" Malachai asked gruffly.

"Wha' frien?"

"Dr. Abernathy. Who the devil do you think I mean? Where's his office, for God's sake?"

"Oh. Jathon. Ith on Thacramen'o and Gran'. I cn drive uth . . . us."

"In what?"

Pooh. Loretta had forgotten she wasn't driving today. For health reasons. If her face didn't hurt so badly, she'd have smiled in irony.

"I'll hail a cab."

And leaving Loretta suddenly to her own devices, Malachai strode off to do just that. Finding herself alone and momentarily bereft of cogent thought, Loretta glanced around, wondering what to do.

She didn't wonder long. Being careful, since it would be totally humiliating to faint, Loretta walked slowly over to where Mr. Peavey sat on some nearby steps. He appeared confused, although Loretta couldn't recall ever seeing the man when he didn't look that way, so she didn't put too much meaning on his appearance. She sat down next to him, using the stair railing as a balance since she felt a trifle unsteady.

"Are you all righ', Mithter Peavey?" she asked gently.

He turned his head and gazed at her with blank, unfocused eyes. "It was the Moors done it," he said.

Oh, dear. Loretta took his hand tenderly in hers and patted it with her other one. "Yeth, Mithter Peavey, it wath the Moors."

He nodded, evidently satisfied that she'd understood him. "Spaniards never had no chance at all."

TEN

When Malachai and his two men, Johnson and Tutwiler, had stepped into the tobacconist's shop to buy a couple of cigars, he'd expected Peavey to follow them. He ought to have been paying closer attention or made sure either Johnson or Tutwiler had stuck with him. Derrick Peavey lived in his own world, and it bore little resemblance to the one occupied by the rest of the denizens on earth.

Therefore, after he'd made his purchase and realized Peavey had wandered off, he'd dashed outdoors. After a brief search, he'd seen a large bully of a man pounding on poor Peavey's head. Malachai, while mad as hell, wasn't surprised. For some reason he couldn't fathom, ever since they'd docked at San Francisco, Derrick Peavey seemed to draw catastrophe unto himself.

Then, when Malachai had seen Loretta Linden charge out of the watching throng and attack the bully with her handbag, he shouldn't have been surprised, but he had been. Although Malachai knew Loretta to be reckless and perhaps unhinged, he still hadn't anticipated her tackling an obviously malicious giant with a handbag.

When the bully had backhanded her and she'd gone flying through the air to land on her luscious bottom on the pavement, he'd seen red. After that he didn't remember anything until he was sitting on some stairs with Loretta in his lap, his heart pounding against his ribs like a storm at sea.

It had taken quite a while for him to calm down enough to behave rationally. That was unlike him. Malachai Quarles was, above anything else, a rational man. He had about as much truck with unreason as he did with ballet dancing. He couldn't leave off holding Loretta, though, for what seemed like hours. It could only have been minutes—even seconds—when he came to his senses, and saw that the man who had attacked Peavey lay unconscious on the roadway.

Had he done that? He couldn't remember, but he hoped to hell he had.

Then he called to the two men who were tending Peavey, "Johnson, Tutwiler, get that man bound and take him to the nearest police station."

"Aye-aye, Cap'n," Johnson called back. And then, like everyone else under Malachai's command, he and Tutwiler had done what their captain had asked them to do, without hesitation or question.

So far, the only person in his life who didn't instantly obey any of his commands, was the woman on his lap. She drove him absolutely crazy.

As soon as he was sure she was able to stand on her own, he went to secure transportation for her. He aimed to make sure she was checked out by a competent physician, and Jason Abernathy was probably the closest one to him at that moment.

"*Cab!*" he shouted into the street, not really noticing if there were any cabs at hand.

A woman nearby screamed in alarm, and he shot her a furious scowl. She scurried away as if he were a scoundrel rather than the hero in the piece. He didn't have time to brood on the irrationality of the average female human being, since three cabs screeched to a halt in front of him. He chose the nearest one and said, "Wait here."

The cabbie said "Yessir," in a frightened-sounding voice, and Malachai stomped back to Loretta.

He found her sitting next to Peavey, with Peavey's hand in hers. He wanted to yank Peavey away from her, but knew he was reacting unreasonably. The damned woman had pushed him to the edge of total insanity.

"The cab's at the curb," he growled at the two. "Can you walk?"

"Of courth," said Loretta.

She would. Malachai frowned down at her, but she only gazed up at him, her eyes bright, her cheek swollen to twice its size, and with the mark of a man's hand standing out in red against the white skin. She was going to be bruised black-and-blue before the day was out. Malachai fought an impulse to follow his sailors and the bully to the police station and strangle the bully with his bare hands.

"Take my hand," he said gruffly, holding it out for her.

She said, "Thass noh nethith—um—never mide." Clutching the stair railing, she heaved herself to her feet, where she stood, swaying, until he caught her shoulders.

"The hell it's not," he growled. And he picked her up. Glancing down at Peavey, he said, "Follow us, Peavey."

Without a word, Peavey, good fellow that he was, rose and followed behind Malachai. He was like a well-trained dog, Peavey was, even when his mind wandered.

At least Loretta didn't struggle. Malachai didn't know whether to be grateful or worried. Loretta wasn't the meek-kitten type. Any other female in the world would have put her arms about his neck, laid her head on his shoulder, and sighed with appreciation, unless she succumbed to a fit of the vapors and loud wailing. Loretta merely tried to frown at him. Because of her swollen cheek, she couldn't manage much of a frown.

Because he was so upset, he snarled, "You're welcome."

"Wha?"

"I said you're welcome. I rescued you, remember?"

Her eyes narrowed, and her pretty little brow wrinkled up, and it was all Malachai could do not to kiss her. She said, "Huh."

With a grin, Malachai said, "So that's the way to keep you quiet, is it?"

She didn't try to talk, but only glared at him.

"I should have thought of it before. Sock you in the jaw, and you can't talk. I'll keep it in mind." Kissing her had worked, too, but that was much more dangerous than hitting her. Backhanding her might lead to legal proceedings against him, but kissing her could lead to a life sentence.

It worried him that the notion of marriage to Loretta Linden didn't alarm him as much as it should have. They were at the curb, however, and he chose not to think about it. Carefully settling Loretta in the front seat next to the cabbie, he helped Peavey into the back seat and climbed in after him. After Loretta gave the cab driver a slow and carefully enunciated address, none of them spoke again until the cab drew to a stop in front of Jason Abernathy's Chinatown clinic.

Malachai looked at the structure doubtfully as he helped Loretta out of the cab. "Are you sure Abernathy knows what he's doing?"

"Who? Jathon? Of courth he dohth!" She was indignant, which Malachai took as a good omen regarding her state of health.

He chose not to meet her indignation with anger. "Good," he said, and he helped Peavey get out of the cab. Poor Peavey had fared worse than Loretta. He limped, and his arm hung at an odd angle, and his face was purpling and swelling. Blood seeped from several cuts.

"Between the two of you, you look as if you've survived a war," Malachai commented as he strode forward and yanked the clinic's door open. He itched to go back and assist Loretta, but she was assisting Peavey.

Damned independent female. Malachai didn't approve of independent women. They were annoying and caused no end of trouble. They were almost as irritating as the women who shrieked and fainted every other minute.

Jason Abernathy jumped up from his desk at the sudden opening of his front door. "Good God!" When he saw the captain, he released a breath and grinned. "I thought you were a hatchet man come to do me in, Captain Quarles. People don't ordinarily open my door with such enthusiasm."

"Sorry." Malachai was a little embarrassed. He guessed he *had* opened the door rather forcefully. "But I have a couple of patients for you, if you have the time."

Jason's smile vanished when he beheld Loretta and Peavey limping into his office. "Good Lord, Loretta, what have you been up to now?"

She gave him an exasperated look as she settled Peavey into a chair. But Jason, Malachai was pleased to note, was not fooled.

"Let me have a look at that cheek, Loretta." Jason took her arm and guided her carefully to the chair beside his desk.

"Look at Mithter Peavey firtht," she said.

"In a minute." Jason gently pressed her down into the chair.

Malachai winced along with Loretta before he steeled his nerves. It was nothing to him if the wench had got herself hurt. Damned fool woman. He had to stifle a cry of alarm at Jason's next question, however.

"Did you lose any teeth?"

"Teef?" Loretta sounded as alarmed as Malachai felt.

About damned time, he thought nastily. And he winced again when Jason began probing. This was stupid. He sat down heavily next to Peavey and tried to concentrate on his sailor. Unfortunately, Peavey's attention was riveted on Jason and Loretta, too.

"How the devil did this happen?" Jason asked, his anger plain to hear in his voice. Then, when Loretta started to answer, he said, "No. Not you. Captain Quarles? Do you know how Loretta sustained this vicious blow?"

"Yeah," said Malachai, in a grump with himself and Loretta both. "She tried to break up a fight with her handbag and got knocked senseless for her efforts."

Jason shook his head. "Loretta, Loretta, Loretta, when will you ever learn?" With a laugh, he added,

"Don't answer that. I don't want you moving this jaw." He glanced at Malachai. "I suppose the guy was twice as big as she?"

"At least."

"Naargh!" said Loretta. It was all she could say under the circumstances.

"Well, it doesn't look as if your jaw is broken, at least, and you haven't lost or loosened any teeth. That's the good news. The bad news is that the inside of your cheek suffered from the collision with your teeth, and your tongue has a nasty bite on it that's going to hurt for a while. Your jaw is going to be bruised and swollen for a couple of weeks, at least. I'm going to dab iodine on the inside of your cheek—don't swallow any more of it than you can help, since it's poisonous—and give you an ice pack. I want you to hold it against your cheek." He shook a finger in her face. "And don't talk."

She glared at him, but she didn't talk as he went to the icebox in a corner of his office and filled an ice bag with chips he hacked from a large chunk of ice. He handed it to her with another admonition. "You really shouldn't attack people who are twice as big as you are, Loretta."

Taking the ice bag, she began indignantly, "I dinn—"

"Don't talk!" he commanded, wagging his finger again. Then he laughed. "You can tell me all about it later—say, in a couple of weeks. Right now, I only want to treat that jaw. It's a real mess."

She sighed in agreement.

Silence reigned in Jason's office while he gently dabbed iodine on the inside of Loretta's mouth. Malachai, watching, was hard pressed to keep seated. He had a mad impulse to rush over to Jason and

Loretta, knock Jason senseless, and carry Loretta off to the Fairfield, where he could tenderly see to her injuries. Damned fool. He was only a little rattled by events and slightly irrational. It wouldn't last.

Even Malachai didn't believe that one. Nevertheless, he remained where he was and didn't make a total ass of himself.

After Jason set aside his iodine bottle, he asked, "Are there any other parts of your body that sustained injury?"

Malachai wondered if Loretta would mention her bottom, but she didn't. She only shook her head.

"You sure? Did you fall against anything and hurt your ribs? Are your legs bruised?"

The combination of a vivid blush and the encroaching blue of the bruising turned Loretta's face into a vibrant sunset of color. She shook her head again, harder.

Jason stood back, put his fists on his hips, and gazed down at her. "I don't believe you. I'll bet you landed on your bum, and you're embarrassed to tell me about it. Well, that's all right. I suppose you're going to be black and blue for quite a while, however, and I expect you to tell me if you experience any trouble. It's possible that your sacroiliac has been bruised or cracked, and that could lead to trouble. Will you tell me if it hurts too badly?"

She nodded.

"You promise?"

Another nod.

"I mean it, Loretta. Promise me."

"I arreahy dih!" she cried indignantly.

Through his grin, Jason said, "And don't talk."

She huffed and subsided into her chair, contenting herself with frowning around her ice bag.

"You're going to have to have complete bed rest for at least a week, and then I'm going to allow you to get up, but you aren't allowed to go downtown or to the soup kitchen for at least another week after that."

"No!" she cried, plainly horrified.

"Yes," Jason said in a no-nonsense voice.

"Fooh."

Jason, who knew her well, said, "I'm serious, Loretta. I'm going to tell Miss MacTavish all about this day's events, and *she'll* tell me if you're keeping anything from me or if you try to disobey my orders."

A powerful scowl met this piece of news. Malachai had an urge to applaud. He was glad he'd brought the injured parties to Jason's clinic, because Jason knew Loretta, and it was obvious that he wasn't going to let her get away with anything.

Gently, Jason took her arm. "I'm just going to move you over to sit beside the captain now, and take a look at Mr. Peavey."

She was limping badly when Jason led her over to him. Malachai rose and assisted her into a chair, using much more care than he generally did with injured people. She didn't thank him for it. Rather, she frowned as if he were some kind of monster and muttered, "I doh neeh hep."

"Nuts," said Jason. To the captain, he said, "I'm going to take Mr. Peavey into my examining room. If he sustained a pounding, he might have cracked ribs, and I want to inspect that arm. He might have dislocated the shoulder, and it will have to be put back into place." He patted Peavey's shoulder. "It's not a pleasant experience, but it'll have to be done."

"Damned Moors," muttered Peavey.

"Thanks," said Malachai.

So Jason led Peavey away, and Malachai and Loretta were left alone in his office. Loretta held the ice pack to her cheek and didn't look at him. Malachai wanted to inspect her various injuries himself. Not that he didn't trust Jason, but he was very worried about Loretta. When he'd seen her flying through the air, he'd nearly had a heart attack. She'd landed hard, too, and he'd bet money that she had more wrong with her than only her cheek. She'd never allow him to fuss over her. Damned woman was such a pain in the ass. Which was probably true literally as well as figuratively now.

After several minutes of silence, he couldn't keep quiet any longer. "You sure you're all right? You probably have a hell of a bruise on your . . . uh . . . leg."

"I'm figh."

The hell she was. Malachai said, "Be sure you keep a watch, though. Sometimes injuries show up some time after the initial blow or fight."

"Uh-huh."

"I mean it," he said, trying to appear both sincere and authoritative. "One of my men got hit by a spar once. We all thought he was all right, but he died during the night. The doc said a blood clot had formed, and that's what did him in. You've got to watch out for clots."

"Uh-huh."

The notion of Loretta developing a blood clot and dying made Malachai's temper rise. "Don't 'uh-huh' me, dammit. I'm serious."

Narrowing her eyes, Loretta pointed at her ice pack. "Cann talk."

"Humph."

Deciding to quit while he was ahead—or at least not too far behind—Malachai clammed up. She didn't appreciate his concern anyhow. He didn't, either, damn it. He couldn't help it, unfortunately.

It must have been at least forty-five minutes that the two of them sat there, Malachai fidgeting and fighting the impulse to cosset Loretta, and Loretta holding her ice pack to a cheek that was becoming bluer and bluer as the minutes passed. It pained Malachai to look at it, but he couldn't help himself.

Loretta noticed his attention. With her frown as firmly in place as her ice bag, she said, "Doh stare ah me."

"I'm not staring."

"Are too."

"Am not."

"Are—Oh, fooh." She stopped pestering him and readjusted the ice pack. Good thing.

When the door to Jason's examination room opened, Malachai leapt to his feet. "Well?" he demanded loudly—much more loudly than was necessary or than he'd intended.

Loretta said, "Hmpf."

Leading Peavey tenderly by his right arm, Jason smiled at the pair. "I see you've been a good girl, Loretta. Of course, with the captain watching over you, I suppose you didn't dare be anything else."

"Wha?" Loretta tried to leap to her feet as Malachai had done, but her leg gave out and she landed back in her chair with a powerful whomp that made tears spring into her eyes. Malachai saw them and wanted to rush out and kill the man who'd hurt her. It was a damned shame he'd told his men to take the bastard to the police station. He deserved to die.

"Aaaah," said Loretta, her face snow-white beneath her bruises.

Jason shook his head. "Dash it, Loretta, *will* you behave for once? You're injured, and you're going to have to stop moving around."

She said, "Huh," but she seemed to have learned her lesson, because that was all she said, and she didn't move again.

Jason helped Mr. Peavey to sit down on the other side of Malachai. He treated the man with great tenderness, and Malachai liked him for it. Jason Abernathy was a good man, in spite of his inexplicable fondness for Loretta Linden.

"How is he?" Malachai asked. Then, believing it to be only courteous, even though he didn't expect much of an answer, he repeated his question, this time to Peavey himself.

"How are you feeling, Peavey?"

"It was them damned Moors," muttered Peavey.

Jason winked at Malachai. "He's sustained a dislocated shoulder, a couple of cracked ribs, and a good deal of pounding. He's going to be at least as black and blue as Loretta, and he ought to stay in bed for a week or so." He turned and frowned at Loretta. "Just like you."

"Aaaah," said Loretta, frowning back.

"Don't be an idiot, Loretta. I'll telephone Miss MacTavish. She'll see that you behave yourself, if she has to hide all your clothes." He brightened. "In fact, I'll tell her to do it before you get home, so you won't stand a chance of disobeying your doctor's orders."

The notion of Loretta without any clothes appealed

strongly to Malachai. He considered this a bad sign. Because he'd sooner appear in public in a tutu than have anyone guess his innermost thoughts, he said, "Good idea. It's probably the only way to keep her down."

She turned her glare on him. He didn't care. Since he was impervious, she transferred her attention back to Jason. "Wha 'bou the soo kish—kish—" She huffed in frustration. "The soup kitchen?"

Malachai and Jason exchanged a glance. "I'll tell them you're laid up," Malachai offered. "As soon as I get you home."

"You don neeh!" Loretta exclaimed indignantly.

Malachai only rolled his eyes.

Jason said, "Don't be silly, Loretta. You need help. Accept it for once, won't you? Your feminist principles won't be violated by accepting help when you need it. In fact, it's only sensible. You'd be an idiot not to. You don't want the world to think all feminists are stupid, do you?"

She looked as if she were as mad as fire, but she bowed to the inevitable. "Fooh."

With another laugh, Jason said, "I'll take that as a yes." He turned to Malachai. "You'll see her home?"

"Yes. But I want to talk to Peavey first."

"Right. He wants to talk to you, too." Jason knelt in front of Peavey. "Will you tell your captain about the man who attacked you, Mr. Peavey?"

"Yeah. Right." Peavey looked at Malachai. "It were one of them Moors, Cap'n. One of the Moors from the dungeon."

Satisfied, Jason stood up. Malachai saw him direct another wink at Loretta, who didn't look as if she appreciated it much. Figured.

But Malachai didn't take time to interpret the dynamics between Loretta Linden and Jason Abernathy. He had more important matters to deal with. Narrowing his eyes, he said, "You mean the man who beat you up today was one of the ones who kidnaped you and threw you in the—the dungeon?" Damnation, but he wished Peavey's brain worked better. They'd searched all of San Francisco, looking for his so-called castle with its so-called dungeon.

Peavey nodded. "He hit me in that kitchen place, too."

"You mean, that guy was one of the men who knocked you out in the soup kitchen?"

Loretta squeaked softly, but both Malachai and Jason ignored her. Peavey was too focused on Malachai to glance her way.

He nodded solemnly. "He were one of them Moors, Cap'n. One of the same ones."

Another squeak from Loretta. Malachai frowned at her. "Keep out of this, will you? You've got to be still."

She was certainly agitated. Worried about her, but believing he was doing the right thing in keeping her mute, Malachai turned away from her. "Did you recognize anyone else today, Peavey? Think hard." He spoke gently, having had a lot of experience with Peavey's flights of fancy.

Obeying his captain, as he always did, Peavey thought hard for several seconds before shaking his head. "Only that one, Cap'n. Didn't see nobody else."

"Hmm." Malachai was frustrated. He wanted to rush to the police station and question Peavey's attacker, by hand if necessary, and then kill him for hurting Loretta, but he also felt a profound need to see Loretta safely tucked away in bed, and to make sure Peavey was safe in his hotel room. Damn. Too bad there weren't more of him.

A smack to his knee made him say, "Ow!" He turned and glared at Loretta, who had hit him with her ice pack. "What the devil's the matter with you? Besides the obvious."

"Ith Tillinghurtht!"

"Aw, Jeez, not this again." Malachai allowed his head to droop for a second. He was weary. Too damned weary to rehash this nonsense.

"It ith, I teww you!" Again using her ice pack for its intended purpose, Loretta pressed it against her cheek.

She spoke to Mr. Peavey very slowly, enunciating carefully. "Mithter Peavey, do you r'member if the cath—cath—oh, pooh! Do you r'member if the cathel where the dungeon was was brick?"

Peering at her closely, Peavey followed her lips, trying to make out what she was saying. "The dungeon? In the castle?"

Loretta nodded.

"Wath—was it brick? The cathel, I mean."

Peavey understood that. He nodded enthusiastically until he hurt himself, and then he said, "Ow." After allowing himself a moment to recover, he said, "Yeah. That's how come I knew it was a dungeon, was 'cause it was underground. The dungeon, I mean. The door was behind a big bunch of bushes."

"An' dih the cath—castle have a big iron gay—gate 'roun it?"

Peavey squinted and seemed to consult his inner memories for several seconds. "An iron gate . . ."

"A bwack—black one," Loretta prompted.

Enlightenment struck Peavey. "Yes! It was a big black iron gate! It surrounded the castle. I had to climb over it. I remember now!"

Loretta sat back, triumphant. She cried, "I *tol'* you it'th Tillinghurtht! I wath righ!"

"Oh, for God's . . ." Malachai took a deep breath and told himself to calm down. It wouldn't help if he blew his top at her. Besides, she might be an idiot, but at the moment she was a wounded one, and it wouldn't be fair to browbeat an injured woman. "Listen, Miss Linden, it might have been anybody's door. Lots of doors are behind bushes, and lots of rich people have big iron gates surrounding their property."

She said stubbornly, her ice pack held firm, "I'm righ. I know ih."

"Fine. You're right. We'll check into it when you're feeling better. Will that keep you quiet? You're injured at the moment, in case you'd forgotten, and you're facing a week in bed."

"Two weeks," corrected Jason.

Malachai approved and smiled at Jason.

"I din forgeh," she said indignantly. "I know I'm righ."

Malachai stared directly into her eyes. She was going to have at least one shiner by tomorrow morning. Holding his wince inside, he spoke slowly and distinctly, mimicking her own manner of speech, but with more clarity of diction. "I promise you, Miss Linden, that I will take you, in a taxicab or by whatever means of transport you prefer, to Mr. Tillinghurst's mansion as soon as you're well enough to snoop. And I'll go with you through his entire grounds. Will that shut you up?"

She frowned, but only said, "You promith?"

"I promith. Iss, I mean! Damn it, now you've got me doing it."

"Huh." Loretta sank back in her chair. Malachai felt certain she wasn't satisfied with his promise, but she was probably too weak to protest further.

He said to Jason, "Listen, Dr. Abernathy, I want to get Peavey settled, but I want one of us to see Miss Linden home. I don't trust her to go to bed and stay there."

Loretta huffed.

Jason said, "You already know her that well, do you? Well, good." He grinned at Loretta. "Tell you what, Captain Quarles. Why don't I see Mr. Peavey to the hotel. I'll call Miss MacTavish and make sure she hides all of Loretta's clothing, and then you can make sure she gets home in one piece—and immediately. Mr. Peavey said you two are staying at the Fairfield?" He lifted his eyebrows as if he were surprised that Peavey, at least, would be staying in so first-rate a hotel.

But Malachai wasn't one to accept finer accommodations than his men, especially if one of them was slightly off-plumb and inclined to wander. He nodded and turned to Peavey. "Do you have your room key, Peavey?"

Peavey squinched up his eyes and thought for a long time before Malachai, interpreting this as an "I don't know," spoke again to Jason. "Ask at the desk. They'll give you one."

Brightening, Peavey said, "That's right! It's at the desk!"

Malachai patted him on the knee. "That's good, Peavey. You go to your hotel room with Dr. Abernathy, and stay there. Don't go anywhere. I'll come to you as soon as I can, and we'll discuss the day's events further."

"Aye-aye, Cap'n." Peavey saluted.

Loretta huffed again, and said, "Call the kishen."

"Right. I'll telephone the soup kitchen and then Miss MacTavish. I'll be sure she knows to hide your clothes."

"There'th no neeh . . ." But Jason had already lifted the receiver from the candlestick telephone on his desk without giving Loretta a chance to argue about having her clothes hidden.

Malachai heard Jason's conversation first with the telephone exchange and then with whoever answered the phone at the soup kitchen. Jason didn't go into details with the soup kitchen staff member.

"That's right. I am Dr. Jason Abernathy, Miss Linden's physician. Miss Linden is ill and will be laid up for at least two weeks." Jason waited, listening to the person on the other end of the wire. "Thank you. Yes, I'll deliver your message."

He replaced the receiver and grinned at Loretta. "Sister Mary Alexander says she'll pray for you, and wishes you the best."

"Thank'oo." She stood up, carefully balancing herself with a hand on the arm of her chair.

Malachai said, "You might as well sit down. You're not going anywhere until Miss MacTavish has your clothes stowed somewhere you can't get at them."

"Fooh!" She didn't sit down, although she couldn't very well go anywhere, since no one had secured a taxicab yet, and she clearly was in no shape to walk.

With a laugh, Jason said, "I'm heading to my telephone now. I guess it's safe to hail a cab."

"I'll wait until you hang up," said Malachai.

Glancing at Loretta, he added, "I want to make sure Miss MacTavish is home before I let Miss Linden loose upon the world again."

Jason gave him a thumbs-up signal and picked up the receiver.

Indignant, Loretta cried, "Fooh on bofe of you!"

Crossing his arms over his chest, Malachai re-sat himself, secure in the knowledge that he was not only doing the right thing, but that Loretta was in no condition to fight with him about it.

We have 4 FREE BOOKS for you as your
introduction to
KENSINGTON CHOICE!
To get your FREE BOOKS, worth up to $24.96, mail
the card below or call TOLL-FREE 1-800-770-1963.
Visit our website at www.kensingtonbooks.com.

Get 4 FREE Kensington Choice Historical Romances!

YES! Please send me my 4 FREE KENSINGTON CHOICE HISTORICAL ROMANCES (without obligation to purchase other books). I only pay $1.99 for shipping and handling. Unless you hear from me after I receive my 4 FREE BOOKS, you may send me 4 new novels—as soon as they are published—to preview each month FREE for 10 days. If I am not satisfied, I may return them and owe nothing. Otherwise, I will pay the money-saving preferred subscriber's price (over $8.00 off the cover price), plus shipping and handling. I may return any shipment within 10 days and owe nothing, and I may cancel any time I wish. In any case the 4 FREE books will be mine to keep.

Name_____

Address_____ Apt._____

City_____ State_____ Zip_____

Telephone (____)_____

Signature_____

(If under 18, parent or guardian must sign)

KN114A

4 FREE

Kensington
Choice
Historical
Romances
*(worth up to
$24.96)
are waiting
for you to
claim them!*

*See details
inside...*

lll..l..lll....ll.l.ll..ll.l..l.l..ll.l.l.l..ll.l.ll..l

KENSINGTON CHOICE

Zebra Home Subscription Service, Inc.

P.O. Box 5214

Clifton NJ 07015-5214

ELEVEN

"Good Lord in heaven, Loretta Linden, what did you do now?" Marjorie rushed down the porch steps and hurried to the cab while Malachai exited his side of the vehicle and stomped to Loretta's side. "I was so worrit when Dr. Abernathy telephoned! I swear, ye're the most contermashious person I've ever met!"

Loretta, already furious with Malachai and Jason, became furious with Marjorie next. "I dinn do an'f-ing," she announced thickly.

"Och, my land!" Marjorie pressed her hands to her cheeks. "Ye look just *turrible!*"

With her own cheek now swollen up like a pig's bladder, it was difficult for Loretta to scowl effectively, but she did her best.

"Did you hide her clothes?" Malachai asked as he reached inside the cab to take Loretta's arm. She tried to swat him away, but he wouldn't let go.

"Aye. I thought Dr. Abernathy was codding, but he said he wasna." She hurried over to assist Malachai. "Is she coggly on her shanks?"

With a chuckle, Malachai said, "Probably, although I don't know what that means."

Marjorie lifted her hands and let them drop. "I'm

sorry. I'm sae upset. It means wobbly on her kegs. Legs."

"Yes," Malachai said, "she's coggly."

An irate Loretta gave in to Malachai's bullying and allowed herself to be assisted in exiting the cab. She was about to look in her handbag for money when the captain preempted her. Drat the man!

"Keep the change," he growled at the cabbie.

The cabbie saluted.

Totally enraged, Loretta grumbled, "Dohth everyone do thah to you?"

He scowled down at her. "Do what?"

"S'lue." She demonstrated.

He grinned. "Only those who know what's good for them."

And with that, he picked her up and carried her up the porch steps, leaving Marjorie standing there with her arms extended and with nothing to wrap them around. Loretta, who would have loved to give the brute of a captain a piece of her mind, couldn't. Worse, she was relieved not to have to walk.

How humiliating. How embarrassing.

How heavenly.

Lord, she was weak. She hurt much worse than she'd admitted to Jason. Her entire left side, from her shoulder to her ankle, felt as if it had been rammed by a locomotive. She was afraid to see what she looked like. Also, Jason had frightened her badly with his speech about sacroiliacs and so forth. Loretta wasn't even sure what a sacroiliac was, but she wouldn't be surprised if hers was cracked, because everything—positively *everything*—hurt.

Marjorie, having caught up, hurried across the porch ahead of them, opened the door and held it wide for the captain. He carried Loretta inside. Her entire household staff lined the entryway. Mrs. Brandeis, her housekeeper, was wringing her hands. Molly and Li, her maids, shrank back against the wall and looked as if they might faint from terror. Even Mr. Hunter, who managed her grounds, had wormed his way indoors and was at present strangling his hat in his two big brawny hands. He looked worried, too.

In a frightened whisper, Marjorie said, "Is it true that a big man knocked her to the ground?"

"Nnnnnn," said Loretta.

"Yes. I saw it myself. Backhanded her, she flew through the air, and landed on the ground several yards away."

"Fee!" cried Loretta, stung.

The captain, still holding her, shrugged, as if she were merely being picky. "Several feet away."

Taking a deep breath—which hurt her back—Loretta tried to reassure everyone. "I'm aw righ."

Molly burst into tears, and Li threw her arms around her. The two maids stared at Loretta, aghast.

Loretta sighed.

"She'll be all right," Malachai said, his tone reassuring. "She needs to stay in bed for a week or two, and I expect every one of you to make sure she does."

Molly and Li let go of each other. Molly wiped her eyes on her apron and looked somewhat calmer. "Oh, sir, we'll do everything we can to make sure she gets well fast."

Loretta would have smiled at her, but her swollen face didn't accommodate smiles any better than it did scowls. "Fank'oo, Mowwy."

Her blue eyes huge, Molly stuttered, "Y-you're welcome, m-ma'am."

With another sigh, Loretta gave up trying to communicate with her staff, knowing that in her present condition, the effort was futile and would probably only upset everyone even more. "Wah go beh," she said, giving in to the inevitable. Better she rest as hard as she could, because it was obvious they were all against her.

Truth to tell, Loretta guessed she did need rest. And, although it might kill her, she'd even tell Jason if her tail bone continued to bother her. Perhaps her tail bone was her sacroiliac. At the moment, it hurt like mad. When she was well enough to pick up a book, she'd look up *sacroiliac* in the dictionary.

"Carry her upstairs, if ye will, Captain Quarles." Marjorie gestured at the staircase, and Malachai started up them, Loretta in his arms.

He was certainly a strong man. If she liked him better, Loretta might be inclined to snuggle. As it was, she was still inclined to snuggle, but she fought the impulse.

After she was well again, she'd consider pursuing her relationship with the captain. He was a beast, true, but he was an attractive one and offhand, she couldn't think of another man to whom she'd rather give up her virginity. And she did rather want to get that over with, if only so as to gain equality with the rest of the women of her acquaintance.

Well, except for Marjorie. Marjorie had made her position on the issue of free love abundantly plain. Then again, there wasn't a single thing about Marjorie's life that *was* free, poor thing.

The captain, however . . . that was another matter

entirely. Loretta wondered if there were South-Sea maidens longing for him at this very moment. Or perhaps there was an ice-blond Danish female who still pined for Malachai Quarles. Why, there were probably dozens—no, hundreds—of women whom he'd seduced and abandoned.

Lord, she wished she were one. The thought made her squirm, which made her tail bone hurt, which drew a brief gasp from her. She was *very* sore.

"Did I hurt you?"

Malachai's question startled her. Did he sound worried? Her eyelids had begun to puff up, impairing her vision, but she could still inspect his face. He looked worried, too. Well, fancy that.

"No," she said. "Fank'oo." Oh, Lord, her speech was getting worse.

"Dr. Abernathy gave me some laudanum for you." Malachai spoke over his shoulder to Marjorie, who was following them up the stairs. "I'm going to stick around until she takes some and goes to sleep. I guess if she's sleeping, she can't get into trouble."

"I suppose," Marjorie said doubtfully.

"Huh." Loretta *wished* everyone would stop talking about her as if she weren't present. It was disconcerting and rude.

"I'm glad the doctor sent something along to help with the pain." Marjorie was very worried about her; Loretta could tell from her tone of voice. And, while she appreciated the concern of her friends, she didn't approve of the way they kept referring to her as an unmanageable idiot. She wasn't. She'd been trying to help Mr. Peavey, curse it.

"And it'll make her sleep." Malachai's voice held a note of satisfaction. "I don't trust her not to act like an imbecile and try to get out of bed."

"Fooh!"

She really hated it when Malachai grinned at her.

As soon as they'd reached the second-floor landing, Marjorie hurried ahead of Malachai. "Her room is right here." She darted to Loretta's door, and pushed it open. "I've prepared the bed."

"She'd better take these clothes off," Malachai said. "Then you can hide them along with the others."

"Fooh," said Loretta.

While she'd never say so—and not merely because she couldn't speak clearly—she really had no inclination whatsoever to move around. Her face was a minor matter to her now. She was in agony, and Jason had truly frightened her with his talk about cracked or broken sacroiliacs—sacroilii? Well, no matter. However fiery a feminist Loretta was—and she was a *very* fiery feminist—she didn't fancy ruining her health.

"Why don't you wait in the hallway, Captain. I'll help her undress and get into bed."

"Fine."

With exquisite care, Malachai set Loretta on her feet. She wobbled, and he held onto her.

"I'm figh," she said, although she wasn't.

"Nuts to that. I'm staying right here until I know you won't fall over when I let you go." Still holding onto her, he said to Marjorie, "Bring over a chair, will you? She's rocky on her pins."

"Aye." Marjorie grabbed the pretty vanity chair that went with Loretta's birdseye-maple vanity table and plunked it down next to Loretta.

"Be careful now," Malachai warned Loretta. "I'm going to sit you down on the chair. Then Miss Mac-Tavish will help you undress."

Loretta wanted to protest but knew better. With a sigh of resignation, she allowed herself to be placed like a doll on the chair. Only then did Malachai release her. She felt a strange sensation of emptiness when he did so, and chalked it up to her injuries.

And then he left the room, and she felt bereft and abandoned—and without even having been seduced first, which was unfair. She scolded herself for being a silly widgeon. "Fanks for your hep, Mawj'ry."

"You're welcome, Loretta. Here, let me take your hat." She pulled out the pins and rid Loretta of her hat, then put the pretty confection on a nearby dresser. "Can ye lift your arms?"

"Yef." She did so with considerable pain, but she didn't flinch.

Carefully and gently, Marjorie pulled Loretta's top over her head. She sucked in a breath. "Oh, my! Look at that bruise on your arm!"

Turning her head, Loretta looked. "Hmm." Mercy, it was quite a mess. She hadn't realized.

"Can ye stand? Use the back of the chair to steady yoursel'."

Gingerly, Loretta obeyed. Marjorie unbuttoned her tweed skirt and worked it down past Loretta's hips. Loretta held her breath. If her hips were the least little bit smaller, her skirt wouldn't hang up so much, and this operation wouldn't hurt as badly as it did. Drat. Too bad she hadn't begun her exercise program a few days earlier.

"There. The skirt's off. Now, let me get that chemise off you."

Again, Loretta lifted her arms. Marjorie pulled the chemise over her head, and Loretta stood there

in her combinations. How mortifying to have to
have Marjorie's help getting undressed.

"Can you sit down now?" Marjorie asked doubtfully. "I probably should remove your stockings and
shoon before you put on your nightgown."

With a sigh, and using great care, Loretta lowered herself into the chair once more. Resigned
to her fate, she stuck out her right foot and allowed Marjorie to untie her shoe. She untied her
garter herself, and rolled her hose down. Then,
bracing herself for an unpleasant experience, she
lifted her left leg. Even lifting it hurt. She almost
didn't want to look at it, although she knew she
had to eventually.

"I'll try to be careful," said Marjorie.

Loretta only sighed again.

The shoe came off easily enough. When Loretta
untied her garter and rolled her black cotton stock-
ing down, however, the full ghastliness of her
injuries revealed themselves. She was fascinated as
inches and inches of purple skin hove into view.
Her left leg, from the hip to the knee and slightly
beyond, was bruised and swollen.

"Och, Loretta!" cried Marjorie, bursting into
tears. "Whatever did ye do?"

Loretta frowned at her. "Noffing," she said stiffly.

Wiping her tears away with a hastily drawn handkerchief, Marjorie shook her head. "Aye, well,
never mind. You'll rest up and it will be better
soon."

Loretta hoped so. At this moment, she wasn't
sure a week's worth of rest would be enough. She
might have to take the full two weeks that Jason had
prescribed. How embarrassing.

After disposing of Loretta's shoes and stockings,

Marjorie flapped a frilly white nightgown in the air and approached Loretta. "Do you want to remove your combinations first?"

Hmmm. Loretta wasn't sure. She knew that Malachai would see her in a few minutes, and she wasn't sure she wanted him to do so when she had only a flimsy bit of white silk covering her body. Well, white silk and the bed clothes, but still . . .

On the other hand, if she intended to perpetrate a seduction on the captain, perhaps the fewer clothes she wore, the better. Malachai hadn't seemed averse to kissing her, but one never knew. Perhaps the kiss had been an aberration. Perhaps she'd have better luck in seducing him if she flaunted herself.

A glance down at her various bruises and a peek in the mirror, where she observed the extent of her face's realignment and recoloration, decided her. "'ake off," she said firmly.

"Very well." Marjorie helped her out of her combinations and slipped the nightgown over her head. "Can ye get into bed, or do ye need help?"

Good question. Loretta eyed her bed. It was pretty tall. But there was a stool. But should she ask for Malachai's help? He could lift her in her frilly white nightgown into bed with those strong arms of his, and he might be enticed.

Then again, he might *not* be enticed. That would be totally humiliating.

Slowly and carefully, Loretta walked to the bed. Marjorie rushed over and pulled out the footstool, and Loretta climbed up, steadying herself on the carved maple headboard. Marjorie had already pulled back the counterpane and the sheets, so Loretta didn't have too much trouble making herself comfortable. Or as comfortable as possible, considering the circumstances. She didn't approve of drug-taking, but she was looking forward to that laudanum.

"Do ye want your robe?" Marjorie asked. She stood beside the bed, Loretta's clothes in her arms.

Frowning at the clothes, Loretta said, "You gonna high 'ose?"

After puzzling over the question for a second or two before she comprehended it, Marjorie said, "Aye. Dr. Abernathy and Captain Quarles are right. You canna be trusted to behave well, Loretta Linden. Just look at you!"

"Fooh."

"I'm going to put these up." Marjorie shook the armful of clothes at her. "And get you an ice pack. Dr. Abernathy said to keep your cheek iced for several more hours."

"Aw wigh." She might as well capitulate with grace, since she perceived no alternative. Wait until she was back in fighting shape, though. Her friends weren't going to escape lightly.

"I'll fetch Captain Quarles. He can watch you while I get the ice pack."

Loretta wanted to say nobody needed to watch her, but knew that protest would be not merely impossible, but fruitless. Besides, even though she knew her face looked like a bloated blue trout at the moment, the rest of her body that showed was shapely and undamaged. If the captain was like people said most men were, he probably wouldn't even care about her face.

Making sure Marjorie's back was turned, she adjusted her bedclothes until they covered all of her except a gentle swell of bosom. She tugged the sheet a trifle lower to expose a teensy bit more cleavage. There. That was good.

The door opened and Marjorie stepped aside. "Come ben, Captain Quarles. I'll just fetch an ice bag. Will ye watch her while I'm gone?"

"Gladly. I don't want her left alone while she's capable of flight."

Flight? Through her swollen eyelids, Loretta eyed her secretary and the captain. Her spectacles were still in her handbag, but she could discern their exchange of confidential grins. Drat them both.

Marjorie vanished into the hall, and Malachai strode to her bedside. Looming over her, he frowned. "You're a damned mess."

So much for gently swelling bosoms. Loretta said, "Fooh." If her cheek swelled up any more, she was afraid the skin on her face would crack. Then there were her eyes. She didn't suppose even spectacles could help her see clearly if her eyes were swollen shut.

Although . . . it was possible that, after she recovered some, she might like to read. Peering up at Malachai as well as she could, she said, "Pease geh my han'bag."

"What?" Malachai's brow wrinkled in puzzlement.

She took a deep breath. "My han—handbag."

"Your handbag? What the devil do you want your handbag for?"

The expression on his face told her as plainly as words that he expected her to grab her handbag and run away. Ha! If only he knew. It would be a long, long time before Loretta Linden would run again. Hobble, maybe, although even that was doubtful at the moment. Lifting her hand, she pointed at her right eye. "Speckles."

"Speckles?" For a second or two, Malachai pondered this odd request, and then enlightenment struck. "Oh! Your eyeglasses!"

"Yeff. Gaffes."

He shook his head. "I guess that's all right. You can't get very far in that silk thing."

"Huh."

This wasn't working out quite as Loretta had hoped it would. It was just like Malachai Quarles to kiss her when she didn't want him to and then ignore her when she was trying to be seductive. A most contrary fellow, the captain. He looked awfully out of place in Loretta's pretty feminine bedroom. She'd decorated it in shades of green and rusty orange, and it was quite delicate.

"Delicate" wasn't a word one would ever associate with Malachai. At the moment, he stood next to her vanity table, looking as if he could thump it with a fist and break it in two if he cared to. His hands were huge as they reached for the handbag Marjorie had laid there. "You want the whole bag or just the glasses?"

She thought about it for a moment. "Gaffes."

Without hesitation, he unsnapped her handbag, and his gigantic brown hand tried to dip within. It wouldn't fit. He muttered a soft, "Damn," and upended the bag over the glass top of her vanity table. Loretta thanked her lucky stars she'd changed bags that morning, because the things that fell out made a most proper and tidy jumble. Handkerchief. Eyeglass case. Change purse. A pencil, two capped fountain pens, and a small notebook.

Malachai picked up the glasses case and marched to the bed with it. "Here."

"Fank'oo."

"You're welcome."

He stood at the head of her bed, frowning down at her, while she tucked the glasses case under the pillow next to her. Was he staring at her bosom? Or at her ugly, swollen face? After a few seconds of wondering, Loretta, whose lack of patience was legendary among her family and friends, said, "Wew? Wha'?"

When he spoke, his question surprised her. "Do you want a book?"

"Book?" She hadn't considered particular reading materials when she'd asked for her spectacles. She'd mostly thought about seeing him more clearly. Which, now that she thought about it, was silly, since she didn't want him to see her in her eyeglasses. Which was also silly. What difference would a pair of eyeglasses make at this point? Ah, well, the human animal was incomprehensible sometimes, even when it was housed in the body of the ever-so-rational Loretta Linden. "Yeff, pease."

"I'll wait until Miss MacTavish gets back with your ice pack. Do you know which book you want?"

Hmm. Under ordinary circumstances, Loretta would probably mention an outlandish book title. *Sister Carrie* was always good, since it was widely considered to be a shocking book. But Loretta had already read that one. Besides, if she was going to be laid up here for several days, she'd really rather read something entertaining and leave her further social education for another day, when she was feeling stronger.

On the other hand, she didn't want the captain

to believe her to be a frivolous female. On the other other hand, she might be stuck with what he brought her, so she'd best choose one she'd be happy with. Loretta didn't like the idea of having to trot down to her library to root around in the books. She didn't like the idea of having to trot anywhere, actually. The mere thought of negotiating the stairs made her bruises throb.

She guessed she'd better ask for the two books she'd been meaning to read for a couple of months and that were downstairs, waiting for her on her library desk: *A Princess of Mars,* by Edgar Rice Burroughs; and *Riders of the Purple Sage,* by Zane Grey. The only problem remaining, therefore, was how to pronounce the titles.

"Well?" said Malachai impatiently.

Loretta tried to glower at him. "I'm finking."

"Fine." Still looming, Malachai reached behind him, grabbed the tiny vanity chair, drew it close to the head of the bed, and sat. "Think away." He waved one of those massive hands in a careless gesture.

Loretta held her breath, but the chair didn't crumple under the captain's weight. Deciding upon the course of least resistance, she said, "Burroughth book an' Grey book. On wibrary tayboo."

A slow grin spread over Malachai's face. Loretta didn't like that look. "Do you mean to tell me you want to read a book by Edgar Rice Burroughs and a book by Zane Grey?"

"Whazzamah wiff 'at?"

"Not a single thing."

Loretta nearly jumped out of her skin when a large, brown hand lifted from where it had been resting on Malachai's lap and reached for her. She drew back a little, although she didn't mean to. She was no coward, curse it!

When his finger smoothed her swollen cheek, she blinked, astonished.

"Poor Miss Linden." His hand cupped her cheek. Loretta would have fallen over had she been standing. "You really should be more careful. I know you were trying to help Peavey, but that man was big. Rushing headlong isn't always the best way to deal with problems."

Curse the man. Not only was he right, but if he kept up being tender and solicitous, she might just start purring.

"You could have set up a screech, you know, and startled the fellow. Or even summoned a policeman. If my men and I hadn't been nearby, the man would probably not merely have pounded you and Peavey into the pavement, but gotten away with it, as well."

"Fooh." His touch was making her mind wander. At the moment, it was wandering hand-in-hand with Malachai through a grassy field full of buttercups and daisies. And birds. And sheep grazing in the distance. And with a blue, blue sky decorated with puffy white clouds overhead.

"You'll be better soon," Malachai said, scattering her thoughts. "You're young. You'll heal fast." His gaze drifted from her face to her gently swelling bosom and, while Loretta felt vindicated, she also wished she hadn't been quite so generous in exposing it. "I hate to see you like this, all bruised up."

She badly wanted him to kiss her. It would hurt, but she still wanted it. His next question drove thoughts of a kiss out of her mind.

"How old are you, Miss Linden?"

She jerked, startled, sending her bruised muscles into a spasm. "Wha?"

His smile was still tender. Loretta couldn't reconcile his smile with that question. "It's not polite, I know, but I'm curious," explained Malachai. "I'll tell you how old I am if you tell me how old you are."

Childish nonsense, Loretta fumed silently. Age was only a number. Loretta Linden didn't give a hang if everyone in San Francisco considered her an over-the-hill rabble-rouser. She'd even heard some people say that she roused rabble because she was getting old and was trying to make up for the lack of masculine attention in her life, which was utter foolishness. *She* didn't consider herself too old for anything. *She* didn't think a woman was a failure if she wasn't married by the time she reached her age. Anyhow, it was ridiculous to be ashamed of one's age.

Who was she trying to fool? Herself, no doubt. Loretta didn't hold with *that,* either, curse it. Unwilling, but following her principles, she muttered, "Twenny-aigh."

"Twenty-eight?"

Did he appear disappointed? Loretta, furrowing her brow for all she was worth, tried to focus more clearly on Malachai's face. It was no use. Her poor eyelids were too swollen.

"Wew?" she demanded.

"Well what?" he asked mildly.

"Wew, izzat too ode for you?"

"Too old? For me?" Malachai was clearly taken aback. "You're a child, Loretta Linden. A mere child."

Her nose wrinkled as she tried to reconcile his

words with her own beliefs. A child? A twenty-eight-year-old, unmarried, unwanted-by-a-man feminist female agitator? "Huh." It was probably a good thing she couldn't speak clearly, since she didn't know what to say.

She did, however, want to know how old he was. If he considered a twenty-eight-year-old spinster a child, he must be older than Loretta had guessed.

Actually, she hadn't guessed. She'd only judged him to be the right age for her.

Whatever was she thinking? She didn't mean that. Or . . . well, she did mean it, but not exactly in the way she'd thought it.

Bother. There she went again, trying to deceive herself. Frustrated, both with herself and with Malachai for not instantly keeping his bargain, she asked, "Wew? How ode are you?"

His hand, which had by this time strayed to her neck and was fiddling with a stray lock of her hair, was sending her innards into a frenzy. If he didn't stop that, she might just have to take action, although precisely which action was unclear to her at the moment. Everything was unclear to her, actually, and she knew her state of confusion was only dimly related to her battered body. It was Malachai Quarles and his massive presence who was the problem here, curse it. Well, and her own treacherous body. Curse it, too.

"I'm thirty-nine. More than ten years your senior, my dear."

I'm not your dear, thought Loretta, although she wasn't sure she meant it. Or, rather, she did mean it, but wished it weren't so and that she really *was* his dear. Which was absolutely pathetic. Loretta was ashamed of her weakness.

Thirty-nine sounded like a rather nice age to her, too, which was unfortunate, because it was her emotions judging and not her intellect. Her intellect knew that age was not important. Her emotions told her that Malachai Quarles was old enough to be a gallant protector and lover. Loretta Linden had lived her life since her sixteenth birthday on the premise that a woman needed neither gallantry nor protection. Love was something else entirely, but she was too weak to contemplate it at the moment.

Fiddlesticks. The man drove her absolutely loony. When she recovered, she'd be able to engage her intellect more fully. Right now, her emotions were basking in his touch, drat them.

Malachai's sigh blended with hers. "Too old for a lovely young lady like you."

Loretta only realized that she had closed her eyes when they popped open. Perhaps *popped* was too lively a word to describe the slits that appeared between her swollen lids. "Too ode?" What was the man talking about?

He seemed to summon his thoughts back from wherever they'd wandered. "What? Oh, I . . . never mind." His hand left off petting her and returned to his lap. Loretta was terribly disappointed. "Why in God's name are we talking about age?" He asked the question sharply, as if it had been Loretta who'd brought up the age issue. "Damned fool thing to talk about. I don't know why women are always so worried about their damned ages."

Indignant, Loretta said, "Fooh!"

TWELVE

Malachai decided to walk to the Fairfield from Loretta's house. He needed to get there quickly and see to Peavey, but he also had to calm himself. After seeing Loretta in her big, lonely bed, he was too wrought up to deal with anything at all, much less poor addled Peavey.

What the devil was the matter with him? He'd seen women before. Lots of them. He'd never been tempted to crawl in bed beside one of them and hold her and comfort her and tell her everything was going to be all right and that he'd take care of her and she didn't have to worry about anything, ever, again in her life.

But Loretta was such an annoyingly independent female. And she was usually so lively and vivacious as she interfered with other people and lectured him about the evils of the world. And she'd looked so pathetic in that big bed, all by herself, and so bruised and battered. When he'd looked down on her, something in his chest region had ached severely for several seconds and then snapped. Obviously, whatever it was had affected his brain.

"Damned fool," he muttered to himself as he clattered down the twisty brick steps lining Lombard Street. A young Chinese man skipped out of his way with a frightened gasp. Malachai glared at him, wondering what his problem was.

When he reached the bottom of the hill and wheeled to his right onto Leavenworth, a plump matron carrying a frivolous parasol squealed like a piglet and jumped right into the street. Malachai reached out, grabbed her by the arm, and hauled her back up onto the sidewalk before she could be hit by an automobile, wondering what had possessed her.

Loretta's poor face. Lord, he hoped she'd be all right. And her lovely bosom. He wished like thunder he hadn't been allowed to view her bosom. Obviously, she was in worse shape than even he'd imagined, or she'd never have exposed so much of her succulent flesh.

Why had he stayed in her room so long? Stupid question. He'd stayed because he couldn't make himself leave.

"Idiot," he snarled. A newspaper boy who had been set to offer him a *Chronicle,* darted into a doorway and covered his head until Malachai passed. Malachai squinted at the boy, and thought it was a damned shame that so shy a child should be forced to hawk newspapers on street corners.

When he reached the Fairfield, he stomped into the lobby and up to the desk and demanded his key. The desk clerk, turning pale, stuttered out a "Y-yes, sir," fumbled with the keys on the rack behind him, dropped Malachai's room key twice, and slammed it onto the counter as if he couldn't get rid of it fast enough. It didn't seem right that so clumsy a fellow should be in charge of so fancy a hotel's guest keys.

When he visited Peavey's room and demanded to

know how he was, Peavey hid under the covers and told him that the Moors were after him.

By the time he entered his own room and threw his key against the far wall, sending a considerable chunk of plaster dust crumbling to the floor, he was convinced that every person in San Francisco was insane, that he was fast joining their ranks, and that it was all Loretta Linden's fault.

Naturally, since his mind had been so badly affected by her, he visited her every day for two weeks while she recuperated. He couldn't help himself. It was a compulsion brought about by the aforementioned mental defect and, while he didn't understand, appreciate, or want it, he didn't even try to fight it. Malachai knew better than to court defeat by attempting the impossible.

November had sneaked up and overthrown October, and on the third afternoon of the month, and in spite of whatever better judgment he might once have possessed, Malachai sat with a bundled-up Loretta on her beautiful patio. The weather was crisp and clear and a breeze blew in from the bay, carrying with it all the scents of a world Malachai had traveled for years, along with the special perfume that was uniquely San Francisco's.

As he sat there, it occurred to him, not for the first time, that, while he had enjoyed seeing the world and investigating its many mysteries, he was tired of traveling. It seemed strange to him that he was peering about him at Loretta's garden and wondering if something like this wouldn't be nice for his own home, the home he had been contemplating building—in San Francisco, by God.

Thoughts of domesticity, as foreign to him as had once been the far East, dribbled into his mind as he

admired Loretta's landscaped yard and patio and
sipped, of all nonsensical beverages, tea. Sweetened. With milk. If anyone had asked him a month
before if he could imagine himself sitting on a spinster's patio and sipping tea, he'd have believed the
question to be a joke.

Some joke. He lifted a flowery teacup and
gulped. Tea. In a flowery teacup. He couldn't stand
it.

"I tell you it's true," said Loretta. She was able to
frown again, Malachai noticed, and quite effectively.

"You've been telling me the same thing for the
past several weeks." He really liked this patio. It
spoke to him. Needed a dog, but it was a nice patio.
"Say, Miss Linden, who did your landscaping?"

"Landscaping?" Loretta looked at him as if he'd
lost his mind, which was appropriate if she only
knew it. "I thought we were talking about the stolen
artifacts."

Malachai sighed. "I just wanted to know who did
your landscaping."

"Somerset FitzRoy, why?"

"Just wondered. He did a good job."

"He's a genius," Loretta said shortly, "but that's
not the point."

"I suppose it is the point if we're talking about
landscaping."

"Landscaping?" She stared at him, and he saw
that she'd actually brushed some face powder over
her cheeks to hide her yellowing bruises.

It was difficult for him to reconcile face powder
with the Loretta Linden he'd come to know. To any
other woman in the world, covering bruises with
face powder would be only natural; for Loretta, it

seemed like some kind of betrayal. Malachai was pretty sure he'd never understand the way her mind worked. But that wasn't the point. "Yes. Is this FitzRoy character a local person?"

"What?"

"FitzRoy. Isn't that what you said his name is? Is he a local merchant?"

"Merchant? What . . . he's a friend of mine, actually. But . . ."

Ah. He might have guessed. "I see. Well, I'll keep his name in mind."

"In mind for *what?*"

Perplexed by her evident anger, he said, "Why are you yelling at me?"

"Because you're not paying attention!"

"I'm not?" He'd thought he was.

"Don't you even care?" She was indignant, as usual.

"About what?"

"About the cursed missing artifacts!" she screeched.

Malachai sighed. She just wouldn't leave the damned artifacts alone. She drove him crazy with her perpetual frenzy about the damned artifacts. "Of course I care. I did all the work, remember? The police are working on the problem."

"The police?" Loretta scoffed. She was good at that. "William Tillinghurst has the police in his pocket."

He shrugged. "That's good. If they respect him, I expect they'll be diligent in searching for and finding the lost treasure and in pursuing the thieves."

She pinned him with her beautiful brown eyes. He was glad they were finally unaffected by swelling. It had hurt his heart to see them swollen shut, imprisoned in puffy black and blue flesh.

Lord. There he went again. Until he met Loretta Linden, he'd been happy in the belief that he didn't possess a heart. At least not the kind the poets were forever ranting on about. Now . . . well, he could only hope he'd get over this . . . this . . . infatuation, he supposed was a good word for it.

"Have you listened to a single thing I've said to you, Captain Quarles?"

"Why don't you call me Malachai. It's so much friendlier."

She huffed, but said, "Very well, *Malachai.* You may call me Loretta."

"Thank you, Loretta." He hoped he'd endowed his thanks with the proper humility. Since she huffed again, he guessed he hadn't. To hell with it. Humility wasn't one of his primary character traits.

"You didn't answer my question," she said accusingly.

"Which question was that, Loretta?" He liked the name *Loretta* for her. It wasn't a name he'd taken any particular notice of before he met her. But it seemed to fit her somehow, being a trifle snappish and crisp, but pretty, too, in an odd way.

Lord, she had more hair per square inch than any other person he'd ever met in his life. His fingers itched to burrow into those thick, silky tresses.

"I *asked,*" she said sharply, "if you'd been listening to me."

"Of course, I've been listening to you. Do you realize that you have more hair than any other woman I've ever met? Your hair is very pretty, Loretta."

Her mouth fell open and stayed that way for a moment before shutting with a snap. "What does my hair have to do with anything?"

He shrugged and sipped more tea. Ugh. It had gone cold and now tasted even more vile than it had when it had been hot. "It's very pretty, is all. It catches the sun, and it looks like there are red and gold sparkles in it."

Her right hand lifted and patted her hair. She said, "Oh," in a disconcerted sort of voice. "I . . . I . . . thank you."

Waving away her thanks, he said, "Your eyes are beautiful again, too, now that they aren't swollen shut. Too bad the skin around them is still green, but at least brown and green go well together."

She gaped at him.

"Does your leg still hurt?"

She continued gaping for several seconds. Malachai didn't have a clue what the matter was. He was only being polite, after all.

At last she burst out, "What are you trying to do?"

"I beg your pardon?"

"You keep changing the subject!"

Honestly puzzled, he said, "What subject?"

"For heaven's . . . I've been *trying* to talk to you about Tillinghurst having stolen your precious artifacts, Malachai Quarles!"

He sighed heavily. "Oh. That again."

"Yes, that again," she said indignantly. "I keep telling you that Tillinghurst is behind the theft."

"Yes, you do."

"Well? Don't you want to know why?"

"Why what? Why he stole the loot?"

"No! Why I know he did it!"

"You've told me why." He thought about that for

a second. "Come to think of it, you haven't told me why. You've only told me that you think he stole it, and I've told you that I think you're crazy." He shrugged. "Has anything changed?"

Irate, Loretta cried, "I did, too, tell you why!"

"You said it was a feeling, if I recall correctly. Have you taken this feeling to the police? I'm sure they'll rush right over to Tillinghurst's place and arrest him. I suppose there's a San Francisco law granting warrants to the police based on ladies' feelings." San Francisco was kind of a crazy place. It wouldn't surprise him much if such a law really *was* on the books somewhere.

Angry now, Loretta leaned closer to him. "That's *not* the only reason, curse you!"

The blanket she'd thrown over her shoulders slipped, exposing her arms. She was wearing a deep-green silk robe that shimmered in the fall sunshine almost as brightly as did her hair, and it clung to her various protuberances enticingly. Smiling with pleasure at the sight, Malachai said, "You ought to wear silk more often, Loretta. And that color is nice on you. Do you call that jade green?"

"What?"

"Is that jade green? Is that what they call that color of green? It kind of goes with the skin around your eyes, but I'm sure that greenish color will fade soon. At least you're not black and blue any longer."

To his disappointment, Loretta sat up in her chair and pulled her blanket over her shoulders. "You aren't listening to a thing I say, are you?"

"Of course I am!" What was the matter with the woman? He was paying absolute attention to her. Lord, if his attentions got any more intense, he'd take the woman right here on her own patio, before God and her servants. Pathetic. He was pathetic.

"Oh, you drive me crazy," Loretta said. "What's the point in talking to you?" She threw her arms up, and her blanket slipped again.

Malachai was charmed. "I don't know."

"Well, I'll prove it to you."

"Prove what?"

Her eyes grew huge, and her cheeks turned crimson. From these symptoms, Malachai presumed he'd missed a clue again. Hang it all, though, it was difficult to concentrate on a conversation when there was so much delicious flesh teasing him. Besides, he hadn't met a woman yet who was worth talking to.

"Prove *what?*" she shouted. "Prove that Tillinghurst is a crook, of course!"

"Ah."

"Oh, you're just impossible! I *will* prove it to you, though. You just wait."

"I'll have to wait, won't I?" Waiting was becoming very frustrating, although he was pretty sure they weren't talking about the same thing. With a sigh, he decided there wasn't much he could do about it.

She glared at him for at least a minute, and neither of them spoke. Malachai was enjoying the view. He didn't know what Loretta was doing—well, except for fuming, which was her natural condition—but he hoped she'd keep it up, because she'd apparently forgotten all about her blanket.

The back door opened, and she pulled her blanket up again. Disappointed but grateful for what enticements he'd been allowed to glimpse, Malachai turned to see which one of Loretta's thousands of friends had come to call. A pretty blond woman, holding the hand of a pretty blond girl, stepped out onto the patio. Malachai stood, thereby proving, if Loretta was paying attention, that he was a gentleman.

Ignoring him, Loretta jumped to her feet. "It's the FitzRoys! I'm so glad you've come!"

"We brought you some books," said the little girl. "Remember, we said we would."

"I remember, sweetheart. You're both dears to think of me."

The pretty blond lady laughed. "My daughter selected the volumes, so prepare yourself for an education."

Both women laughed. The little girl smiled, but Malachai sensed her heart wasn't in it.

"I selected a number of books, both entertaining and educational, Miss Linden. Mama's just teasing."

She must be Eunice, Malachai deduced. Dr. Abernathy had told him about Eunice FitzRoy, the child genius. He smiled, prepared to meet the newcomers.

"Come over here and meet Captain Malachai Quarles. You remember I told you about Captain Quarles' treasure-recovery expedition, Eunice."

The child's eyes brightened. "Oh, my, yes! Oh, Captain Quarles, I should be so happy to discuss your adventures on the high seas."

So Malachai spent the rest of his visit with Loretta answering the most amazing set of questions he could have imagined, all posed to him by a nine-year-old girl. Eunice was almost—but not quite—enough to make him reconsider settling down.

* * *

Loretta was a little nervous, but not nervous enough to change her mind regarding her mission. She hadn't dared tell Marjorie about her plans, because she didn't trust her secretary not to blab. Marjorie always thought she knew best, but her decisions were invariably made according to her frightened, narrow-minded view of the world.

Well, Loretta was neither narrow-minded nor frightened, although she had to admit to the aforementioned trace of nervousness. It wasn't, after all, her customary practice to climb over people's tall black iron fences and snoop around in their gardens for stolen historical artifacts.

She'd prepared herself as well as she could for the adventure. She'd even gone so far as to don a pair of men's trousers. No sense climbing fences in a dress, after all. Besides, why should women be forced to wear cumbersome skirts and petticoats? Her feminist soul took great joy in the freedom of movement her trousers allowed.

Her more conventional side, the one she tried to keep hidden from society and, more important, from herself, was grateful for the darkness under which she aimed to perpetrate her search. She'd have been mortified to have been seen in public wearing such scandalously revealing apparel.

She'd also brought along one of those newfangled, battery-operated torches—flashlights, some people called them. She'd attempted to stuff her hair under a cloth cap, but she had too much of it to stuff effectively. Therefore, she'd drawn her hair back into a bun and tacked it to the back of her head, and plopped the cap on top. It was dark, and she didn't expect to be observed, so she felt sure her hair wouldn't be a problem.

It had taken her a long, hard session of soul-searching and deep thought before she'd opted to take a cab and not her Runabout on the night's adventure. Ultimately, she decided upon riding to Tillinghurst's estate in a cab. If she awakened a servant to crank up the Runabout, the whole household would know about her adventure come morning—and if she cranked it up herself, the noise would probably awaken the whole household anyhow. Therefore, she considered taking a cab the more prudent course of action to follow.

And then there was the problem that should, by some remote possibility, anything happen to her, nobody would know where she was. After all, if Tillinghurst was a wicked criminal, he might not balk at murder. With that possibility in mind, Loretta decided to leave a note.

A shudder slithered down her spine as she pinned the note to her pillow. Marjorie would faint dead away when she read it, but at least they'd know where to find the body.

She told herself not to be ridiculous. There was no need even to think about bodies. Nothing was going to happen to her. She was only borrowing trouble and acting hysterical, two behaviors that were most unlike her. After giving herself one last severe inspection via mirror, she crept downstairs and out of the house.

When she gave directions to the cabman, she disguised her voice, which was perhaps unnecessary, but she didn't want to take any chances. She also gave him a lot of extra money and extracted a promise that he'd wait for her outside Tillinghurst's gated estate so that she'd have a ride home. She didn't fancy being caught out of doors in her britches, no matter how enlightened she considered herself.

Besides which, if she ended up injured or dead, perhaps the cabman would tell someone.

Stop it!

Peeved with herself, Loretta frowned and tried to see the countryside from the cab's windows. Given the state of night, she couldn't do it, but squinting took her mind away from ugly thoughts.

Her heart sped up as the cab approached Tillinghurst's estate just outside of the city. The area was rural and woodsy. It didn't seem quite as welcoming as it had when Loretta had visited during the daylight hours. When she'd come here before, she'd enjoyed the twittering of the birds in the trees and the chattering of the squirrels. Now she wondered if the trees hid bears. Or, worse, human predators.

But that was silly. It was mere fancy that made the trees loom taller and darker and more menacing than she thought they should. Trees were trees. They couldn't hurt her.

Anything hiding behind them might. Again, Loretta scolded herself for cowardice.

"We're here," the cabman said as his automobile rounded a bend in the road and the iron bars on Tillinghurst's gate flashed in the headlamps. "You want I should let you out at the gate?"

"No," Loretta said in her altered voice. "Go on about a hundred yards and pull over."

"Yes, ma'am."

Ma'am? Loretta stared at the back of the cabman's head, dismayed. Fiddlesticks. She'd thought she looked so masculine, too. Well, it couldn't be helped. With luck, no one else would see her.

Following Loretta's instructions, the driver pulled over and stopped the cab in a small clearing among the bushes and trees approximately a hundred yards from Tillinghurst's gate. Taking a deep breath for courage, Loretta slid out of the cab before the cabman could open the door for her. At least the moon wasn't out yet, and it would only be a sliver when it showed up. And there was lots of shrubbery to hide her from any passing motorists.

Passing motorists? Loretta wondered at her mental processes. No one came out here at night.

Well, that was a good thing. She slipped into the bushes, noticing as she did so that they were *quite* dense. Thank God she'd worn long sleeves, or she'd have scratches to remind her of the night's escapade from here to kingdom come.

Climbing tall iron fences, Loretta soon discovered, wasn't a job for the weak-willed or unhealthy. It would have been easier for her to do if she hadn't been laid up for the past two weeks, because her strength had ebbed substantially during her period of enforced idleness. Her determination was at least as strong as her body, however, and she managed to heave herself over the top of the fence after a struggle.

She then found herself dangling, and wished she'd given more thought to trajectory. With a little more effort, she managed to scoot along the top of the fence, hand over hand, until her feet barely touched a bush beneath her. Then, holding her breath and praying she wouldn't break anything, she let go of the fence.

It was a prickly bush. Fortunately, it didn't sport

any actual thorns, the prickles having mainly to do with broken twigs, and she managed to disentangle herself without sustaining too many scratches. *Thank God for gloves.* Too bad no one had invented a glove for one's face.

Once she'd gained entry to the estate grounds and brushed herself off, Loretta engaged her flashlight only long enough to take her bearings. She knew where she aimed to search once she figured out where she was in the overall scheme of things.

She heard a dog bark and nearly suffered a spasm. She hadn't recalled that Tillinghurst owned dogs. Were they guard dogs that were only released at night? Were they trained to attack intruders?

Lord, she wished she'd remembered to have Marjorie ask Tillinghurst about his estate's security measures. It would have been perfectly within the supposed scope of their visit.

But Marjorie would probably have fumbled the question. Loretta had grave doubts about Marjorie's effectiveness as a collaborator.

Malachai Quarles would make a good partner in crime, she imagined, if he could only be persuaded that the cause was just. Unfortunately, he had an incredibly thick head when it came to seeing things Loretta's way, curse him.

She stood still for what seemed like an hour at least, before deciding that the dog wasn't a threat to her. Its bark faded and stopped, and Loretta guessed it was outside Tillinghurst's gates. Thank God. She wasn't sure what she'd do if Tillinghurst used, say, a bull mastiff to ward off intruders. She'd end up a doggie snack, is probably what she'd do. The notion held no appeal, and she vaguely wished that she hadn't read *The Hound of the Baskervilles* so many times.

As she began wading through bushes and trees, making a terrible racket and wishing she'd chosen a less thickly planted area, she contemplated Malachai Quarles with rancor. If he weren't so stubborn, she wouldn't have to risk herself this way. She could have left it to him to explore his partner's estate. But no. Malachai Quarles seemed intent upon thwarting Loretta at every turn in the road, blast the man.

Wouldn't he be surprised when she told him where Tillinghurst had hidden the stolen artifacts?

Another bark sent her thoughts flying through the air like dandelion fluff. Again, Loretta paused, trying to determine where the bark had come from. She couldn't. Not only was it so dark as to confuse her sense of direction, but fog had begun to creep in through the iron railings of Tillinghurst's massive fence and blur the edges of her sharp wits.

The wretched estate was starting to resemble the castle of an evil king in a Gothic romance novel, and Loretta, whose sensibilities were exquisite, although she endeavored to keep them under control most of the time, was feeling an increase of her heretofore slight nervousness. Just because the place *looked* ghostly in the foggy night, didn't mean it was haunted. There were no such things as ghosts.

There were such things as guard dogs, fog or no fog.

Loretta gave herself a hard mental slap and, sucking in a deep breath, only slightly fog-laden, she commanded herself to keep her wits about her. It would do nobody any good if she panicked. Loretta

Linden, she reminded herself, was not the panicking kind.

That being the case, and since she heard no more barks, she crunched forward through the bushes, wishing she could stride. She felt much more like herself when she was striding through the world with vigor. This creeping about was for a personality less inclined to take charge than hers. Marjorie was the creeping-around type, not Loretta.

She nearly wept with relief when she finally maneuvered herself out of the underbrush and onto a paved driveway. At least she thought it was a driveway. Allowing one more tiny flick of her flashlight, she saw that she was right, and that she only needed to walk another hundred yards or so to be in the area where she believed her success might lie.

As quietly as possible—she was glad she'd worn rubber-soled shoes for this evening's work—Loretta traversed the drive to a building sitting several yards beyond the back of Tillinghurst's mansion, almost hidden by thick bushes and a tall hedge. Slowly, she edged around the building, searching for the door she'd espied right before Captain Quarles had thwarted her first search.

Ah. There it was, looming large and black before her.

Loretta wished she hadn't thought the word *loomed*. Loomed was such a . . . a dangerous word.

Well, never mind. She'd found what she'd been looking for: a recessed area that, during the day, was shaded by thick bushes. If she hadn't inspected them during her first visit, with Marjorie, to Tillinghurst's estate, she'd never have discovered, behind the prickly hedge, steps leading down to a door. That door must open into a room underground, and it was so well hidden that Loretta couldn't think of a better place to hide stolen loot.

That being the case, she tiptoed down the stairs until she stood before the door. Silently, she tried the knob. Locked. Disappointing, but not unexpected. Feeling with her hands, she tried to determine if there was a window in the door. There wasn't. She muttered a soft, "Damn," under her breath.

Her heart nearly jumped out of her chest when, from the other side of the door, she heard a whispered, "Cap'n? Is that you, Cap'n Quarles?"

Loretta was halfway up the stairs before she recalled that she'd probably just found what she'd been looking for, at least in part. Swallowing her heart and pressing on her chest to keep it where it belonged, she edged back down the stairs. Her nerves were still jangling when she put her lips close to the keyhole and whispered, "Jones?"

A voice responded, "Cap'n?"

"Are you Jones?" Loretta tried again.

The voice said, "Is that you, Cap'n Quarles?"

Curse the man! Why wouldn't he answer her question? A tiny bit louder, Loretta said, "Are you Mr. Jones? Mr. *Percival* Jones?"

A pause ensued. Loretta was about to bolt up the stairs again when the voice said, somewhat pettishly, "The name ain't my fault."

THIRTEEN

Malachai sat in his hotel room, his feet propped on an ottoman, and a feeling of incompleteness bothering him. He ought to be perfectly content, and he knew it.

Here he was, relaxing in the most magnificent surroundings he'd ever inhabited, in a first-class hotel, with a fire burning in the grate and a lively city right outside waiting to clasp him to her bosom. He'd bought himself a stack of books so that he could catch up on his reading—treasure recovery didn't leave a man with much time to fritter away—and he'd been looking forward to an evening to himself.

More, he'd assured his future absolutely and beyond doubt. If anything should give a man a feeling of contentment and completion, it was that. This latest expedition, even though some of its fruits had gone missing somewhere, had capped a career that was revered in ship-recovery circles. He'd made his fortune beyond any chance of doubt, and he was looking forward to settling down at last.

Security. He loved that damned word. So few people understood or appreciated it, probably because they'd had it from birth. Only someone who'd grown up like he had could value security the way it ought to be valued.

So why wasn't he able to get lost in Chesterton's latest *Father Brown* mystery story? Why did he feel the faintest bit itchy, sitting here in luxury and comfort?

Why the devil did visions of Loretta Linden keep plaguing him, confound it?

"Damn her," he muttered without a care for Chesterton's sleuth in holy orders. "The damned woman drives me crazy."

What really drove him crazy was remembering her in her beautiful garden, with that green thing slipping from her shoulders, and her amazing dark hair carelessly piled on top of her head, and her huge chocolate-brown eyes sparkling at him as she decried the world and its failures.

When they'd first met, he'd believed that he'd met women like her before: women who crusaded for causes they knew nothing about and who would shrink from actually *touching* a poor person or a person with some hideous disease. He'd been wrong about her. Loretta not only got right down in the gutter with the people she wanted to save, but she even served them soup.

Malachai grinned. Soup, hell. When she saw an injustice being perpetrated, she went after it with her handbag. His grin dried up when he remembered her bruised flesh.

Damned woman had no sense. She had brains, he guessed, but she possessed the common sense of a gerbil. She needed somebody to take care of her, damn it, whether she knew it or not. And she didn't know it, of course.

She'd swear until she was blue that she didn't need anyone or anything and that she could take care of herself, but she was wrong. Malachai had seen proof of it more than once, the first time being on the very night they'd met. If he'd been a shade more impulsive, Loretta Linden would be dead now.

Impulsiveness wasn't one of Malachai's weaknesses, however. He'd overcome any tendency in that direction as a boy, when he'd learned that being impulsive generally led to switches being applied to the backs of his legs by those rotten nuns.

Nuns. The mere thought of them made him shudder, even all these years later. He'd discovered long since that most nuns weren't mean like that, but he still had no use for the Catholic church. It bothered him some that Loretta's precious soup kitchen was affiliated somehow with nuns, although he tried not to let it.

He picked up his book once more and swore at himself to pay attention. No sense thinking about Loretta, even if she was the most aggravating female in the universe. Besides, he'd see her again tomorrow.

That notion soothed his irritated nerves a little bit until he realized there was no reason for it to do so. Of all the women in the world, Loretta was the only one he'd met thus far in his increasingly long life who was guaranteed to ruffle his calm. Therefore, the notion that seeing her should soothe his nerves vexed him. He thumped Father Brown on his engagingly illustrated rump and frowned into the fire. Nothing about his reaction to Loretta Linden made sense to him, and he didn't like things that didn't make sense.

He hadn't pursued this line of thought to its conclusion when—fortunately, because it was an unprofitable one—he was interrupted by a peremptory knock at his door. Pulling off his reading glasses and thrusting them at the chair-side table, Malachai squinted at the clock on the mantel. Who the devil could be knocking on his door at seven minutes past midnight on a Thursday?

Muttering, "Christ, what now?" he rose from his chair, made sure his dressing gown's belt was tied, and shambled to the door. Prepared for just about anything from Derrick Peavey to one of Peavey's Moors in full fighting regalia, he flung the door wide, his mouth open to ask whoever had knocked his business. The words died on his lips.

"I found it!"

Malachai gaped at Loretta, who stood before him in the most outlandish outfit he'd ever seen on a woman; with her hair frowzy, windblown, full of what looked like twigs and leaves, and with a cloth cap sliding sideways over her ear; her cheeks scratched; the knees of her trousers—her *trousers?*—ripped out; one sleeve of her flannel shirt torn half off her shoulder; and with a smile a mile wide on her face.

"Great God in a gun boat, what happened to you?" he bellowed.

Her smile shrank considerably. "I *said*," she said, "that I found it."

"Found what?" Taking a quick look up and down the hall, Malachai didn't wait for her answer. Shooting out a hand, he grabbed Loretta by one scruffy arm and yanked her into his room.

"Ow! Unhand me, you brute!"

He did. Slamming his fists on his hips as soon as he'd slammed the door, and with his heart battering against his ribs like a Gatling gun, he glowered down at her with all his might. "What the hell have you been up to now? Dammit, Loretta, what the devil are you doing out on a night like this dressed like that?" He swept one arm out in an all-encompassing gesture. "You look like a damned wharf rat!"

"Don't swear at me." As if she felt that was weak, she went on indignantly, "I told you I'd find it, and I found it!"

"Found what? Are you talking about the damned treasure?"

"Of course, I'm talking about the treasure!" Her face began to flush with rage. "What *else* would I be talking about?"

"I have no idea." Fearful lest he grab and kiss her, Malachai turned abruptly and stomped to a table which the Fairfield Hotel had conveniently stocked with a tray, glasses, and several bottles. He grabbed the first one, which purported to contain cognac, and slopped some into a glass. Picking it up, he carried it to Loretta. "Drink this."

"I don't need spirits!"

Losing the battle with his temper, Malachai set the glass down with a crack and picked her up. Her eyes went huge and she gasped, but he didn't give her time to make words. Rather, he shook her as if she were a rag doll.

"I swear to God, Loretta Linden, if you've been out to Tillinghurst's estate on your damned crazy quest dressed like that, I'll turn you over my knee and paddle you until you howl!"

After her head stopped bobbing, Loretta returned his glower with one of her own that was as intense, if not quite as large, as his. "Put me down. And what do my clothes have to do with anything?"

He complied, more gently than he thought was warranted, but not wanting to do her any injury. Any *further* injury. Obviously, she'd sustained in-

juries already tonight. Scarcely able to pry his jaws
far enough apart to push words out, he said, "Why
are you in trousers?"

Because she didn't seem to want to obey his
wishes, he took the option out of her hands, picked
her up once more, and deposited her on the lavish
sofa in front of the fireplace. With a swipe of his
hand, he grabbed the glass containing cognac and
held it out to her. She took the glass, probably because it was the only way to get his fist out of her face.

"Drink it," he commanded.

She sipped and made a face. "It's awful, and I
don't need it."

Feeling slightly less likely to explode, Malachai
took a chair opposite the sofa. He noticed that
Loretta's legs weren't long enough for her feet to
rest on the floor. With another swoop, he snagged
the ottoman and shoved it in front of her. She
frowned, but, probably understanding that to object would be fruitless, she rested her feet on the
ottoman. She was wearing rubber-soled shoes,
Malachai noticed. They were the kind people
called tennis shoes, he thought, although he wasn't
certain.

Because he feared that if he used too many
words, they'd get away from him and form sentences he'd regret, he said shortly, "Explain
yourself."

"I was *trying* to explain myself when you—" She
broke off suddenly, perhaps because she saw
Malachai's jaw bulge as he ground his teeth.
"There's no need for such anger, Captain Quarles.
I came here to tell you that I was right all along,
and that Mr. Tillinghurst is the villain. *He* stole your

precious artifacts." She sat back against the sofa cushions, a smug expression on her face.

All at once, Malachai thought of something that nearly made him gasp aloud. "How the devil did you know which room was mine?" A sense of impending doom pervaded his body and soul. If this meddlesome woman had asked at the front—

"I asked at the front desk, of course."

Malachai buried his face in his hands. Impending, hell. Doom had come upon him as surely as it had the Lady of Shalott.

"There's no need for hysterics, Captain," Loretta said shortly, for once correctly understanding the cause of his upset. "No one knew it was me. I, I mean."

He allowed one of his eyes to peer through his fingers. There she was: Doom personified. And she was telling him there was no need for hysterics. "I suppose we can find a justice of the peace somewhere." His voice, he noted, carried none of the turmoil he felt. That was something, anyway.

Her eyes narrowed, and she looked at him as if *he* were the one in the room who was crazy. "Whatever in the world do you want a justice of the peace for? What we need is a police battalion."

"To marry us. I can't perform the service for myself, I don't think."

Her mouth dropped open and her eyes, which had been little suspicious slits, opened wide. "To *what?*"

Deciding to face his fate head-on, Malachai straightened in his chair, lowered his hands from his face, and frowned at the woman who had ruined his life—and who sat there as serenely as if she hadn't done it.

In his most bitingly sarcastic voice, he said, "In case it has failed to register with you, Loretta Linden, by the time the sun rises this morning, the entire city of San Francisco will know that you, a single woman, visited my hotel room in the middle of the night, without an escort of any kind. You made sure the news would get out when you asked at the front desk for the number of my suite. Therefore, in order to salvage your honor—*your* honor, mind you—I will do the gentlemanly thing and marry you. If I were less honorable, I'd let you swing on your own."

She'd begun to sputter before he'd come to the end of his declaration, but Malachai forged on relentlessly. If there was one thing he was really good at, it was overpowering his opponents by the force of his personality. "If you think I'm going to allow you to tarnish my reputation as an upstanding man in the city in which I plan to settle down, you're even more of an idiot than I took you for."

"I—I—"

"And furthermore, I don't believe for a minute that William Frederick Tillinghurst stole the artifacts, but if he did, why the devil didn't you go and tell it to the police instead of me? I doubt even you could compromise an entire police department!"

"Compromise! Why, you—"

Malachai jumped up from his chair and started pacing before the fireplace. "I can't believe you asked for my room number at the front desk!"

"Nobody will ever know that was me!" she cried, propelled from the sofa by the same outrage fueling Malachai. "The boy thought I was a *man!*"

Malachai stopped pacing. Turning slowly, he directed a withering glance at her, raking her from tip to toe and back again. "There isn't a man alive today," he said in his most biting tone, "who would ever take you for a man, even dressed in that ridiculous costume."

She threw out her arms and looked down at herself. "It's not ridiculous! I looked just like one of those runners the lawyers use!"

Even she, whom Malachai believed to be a mistress of self-deception, among other things, couldn't say that and sound convincing. He snorted to tell her so.

"Well, I did when I started out earlier this evening," she said, less vigorously. "It's dark, after all, and—"

"Is it dark in the lobby?"

He had her there, and he knew it. She gulped. "Well . . . That boy at the desk doesn't know who I am. He'll probably think I'm one of your . . . your sailors."

Malachai rolled his eyes.

"Or a . . . or a prostitute!" Loretta's face flamed. "Anyhow, he'll never recognize me again in a million years! I'll never wear these clothes again!"

It was too much for Malachai. Her total lack of sense, her silly costume, her stubbornness, her blithe belief in her sleuthing powers, and her smug satisfaction about having been right—damn her—sent him over the edge. With one powerful stride, he blocked her path, and with a single sweep of his powerful right arm, he picked her up.

"You are, by far, the most troublesome female I've ever met in my entire life, Loretta Linden." And with that, and because he couldn't help himself, he kissed her.

* * *

Offhand, Loretta couldn't remember the last time she'd been this outraged, although she knew it must have been recently. Malachai Quarles was the only human being she'd ever met who could infuriate her this much, and she hadn't known him very long.

Then he kissed her, and her rage flew off like a leaf in a high wind.

It was going to happen tonight! She hadn't really come here with seduction in mind—this was particularly true when she remembered the clothes she wore and considered how she must look—but perhaps her unconscious mind had taken care of the problem for her. He was kissing her, and she didn't aim to let him stop until he'd done his duty by her as a woman and an advocate of free love.

She was hanging from his embrace like a rag doll, so she wrapped her legs around his waist to give herself more leverage, and she kissed him back with enthusiasm. He might be the most irritating man in the world, but he was wildly attractive.

His embrace was rather crushing, and Loretta wiggled slightly to get him to loosen his grip a little. She didn't want to interrupt him, God knew, but it would help her overall state of being if he—

"Uff!"

Loretta's feet hit the carpet with a thump. Gazing up at him in befuddlement, she said, "Wh-what?"

"What the devil do you have in your hair?" He shook his hand, and Loretta noticed that he'd scratched it, probably on one of the twigs she'd inadvertently picked up at Tillinghurst's estate.

"My hair?" Curse it, he wasn't going to stop because her hair was a mess, was he? "I . . . I think some leaves got in it when I was running away from the dogs."

His eyes widened. "You were chased by dogs?"

She nodded. Blast and hell, why had he become distracted? This wasn't fair! "According to Mr. Jones—"

"*Jones!*"

Loretta clapped her hands over her ears. "Don't shout so loudly! You'll break my—"

He had her by the shoulders again and had started shaking her, so she couldn't expand upon her request.

"Do you mean to tell me you were chased by dogs and you found *Jones?*"

"S-stop sh-shaking me!" Offended, Loretta wrenched herself out of the captain's hands, sure she would have a whole new batch of bruises. After backing far enough away to avoid a snatch, she propped her fists on her hips and said, "You're a brutal man, Captain Quarles, and I don't know why I put up with you!"

Malachai seemed to be trying to regain control of himself. Curse him, she didn't want him in control. She wanted him out of control with desire for her.

"I beg your pardon," came, stifled, from his lips. "Did you say you found Mr. Jones?"

"Yes, I did."

"And that you were chased—" He had to pause and take in air. Loretta watched, fascinated, as his chest expanded to accommodate it. He was *such* a large man. "—by dogs?"

"A couple of bull mastiffs, according to Jones, although I couldn't verify their breed since I was occupied in running away from them at the time."

"Bull—" Again, Malachai stopped speaking, as if compelled to do so by a strong outside force. Again, he sucked in air.

"Mind you, Mr. Jones might have been correct. Their growls and barks were quite deep and ferocious." Loretta laughed self-deprecatingly. "I have to admit that I was quite frightened at the time. Fortunately I remembered the way back to the fence, where there were trees I could climb."

She chose not to confess to this man that she hadn't climbed a tree before in her life, because it sounded pathetic in her mind. She felt the lack of prior tree-climbing experience keenly tonight, and wished she'd had more brothers—brothers unlike the one she possessed. What she'd needed was the Tom-Sawyer-Huck-Finn-kinds of brothers: brothers who did things like climbing trees and running away from dogs and who would take their kid sister with them on their adventures. Her real brother's idea of adventure was speculating on the stock exchange.

The captain passed a huge hand over his face, as if he couldn't quite take everything in. Loretta felt obliged to explain further.

"The dogs are the reason Mr. Jones hasn't tried to escape, you see. He believed Mr. Peavey had been mauled by the dogs. Evidently, his captors told him so, and he thought he'd heard them chasing Mr. Peavey and Mr. Peavey yelling." She frowned slightly. "Perhaps Mr. Peavey climbed the same tree I did." It would be interesting to find out.

"Jones is at Tillinghurst's place?"

Loretta nodded energetically. "That's what I've been telling you! He's been there ever since he and Mr. Peavey were kidnaped."

"By Tillinghurst."

"Well, by Tillinghurst's men," Loretta temporized, although hiring people to kidnap other people was as bad as doing the deed oneself in her opinion. Perhaps it was worse.

Suddenly the captain turned his back on her. Dismayed, Loretta stared at his broad shoulders and tried to think of a way to renew his interest in her body. She wished now that she'd taken the time to change her clothes and clean her scratches. She had no idea Malachai Quarles could be so easily distracted from so intense an instinct as that of mating. After a few minutes of gazing at his shoulders and speculating how they'd look naked, she decided that tonight wasn't the night after all, curse it, and that she might as well head for home.

"Well, I'd better be going now." Her voice, she noted with disgust, reflected her disappointment.

Her comment managed to get him turned around again, however, which was nice, because Loretta found his face fascinating. She imagined it reflected a map of all the interesting places he'd been. It wasn't a handsome face, exactly, but it was a very interesting and attractive one, full of hard planes and deep lines. And then there was that earring. That earring alone proclaimed a man who had strayed far from the beaten path stamped out by the more conformable of his masculine kin.

"You can't go home alone," he said flatly, as if that settled the matter.

Loretta shook her head in disgust. "For heaven's sake, don't start in with that nonsense! I can and will go home alone if I choose to do so."

Malachai's frown would have been more impressive if Loretta hadn't seen it so often. "At least tell me about Jones. You can't come here in the middle of the night, say you've found a man who's been missing for four weeks, and then walk out again. Did you find the treasure along with Jones?"

"Not exactly." Loretta decided that as long as they were going to chat some more, she might as well sit. She selected the sofa again. "I couldn't get into the room where Mr. Jones was being held."

Malachai took the chair opposite the sofa where Loretta resided. Their knees were so close they nearly touched, and Loretta suppressed a mad impulse to fling herself into his arms. She sighed, wishing things were otherwise.

"How do you know it's Jones?"

She clucked disgustedly. "For heaven's sake, what a stupid question. He told me so. I asked him."

Malachai didn't react to her disdain. "How do you know the treasure's there?" Malachai asked.

"Mr. Jones told me so."

He rubbed his cheek with one of his large hands. He hadn't shaved for a while, Loretta noticed, his beard was coming in thick and dark, and she heard the scritch as his callused hand scraped across the short whiskers. She wondered if there would be any gray in his whiskers should he allow them to grow. He was approaching forty, after all. Didn't men begin to go gray around forty?

She wished she knew, but the truth was that she knew precious little about men, except in the philosophical sense. For instance, she knew that men ruled the world, were carelessly cruel, and lacked any understanding about women's worth; and she knew that she despised her brother because he was thoughtless, frivolous, and looked down upon her and her works. She forgave her father for exhibiting the same qualities, because he was from an earlier generation and set in his ways. She couldn't find any excuses for her brother.

"So I guess Tillinghurst is the villain of the piece after all." Malachai spoke grudgingly.

"I told you he was," Loretta reminded him, unable to keep the satisfaction from her voice.

"I know you did. You needn't rub it in."

Rub it in. Oh, my, she wished she could. But he didn't seem interested in her as a woman any longer. With a deep sigh, she reached for her cloth cap, which had become quite loose and was now sort of hanging from her hair by virtue of two hairpins that were pulling painfully at her scalp. She must have made a grimace, because Malachai, who had been staring at his feet, glanced up. She saw his gaze sharpen.

"What are you doing?"

"Taking off my hat. It's pulling my hair out."

She saw him swallow. "Be careful."

She laughed softly. "Don't worry. I won't hurt myself. I have too much hair, and it's curly, and I guess both my hair and the hat got caught on some twigs when I was climbing up the tree."

The memory made her shudder unexpectedly. It truly had been a scary experience. She never did get a clear look at the dogs, but she heard them snapping and growling at her heels, and her mind's eye featured ravening beasts frothing at the mouth and with fangs as long as cavalry sabers.

"The tree," Malachai repeated. His gaze was intense as it focused on her hair. It gave Loretta a trembly feeling in her middle.

"Wh-what are you looking at?" Her voice had gone low and slightly squeaky.

"Your hair."

He licked his lips, giving Loretta the impression of a bear about to spring on its prey and devour it. She stopped fiddling with her hairpins, and her arms dropped to her lap. She felt her eyes open wide when Malachai lunged out of his chair and plopped himself beside her on the sofa.

"Let me do that." His voice was hoarse. Without waiting for her consent, he reached for her hair.

Loretta winced a little, but his big hands were gentle. Carefully, he maneuvered the hairpins out of her tangled tresses. Gently, he removed her silly cloth cap. And then, with exquisite care, he burrowed his fingers into her hair and began combing out the tangles. Her eyes drifted shut.

"Your hair . . . I like your hair."

"Thank you." She'd whispered, although she knew not why.

"There's so much of it."

"Mmm."

"It feels like . . . like silk."

"Mmm."

"I've been wanting to do this for a long time."

"Mmm?"

"Touch your hair."

"Mmm."

"Feel your hair."

"Mmm."

"Kiss your hair."

What? For the briefest instant, Loretta's eyes popped open, but at the feel of Malachai's lips following his fingers on her hair, they closed again. She felt herself slump against his huge, warm body, and then he held her in his arms.

Oh, yes. This is what she needed. Turning her face to his, she sought his lips with her own, found them, and decided this was going to be the night after all. Hallelujah!

She made herself stop thinking then, because she didn't want to spoil the moment. Her body tingled with anticipation, and her heart soared, and she threw her arms around Malachai Quarles and swore she wouldn't let go of him until he'd fulfilled his purpose in her life.

His body was like a rock. A hot rock. He was so hard. Everywhere. She explored his contours almost frantically in her quest for education and satisfaction. She'd never even wanted to do this with another man. Even at her most curious, the notion of rolling around naked with any of the other men she knew hadn't appealed one little bit.

Malachai Quarles, however, had piqued her interest from the very beginning. Even when she was furious with him, she'd wanted him. Her hands, which had been investigating his incredibly broad shoulders, found his face.

"You've got a craggy face," she murmured, pressing kisses on the lines radiating from his eyes. She felt as if she were kissing a gift from the sun.

He gasped and said, "Is that bad?"

"No," she said. "No, it's not bad. Your face is like a work of art. Like a sculpture shaped by the sea and the sun and the wind."

"Huh."

Worrying lest she get too carried away and contribute to his already enlarged ego, Loretta gave up on extolling his face. No matter how much she adored it. Anyhow, he'd covered her lips with his, so she couldn't talk anymore if she wanted to.

When his hand covered her breast, she very nearly fainted dead away on the sofa. Recovering at once, she thrust herself at him, begging him with her body to fondle the other breast while he was at it. Fortunately, the captain, being a man of quick intelligence, understood at once. Loretta heard fabric rip and a soft curse.

"Damn it, get this thing off."

Without waiting for her to comply, he tore the shirt right off her back. Loretta didn't mind. All she wore beneath the shirt was a short camisole. She hadn't bothered with her combinations this evening, since she was wearing trousers, and was clad underneath only in her camisole and a pair of short drawers. As far as she was concerned, the captain could rip them all from her body—and the sooner, the better.

In order to facilitate whatever he aimed to do with her clothing, Malachai had knelt on the floor. He pushed the ragtag ends of her shirt back from her shoulders, lifted her camisole over her head and feasted his eyes upon her. Loretta probably would have been embarrassed if she'd been thinking. Fortunately, she wasn't. His gaze, hot and possessive, fed something deep in her soul that had been starving for years.

"God, I've wanted to do this for weeks now."

Thank heaven! What he'd wanted to do was lave her breasts with his warm tongue. Loretta hadn't expected anything ever to feel so good. She allowed her head to drop back, and she reveled in the feel of being loved by a man—and not just any man, either. By Captain Malachai Quarles, the bane and boon of her existence, and the only man in the world for her.

"Damn, I shouldn't be doing this," Malachai muttered, leaving off kissing her breasts and pressing his face into them.

Loretta didn't like the sound of that. "Yes, you should." Curse it, why in the world had she fallen in lust with a man of honor? Any other man in the world wouldn't have any scruples at all about ravishing a willing woman.

"No, I shouldn't."

The damned man *would* argue with her, wouldn't he? "Yes, you should. I want you to."

"You do?"

Loretta felt his eyebrow quirk against her bosom. "Yes. I do. If you stop now, I'll never speak to you again."

As soon as she heard his rough, low chuckle, she guessed she should have offered him another threat.

"Well . . . as tempting as it is never to be spoken to again by you . . ."

Loretta held her breath.

Suddenly Malachai stood up. To Loretta's surprise, he took her with him. "To hell with it," he said. "I'm already going to hell and I'm already going to have to marry you, so why not?"

Loretta couldn't follow his reasoning, primarily because her body's scream for fulfillment was way louder than her brain's feeble attempt at thought. But, when she realized he was carrying her to the bedroom of his suite, she didn't care. In fact, she was overjoyed.

"Oh, good!" she cried. "I've been wanting to do this for the longest time!"

He squinted down at her. "You have?"

"Yes." She snuggled close to him and, since he seemed to appreciate her bosom, which Loretta herself had always considered was slightly too large, she pressed her breasts against his chest. She felt his heart pounding away like a jackhammer, and she knew she'd done the right thing.

He fell upon the bed with her still in his arms, and they both bounced. Loretta, finding herself free from his embrace, took the opportunity to unbutton her trousers. They snagged on her hips when she tried to slip out of them. "Curse it," she muttered.

"Here, allow me." Malachai lifted her hands from the trousers.

Peering at him closely, Loretta frowned. "Are you laughing at me?" *Were* her hips too big? Curses!

"Never."

She distinctly heard him chuckle. "You are, too!"

"Shut up, Loretta."

As he started tugging her trousers down her legs, kissing the skin thus exposed as he went, Loretta forgot her grievance and shut up. His lips on her body felt heavenly. She sighed deeply. Lord, no wonder all of her bohemian friends extolled the wonders of free love, if it was like this. Maybe it didn't even have to be free. What did she know? Well, she knew more than she had an hour ago, thank God.

"That feels so good," she said upon a sigh. Then he kissed the very most secret place on her body, and her eyes flew open. Good Lord, could a man kiss a woman *there*?

He could. And he did. And he added some tongue. And Loretta thought she must have died and gone to heaven. "Oh, my *God!*"

"Does that feel good?"

Stupid question. Loretta's hips arched like a bow, and with very little work on Malachai's part, she shot over the brink of excitement into a shattering climax the likes of which she'd never even dreamed of.

In a flash, before she'd had a chance to collect her bedazzled senses, Malachai had rid himself of his robe and pajamas and was naked beside her. Loretta barely had the chance to register the magnificence of him and his body before he had driven himself home in her.

It didn't hurt. That was her first surprising thought. It was also her last, because Malachai drew himself halfway out of her. She was poised to cry out in protest when he plunged in again. And he did it again. And again. And he established a smooth rhythm with which she attuned herself almost instantly. And then, with a harsh groan and a massive shudder, Malachai's release came.

Loretta had never felt so triumphant in her entire twenty-eight years.

FOURTEEN

Malachai told himself that, although he was an ass, at least he was a satisfied one. Loretta Linden had met all of his expectations and even exceeded them. She was spectacular. And her body . . . He groaned, remembering.

Then he groaned again when he realized what was in store for him. He truly, truly was an ass. He tried to comfort himself with the thought that it wouldn't have made any difference. He would have had to marry the wench anyway, since she'd showed up at his hotel room, alone, after midnight. He might just as well marry her a happy man as a frustrated one.

"Oh, my."

He turned to see what Loretta was oh-mying about. With a grin and a feeling of masculine pride filling his large, seafaring chest, he saw that she looked rather like a kitten who'd just lapped up all the cream. "Enjoy yourself?" he asked with something of a smirk.

Her eyes had been closed, but they opened at that, and she turned her head and smiled at him. "Oh, my goodness, yes!"

"Good." He couldn't help himself; he grabbed her and squeezed her in a bear hug. She was absolutely perfect for him! How strange, he thought, that a fiery, rabble-rousing do-gooder should be the one woman in the world he didn't especially mind the thought of being shackled to for life.

"Did you enjoy it?" she asked, sounding shy.

It was far past time for shyness in Malachai's considered opinion, but he thought it was sweet that she was worried that he hadn't been satisfied. As if there were any question about it! "Yes," he said, striving for a sober tone. "I enjoyed it."

"Oh, good."

She sighed and subsided into his arms as meekly as if she weren't the most aggravating female Malachai had ever met in his entire life. They remained like that for several minutes. Malachai had almost drifted off to sleep when Loretta spoke again, with another sigh. "I suppose I should go home now."

He yawned hugely. "Why bother? Let's just call in a justice of the peace, and we can get married right here, right now. Save you the embarrassment of showing up at your house looking like a ragamuffin." A ragamuffin who'd just been thoroughly and excellently loved, he added silently. He wouldn't embarrass her by saying it out loud, although his masculine pride scooted up another couple of notches.

He realized she hadn't spoken and craned his neck to look at her. "Is that all right with you?"

Still she didn't speak. Worse, she frowned. What the devil was the matter with the woman? What was there to frown about? She wasn't going to insist on a big wedding, was she? With bridesmaids and formal gowns and black monkey suits and attendants and all that rubbish? Malachai loathed ceremonies. He didn't want to go through with

one on account of his having been an ass, damn
it. Marrying her was punishment enough, for
God's sake. He shouldn't have to be humiliated
into the bargain.

At last she spoke. "I beg your pardon?"

Ah, hell. She was going to be difficult. Aiming for
a conciliatory note, which wasn't easy, he said, "I
just thought you might not want to bother with a
big ceremony, since we'll have to get hitched right
away." He shrugged in an effort to show how little
it all meant to him.

"Ceremony?" she said. "Hitched?"

"Yeah. You know, a big wedding."

"Wedding?" Her voice had risen.

What the devil was her problem? "Yeah. We'll
have to marry now. I mean, you might possibly get
away with calling on me at my hotel room in the
middle of the night, but you've stayed far too long
now for anyone not to guess what went on."

Her eyes began flashing sparks. Malachai considered that a worrisome signal. "Well?" he demanded,
still attempting a reasonable tone. "You know it's
true."

"I," said Loretta in her most annoying fire-eater's
voice and sliding to the edge of the bed, "know
nothing of the kind." She popped out of the bed
and stood, her perky breasts bouncing and sending
a spike of lust through Malachai. "That's the most
ridiculous thing I've ever heard, Captain Malachai
Quarles. I won't marry you. I won't marry *any*
man."

It was Malachai's turn to jump out of bed. He
probably didn't appear as formidable as he'd have
liked to, since seeing her there in the altogether
had stimulated his masculinity and it was now

standing proudly at attention, but he couldn't help that. "You'll damned well marry *me!*"

"I won't. I," she said, her chin lifting, "am an advocate of free love, and I won't violate my principles for anyone. Why is it necessary to formalize these unions, is what I want to know." She looked around on the floor, presumably for her clothes, not that they'd do her any good since they were now in shreds.

Astounded, Malachai actually stuttered. "F-formalize th-these unions? What the devil do you mean by *these unions,* damn it?" He snatched up his dressing gown, which had somehow or other ended up dangling from the lamp stand. He was enraged when he realized he'd put it on inside-out, and he tore it from his large frame, shook it violently, and put it on again the right way. He nearly cut his body in half yanking the belt as he tied it. "I'm a man of honor, damn it! It's my duty to marry you now, and I'll damned well do my duty!"

She looked upon him with what Malachai could only describe as scorn, her nipples peeking out of the ripped-up shirt she'd donned. "There's no need for you to shout, Malachai. And you needn't consider me your *duty.* I refuse to be any man's *duty.*" She huffed. "Stupid word."

"I didn't mean it like that," he said, knowing full well that he had. "What we did now requires formalization, that's all. It's . . . it's expected. You can't go around bedding men and not marrying them. It's not done!"

Another pitying look slapped him. "I've told you before that I am a forward-thinking woman, Malachai Quarles. If I advocate free love, I am obliged to act upon my principles." She frowned down at her nipples and tried to adjust the fabric over them. Malachai tried not to notice.

"Principles! *Principles?* Since when does a woman have principles? That's the stupidest thing I've ever heard!"

She stopped attempting to make her shirt decent. It was an impossible task, although Malachai didn't think that was her motive in stopping, since common sense wasn't one of her outstanding characteristics.

"How dare you?" Her voice throbbed with passion. "Women do, so, have principles. Why, if it weren't for women, the world would be in even worse shape than it is! *We're* the ones who care for the poor! *We're* the ones who bandage and nurse you *men* after you fight your stupid wars! *We're* the nurturers! *We're* the ones who suffer when a man decides to drink his wages. *We're* the ones who— Uff!"

She couldn't continue her diatribe because Malachai grabbed her. "I have my principles, too, damn it, and I'll be damned if I'll bed a woman and not marry her!"

He nearly dropped his teeth when she laughed. She *laughed!* At *him!* It sounded like a genuine laugh, too. He could scarcely believe his ears.

"That's silly, Malachai. I know good and well I'm not the first woman you've bedded. How many wives do you have, anyhow?"

Putting her down again, he felt a little bit—only a little bit—abashed. "You're the first decent woman I've bedded."

"Ah, I see. Until now, you've only bedded indecent ones."

Sarcasm dripped from the words. She turned and

started scavenging for her trousers. He guessed she'd given up on the shirt. He watched her lush bottom twitch and longed to feel it again. His mind's eye imagined her riding him, guided by his hands on that part of her anatomy, and he almost forgot the subject of their argument.

He shook himself in an effort to clear his lust-blinded vision. "It's the truth," he insisted. "Hell, you don't think I bed the virgin daughters of millionaire bankers every day of the week, do you? How do you think I've remained single until my fortieth year?" Damn, he wished she were wearing more clothes. It was difficult to keep track of his points with her parading around nearly naked.

As she stepped into her trousers—she didn't bother with her drawers, he noticed—she gave him another scornful glance. "I see. So it's only the virgin daughters of millionaires who have been safe from you thus far in your colorful career?"

"That's not what I meant! Damn it, I'm not a monster. I don't go around ravishing females!"

"I see. You only fornicate with the willing ones who aren't from the upper echelons of society, I suppose, or the ones who don't have any choice in the matter. And if they're women of color, I imagine that's even better, since *surely* no white man is *ever* expected to be responsible for ravishing colored women!"

Malachai's rage shot up like a bullet from a gun. He trembled with it. It was perhaps the first time in his life he'd been this angry and, at the same time, unable to hit the person who'd enraged him. His fists clenched. His teeth ground together. He felt his jaw muscles bulge. He spoke carefully and distinctly for fear that if he let himself go, his roar would shatter the glass windows. "I have never raped a woman in my life."

"I see. Until I came along, I presume you only bedded those women who are forced to earn their livings on their backs? Or married women. I'm sure there are bored married women out there who might think it a thrill to bed the dashing Captain Quarles—as long as their husbands don't find out."

He shuffled his feet. "I wouldn't put it like that." It sounded so bad, the way she said it.

Loretta sniffed. "I'm sure you wouldn't. However, I still don't see why that makes it necessary for us to marry."

She frowned at her ensemble, which was pathetic. Her hair was a mess, too. Malachai ached to run his fingers through it again. Fortunately, he was unable to do so even if Loretta wanted him to, since he couldn't unclench his fists.

"You are the most aggravating—" Malachai sucked in a huge breath and tried to tamp down his ire. It couldn't be done. "You're making me sound like some bag of scum who takes advantage of women all the time. I'm not, and I don't!"

"I'm glad to hear it." After tugging fruitlessly at her shirt, she added, "I'm going to need to borrow a shirt from you."

He stomped to the closet, yanked the door open, and snagged a white shirt from a hanger. "Here." He threw the shirt at her. "Use that."

She caught the shirt. "Thank you."

"Want a collar?"

"That's not necessary, thank you." As she put on the shirt, she said, "I don't know why you're so angry. You didn't expect any of your other women to—"

"I don't have other *women!*" Because he had to do

something or burst, he reached into the closet again and snabbled another shirt. After jerking his robe off and throwing it from him, he stabbed his hands into the shirt's sleeves.

"Well, you've certainly bedded other women, and you apparently didn't think you had to marry *them.*"

"Of course I didn't!"

"Why? Were they all married to other men? Were they all unworthy of your name? Or did you consider them beneath you." She frowned, evidently pondering her choice of words. "In a manner of speaking."

Malachai grabbed a pair of trousers and flapped them furiously so that he could stick his legs into them. "They weren't *beneath* me. They just didn't expect marriage from a man just because they went to bed together."

Loretta finished buttoning Malachai's shirt. It was miles too big for her, but she looked up and shot him a beaming smile. "There! You see? I don't, either, so you're off the hook."

"Off the . . ." He paused in the act of buttoning his trousers, and realized suddenly that he didn't want to be off the hook. He watched as Loretta tried to manhandle her hair into some semblance of order and it struck him that he actually *wanted* to marry her. All that stuff he'd been spouting about honor and duty was so much bilgewater.

Damn, but he hated to admit that. Because his last series of thoughts had so disconcerted him, he gave up the argument for the nonce. "We'll talk about this later. I'll see you home now."

"There's no need for—"

"Don't say it!" he roared. "I'll see you home, whether you want me to or not!"

She clucked her tongue. "Oh, very well."

* * *

Loretta couldn't recall the last time she'd felt this wonderful. It might perhaps have been when she'd realized she wasn't going to drown the night the *Titanic* sank, but she doubted it, since it had been difficult to take comfort from her own survival when so many others had perished.

She didn't think it was when she'd met Mrs. Pankhurst. That had been an exciting moment, but it hadn't filled her with this sense of . . . of . . . joy and fulfillment, she guessed were the best words for it.

She knew it wasn't a valid sentiment, but the fact that she'd now experienced sexual congress with a man—and *such* a man—made her feel like a true woman. A woman in every sense of the word, even though Loretta would be the last female on earth who would actually *say* that a woman had to have a man in her life to be fulfilled or worthwhile. Why, often the reverse was true.

It made no difference. Even though she knew in her heart that if she'd lived her entire life without knowing, in the Biblical sense, a man, and died a virgin, her life would have been full and useful, she was still ecstatic.

Not only had she been bedded by Malachai Quarles, the only man she'd ever met for whom she'd felt honest lust, but it had felt *wonderful!*

She really hadn't expected that. Her mother had never spoken to her about the physical aspects of marriage. Loretta hadn't expected her to, since poor Dorothea Linden became embarrassed at the least little thing, but she'd listened to other women talk. She'd heard that it invariably hurt the first time, and often hurt forever, no matter how often one did it, but it was a duty when one was married, so one did one's duty. But the fusspots had been wrong. Dead wrong.

At the moment she sat on Malachai's bed, waiting for him to return to her. He'd made her promise to sit still and not move while he secured a cab. As much as she hated to admit it, she was glad he hadn't left it up to her to do that, mainly because she looked decidedly odd.

As soon as the door had closed behind Malachai, she'd jumped off the bed and inspected herself in the mirror. Her cheeks were flushed, her eyes were bright, and she had a silly smile on her face, but the rest of her was a total disaster. Her hair had never been so messy, and her clothes were beyond description. It was just as well that she hadn't had to rustle up a taxi, because any one of San Francisco's cabbies, a canny lot, would probably have pegged her for a runaway rich girl and tried to take advantage of her. And, while Loretta trusted herself to win any verbal confrontation she found herself in, and could probably hold her own in a physical fight, she didn't want to do battle tonight. Or this morning, rather. She wanted to gloat over the fact that she'd got what she wanted from Malachai Quarles.

She was actually humming to herself, something she seldom did since she couldn't hold a tune, when she heard the key in the lock of his hotel room door and experienced a mad impulse to rush to the door and greet him with a kiss. She held herself back because, after all, they weren't *really* lovers. Not in the sense that they bedded each other regularly and had strong emotional feelings for each other. Not yet, anyway.

For the briefest of moments, Loretta thought of

all the lovers she'd read about. Wouldn't it be something to have a real, long-lasting, true-love match, like the one George Eliot had with the man with whom she'd lived? Or Lord Nelson and Lady Hamilton?

But she couldn't continue daydreaming, because Malachai pushed the door open, stumped in, and said, "What the devil do you mean to do about Tillinghurst?"

So far had her thoughts strayed from Mr. Tillinghurst, the stolen artifacts, and Malachai's lost sailor Mr. Jones, that she could only blink at him for several seconds before understanding struck. "Oh, um . . ."

"What I suggest is that you do nothing for a day or so. I want to check out your story first."

Euphoria vanished in a flash of temper. Loretta jumped down from the bed. "Do you think I was *lying* to you?"

With a disgusted look on his face, Malachai threw a pea-coat at her. "No, but there's no sense going off half-cocked. I want to make sure you saw what you say you saw before I go running to the police."

"Fine," she said, feeling disgruntled as she noticed a good six inches of the pea-coat's sleeves flapping in the breeze after her hands ended. She had to raise her arm and shake one sleeve down before her fingers appeared and she could try to roll the other sleeve up. The fabric was thick wool, however, and didn't want to roll. "Curse it," she muttered, and resigned herself to flapping sleeves.

"Fine?" Malachai stopped in the process of putting on his own coat and stared at her, incredulous. "You mean you agree with me?"

She gave him a withering frown. "Of course, I

don't agree with you. However, if you don't want to go to the police, that's fine with me. I'll go myself. I'm the one who discovered Mr. Jones, after all. I should be the one to take the credit."

"Credit? What credit?" He reached out, grabbed one of her sleeves and rolled it up as if the fabric were as sheer as linen and not as thick as a log. Loretta watched him do it and felt inadequate.

"I didn't mean credit, exactly. What I meant was that since I'm the one who discovered Mr. Tillinghurst to be a kidnapper and thief, I'm the one who should report it."

Taking her by the hand and exiting the room, making her trot to keep up with him, Malachai muttered, "You see? That's just what I mean. You're assuming that since you found somebody who calls himself Jones at Tillinghurst's place, you've solved the entire problem of the missing artifacts. But you don't know that, and *I* don't know that. You didn't actually see anything at all, much less Jones or any artifacts. If you send the police out to Tillinghurst's place and they discover there's a reasonable explanation for somebody named Jones being there and don't discover the missing treasure, you're going to feel like a fool. And a good thing, too."

"That's not fair! What was Mr. Jones doing there, being held captive, if he hadn't been kidnaped? He said that's what happened. So did Mr. Peavey."

Malachai grunted. "That's what you *think* happened. For all you know, Jones is there because he wants to be, and you must have figured out by this time that nothing Peavey says can be taken at face value."

Curse it. Loretta hated it when people got sensible on her. After trying to think about it—the captain was setting a very rapid pace, and most of her concentration was centered on keeping her feet pumping as Malachai sped her across the lobby carpet—she said, "Well . . . I suppose you *may* have a point, although I know I'm right."

"Huh."

A sleepy-looking doorman in a natty uniform saw them coming and, without acknowledging the state of Loretta's person by so much as a raised eyebrow, he opened the door. The damp, heavy fog of November smote her in the face as soon as she stepped out of the hotel. The air smelled of ocean and salt and creosote.

There was something eerie about this time of day, Loretta thought. She'd only been awake at three or four o'clock in the morning a few times in her life, but those few times had struck her as spooky. This time did, too. She scurried a trifle closer to Malachai's comforting bulk.

Fog swirled around their feet, and street lamps shone through it in weird smudges of dirty yellow, providing very little actual light. She heard footsteps heading their way and her heart sped up, her imagination instantly featuring armed thugs bent upon mayhem.

A policeman, swinging his nightstick, gradually appeared from out of the fog. He nodded and smiled at them, and Loretta silently called herself a fool. And there was the cab looming in the mist and looking like something from out of a Gothic romance. It was a horse-drawn number for a change. Most of the daytime cabs were motorized these days, she supposed because during the day people were in a hurry to take care of their business, whatever it was. She guessed all the old cart horses had been relegated to nighttime service.

Malachai nodded at the policeman, gave Loretta's address to the cabbie, and opened the cab door. Reaching inside, he flipped down the stairs for Loretta to climb. "I'll ride with you and see you safely home."

She was about to say she didn't need an escort when a brilliant thought occurred to her, and she swallowed her protest. It wouldn't have done her any good to voice it anyway. As she slid onto the seat she cried, "I have it!"

Climbing in after her, Malachai sat with a grunt and said, "You have what?"

It didn't sound to Loretta as if he gave a hang, but she answered him anyway. "I know what we should do."

"About what?"

She saw his eyes watching her keenly, and realized he was thinking about the supposed wedding problem. Since she didn't want to argue with him anymore about that, she hurried to explain. "About Mr. Tillinghurst and Mr. Jones and Mr. Peavey."

After expelling an exaggerated sigh, Malachai said, "All right, go on. I suppose you're going to tell me even if I don't want you to."

"Indeed, I am," said Loretta, offended. "I thought you cared about your men, Malachai Quarles."

"I do." She saw him cast an obviously patient glance at the tattered ceiling of the cab, and ire swelled within her.

"All right, then. Since you don't believe me, we'll just take Mr. Peavey out to Mr. Tillinghurst's estate and let *him* tell us if that's the place."

"Huh. And how do you propose to get this

scheme to fulfillment? Ask Tillinghurst if we can bring a crazy man into his home to prove that he's a thief?"

"Of course not! But you've been taking Mr. Peavey all over San Francisco, why not take him out of town to Mr. Tillinghurst's estate? He might recognize something."

"We're talking about Peavey here, remember." Malachai tapped his forehead with a gloved finger. "He's not *that* bad off."

"Yes, he is. I doubt that he'd recognize his so-called castle even if he suddenly turned clearheaded. He's been bashed around a lot lately, remember."

Loretta fingered her cheek, where traces of her own injury remained. "Well, it's worth a try."

"Maybe."

Feeling defiant, Loretta added, "And if you won't agree at least to test my theory, I'll have no choice but to go to the police and let them sort things out."

"For God's . . . All right. If it will shut you up and keep you from making a damned fool of yourself, we can take Peavey to Tillinghurst's place."

"Good." A huge yawn caught Loretta by surprise.

"You need to get some sleep. You've had a busy night, and you haven't fully recovered from your injuries yet."

Was that concern in Malachai's voice? Loretta couldn't credit her ears.

"Only you would do such a damn-fool thing as climb over somebody's iron gate in the middle of the night and search for stolen treasure on private property. It's a damned good thing you didn't get mauled by those dogs."

Any hint of pleasure at the notion that he might care about her vanished like smoke. "At least I did something! That's more than you've done so far. And I, don't forget, found Mr. Jones."

"We'll see about that."

"You're impossible, Malachai Quarles, did you know that?"

He snorted. "I guess that means we're well matched, then, since you're the most impossible female it's ever been my misfortune to meet up with."

Deciding silence would be her best friend at the moment, Loretta opted to keep mute. His words—about them being well matched, not the ones about her presumed impossibility—had thrilled her, though.

FIFTEEN

Malachai sprawled on one of Loretta's back-porch chairs and eyed her fading autumn garden with an eye to the future. He really liked her house. And this garden, even in its present condition as winter loomed, touched something in his soul that he'd thought dead long since.

But it hadn't died during those hard years, it had only been hibernating. It was ready to crawl out of its cave and perk to life here, right here. In Loretta Linden's garden. Since he didn't have anything else to do, he puzzled over this phenomenon for several moments.

It was a little early in the day to come calling, since Malachai knew for a fact that Loretta hadn't gotten to bed until after four in the morning, but since he'd been too keyed up to sleep, he figured he might as well tackle the stubborn woman again about marrying him. Maybe lack of sleep would have lowered her resistance, and she'd agree that marriage was their only option now that they'd done the deed.

And if they could get hitched today, so much the better. He wouldn't have to worry about it any longer. Not that he was worried, precisely.

Oh, hell, who was he trying to fool? He was, so,

worried. If Loretta continued to refuse him, he didn't know what he was going to do. He should celebrate. That's what any sane man would do, but Malachai guessed he was no longer sane. His association with Loretta had addled his wits, and he also feared that if she couldn't be made to marry him, he might just . . . well . . . suffer. A lot.

Revolting thought.

Fancy her refusing to marry him! He scowled at the rose garden, still abloom here and there. That fellow who'd designed it, Fitz-somebody, had done a great job with it. Malachai liked the hedges lining the paths and the trellises, and the way he'd had wood chips put down on the walkways. It was real pretty. Homey. It's exactly how he'd have done it himself, if he'd ever had a garden. He wanted one badly. This one, in fact, although it was beginning to look as if he might have to plant his own somewhere else. Damn Loretta Linden!

Women had no business with principles. And to have found one who had principles and actually acted upon them was so unusual in his life that he couldn't quite believe it. He guessed he liked her for it, in a way, but to refuse marriage after giving up her virginity wasn't principled. It was nuts. It was also causing him grief, and he didn't appreciate it one little bit.

The back door opened, and Loretta, looking like a spring bloom on this gloomy November day, bounced out onto the porch, smiling gaily. Malachai frowned at her, thinking she had no right to be so damned happy.

She was dressed in yellow today, and her dark brown hair gleamed where the few rays of sunshine that managed to struggle through the clouds and fog touched it. She'd washed her hair, obviously. Malachai wished he could have been there and brushed it out for her.

Great God in a gun boat, he really *had* lost his mind!

"Malachai!" she cried, holding out both hands to him. "How nice of you to call."

He took her hands and peered down at her, puzzled. "What the devil's the matter with you?"

Her smile vanished. "What do you mean?" She bypassed confusion and went straight to rancor. "Why must you always be so cursed unpleasant, Malachai Quarles? I thought we'd advanced slightly in our relationship."

"At least you admit we have a relationship," Malachai said bitterly.

"Don't be silly. Of course we have a relationship!"

A daffodil. That's what she looked like. "Nice dress," he said somewhat stiffly. He wasn't accustomed to paying women compliments. Realizing he still held her hands, he squeezed them briefly and released them.

Loretta, shaking out her hands—he hadn't squeezed them *that* hard, damn it—said, "Thank you. I like yellow. It's a cheerful color." She flounced over to a chair and sat, then looked around her yard as if searching for something. "Where's Mr. Peavey?"

Malachai's brow furrowed. "Peavey? How the hell should I know where he is? At the hotel, I expect."

Her eyes were as clear and bright as if she hadn't been up all night. Malachai thought that if she had any modesty at all, she ought at least to look sleepy. Or blush, for God's sake. After all, he was the instrument of her ruin. Fool woman. Had no more common sense than a sea horse.

Those sparkling eyes narrowed now. "I thought we were going to take Mr. Peavey to Mr. Tillinghurst's estate?"

Oh, hell, he'd forgotten all about that idiotic plan. "Yes, yes," he said, unwilling to admit his forgetfulness, since Loretta would certainly object. "We'll do that."

"We ought to do it today. There's no telling what Mr. Tillinghurst might do after last night's commotion with the dogs. I don't think he'll chalk it up to chance."

Malachai let out a heavy sigh. "No, he probably won't. You really fouled everything up, didn't you?"

She bridled instantly, and Malachai scolded himself for maladroitness. He was so accustomed to dealing with his sailors, who knew him to be a plain-spoken man and never expected him to coddle them, that he'd gotten out of the habit of placating anyone. Loretta, however, was a special case, and even more prickly than most women.

Hell, he thought with an internal grin. He never had trouble with most women, because they were stupid and didn't expect a man to actually *talk* to them. It was enough for most women if a man was strong and silent. Not Loretta.

"I did not foul anything up! I discovered your missing sailor, let me remind you, and probably the stolen artifacts, too. That's not fouling things up!"

He held his hands up, palms out. "All right, all right. I take it back. You didn't foul things up. But we have more important things to talk about today. The artifacts will hold. They've been around for a thousand years, and I expect they'll stay around for another thousand."

She jumped up from her chair, her fists clenched. "They might remain on this earth, curse you, Malachai Quarles, but *where*? If you think Mr. Tillinghurst is going to oblige us by keeping everything there after the commotion last night, you're crazed."

"Calm down, will you?" Damn the woman. She could go off on tangents better and quicker than anyone else he knew, including Derrick Peavey. "We can pick Peavey up at the hotel and go to Tillinghurst's place, but first we need to clear up the marriage issue."

She sat down again with a plop and looked at him as if she didn't know what he was talking about. She would. Malachai perceived that he wasn't going to win this one without a battle. But, since marrying Loretta Linden had become the most important issue in his life, surpassing even the stolen artifacts and the kidnaped Mr. Percival Jones, he was willing if not eager to wage it. He didn't intend to be defeated, either.

"There is no marriage issue," Loretta stated flatly.

Before Malachai could once more, and with exaggerated patience, explain to her that there was, too, a marriage issue, and that **he** didn't intend for it to go away until she bowed to his wishes in the matter, the back door opened. A flushed Marjorie MacTavish and a grinning Jason Abernathy came out onto the porch. Reluctantly, Malachai rose to his feet. Damn it, he hated being interrupted during important arguments.

"Good afternoon, Captain Quarles," Jason boomed in his heartiest voice. "How-do, Loretta?"

"Oh, Jason, how good of you to visit today. We may need you."

"Oh?" The doctor's bushy eyebrows arched over his twinkling blue eyes.

"I dinna know why," muttered Marjorie. "He'sna good for naught."

"Pooh, Miss MacTavish," said Jason with a chuckle, and Malachai perceived that the two had been having words. According to Loretta, having words was a normal state of affairs for them.

Suddenly, Malachai decided to put this interruption to good use. "Good to see you again, Doctor," he said, shaking Jason's hand with vigor. "I think Loretta may be right. We probably *can* use you."

"Good, good." Rubbing his hands, Jason sat between Loretta and Malachai after shoving Marjorie into another chair. She shot him a furious scowl that affected him not. "What can I do for you?"

"You can accompany us to Mr. Tillinghurst's estate," said Loretta.

"You can stand as a witness to our nuptials," said Malachai at the same time.

"Nuptials?" cried Marjorie, having zeroed in on the item that was of interest to females. Most females. Not Loretta.

"Tillinghurst?" said Jason, clearly puzzled.

Anticipating Loretta's angry frown, Malachai met it with a grin. "You know it's true," he said.

"Pooh," she said.

"Did you say something about nuptials?" Memory jogged, Jason's furry eyebrows soared like two rainbows over his blue, blue eyes.

"Yes," said Malachai.

"No," said Loretta.

Marjorie, clasping her hands to her bosom,

whispered, "Och, my," and looked as if she might be experiencing an ecstatic vision.

Not Loretta. Giving her friends—and Malachai—a general, all-purpose glower, she jumped out of her chair, stamped her foot and said, "I will not marry you, Malachai Quarles! I don't care if we *are* lovers, I won't do it."

Marjorie's gasp of horror brought Loretta's diatribe to an abrupt end. Loretta hurried to her secretary's side, clasped her hand, and said, "It's nothing, Marjorie. Don't fret yourself. You know my feelings on the subject of free love."

Marjorie, her green eyes starting out of a face that had gone white as chalk, stammered, "But—but I dinna think you *meant* it."

Malachai, feeling moderately vindicated—it was good to know a woman didn't trust her sex to act upon its convictions any more than he did, not that it had any convictions for the most part—said, "She doesn't."

Turning on him in a flash, Loretta shouted, "I do, too!"

"Oh, brother." Malachai would have liked to throttle the woman. Again.

"You mean . . ." Jason, frowning, looked from Loretta to Malachai. "Now see here, Captain Quarles, I know that Loretta is a handful—"

"I am not!" Loretta slapped Jason's arm, something she often did in fun. Malachai sensed there was no fun in her at the moment.

Jason ignored her. "I know she's a little—oh, very well, more than a little—difficult sometimes, but see here, man, if you think you can come in here and—"

Malachai held up a hand to stop the good doctor's

protest. "I know what you're thinking, and you're right. I was a cad. But I'm attempting to rectify the situation now. She claims she won't marry me."

"I won't!"

"Still . . ." Jason was unmollified. "There's such a thing as honor, man, and if you think you can get away with—"

"How dare you?" shrieked Loretta. This time everyone ignored her.

Feeling about on a par with dirt and worms and maggots and other disgusting creatures of the earth, Malachai muttered, "I know. I was a rascal. A cad. A lout. It was not only an ungentlemanly thing to do, but it was extremely foolish." Damn Loretta Linden anyhow! It was her fault he was having to admit his sins in front of strangers. The urge to strangle his beloved intensified.

"I should say so," said Jason, although the tone of his voice had eased up slightly from the censorious one he'd adopted at first.

"I should say *not!*" exclaimed Loretta, still being slighted by the three other people on her porch.

Not that Malachai blamed Jason for his censure. He himself thought he ought to be horsewhipped. He'd allowed himself to succumb to base lust, defying social wisdom, custom, practice, not to mention common sense and his instinct for survival, and that was something he'd never done before. "But my intentions are honorable. I said I'll marry the woman." He frowned, his choice of words and the voice in which he'd said them having plopped rather uncongenially into the early afternoon air.

"I wouldn't have you on a *bet!*" cried Loretta, turning on him like a termagant inflamed.

Jason, continuing to disregard Loretta, nodded

thoughtfully. "I see. Well, I guess that as long as you're willing to face up to your—"

"*I'm not his responsibility!*" shrieked Loretta.

Malachai and Jason exchanged a knowing look.

Relief came from an unexpected source. Marjorie, who had fallen into a chair as if her knees had given out beneath her, said in a voice that rasped, "It'sna his fault. You ken that, Dr. Abernathy. It'sna his fault." She stared at Loretta as if she were looking upon Satan himself. "It's Loretta. She's been begging to go to hell for years now. The poor captain is only her choice of vehicles."

Loretta was still fuming as the taxicab pulled out of her driveway, although she was no longer screaming at the top of her lungs, having gone hoarse. She remained defiant, however. She'd be cursed if she'd marry Malachai just because they'd gone to bed together. Why, that sort of thinking was not merely old-fashioned and ridiculous, but it defied every single one of the tenets by which she lived.

Because she couldn't contain her wrath, even if her throat hurt, she spat out, "The sexual instinct is inbred in all of us. In this modern day and age, there's no earthly reason men and women have to be married in order to express it."

Malachai heaved a sigh that all but rocked the cab. "I agree."

She stared at him, disbelieving. "Then why are you insisting that we marry?"

Seated next to her in the back seat of the cab, he'd crossed his arms over his massive chest, planted his feet on the floor, and hulked there not unlike a gigantic marble slab that someone had shoved into the cab. He was looking at her slant-ways, as if assessing her mood. Her mood was savage, actually, but Loretta knew she couldn't screech in a taxicab. By the time her voice had given out on her back porch, her entire household staff, and probably the whole of Russian Hill, had learned that she was no longer a virgin. If she resumed shrieking now, all of San Francisco would know it.

Already, the telephone wires were probably humming with neighbors calling her mother to relate the latest gossip about Dorothea's unruly daughter. The notion of dealing with her parents almost made Loretta relinquish the battle and agree to marry Malachai.

But no. She couldn't do that and remain true to herself and her causes.

It was all, frankly, embarrassing, although, Loretta told herself, not for the reason an ordinary, conventional person would think so. No. The reason for Loretta's embarrassment stemmed from the fact that she'd remained a virgin until she was approaching the age of thirty. That seemed pitiful to her.

Still squinting at her out of the corner of his eye, Malachai said, "I'm insisting we marry because it's time for me to settle down."

She gaped at him, disbelieving. "I beg your pardon?"

"I've been thinking for some time now that I'd like to settle down. You know, have a home of my own. A settled place where I can have . . . well . . . a garden. And dogs. I like dogs, and I like San Francisco."

An odd sinking sensation engulfed Loretta. Of all the reasons he might have given her for desiring marriage, this wasn't one she'd even thought about. "You . . . you want to settle down? Have a dog? Leave the sea?"

His smile struck her as quite unpleasant. "Is that so odd?"

"Odd? Well, yes. Or no, I mean. I don't suppose it's particularly odd." Unexpected, maybe. And . . . well . . . unemotional. Passionless.

Boring.

It was a word she would never have associated with Captain Malachai Quarles in a million years. Until this minute.

Disappointment warred with rage in her breast. Did he mean to say that *any* old woman would do for him at this point in his life? Did he mean that he was only insisting upon marriage because it suited his current plans? She wasn't even sure how to ask the question. Or if she wanted to know the answer.

Because she found it very difficult, even under the most favorable of circumstances, to hold her tongue, and because she couldn't seem to help herself, she said, striving for a coolness she didn't feel, "I see. I'm convenient."

The unpleasant smile evaporated, and Malachai roared, "Convenient? You're the most damned *in*-convenient female I've ever met in my life!"

Borrowing his pose, Loretta folded her arms over her breasts. She might have planted her feet on the floor, as well, except they didn't reach. "Well, then, I'm sure you would rather not marry me, since I'm so unsatisfactory."

When she slid a glance at his face, his eyes seemed to be glittering strangely. Uncomfortable with this new phenomenon, she eased a little farther away from him on the seat of the cab.

"I didn't say you were unsatisfactory, Loretta."

She swallowed, suddenly aware that the air between them seemed rather thick. "Um . . ." But she couldn't think of a thing to say.

"I don't think you're unsatisfactory at all."

"Oh."

"You're a pain in the ass, but you're far from unsatisfactory."

Ah. Familiar territory. Loretta had puffed up and was about to give vent to a rant about how men always consider women who think for themselves and have opinions uncomfortable, but she didn't get any farther than the first indrawn breath. Suddenly, she discovered herself on Malachai's lap, being kissed with a thoroughness that drove all thought from her head.

His tongue pried her lips apart and drove home, and Loretta's stiff posture dissolved until she felt like chocolate melting over a slow flame. Gradually, her own internal fire grew, until it totally engulfed her, and her hands began a frantic perusal of the planes of Malachai's face. He'd shaved since they'd last been in each other's arms, she noticed in passing.

His hand closing over her breast brought a moan of pleasure from her, and she reached for the evidence of his arousal. It felt something like an oak log, actually, and now that she knew what it was good for, Loretta squirmed to get the full benefit of it between her legs. It was Malachai who groaned this time.

She had no idea how long they played with each other in the cab, or how far they would have gone. On her part, she'd entirely lost track of their whereabouts. She knew for a fact that she'd have gone on to completion if Malachai hadn't suddenly thrust her away as if she were a pesky gnat.

Blinking in confusion, Loretta hadn't composed herself enough to ask why he'd stopped when she realized the cab no longer moved. Too, the back door had opened, God knew when. When she swivelled her head to ascertain what had happened and why, an amused voice shattered the remains of her mood as if it were a hammer cracking spun sugar.

"The Fairfield Hotel, sir."

"Right."

Loretta, squinting at Malachai through the wisps of lust-fog lingering on the edges of her senses, decided that he appeared too composed and collected. It didn't seem right to her. It didn't seem fair.

However, in justice to herself and all of womankind, she could but pretend to be as cool and composed as he. With hands that, she was disgusted to notice, trembled slightly, she arranged her pretty yellow woolen suit, tugging the skirt down to discreetly cover her ankles. She hadn't even realized that Malachai had slid it up, and she wondered briefly how much of her leg the cabbie had seen. How embarrassing.

Lifting her chin, Loretta swore to herself that she'd not lose her head again in Malachai's presence. Because he'd exited the cab to pay the cabbie—it was a measure of her discomposure that she hadn't beaten him to that punch—and was now holding his hand out to her, she decided not to buck convention any more at the moment, and took his hand. He was gentle in helping her get out of the cab, and she appreciated him for it, although she'd never tell him so. After all, it was his fault she'd been caught with her skirt up in the first place.

With a grin and a quick salute, the cab driver squealed away from the curb. Loretta prayed her face betrayed none of her inner chaos. "You think Mr. Peavey is here? You don't think he might have gone out?"

"Peavey doesn't get around much, except at sea. He prefers to remain where he's comfortable, and he's only comfortable in familiar surroundings. He likes to read, and I gave him a couple of books and some newspapers."

"I hadn't pegged Mr. Peavey as a reader."

Malachai's deep chuckle did strange things to Loretta's internal confusion. "Oh, sure. Peavey loves rip-roaring tales of the sea and things like that. He's a big fan of Robert Louis Stevenson. He doesn't go in much for intellectual stuff."

"Oh." There was no getting around it: Mr. Peavey was a very odd duck. "Well, then, we shouldn't have any trouble locating him."

"Naw. He'll either be in the restaurant or in his room."

Malachai took her hand, placed it in the crook of his arm as if he were a normal, courteous, everyday sort of gentleman, and led her into the lobby of the Fairfield. Rather than speeding off, as was usual for him when he and Loretta were together, he slowed his long stride so that she didn't have to scurry behind him. Her heart fluttered like a hummingbird, and Loretta was annoyed with it. It had no business behaving like a so-called normal female heart; Loretta's heart ought to be tougher than that.

In an effort to disguise her reaction to his touch,

she said, "Let's look in the restaurant first, then, since it's on this floor."

"Good idea."

She waited, but he didn't add anything to moderate this expression of approbation. This was very strange. Loretta wasn't sure how to react to Malachai when he wasn't being provoking. It was just like him to confuse her this way.

"Are you hungry?" he asked, interrupting her flow of thought.

Peering at him closely, she discerned no suggestive twinkle or mocking intent. "No, thank you."

"You sure? The Fairfield has a good restaurant."

"Yes, I know. Thank you." Loretta heard the mistrust in her voice.

His grin came out of nowhere, and his white teeth flashed against his tanned face. "I'm not trying to trick you, Loretta. I'm really acting like a gentleman, foreign as the behavior is to me."

Because she couldn't think of a retort cutting enough, Loretta contented herself with a soft huff. He chuckled again, and she could have screamed if her throat weren't still sore. Every time he laughed like that, deep in his chest, she wanted to climb into his arms and curl up and purr. It wasn't fair that she should have such a strong reaction to him. She'd have a chat with God about it, even though she wasn't sure she was supposed to believe in God since so many of her friends purported not to. This attitude always rather shocked Loretta, although she tried not to show it. And she still attended church because she couldn't force herself not to, mainly because she'd have to explain her decision to her parents, and she didn't think she could.

Malachai waved away the maître d'hôtel, and

searched the restaurant. Loretta stood on tiptoes and scanned the room, as well. This wasn't the Fairfield's fancy dining hall on a lower floor, where Loretta's friend Isabel used to dance for a living. It was the more casual coffee room, where hotel guests could take breakfast or luncheon if they were so inclined.

"I don't see him," she said. "Do you?" He was considerably taller than she, so she didn't mind asking him. Too much.

"No. He's probably in his room, reading or sleeping." Again, he took her arm, this time to lead her to the elevator cage.

The notion of Mr. Peavey sleeping reminded her of something. "How's his arm?"

"Fine. Your friend the doctor fixed him right up."

"Jason's a good doctor."

"Seems to be." They stepped into the gilt elevator cage, and Malachai said, "Six," to the uniformed elevator attendant.

As if he were really the gentleman he was pretending to be, Malachai stepped aside and bowed slightly when the elevator clanked to a stop on the sixth floor. Loretta swept out ahead of him, thinking that if they *were* married and, say, on their honeymoon or something, this might well be a hotel in Paris or London or Austria, or even Cairo—she'd always wanted to go to Egypt. She gave herself a short, sharp mental slap, and reminded herself that if she wanted to go to Egypt, she could jolly well go by herself. She was a modern American woman and didn't need things like weddings and honeymoons.

You might not need them, her mental self answered back, *but wouldn't they be fun?*

Curse it, she didn't need arguments from herself

as well as her friends and parents and Malachai.
Loretta consciously thrust thoughts of marriage out
of her mind and concentrated on Mr. Peavey. With
him present to confirm her suspicions, Malachai
couldn't balk any longer at the notion that Mr. Tillinghurst was a thief and a villain. He'd *have* to
admire her intelligence and cunning then, whether
he wanted to or not. The notion of Malachai begging her to forgive him gave her a warm, fuzzy
feeling in her bosom.

The feeling fled when Malachai next spoke, in a
voice that had a strange note to it. "Something's
wrong."

Her heart, which seconds earlier, and been
singing, if slightly off-key, gave a hard spasm. "What
do you mean?"

"The door's open."

That didn't seem so awful to Loretta. Given Mr.
Peavey's unusual inclinations, she wouldn't have
been surprised to discover that he'd left the door
open on purpose to rid himself of Moors. Or
merely forgotten to close it.

Abandoning gentlemanliness, Malachai dropped
Loretta's arm and sprinted the last few paces to
Peavey's door. Loretta didn't like the look on his
face when he came to a halt and stared inside.

Hurrying to catch up with him, she asked, "What
is it?" Her nerves started to jump.

"They've got him."

Loretta gasped. Reaching his side and clasping
hold of his arm, she, too, stared into the room.It
had been all but demolished, and Derrick Peavey
was nowhere to be seen.

SIXTEEN

Malachai had shaken her hand off and raced back to the elevator before Loretta had time to collect her thoughts. She'd rushed after him, but didn't get there in time to hear what he'd asked the elevator operator. She quickly learned.

"No, sir," the elevator operator said in a shaky voice. "I didn't take him downstairs in my elevator."

Loretta noticed that he'd backed himself into the corner of his cage and seemed to be cowering. She couldn't blame him, as Malachai loomed very large and dangerous before him. Stepping up to the bat, as it were, in an effort to assuage the poor elevator boy, she smiled as sweetly as she was able. "We don't think you had anything to do with Mr. Peavey's disappearance—"

"Disappearance?" The elevator boy looked shocked. "He's disappeared?"

Loretta cursed her thoughtless words. "Well, not to say *disappeared* exactly—"

"Disappearance is exactly what we mean," roared Malachai. "And if they didn't take him down the elevator, where the devil *did* they take him?"

"I d-d-don't know, sir." The boy saluted Malachai, plainly recognizing his authority, even though he was clad in a stylish heather-and-brown checked suit and derby hat and not his captain's uniform today.

Loretta tugged on Malachai's coat sleeve. "Stop shouting at the boy, Malachai. You're frightening him."

Malachai said, "Balderdash!" even as the boy nodded and shrank into as small an object as he could manage.

Trying and failing to shove Malachai aside—he was not unlike a mountain, she noticed not for the first time, and fairly unshovable—Loretta stepped into the elevator cage and perked up her smile for the cowering lad. "You see, a friend of ours was staying in room 612, but he's not there, the door's open, and the room is a mess, as if a struggle had taken place."

"Jeepers!" breathed the boy. "Want I should tell someone to call the cops?"

Loretta looked over her shoulder at Malachai. She had to admit that, if she didn't know him, his fierce scowl and immense presence would frighten her. Small wonder the elevator boy was all atremble. "Do you think we should involve the police?"

Malachai's glower grew fiercer. "I don't know . . . . No. If I decide to call in the police, I'll do it myself."

That was probably a good idea. The police would be much more apt to do Malachai's bidding than an elevator operator's. Stepping back out of the cage, Loretta continued smiling at the lad. She wondered if animal trainers worked like this: comporting themselves gently and tenderly in an effort to calm the shattered nerves of the animal they were attempting to subdue. "Are there some back stairs where someone might go downstairs without using the elevator?" she asked sweetly.

The lad nodded and pointed westward. "Down that way." He seemed to be bucking up after his initial panic. "Want I should help you?"

"That won't be necessary," growled Malachai.

Noticing the boy's stricken look, Loretta added, "We don't want you to get into trouble with Mr. Balderston, but we certainly do appreciate your offer of assistance." Joseph Balderston, a childhood friend of Loretta's, owned and ran the Fairfield Hotel.

"Okay," said the lad. "Thanks."

"You're very kind to offer," Loretta added, sensing the boy's disappointment. They were, she realized, depriving him of an adventure.

A little more brightly, the boy said, "You want me to keep mum about this? I won't tell nobody if you tell me not to." There was an eagerness in his voice that might have amused Loretta under different circumstances. She thought it would be fun to have a high-spirited, adventurous boy, as long as she could rear him to respect women.

She tried to catch Malachai's eye to determine his view on the issue of silence, but he went ahead without her and answered the boy. That figured. Naturally, *he* wouldn't think of consulting *her* before making a decision, curse him.

"Yeah. It would be better not to advertise this. Thanks." Pulling out several coins from his pocket, Malachai handed them to the boy. "I'll let you know what happens."

Saluting again, the lad cried, "Thank you, sir!"

He completely ignored Loretta, who didn't think she'd ever become accustomed to being treated as if she didn't exist. And here she'd wasted so many smiles on the young thug.

Malachai grabbed her hand and started off down the hall before her grievance could grow too large. "Let's see if the back staircase can tell us anything."

Scrambling to keep her feet under her, Loretta panted, "What are we going to do?"

"I'm not sure."

"I'm sure," she said as firmly as she could, given that she was having to concentrate on keeping up with Malachai. "We ought to get out to Mr. Tillinghurst's place instantly. Before he has a chance to clear out with the artifacts and your two sailors."

"I know what you think," Malachai snapped. "I want to make sure we do the right thing."

"That *is* the right thing, curse you!"

"Huh."

They'd reached the door to the service stairs by this time, and Malachai yanked it open. Elbowing him in the ribs to get him to step aside so she could see, Loretta stuck her head in the passageway.

She saw a flight of stairs going up and a flight of stairs going down. No discarded items of Mr. Peavey's clothing lay scattered about. No gruesome streaks of blood stained the walls. No messages scrawled in code by means of a finger dipped in gore met their eyes.

"Damn," said Malachai. "Wonder if it's worth going down to see if we can determine if this is the way they took him out."

"It must be the way," Loretta said reasonably. "If they didn't take the elevator, there's only one way down." She gasped, a horrifying thought having struck her.

"What the devil's the matter with—"

But Loretta didn't wait to hear the end of his question. She knew what it would be anyway. She ran back to Mr. Peavey's room, her heart in her throat, and scrambled over the upturned furniture and scattered bed linens until she got to the window. Throwing up the sash, she leaned out. Only then did she sigh with relief.

"What do you think you're doing?" Malachai thundered, storming into the room after her. When he saw her leaning out of the window, he said, "Oh."

"It's all right," Loretta said, this time with a genuine smile on her face. "If anybody had been thrown out of the window, there would be tons of people milling about, and there's no one there." And there was no flattened, bloody corpse on the sidewalk, either, thank the good Lord.

Nodding, Malachai said, "I suppose we'd best go to Tillinghurst's place."

At last! "Good idea," said Loretta. She couldn't resist adding, "Even if it *was* mine."

He only grunted. "I'm going to take a quick look around in here first, though. Peavey had some Moorish coins, and I want to see if they're still where he was keeping them."

Loretta joined him in picking things up and peering around. "I thought you'd scooped up all the coins from the floor at the soup kitchen."

"Those weren't the only ones. Peavey told me he pocketed about a dozen of them before he skedaddled out of his so-called dungeon."

"He didn't mention dogs, did he?" Loretta asked, wondering for the first time how Mr. Peavey had eluded the ravening beasts that had almost been the instruments of her own demise.

"I guess he got the dogs after Peavey escaped."

Loretta stood up abruptly. "Aha! So you *do* think Mr. Tillinghurst is behind all of this evil-doing!"

"I didn't say that," grumbled Malachai.

"But you think it, or you wouldn't have connected the purchase of the dogs to Mr. Peavey's escape."

"We'll see," he said gruffly.

But Loretta didn't have to wait and see. She *knew*.

"I tell you, you're wasting time!"

Malachai, glowering for all he was worth and wondering for approximately the fiftieth time why his glowers didn't work on Loretta the way they did on everyone else in the world, said, "You're crazy."

"I am not!"

"All right. You can call Dr. Abernathy from the police station, but we're not making a detour to Chinatown to pick him up."

"We don't need the police," Loretta said stubbornly, crossing her arms over her chest, thereby pushing her luscious breasts up slightly.

Malachai commanded himself not to think about her breasts. "No? You think Tillinghurst and his men will collapse and give themselves up when I tell them to?"

"Well . . . No, of course not. Not that, but . . ."

"But what?"

"Well, but we're taking so much time."

"Better take the time now than get killed because we don't have anybody but us to fight our battle. Anyhow, we'll have to get a search warrant if we aim to scour his house and grounds."

"A search warrant?" Loretta had heard of search warrants. She'd read about them in novels. At least she thought she had, but she wasn't sure what one was.

"You think Tillinghurst will invite us in and give us free rein to inspect his house and grounds?"

"Of course not!"

"Then we'd better be prepared with a search warrant and the men to carry it out. Providing you're right about Tillinghurst, which nobody's proved to me yet."

"You're the most stubborn male human being I've ever met!"

"Likewise, I'm sure, on the other side."

"Bother."

In a tiff, Loretta gave up arguing and stared out the side window of the taxicab. Malachai figured it was only a temporary reprieve. He'd come to know his beloved well.

Since he couldn't think of anything better to do, he stared out the window on the other side of the cab. Nob Hill was quite a place. If the United States had royalty, he bet they'd choose to live here, on Nob Hill, in San Francisco, California. Why bother with Washington, D.C., and all its weather, when you could live here? In one of those incredibly fancy estates with their rolling lawns and birthday-cake trim.

The whole of San Francisco was quite a place, actually. Ever since he'd escaped from the damned orphanage, Malachai had been everywhere, pretty much, and seen pretty much everything, but he'd never found a city he liked as well as San Francisco. A man could be happy here, within reach of the ocean and foreign shores if the wanderlust grabbed him, yet with roots. Yes, indeedy, San Francisco had everything Malachai figured he needed for a happy rest of his life.

With a sideways squint at his cab-mate, he silently
acknowledged that even Loretta was part of the
everything he'd need. She'd at least assure that he
never got bored with the stability of a home and
family. He'd bet anything that she'd take to motherhood, too. Her vivacity, energy, and intelligence
would guarantee that her children were exposed to
every type and kind of educational experience.
And, since both she and he had money, the kids
would never go hungry, either.

Recalling his own bleak childhood, Malachai
shivered involuntarily.

"Is anything the matter?" Loretta asked him.

He hadn't realized she'd stopped watching the
outdoor scene and had begun inspecting him. "I'm
fine," he said.

"Why did you shiver? Are you cold? It's a chilly
day."

"I'm not cold."

Loretta herself still wore the pretty yellow thing
she'd had on when he'd called on her that morning. She'd topped it with a brown woolen coat and
a silly brown hat with yellow flowers on it. He'd
asked if she had a fur coat, because he didn't want
her to get chilled, and she'd given him a lecture on
how evil it was to kill animals in order to decorate
women's fashions. "It's not as if we're cavemen and
women," she'd said hotly. "We don't need to kill animals in order to cover our bodies. We have *wool!*
We have *cotton!*"

He'd agreed, and meekly, too, which had only
served to incite her to a longer lecture. He grinned,
remembering. Ah, Loretta. However had he lived
without her? And yet he'd only known her for a few
weeks.

"Are you sure?"

He'd forgotten what they'd been talking about, and his face must have given him away, because Loretta huffed.

"You shivered," she snapped. "If you're not cold, perhaps you're getting sick."

"I'm not getting sick."

"Well, then, why did you shiver?"

"How the devil should I know?" he demanded, becoming testy. He didn't want to talk about his miserable beginnings. He wanted to forget them.

"Hmph." Loretta sat back and crossed her arms over her chest again. She resumed staring out the window.

Damn the woman. He'd never known anyone else who could provoke him so much in so little time. Looking out the window on his side, he saw the police station ahead. Good. He aimed to gather reinforcements, and quickly.

"We're about there," he said.

"At the police station?"

"Yes."

"Good. I'll call Jason as soon as we get there."

Malachai heaved a huge sigh. "I still don't see what good it will do to have a doctor on hand." He saw her puffing up and held out a hand before she could tell him. "But I'm not objecting. I suppose we can use all the men we can get."

"Men?" There was an ominous tone to her voice.

God preserve him from feminists. "Armed human beings," he amended, trying not to grin.

She sniffed, but she didn't pursue the matter.

* * *

Although she considered herself a coward for it,
Loretta was glad to espy Marjorie MacTavish waiting
for them and their police cohorts at the gate of Mr.
Tillinghurst's estate.

Not that she *needed* Marjorie. Heavenly days,
Loretta didn't need anyone. Still and all, it was
comforting to know she'd have a woman friend by
her side during the impending confrontation.

It hadn't taken Malachai three minutes to convince the police to take a hand in their proposed
scheme. In fact, to Loretta's disgust, three of the policemen had saluted Malachai, as if he were their
leader. She'd wager she'd still be arguing with them
if Malachai had left it up to her to convince them
they needed help. The cursed man had everybody
twined about his little finger. It wasn't fair.

Out of nowhere, Loretta wondered what kind of
father Malachai would be. She'd bet he'd be the
sort of hard man who turned to mush around his
own children. It would be interesting to find out if
she was right.

Good Lord, wherever had that thought sprung
from? Giving herself a good hard mental shake,
Loretta forced her mind back to the present.

Malachai caught sight of Marjorie, too. "Good
God, why did the damned fool bring that woman
along?"

Glad to be diverted from her previous thoughts,
Loretta said firmly, "Jason is not a fool, and Marjorie can be of use to us."

"I don't see how," he growled. "But I guess there's
no help for it now."

The police car pulled up in front of Jason's Hudson automobile, and Loretta didn't wait for a
policeman or Malachai or Jason to open her door

for her. Ridiculous tradition, that. She shoved the door open and leaped out, fortunately missing a clump of cactus. She reminded herself that, while women were every bit as competent as men, they were still well advised to look before they leaped.

Marjorie hurried up to her. "What's going on, Loretta? Jason—Dr. Abernathy, I mean—said there's something amiss at Mr. Tillinghurst's estate."

"Amiss, my foot. He's a villain, and he's kidnaped Mr. Peavey again!"

"Merciful God." Marjorie pressed a hand over her mouth.

"We don't know that," Malachai said gruffly. "But we're going to find out right now."

"How are we going to work this?" Jason, who had walked over to join them, asked.

Before Loretta could explain, Malachai spoke. "I'm going to ring the bell and have the gatekeeper admit me. We're all going to enter as soon as the gate is open, and then everyone is going to hang back and surround the house while I talk to Tillinghurst."

"Hang back?" Loretta hadn't been informed of this particular plan. She didn't like it. She wanted to be in the forefront of the action. After all, it had been she who'd first pointed at Tillinghurst as the thief.

Turning and using his great bulk to loom over her, Malachai said, "Yes. Hang back. I'll be damned if I'm going to let you get kidnaped too. How the devil do you suppose I can find out anything if you're in danger?"

"I won't be in danger!" cried Loretta, vexed. "Mr. Tillinghurst doesn't have the least idea that we suspect him of anything at all."

Jason stuck an oar in. "She's right, you know," he said, thoughtfully stroking his upper lip. "In fact, she might give you a good excuse to come visiting. You can tell Tillinghurst that you're engaged to be married or something."

Loretta's upper lip curled. "Married? Jason Abernathy, you know good and well—"

"Yes," he interrupted, sounding exasperated. "*I* know, but does Tillinghurst? You don't have to mean it, you know. It's a ruse. You've heard of ruses, certainly, Loretta."

"There's no need for sarcasm," she muttered.

Malachai huffed. "Can't you shove your blasted principles aside for the sake of Peavey and Jones? It won't take us long to find out what we want to know. While we're talking to Tillinghurst, the police will be searching the grounds."

Deciding that now wasn't the time to argue principles, Loretta conceded graciously. "Very well. And that way I can make an excuse to search the upper story."

Malachai turned on her like a grizzly bear. "Damned if you will!"

"Oh, for heaven's sake, Malachai Quarles, why not? If I beg leave to use the facilities, nobody's going to follow me to see if I'm really searching the upper floor."

"Actually, she might have a point there," said the sergeant of police, the highest ranking officer present. "She can get inside without arousing his suspicions, and we can't."

Loretta had never been particularly fond of the police, believing them to be the puppets of an unjust government, but she smiled upon the sergeant. "Exactly."

"And you can drive to the door in my machine," Jason said with a grin. "If you drive up in a police car, they might suspect something."

"They might," said Malachai sardonically.

"I should have driven us here in my Runabout," said Loretta.

"No, you shouldn't have," chorused Malachai, Jason, and Marjorie, as one.

Loretta resented her friends' insistence that she was a poor driver. She only gave them a disgruntled frown. Malachai, she noticed, was standing there and scowling, looking not unlike a monument to some angry Roman god who was about to throw a thunderbolt and destroy a city. "What's the matter with you?" she asked without bothering with courtesy.

"Are you absolutely set on going in with me?"

"Yes."

"I don't like it," Malachai said under his breath.

"Well, I do, and I aim to do precisely as I said." Loretta sniffed and lifted her chin.

"I'm sure you would anyway," he said nastily.

"All right, children, let's not fight." Jason laughed as he said it.

"Huh." Leaving the huddle, Malachai marched to the gate and rang the bell. When a crackling voice asked who he was to be demanding entry, he growled, "Quarles. And Miss Linden."

"Doesn't sound much like a happy bridegroom-to-be, does he?" Jason asked. Loretta couldn't tell if he was amused or worried.

"No, he doesn't," she said. "But then, he wouldn't, would he?"

Marjorie clucked her tongue.

As the gate began sliding open, Malachai stomped

back to them. "All right. Get in the machine, Loretta."

Marjorie clasped Loretta's hand. "Take care, Loretta. Try not to be a gudgeon."

"Ha," said Malachai. "That'll be the day."

Jason laughed.

"Oh, for heaven's sake!" said Loretta.

They didn't speak as Malachai got behind the wheel. Jason cranked for them, and they were soon rattling along on the long, tree-lined drive, heading for William Tillinghurst's front door. The police contingent, on foot, along with Jason Abernathy, rushed through the gate after them. Malachai didn't see Marjorie, but he held out little hope that she'd had sense enough to remain behind. She was probably in the one lone police car that came through the gates last.

"If we don't find anything, I'm going to have a lot of explaining to do to my business partner, you know," he mumbled.

"If the men and the artifacts aren't here, Tillinghurst has moved them. I know he's the one."

"How?"

She turned in the seat beside him and frowned at him. "What do you mean, *how?*"

"How do you know? You have no proof. All you've told me so far is that you think Tillinghurst is a bad man and somebody answering to the name Jones, whom you couldn't see, spoke to you from behind a locked door a couple of nights ago. That's not a whole lot to go on, unless you want me to believe that you have second sight."

"Fiddlesticks! It only makes sense!" She threw her arms out in an extravagant gesture, as if to convince him.

He wasn't convinced. Well . . . maybe he was, but not because he believed in Loretta's fine understanding of human nature. But things had begun to stack up against Tillinghurst, and Malachai, who didn't like the man personally, and who always interacted with others warily, wasn't one to give anyone the benefit of the doubt. He'd learned that hard life lesson as an infant.

"We'd better plan what we're going to do when we gain entrance to Tillinghurst's house," Malachai said.

"Plan? What do you mean?" The afternoon sunlight reflected on the lenses of her eyeglasses, but Malachai could detect the gleam in her eyes. The dashed woman was actually enjoying this!

He gave her an exasperated glance. "We're not going to storm in and take over the place as if we're besieging Peavey's precious castle, for God's sake. What I propose is that we pretend to be engaged, and that we're paying a sociable call on my business partner in order to tell him the happy news."

Without looking, he felt her doubt. Annoyed, he said, "We don't have to mean it, for God's sake. As your friend Jason said, it's a ruse. You've heard of ruses, haven't you?"

For a moment the only thing Malachai heard was the noise of the Hudson's engine. Then Loretta said, "I don't trust you."

It was, possibly, the worst thing she could have said to him. Turning on her, he said with venom, "I am the most trustworthy man you'll ever meet, Loretta Linden, and don't you ever forget it. I've spent my entire life being trustworthy. How the devil do you think I've gained and kept the loyalty of my men? It certainly wasn't by deceiving them or cheating others."

He could tell he'd startled her, because she actually flinched from his wrath, something Loretta seldom did even when Malachai was at his most truculent. "I didn't mean it that way."

"No? How the devil *did* you mean it?"

"Well . . . As long as you know we're not really engaged."

"Oh, for . . . Listen to me, Loretta Linden. This is a *ruse.* A *scheme.* Can't you get that through your head? I thought you were supposed to be smart!"

She sniffed. "I am smart."

"Well, then, act like it, can't you?"

"There's no need to be rude, Malachai. I only wanted to make sure we both knew the truth."

If he hadn't been driving, Malachai would have pounded his fists against something. But Tillinghurst's drive was long and curvy, and he didn't fancy running the good doctor's nice Hudson automobile into a tree. He allowed himself one frustrated, "God," before deciding that talking sense to Loretta Linden was approximately as useful as lecturing a school of fish. Or Derrick Peavey.

"But you need to discuss something in the nature of business with him, too, Malachai," Loretta pointed out, pushing her spectacles up her pert nose absently.

"Why?"

"To give me an excuse to leave the room and look around."

"But I don't *want* you leaving the room and looking around."

"Fiddlesticks. Who else is going to do it?"

"How about the police?"

"They can look around later! For heaven's sake, Malachai, we need to find *something*. I know Tillinghurst is the thief and kidnaper, but we still have to prove it."

"That's the police's job."

"Darn you! I want to search his house."

"You and all his servants?"

"Pooh. I can avoid the servants."

"We'll see."

"If you don't make an excuse for me to leave the room, I will," she promised him. Or perhaps it was a threat.

He gave up the fight. Might as well, since arguing wouldn't do him any good. "Fine. Snoop."

"It's not snooping."

"Huh." He pulled the Hudson to a stop in front of the huge front porch and hissed, "Stay there until I open your door."

"I don't need you—"

"Damn it! I know you don't need me to open your damned door! *Pretend,* will you?"

Another sniff, then she said, "Very well."

"I have never in all my life met anyone as troublesome as you, Loretta Linden. I hope you know that."

She lifted her chin and said, "Thank you."

Malachai almost laughed out loud.

Loretta felt rather silly, and she guessed Malachai and Jason were right, at least this time. She probably ought to subdue her feminist principles for as long as it took them to fool Mr. Tillinghurst into believing they were only making a social call. With luck, and with their reinforcements working together, they should be able to end this entire thing today, free Malachai's sailors, arrest Mr. Tillinghurst, and recover the stolen artifacts. She fingered her purse and was surprised to encounter something sharp.

"What are you doing?" Malachai asked. He'd opened the door on her side of the machine, and stood looking down at her.

"I pricked my finger." She stuck it in her mouth as she put her hand in the bag to find her handkerchief. She pulled out the Chinese knife. "Bother. I thought I'd put this up."

"What the devil are you doing with a damned knife?" Malachai demanded. "I can just picture you trying to fend off any number of large, armed ruffians with that tiny ornamental thing."

Irked that he should think so little of her common sense, she said, "Don't be ridiculous. It's not really a knife." She climbed out of the automobile and stuck the knife back in her handbag. "Well, it *is* a knife, but I didn't put it in my purse with the intention of using it."

"Give it to me." He held out his hand.

"I will not! It's mine, and besides that, it's only in my bag because I forgot to take it out. I'm not planning to use it." She made sure her scorn could be heard in her voice. "Except, perhaps, on you, if you keep being rude."

"Good God." Turning without bothering to make sure she was at his side, he ran up the porch stairs.

Frustrated, she trotted up them after him. She guessed he was as frustrated as she—or perhaps it was his nerves acting up— because he mashed down on the electrical doorbell approximately seventeen times.

A red-faced butler opened the door. "Captain

Quarles! We thought the cavalry had attacked. You were quite vigorous with the bell, sir." He caught sight of Loretta and smiled. "Good afternoon, Miss Linden."

"Good afternoon." She bestowed a gracious smile upon him and sashayed into the house as if she owned it. She heard Malachai stomping in behind her and presumed he didn't appreciate her attitude. Too bad.

SEVENTEEN

"To what do I owe this pleasure, Quarles?" William Tillinghurst's ferret face strained to produce a smile. "And Miss Linden, too, I see."

They'd obviously caught him off guard. When Loretta had swept ahead of the butler and marched into Tillinghurst's front parlor, Tillinghurst had wheeled around, startled. Malachai noticed that he held a bronze statuette that Malachai had last seen on the deck of his ship, *The Moor's Revenge*. That statuette ought, by rights, to be among the treasures in the Museum of Natural History.

He opted not to mention it. If everything went well—which seemed unlikely, but a man could hope—all of the stolen loot would be in its rightful place soon.

Damn, but he hated to admit that Loretta had been correct about Tillinghurst all along. Ah, well, there was no help for it.

Loretta actually curtseyed at their reluctant host. Malachai could hardly believe his eyes. "How nice to see you again, Mr. Tillinghurst."

Tillinghurst grunted as if he didn't believe a word of it, and tried to hide the statuette among the folds of his dressing gown. "I'm not exactly dressed for visitors," he muttered ungraciously.

"You might use the telephone before you stop by next time, Malachai."

"Oh, la, think nothing of it," trilled Loretta. "I do think spontaneity is such a refreshing thing, don't you?"

Swallowing a bark of laughter—Mr. Tillinghurst clearly preferred to leave spontaneity to others—Malachai said, "Just a social call, Tillinghurst." He didn't like his business partner, and he was pretty sure Tillinghurst didn't like him. Glancing around Tillinghurst's front parlor, he noticed signs of disarray. "Going somewhere?"

For the first time in their acquaintance, Malachai detected traces of nervousness in his partner, although Tillinghurst was quick to don his usual suave manner. "Just cleaning up a trifle," he said vaguely. "Things tend to get out of hand, don't you know."

Malachai didn't know, but he deemed it better not to say so. "Miss Linden and I thought you ought to be among the first to know, Tillinghurst." Malachai grabbed Loretta's hand, vexed that it should be necessary to do so. Any normal woman would be simpering and hanging onto him like a limpet onto a ship's hull. "We're engaged to be married."

When he looked, he saw that Loretta had managed to produce a rather grim smile. Dash it all, the least she could do is *act* happy to be engaged to him. He'd have to have a chat with her about her acting ability one of these days. Not that she'd need it again. He'd make sure of that, by God, or know the reason why. He was going to keep her safe from now on, with or without her permission.

"Married?" Tillinghurst looked at him as if he

were trying to determine if Malachai were drunk or merely insane. "Uh . . . how nice."

"We wanted you to be the first to know," said Loretta brightly. "Since you and dear Malachai are partners and all that."

"Right." *Dear Malachai?* Malachai felt more foolish than he could remember feeling for a long, long time.

"Oh?"

From the expression on Tillinghurst's face, Malachai judged that he'd reached a decision on the alcohol-versus-sanity issue, and believed that both Malachai and Loretta had lost their minds. He might be right.

Before he could think of anything to say that might gloss over the situation and make their sudden appearance at Tillinghurst's estate seem anything other than odd, Loretta stepped into the breech.

"We thought it might be good publicity, you see."

Tillinghurst stared at her. So did Malachai. Her cheeks took on a becoming pink color. What with her yellow dress and brown coat, she looked rather like a blooming spring bud.

"I mean, you know, you want to have people visit your exhibition at the museum. Wouldn't it be sweet to have a photograph of the two of us taken among the artifacts? In the newspapers, you know."

Her trilling laugh sounded hollow, but Malachai had to give her credit for trying. "Right," he said, following her lead. "You never know who'll be reading the society pages, old man. Some wealthy dowager might decide to fund another treasure-recovery expedition if we touch her heart." Good

God in a goblet, he couldn't believe such tripe had actually issued from his mouth.

"Er . . . I see." As if he didn't quite know what to do next, Tillinghurst stood there, frozen, his glance passing between Loretta and Malachai. He looked as if he were trying to determine which of the two of them was the more dangerous lunatic.

Again, Loretta saved the day. "But we have other business with you, too, Mr. Tillinghurst."

Warily, as if he weren't sure he wanted to know what that business might be, Tillinghurst said, "You do?"

Malachai barely stopped himself from echoing Tillinghurst's question.

"Why, yes. My parents are thinking of funding another expedition, this time in the area of the Hawaiian Islands. We thought that, if we could garner enough publicity for the venture, others might be interested in joint funding."

For the first time since they barged in on him, Tillinghurst looked almost interested. "Oh?"

God bless the woman, she really could think on her feet. Too bad she didn't know what she was talking about. Ah, well, she couldn't be faulted just because she wasn't well versed in sailing and treasure-hunting lore.

Malachai, hoping Tillinghurst was as ignorant of such things as she, picked up the line and ran with it. "Right. Mr. Linden and some of his business allies thought it would be worthwhile to explore along the coasts of a couple of the islands. Chinese trading vessels have been lost there, going back centuries. The islands were a stop on the trade routes, you know."

"Oh? Well, I guess that's so." Tillinghurst didn't

sound exactly sure of himself. "I hadn't heard about the lost vessels. Were they carrying anything worthwhile?"

"Oh, tons of it. Gold, silver, bronze." Loretta's contribution. She glanced around the room with interest. "But why don't we sit down and discuss it, Mr. Tillinghurst? I hope we're not interrupting anything too important." She gave another inane burble of laughter.

Tillinghurst sneered and looked as if he would have liked to shoot her. Malachai, who understood this reaction to Loretta, having had it himself a time or two, hastened to intervene. "Er, why don't you go outside and look at the gardens, Loretta. Tillinghurst and I need to discuss some technical details."

For only a moment, Malachai feared Loretta would rebel. The familiar mulish look visited her face, and he held his breath. But she recalled their purpose before commencing to lecture, and smiled vacuously. "Oh, of course. We women can't *possibly* understand technical details."

"There's nothing in the gardens," Tillinghurst said. His glance began darting around the room. Malachai suspected he was looking for a hiding place for the stolen statuette. "It's November."

"True, true," said Loretta, "but I still love to walk. Nothing like an invigorating walk, don't you know."

"Right." Tillinghurst wasn't buying it.

Quickly, Malachai said, "Go on along now, Loretta. We men have to talk."

"Of course." With a smile that could have sweetened a gallon of lemon juice—or curdled milk—Loretta left them.

* * *

How galling it was to be forced to act like a blithering idiot! Loretta paused for a moment outside the parlor door in order to collect herself and pour figurative water on her inflamed temper. She reminded herself that Jason and Malachai were correct in this instance, and that she needed to play a role.

She made her way to the front entry hall, an elaborately tiled room that would have been right at home in Mr. Peavey's castle. A twisting stairway, carpeted with a lush scarlet Oriental runner, led to the upper story. Pondering her options, Loretta decided she probably ought to start her search upstairs. A villain would be more apt to hide his loot away from more public rooms.

"May I help you, Miss Linden?"

Loretta jumped a foot and whirled around. The butler, looking very dignified, stood behind her. He held a candlestick in his left fist. Loretta eyed it with misgiving. Surely, he didn't aim to bash her with it, did he? Ridiculous!

Her nerves leaping like frightened frogs, she commanded herself to play her part and smiled, she hoped benignly. "Oh, hello there. I . . . ah . . . wondered if you can tell me where the powder room is." Honestly embarrassed to have asked a man directions to the toilet, Loretta blushed.

The butler's stern demeanor softened, as if he comprehended how a delicately reared young lady might shrink from asking such a question. "Certainly, ma'am. Right upstairs and to the left." He gave her an understanding smile.

Resenting the smile, but ecstatic to have been given permission to snoop upstairs, Loretta simpered fatuously. "Thank you so much."

"Certainly, ma'am."

Before darting up the stairs, she asked, "Er . . . is Mr. Tillinghurst planning a journey?" She eyed the candlestick in the butler's hand.

He glanced down at it and back at Loretta. "Mr. Tillinghurst has been called back east, ma'am. We're packing the household, as he expects to be gone for some time."

"Back east, eh?"

"Yes. A family emergency."

"Oh, I'm so sorry." A likely story. Loretta credited Mr. William Frederick Tillinghurst with about as much family feeling as a rattlesnake. And did he aim to take Messrs. Peavey and Jones with him? She simpered again, hating herself even as she did so. "I should so like to journey to New York again."

"Yes, ma'am."

The man's stolid, butlerish mien had returned, and Loretta guessed she'd be better off not trying to pry further information from him. Although it seemed unlikely, the butler might be in cahoots with Mr. Tillinghurst. Perhaps she'd find a maid upstairs whom she could question. Women were ever so much easier to talk to than men.

"Thank you," she said, and skipped up the stairs.

Mr. Tillinghurst didn't stint on his furnishings. Loretta had been in his home before, when she'd accompanied her parents to parties here, but this time she paid more attention to the way the place was decorated. Chinese silks had been hung on the wall in the upstairs hall. When she walked up to scrutinize one of them more closely, she thought it looked as if it might well be ancient. Denise had something like it in her art gallery. Loretta wondered if Tillinghurst had stolen them from a gallery somewhere, or from an art collector.

Then there were the *objets d'art* placed here and there in pleasing arrangements. And the carved ebony chairs with the luscious silk-embroidered cushions. Loretta squinted down at one of the cushions and was sure she'd seen something similar to it in a museum in London.

Goodness, but Mr. Tillinghurst must be a very rich man. Or a very dishonest one. Or both.

Her parents' house was furnished expensively, and her father enjoyed antique Chinese and Persian accessories, but his home was nothing like this. This might as well be another museum.

Having read about such things in various newspapers and magazines, Loretta had a hunch that many of Mr. Tillinghurst's trimmings had come from archeological sites or treasure-recovery operations like the one Malachai had carried out for him. He was a well-known supporter of such expeditions. Also, unless Mr. T. kept immaculate records, the provenance of the items was probably murky at best.

Loretta shook her head sadly, and wondered if this magnificent chair might have come from an ancient Oriental potentate's palace. It ought to be on display somewhere. Somewhere accessible to the public, who could be educated as to the potentate's culture and career. It didn't seem right to her that a person should hoard up beautiful and historical objects like this. They should be in museums, where everyone could enjoy and learn from them.

Grimly, she remembered the time she'd told her father something like that, and he'd told her not to be an idiot, that a man deserved the trappings of his success and if he appreciated antiquities, then he should be able to enjoy them in peace, without a bunch of rabble-rousers pestering him. Her father was not, Loretta reminded herself, a scholar.

That, however, was neither here nor there at the moment. Pushing her eyeglasses up her nose, she ventured down the hallway, deciding to begin with the room farthest away and work her way back to the staircase. Then she could tackle the other wing.

As she had anticipated, the search wasn't all that simple, since Tillinghurst's house was a mansion, and it didn't have mere rooms and a hallway, but suites of rooms and several hallways. And in each one of them, Loretta found evidence of hasty packing. A couple of the rooms—they looked to her like a sitting room and a bedroom—were stacked with boxes, and all the pictures and hangings had been removed from the walls.

If Mr. Tillinghurst had indeed been informed of a family emergency, it looked to her as if he planned to move in with it.

Family emergency, my foot. He's escaping, is what he's doing.

So fascinated was Loretta by her adventure that she lost track of time.

"Well," said Tillinghurst ungraciously. "You might as well sit down, Quarles." Tillinghurst himself took a seat on an overstuffed chair and surreptitiously jammed the bronze statuette behind a cushion.

"Thank you. Don't mind if I do." As he did so, Malachai decided it was silly to pretend any longer, and that there was no point in mincing his words. After all, if Tillinghurst tried to escape, the police were surrounding the house even as they sat here.

"All right, Tillinghurst, what are you up to? I can tell that you're packing up your household. Why?"

Tillinghurst jerked in his chair, completely taken aback. "I beg your pardon?"

"Why are you leaving? Did you aim to tell anyone before you bolted?"

"Well, of course! And I'm not bolting, as you call it. I-I-I . . ."

"Huh." Malachai decided it would be better not to give him the time to think up an excuse for all this hasty packing. Opting for the direct approach, he said, "I know you kidnaped my men. I'm pretty sure you stole the missing artifacts, too. Where are they?"

Tillinghurst, whose thin face now sported two vivid banners of red across his sallow cheeks, giving him the look of a pileated woodpecker, sat up straight in his chair and tried to appear offended. "Good God, man, I'm sure I don't know what you're talking about!"

"I saw you stuff that statuette behind the cushion, Tillinghurst, and I recognized it from the artifacts I recovered in the Canaries. I know damned well it's not the only artifact you stole. You can't escape now. Your whole place is surrounded by the San Francisco police department."

"*What?*" Tillinghurst leaped to his feet and scurried to a window, bringing to Malachai's mind images of rats rushing across the deck of a sinking ship.

He rose, too, and followed his erstwhile business partner to the window. Sure enough, the place was swarming with coppers. What a refreshing sight! "The game's up, Tillinghurst. Tell me where my men are."

"I . . . I don't understand. What are those people doing inside my gates?"

"Searching for the stolen treasure and Jones and Peavey would be my guess," said Malachai dryly.

"S-searching? But, good God, man, they can't do that!"

"Can, too. Got a search warrant from Judge Fellows. You remember Fellows, Tillinghurst. He's the chap who gave you the key to the city a few weeks ago, along with the mayor."

He recalled the scene with delicious irony. Malachai, too, had been given a huge, symbolic key to San Francisco that day, amid much pomp and circumstance. Not a man who enjoyed ceremonies, Malachai had barely been able to tolerate that one, but Tillinghurst had basked in the day's glory. He heard Tillinghurst gulp.

"But . . . but this is incredible!"

"Fairly," agreed Malachai.

Tillinghurst spun around. "This is absurd, Quarles! This is all your doing too, isn't it?" All of the creases on his bony face quivered, and the patches of color on his cheeks were now a sickly burgundy-orange shade.

"Not really. The credit belongs to Miss Linden."

"Miss Linden!" Tillinghurst spat Loretta's name out as if it tasted bad. "That silly bitch."

Malachai's humor fled. "Don't call her names, Tillinghurst. I won't allow it."

"You won't allow it?" Tillinghurst, while resembling a rodent, could spew scorn with the best—or the worst—of his fellow beings. "I'll be damned if I'll let you get away with this!"

"You don't have any say in the matter anymore," Malachai pointed out. "The police are already conducting a search outdoors, and my beloved is searching upstairs."

"She's *what?*"

He made as if to dart past the large obstacle in his way, but Malachai was too quick for him. He grabbed Tillinghurst by the collar of his dressing gown. "Not so fast, partner. Before I let you go anywhere at all, you're going to tell me where my men are."

Helpless, Tillinghurst dangled from Malachai's big fist for a second before gurgling something incomprehensible. Realizing he was choking the man, which wasn't a bad idea but would have to wait, Malachai set him on his feet again, although he kept a firm grip on his skinny shoulder.

"All right, where are Peavey and Jones?"

Dropping defiance for the moment, Tillinghurst said sullenly, "I don't know what you're talking about."

Malachai gave him a sudden hard shake, making his head pitch violently and his teeth clack together. "St-stop it!"

"Not until you tell me where Peavey and Jones are." Although he wouldn't have minded snapping Tillinghurst's worthless neck, Malachai quit shaking him. No sense killing him until he had the information he needed. "Well?"

Tillinghurst put a hand to his throat and gasped several times, as if he were unable to speak. Malachai didn't believe it. "Well?" he demanded again.

"I don't know who you're talking about." Seeing Malachai's hand reach out to clasp him again, Tillinghurst backed away from his opponent, raising a shaking hand. "I mean it. I don't know the men's names."

"Ah." Malachai took a deep breath. By God, Loretta was right on all counts. However would he live this down? She'd be lording it over him for the rest of his life. "But you know who I'm talking about."

"Well . . ." Another step forward on Malachai's part sent the words scuttling out of Tillinghurst's thin-lipped mouth. "Yes. Two of your men. They—"

He broke off suddenly. Malachai understood how difficult this confession was for the bastard, although he couldn't summon up any sympathy for him.

"Let me at least sit down, can't you?" Tillinghurst said querulously.

Malachai gestured for the man to take any old seat he wanted. "Feel free."

Tillinghurst went over to a teakwood chair covered in a fabulous bright red brocade. He sat with a huff and said nothing.

Malachai cued him. "Go on, Tillinghurst. My men what? Saw your men stealing the artifacts from the ship?"

"Saw them? They did it!" For a brief moment, Tillinghurst looked defiant.

With a sneer that doused his partner's flare of defiance, Malachai said, "I know damned good and well they weren't involved in the theft. But they saw your men taking artifacts, didn't they?"

Scowling hideously, Tillinghurst snapped, "Yes."

"I see. Clever of you to steal the treasure before it had been inventoried by the university or the museum. However, lest you expect to escape with anything at all from *The Moor's Revenge*, Tillinghurst, let me tell you that I'm a businessman."

"Of course you are." Tillinghurst sounded like a

whiny schoolboy. "That's why I allowed you to go into partnership with me."

"Bilgewater. You thought I was a dim-witted sailor who didn't know how to run a real business operation. If you'd known the truth, you never would have gone into business with me." He saw from the nasty grimace Tillinghurst shot him that his assessment of his partner was correct. "That was an error on your part, Tillinghurst. I've been on my own since I was fourteen, and I haven't lived this long or prospered this well by being an ordinary roughneck sailor."

Tillinghurst grunted, acknowledging the unhappy truth.

"Too, this isn't the first treasure-recovery expedition I've handled. Every single item that my men find is documented by me personally as it comes out of the water. You didn't know that, did you?"

It was just as well that he didn't expect an answer, because he didn't get one. Tillinghurst sat like a lump, staring at the expensive Turkish carpet under his slippered feet.

"When the police recover all the artifacts you've got stashed, I'll check them against my inventory. If anything's missing, you'll have to explain it. I suspect you've already sold off some of the better items."

Again, he got no answer.

"You son of a bitch." Although Malachai was trying his best to keep his temper under control, the perfidy of William Frederick Tillinghurst chafed him. The knowledge that Loretta had been right all along also grated on his disposition, which was, according to others, irascible even under the most favorable conditions. Malachai had never considered himself touchy, but he felt his dander rising as he watched the man cowering before him in a chair that probably cost more than most people earn in a lifetime. Malachai recognized it as very like one he'd seen in Japan once. He imagined Tillinghurst had stolen it. Maybe from an art gallery somewhere.

Silence reigned in the opulent room. Malachai glowered and Tillinghurst sulked, and, Malachai presumed, Loretta was busy rooting around upstairs. He supposed she'd be all right up there. Tillinghurst wasn't a trusting sort of man; he probably hadn't enlisted his household help with his vicious scheme. The fewer people in on his wickedness, the fewer there were to turn on him when he was cornered.

He didn't know how long they sat there, but it was several minutes before Tillinghurst became restless and stirred in his chair. "Look here, Quarles, this is ridiculous. Why don't I simply tell you where you can find your men. I had planned to release them as soon as I'd made . . . er . . . arrangements."

"I'll bet."

"It's true. I don't want to hurt anyone. I only wanted the rewards of my own efforts."

Malachai could hardly believe his eyes, when Tillinghurst's expression altered from one of defeat to one of self-righteous indignation. "*Your* efforts?"

"My money, then." Tillinghurst sniffed significantly. "You want to make a profit from our venture, too, don't you? Why don't we go into partnership?"

"We already did that," Malachai pointed out grimly. "It didn't turn out so well."

"That's only because I . . ." He paused, presumably to think up an excuse to explain his perfidy.

"Yes?"

"I didn't know you were an intelligent businessman."

"Insulting me isn't likely to win me over to your
side, you know."

"It wasn't an insult!" Tillinghurst sat up straight
and tried to look dignified. Since he was clad in
dressing gown and slippers and had been caught
out in a crime, the effort wasn't too successful. "You
said yourself that no one would have figured you
for an astute businessman."

"Huh."

"But, see here, Quarles, we can go into business
together long-term. You can see for yourself that I
know how to make money." He swept his arm out
in a gesture meant to indicate his lavish estate.

"I do, too, and I don't have to worry about the
police taking it all away from me and locking me in
jail."

"That's nonsense." Tillinghurst's cheeks flamed
again. "I have most of San Francisco's politicians in
my pocket."

"That won't get you far when news of your nefarious activities makes it into the newspapers. The
politicians will trip over each other trying to distance themselves from you."

The shaft hit, and Tillinghurst winced. "It doesn't
have to be like that," he said without conviction.

"My sentiments exactly."

Their conversation ended abruptly when a series
of gunshots shattered the quiet of the day.

So far, Loretta hadn't encountered any maids to
question or footmen to avoid. She hadn't found
any treasure, either. In fact, she was muttering to

herself in frustration as she opened door after door, gathering her courage in both hands each time, only to find nothing but boxes, packed and ready to be sent somewhere. She wondered where. She also considered this exercise a considerable waste of good courage.

"I know he's the one," she grumbled. "But where is the cursed loot?"

Muffled voices came from the other wing of the house. Loretta presumed Mr. Tillinghurst's staff, having finished in this wing, were now packing the other one. Curse it, she couldn't very well walk over there and ask his minions if they'd packed up any stolen treasure, could she? Even if she managed to couch her question in more subtle terms, she doubted that the maids and footmen were in on the game.

Borrowing an epithet from one of her best friends, she muttered, "Bloody hell."

Her heart nearly flew out of her mouth when she heard gunshots rip through the air.

"Malachai!"

Her feet racing to catch up with her heart, Loretta fumbled in her handbag as she ran down the hallway to the staircase. As she rounded a corner, she saw the maids she'd previously envisioned, charging toward the staircase from the other wing.

Loretta beat them to it. She had just managed to disentangle her Chinese knife from her handkerchief—and why she hadn't thought to bring a revolver, she'd never know—when she came to the head of the stairs. Before she could lift her head or determine her precise bearings, somebody running upstairs from below hurtled into

her, slamming her against the far wall of the hallway.

She screamed, sure she was a dead woman.

A man cried, "Oof! Agh!"

And then she heard Malachai's cherished voice.
*"Loretta, God damn it, what the devil are you doing
now?"*

Tears sprang to her eyes with the knowledge that
Malachai hadn't been the recipient of any of those
shots she'd heard. She whispered, "Thank God."

And then she saw William Frederick Tillinghurst
stagger away from her. His eyes bulged from his
bony, pasty face. His mouth formed an incredulous
"O."

Then her eyes took in the fact that his hands had
flown to the hilt of a Chinese ceremonial knife that
was sticking out of his dressing gown at about stomach level. Even as she watched in horror, she saw
thick red blood ooze over the fabric and onto his
hands and begin a relentless drip, drip, drip onto
the hall carpet.

"Loretta!"

Malachai's voice had come closer, and she realized he'd pounded up the stairs after Tillinghurst.
His huge hands grabbed his partner's shoulders before Tillinghurst could fall backward downstairs.

Loretta said, "Malachai?" in a voice she didn't
recognize as her own.

"Loretta!" Malachai thrust Tillinghurst aside as if
he'd been a sack of potatoes instead of a man, and
he reached for Loretta.

And then the world went black.

EIGHTEEN

"She fainted?" Marjorie MacTavish's green eyes fairly popped from their sockets.

"She fainted."

"Sweet Jesus, have mercy," whispered Marjorie.

Loretta glanced from Marjorie to Malachai, not liking the note of disbelief in Marjorie's voice and actively resenting the jubilance she heard in Malachai's. "For heaven's sake, I'd just stabbed a man," she snapped. "It was a shocking thing to do, even if I didn't do it on purpose."

Jason laughed. "What was it you didn't do on purpose? Stab the fellow or faint?"

She felt heat creep into her cheeks. "Both."

At the moment she was residing indecorously on Malachai's lap with his arms firmly around her, and the four of them, along with several representatives of San Francisco's police department, were gathered in William Frederick Tillinghurst's front parlor. Tillinghurst himself, after having been examined by Jason and pronounced able to travel once his wound had been stitched and bandaged, was on his way to the jail ward of the hospital.

Other representatives from the police department were in the process of interviewing Mr. Derrick Peavey—Loretta feared they wouldn't get

much information of a useful nature out of him—
and Mr. Percival Jones. Mr. Jones seemed a
clear-headed individual, so they would probably
all know exactly what had happened soon.

Loretta squirmed slightly. She didn't really want
Malachai to shove her off his lap, but she was conscious of the indelicacy of their situation. She
wished she wasn't, as she was a modern young
woman, and modern young women weren't supposed to be embarrassed by public displays of
affection, but she was anyway. Her feelings didn't
matter, however, since Malachai seemed to have no
inclination to release her. She repressed the urge to
snuggle into him.

"So you were right and all." Marjorie still
sounded disbelieving. "Whoever would credit it?"

Loretta sniffed. "Anyone with half a brain."

"I've got an entire brain, and I didn't believe
you," Jason pointed out. "Tillinghurst has been one
of San Francisco's leading citizens for years."

"Leading?" This time Loretta snorted. "He's one
of the richest, but do you honestly believe him to
have been a leader?"

Jason and Marjorie exchanged a glance, and
Jason said, "Uh . . ."

Fired up now, Loretta declared vehemently, "He
was a scoundrel and a beast who ran sweatshops
and oppressed his workers, particularly the women
who worked for him. Anybody who does that isn't
any kind of leader, in my book. And, what's more,
if a man is dishonest and despicable in that way, he
certainly can't be above committing other crimes."

This time, it was Malachai and Jason who exchanged a glance. She elbowed Malachai in his
tummy. She didn't do it hard, because she wanted

to remain on his lap, but she made sure he felt it. He let out a startled whuff, so she was satisfied.

"Did they find the missing artifacts?" Marjorie asked quickly, as if hoping to avert all-out war.

Malachai tackled this one before Loretta had drawn breath. "Some of them, at least. I don't know yet if they've recovered all of them. I'm pretty sure Tillinghurst sold some of the more valuable items—"

"The rat," Loretta interrupted, believing Malachai's narrative to be a trifle lacking in colorful commentary.

With a grin, Malachai went on. "Right. Anyhow, I think Jones is helping the police take an inventory. He was locked in the room where Tillinghurst had stashed the stuff. We won't know for sure what's there and what isn't until we compare this inventory with the master list."

"Why did he keep it here on his estate?" Jason wanted to know. "It seems a rather foolish hiding place to me."

"Humph," snorted Loretta before Malachai could go on. "Mr. Tillinghurst doesn't trust anyone, and I think he liked to keep his ill-gotten gains close at hand so that he could gloat over them."

"You're making the man out to be a villain in a Gothic novel, Loretta. He isna *that* gormless, surely."

Malachai preempted Loretta's rebuttal. "I don't know about that, Miss MacTavish—"

"Whatever gormless means," Jason thrust in. Marjorie frowned at him.

After chuckling, Malachai went on, "From everything I've learned so far, I believe he was planning to stow most of the stolen loot elsewhere, but something went wrong and he didn't get the chance. I know for certain that he didn't anticipate that the original theft would be witnessed by two of my sailors. He reacted by having them kidnaped, although I doubt he'd have done that if he'd considered the matter longer. No one would have connected the thieves to him, as long as they weren't caught. And then when Peavey escaped, his nerves started to go. He's not a brave man."

"Seems to me he went into the wrong business, then," said Loretta with another significant sniff. "A criminal ought to be fearless. Or stupid. And as much as I detest the man, I know he's not stupid."

"No, he's not," agreed Malachai. "Until now, he's done very well for himself, both legally and illegally—"

Naturally, Loretta couldn't let that pass by without comment. "Even his legal activities are immoral."

A short pause preceded Malachai's, "Right. At any rate, both his legal and his illegal careers are over now."

"What will happen to his businesses?" Jason said. "This might throw a lot of people out of work. Even if it's lousy work, they probably need their wages."

"Oh, my!" Loretta struggled to sit upright. Losing the battle against Malachai's greater strength, she nevertheless kept on subject. "I hadn't thought about that, Jason, but you're right. I shall take care of them."

"You?" Malachai stopped her elbow on its way to his stomach by catching its sharp point in a big hand. "How the devil are you going to take care of them?"

She shrugged. "Why, I shall take over his businesses, of course. Buy him out, if necessary. I'm

sure my father will assist me with the details." A trifle disgruntled, she added, "He'll probably be glad
to think that I'm turning my energies away from social causes and onto the pathway of business,
although I'm sure he won't like it that I aim to run
the businesses according to modern, enlightened
precepts. And by myself. But he'll be wrong. I shall
right the evils Mr. Tillinghurst perpetrated while
at the same time proving that a woman can be a
sound businessman . . . er . . . businesswoman."

"Lord God protect us all," muttered Marjorie.

"He'll have to," Jason said with a laugh. "With
Loretta at the helm, those poor workers will need
all the mercy they can get."

"Jason!" Loretta hated when her friends laughed
at her. She didn't have time to berate him, because
the sergeant of police entered the parlor at that
point to question them.

Loretta was pleased to explain herself. She perse-
vered even in the face of the sergeant's astonished
cries and questions.

Loretta thought she could get used to being in
bed with Malachai. In fact, the notion was quite
comforting. And exciting. It was the excitement
that claimed her now.

"I was afraid he'd shot you when I heard all that
gunfire," she said, stroking his ear and fingering his
earring. It was quite dashing, that earring. Loretta
hoped he wouldn't stop wearing it once he left the
seafaring life for settled calm in San Francisco.

Malachai paused in his ministrations to her body.
They'd thrown off their clothes as soon as the door
closed behind them and they fell onto Loretta's

bed, leaving Jason and Marjorie belowstairs and shocked. Well, Marjorie had been shocked. Loretta doubted that Jason was, since he knew her so well. "How the devil could he shoot me? He wasn't armed."

"I didn't know that."

She didn't look, but she was pretty sure he was rolling his eyes. "He was in his dressing gown, for God's sake."

"Well, he might have had a derringer."

"Jones told me that it was some of Tillinghurst's men who were trying to escape who'd started shooting at the police. No one was hurt."

"That's a silly thing to do. It would be bad enough to be caught in the perpetration of a theft. But if a fellow actually shot a policeman—"

"Shut up, Loretta." To assure himself that she would follow his command, he covered her mouth with his.

Loretta gave herself up to the marvelous sensations he elicited from her body. She particularly loved his hands on her breasts. When he caressed her nipples, such a bolt of lust shot through her, she wasn't sure she could contain herself. Then she decided she didn't need to.

"Oh, Malachai!" she cried, and with a lunge she wrapped her legs around his and climbed on top of him. She didn't even object to his knowing grin.

"You like that, do you?" he asked smugly.

"Yes," she said. "And so do you." To prove it, she reached for his long, hard, silky shaft and derived great pleasure from his moan of delight and the drifting shut of his eyelids. His hands closed over her buttocks, and he guided her to where they could do each other the most good.

Before meeting Malachai, Loretta had attempted by various means to learn about the sex act, but she'd never quite envisioned anything like this. She hadn't believed it would be so wonderful. When she felt her dark wetness slide over him, she imagined herself as a pagan princess. And when she rode him, his hands on her buttocks guiding her, and when he lifted himself so that he could feast upon her breasts, she thought that life couldn't get much sweeter than this.

"God, Loretta, you feel so good."

Yes, by gum, she did, although she sensed he meant something else by his comment. Throwing her head back, her hair streaming over her shoulders like a silky veil, she gave herself up to the sensation of being gloriously, absolutely, and completely loved. Since she was on top, she also felt a good deal of control for a few moments. Then, when the pressure began building to a heated climax, and when Malachai, with a mighty heave, turned her over with him on top, she guessed the feeling had been illusory. And she didn't even care.

"God, you're wonderful, Loretta," Malachai mumbled into her ear.

"So are you," she mumbled back.

And then everything in her exploded in a burst of pleasure so great, her body bucked both herself and Malachai up off the mattress. She hadn't known she had that much strength.

With a wild cry, Malachai joined her in completion with spasm after spasm of release.

They both lay on her bed panting like racehorses for several minutes afterward. Then, with a mighty groan of effort, Malachai turned onto his side, stroked her sweaty breasts and stomach, and grinned. "What say we visit the justice of the peace tomorrow, Loretta? You don't want a big ceremony any more than I do, do you?"

Exhausted and feeling utterly spent, Loretta couldn't bear the thought of having her peace interrupted. Therefore, she opted not to argue with him now. "Let's talk about it later." She was so tired, the words were slurry.

"All right, sweetheart. We'll decide later."

Bother. Right before she slipped into slumber, Loretta mentally smacked Malachai upside the head for continuing to deny her principles.

"What do you mean, you won't marry me?" Malachai hadn't exactly meant to bellow, but Loretta was such an exasperating woman, he couldn't help himself.

Loretta covered her ears with her hands. "Please, Malachai, there's no need to shout. I've told you before that I won't marry you. Why do you keep bringing up the subject? Why do you keep insisting I deny my principles?"

She looked good enough to eat this morning. He'd slept late, for the first time in a long time completely relaxed and without a worry in the world.

Last night, before he and she had returned to Loretta's house, they'd all accompanied the police to the station and signed various reports and on-site inventory lists. Malachai had made arrangements for the recovered artifacts to be locked away pending the final inventory. Then they'd taken care of Peavey and Jones, making sure the two men were safely bestowed in their respective hostelries.

The result of all this activity was that they hadn't

returned home until the early hours of the morning. Then Malachai and Loretta had left Jason and Marjorie to their own devices and gone upstairs where they'd made spectacular love.

And now the woman, standing before him in a peach brocade robe of Chinese design, with her gorgeous hair spilling down her back and her dark eyes bright and beautiful, was once more refusing to marry him. She drove him *crazy!*

Lowering his voice but not his intensity, he hissed, "Because your principles are insane!"

He snatched the hairbrush from her hand and turned her around. He'd been wanting to brush her hair since the moment he'd seen her in that damned soup kitchen.

"They are not," she said, indignant.

Her hair gleamed. Because he wanted to see it in the sunlight, he picked her up—she gasped in surprise, but he didn't care—and carried her to the window, where he flung the curtains aside. Ah, good. No fog. Late morning sunlight streamed in through the sparkling panes—Loretta's staff was good about keeping the windows washed—and brought out all the red and gold highlights in the thick dark mass.

"God, I love your hair," he said. Then he mentally chastised himself for using the word *love*. A man couldn't be too careful with that word around a woman.

Although, he thought suddenly, it probably didn't matter anymore. Not with Loretta. Hell, a man was supposed to love his wife, wasn't he? He opened his mouth, thinking to declare himself, but the words wouldn't come. They were too frightening for a man who had avoided entanglements for almost forty years to blithely fling around, even at the woman he wanted to marry.

"Thank you." She sounded sarcastic, although Malachai couldn't imagine why. "I still won't marry you."

"Dammit, why not?" He'd hollered again. Hell, the woman frustrated the daylights out of him!

"Because I believe in free love, and I won't violate my precepts for you or anyone else, Malachai Quarles." She hesitated for a second or two. "However, I should like us to continue to be lovers."

"That's something, anyhow," Malachai said scathingly.

"Yes, I quite like having you as a lover." And, turning into his arms, she proved it.

Various conflicting emotions sparred with each other in Malachai's breast as he strode away from Loretta's Russian Hill abode shortly after noon on the day after William Frederick Tillinghurst's arrest.

He was glad Tillinghurst had been caught. He wasn't glad that Loretta had been proved correct about him.

He was delighted that Loretta enjoyed the physical aspects of their relationship. If she didn't agree to marry him, he wasn't sure what he'd do, but he was very much afraid he'd lose his mind. What was left of it.

He was overjoyed that his men, Peavey and Jones, had been found and were safe and healthy. He wasn't sure what to do with them now. Sure, he knew they were grown men and grown men were supposed to be able to take care of themselves. And

Jones could. Peavey was another matter entirely. Malachai wasn't sure what the poor man would do now that Malachai was retiring from the treasure-recovery business. They'd been together for twenty years or more, and Peavey depended on him.

"Damn it," he muttered as he stormed along, scattering dithery old ladies and frightened young men as he went, "if she'd only agree to marry me, Peavey could work in our home. I could find something for him to do."

Of course, since Malachai aimed to set up house-keeping in San Francisco, Loretta or no Loretta, he supposed Peavey could still work in his home.

The notion of setting up a bachelor establishment in the same city in which Loretta lived gave him a cold, achy feeling in his chest. He thumped on it a couple of times in an effort to make the pain go away. He succeeded in startling a young Chinese man so badly, he fell off his bicycle. Absently, Malachai bent and plucked him off the pavement with one hand, righted the bicycle with another, said, "Careful there, man," and walked on.

There had to be a way to get her to marry him. Malachai, not accustomed to failing at things, pondered possibilities as he made his way to the Fairfield Hotel to see how Peavey was getting along. He'd meant to do so earlier, but Loretta had distracted him. The ache in his chest gave way to a brief spate of delicious remembrance before kicking in again.

Curse the woman. And curse him, too. Why had he fallen for a damned feminist do-gooder?

The notion that he'd fallen for any woman stopped him in his tracks. He didn't stay stopped for long, but it was sufficiently long enough for a young mother to panic, snatch her son up from the walkway, and dart off in the opposite direction. Malachai stared after her, frowning, and decided that was the reason, right there, in the form of that obviously weak-minded woman and her sailor-suited son.

Loretta wouldn't be frightened by the sight of a large man standing still in front of her. If such a thing happened in *Loretta*'s vicinity, she'd just shove him aside, or try to. And she'd never dress a son in so silly an outfit as that blue-and-white sailor suit. Or allow the lad to run around with his golden curls long enough for him to be mistaken for a girl. God bless the woman, Malachai didn't know how he'd survived this long without her.

It was a dismal certainty in his mind that he'd have a hard time surviving without her now that he'd found her. What a calamity! He, Malachai Quarles, a man who'd survived an orphanage, life on the streets, and twenty-five years at sea, had been laid low by a woman. He shook his head, marveling at how the mighty had been felled—and not by a sweet-tempered, empty-headed blonde, either. He'd been singularly unimpressed by all the females of that description he'd met over the years.

He sighed lustily, sending a young lad who had been sweeping the sidewalk scuttling inside the store he worked for. Deciding he could use a cigar, Malachai swerved into the same store.

"What the devil are you doing cowering there behind the counter?" he demanded of the lad, who peeked out at him with huge, alarmed blue eyes.

"N-nothing, sir," the boy stammered.

"Then pick yourself up and sell me one of those Havanas." Malachai pointed.

Trembling, the boy did as he'd been commanded, laid the cigar on the counter, and backed up against the shelves behind him. Malachai, concerned for the boy's nervous state, slapped a silver dollar on the counter next to the quarter for which he paid for the cigar. "Here, boy, get yourself something to eat." It was obvious to Malachai, if not to the store's owner, that the youngster helping him was shaking from fatigue and hunger.

The boy's quavery, "Th-thank you, sir," followed Malachai out onto the sidewalk again.

As much as he hated to acknowledge it, he guessed Loretta was right about the general lack of caring demonstrated by San Francisco's business community, if that pathetic child was anything by which to judge. Malachai couldn't imagine employing a boy like that and not making sure he was fed properly.

"Hell, I suppose I'll have to talk to her father," he grumbled, biting off the end of the cigar since he didn't have his cigar-clipper with him. He spat the end into the street, causing a milk-wagon driver to pull his steed up abruptly.

Malachai glared at the man. "Careful with that horse, man!" He hated seeing animals mistreated.

Animals and children. And women. The notion that a business partner of his had taken unfair advantage of his female employees galled Malachai. He ought to have seen Tillinghurst for the villain he was long before the truth had slapped him in the face. Any man who could abuse women and children was as foul a creature as lived on earth. Malachai had bitter experience with such, and he was ashamed that Tillinghurst's name should even remotely and in another context be linked with his.

But he'd take care of that problem.

Now, if he could only figure out how to take care of the problem of Loretta . . .

NINETEEN

Several weeks later, on a cool evening in early December, Loretta sat beside Malachai in her parents' large back parlor, listening to an ensemble that specialized in Baroque and early music. She and he sat in the second row, right next to her mother, who beamed upon them with myopic approval.

The room had been decorated in spectacular fashion, with tons of potted plants and flowers and yards of ribbon draped on the chairs that had been rented for the purpose. The chairs formed six rows that seated ten people each, and the people occupying them were dressed in the very latest modes, Loretta and her mother included.

Loretta hadn't known either of her parents to take an interest in early music before this. Or any other type of music, for that matter. She suspected they'd been influenced by reports of her relationship with Malachai and wanted to investigate it for themselves. She wondered if it had been Marjorie or Jason who'd spilled the beans.

Squinting around the room, sans spectacles, since she wanted to look good for Malachai, she couldn't make out expressions on anybody's faces, much less those of Jason or Marjorie who sat together in the back row. Drat her poor vision anyhow!

She could see Malachai perfectly. He seemed totally absorbed in the music. He would. Every time Loretta wanted to talk to him—well, scold him, really—for buying William Tillinghurst's businesses out from under her feet—*with* her father's blessing, naturally—he got involved in something else. The only thing *he* ever wanted to talk about was marriage, curse it.

Suddenly, she wondered if it had been Malachai himself who'd reported to her parents that she refused to marry him, even though they were lovers. She wouldn't put such a low scheme past him.

Squinting was making her feel slightly queasy— Loretta believed she'd picked up some kind of bug at the soup kitchen—so she opted to put on her spectacles. She fished them out of her small handbag and arranged the gold earpieces. Ah, that was better.

Being able to see clearly was a blessing. She supposed she ought to thank her lucky stars that someone had invented spectacles, even though she couldn't help but regret not having been endowed with clear vision to begin with. Such was life. And she really wanted to know how much Malachai had told to her father as he'd been stealing her businesses.

Leaning sideways and whispering in his ear while, at the same time, trying to appear as if she were interested in the music, she said, "Did you tell my father about us?" She settled back in her chair immediately, since she didn't want her mother poking at her to be still.

Her question caught his attention. His head whipped around and he stared at her. Leaning over in his turn, he whispered, "Do you think I'm crazy?

Or that I want to marry you at the barrel of a shot-gun?"

She frowned at him. Perhaps he hadn't been the one who'd let the cat out of the bag.

Catching her mother's sideways glance, Loretta settled back in her chair with a sigh. She believed she looked her best this evening, even if she was wearing her spectacles and didn't feel especially well.

She didn't usually wear black because she deemed it to be a boring color, but this ensemble had caught her fancy when she'd seen it in *Vogue*. She'd had her dressmaker sew it up for her. It was rather revealing, with a strapless black satin under-bodice with a straight skirt and an uneven hem that showed a good deal of ankle. Loretta felt a smug satisfaction in the fact that she could support a strapless under-bodice, being fully endowed in that area of her anatomy. It was one of her endowments that Malachai seemed especially fond of, what's more. The under-bodice was topped with a filmy black chiffon over-bodice with black silk edging and a black silk cummerbund. To top everything off, Loretta wore a black silk flower in her hair.

She felt both elegant and feminine, and she trusted Malachai judged her so, although they hadn't had a chance to speak before the music began. Jason's eyes had bulged when he'd seen her, and he'd let go of a low whistle, so she knew that at least one member of the opposite sex found her attractive—even if he might as well have been a brother to her.

She didn't think Marjorie had approved, but that was Marjorie. If Marjorie had her way, neither one of them would ever appear in public unless they were covered from top to toe. And they'd probably be wearing veils, like those Arabian Mussulman ladies did, as well.

In spite of her quirks, Marjorie looked quite well this evening, too, although her gown might as well have been a nun's habit compared to Loretta's. Still, Marjorie always looked good in green, and the dark, shimmery satin was particularly stunning with Marjorie's pale skin, hazel-green eyes, and bright red hair. Loretta was sure the poor woman was dying inside, no matter how good she looked, because Marjorie was always embarrassed to be noticed, and the gentlemen in the room were definitely eyeing her with approval.

Jason, Loretta observed with an inner grin, hadn't left her side. He was such an odd duck, Jason. Loretta couldn't understand why he didn't simply declare himself to Marjorie and be done with it. Of course, Marjorie would surely reject him without a second thought. Silly woman. Jason was a wonderful man, and she ought to appreciate him.

It was all ridiculous. If Loretta felt stronger, she might just speak to one or both of them about it. Along with her queasiness, however, she'd been visited by a strange lethargy of late. Loretta, who prided herself on her pep and energy, disapproved. But she was sure the malady, whatever it was, would go away soon. Loretta was never ill for long.

The music stopped, and Loretta's attention snapped back to the ensemble. She applauded politely, along with everyone else, although since they were all wearing gloves, the applause was muffled. Wryly, she thought about other musical evenings she'd attended at friends' houses, with Negro bands playing ragtime tunes, and everyone ungloved and happy. When *they* clapped, the band *knew* it was being appreciated.

However, she supposed one shouldn't expect people who played early Baroque music to anticipate thunderous ovations. The leader of the group, a gentleman named Joshua Pearlman, bowed low before the assembly.

Loretta wondered if the poor man had rented his shiny black suit. She knew from her friends that musicians as a group struggled mightily to be heard, rather like novelists struggled mightily to be published. And then, even if one were heard or published, there was no money in it. Perhaps she ought to put her money behind Mr. Pearlman's group. She'd met him earlier in the evening, and could tell he'd been taken with her.

"And now we will play music by Henry Purcell." He smiled at Malachai, who shifted uncomfortably. "We thought the piece would be appropriate, given Captain Quarles' recent triumphant recovery of lost Moorish and Spanish treasure. This is incidental music composed in 1695 to accompany a theatrical play called *Abdelazer,* or *The Moor's Revenge.*"

Loretta slapped a hand over her mouth and turned to stare at Malachai, who gave a visible start, clearly as surprised as she. She couldn't help it when she began to giggle. Striving manfully—or womanfully—to stifle her amusement, she refocused her attention on Mr. Pearlman, who was gazing at her with a bruised-lamb expression on his sensitive face. She vowed to herself that she would apologize to him as soon as possible and explain why she'd been so diverted by the title of the piece.

Then she'd throw some money at him; money seemed to be the universal salve.

Abdelazer was a lovely bit of music. Loretta, who had been forced to take piano lessons as a girl, but who had successfully resisted acquiring the skill, appreciated it. She applauded lustily when it came to an end, silently cursing her gloves.

Mr. Pearlman bowed, thanked everyone for their attention, gestured at his small band of musicians, all of whom stood and bowed, there was more applause, and then the assembly broke up. Refreshments were being served in the front parlor and the dining room. Loretta attached herself to Malachai.

"The Moor's Revenge," she said, "fancy that!"

"Funny coincidence," he acknowledged, his gold earring glinting in the light from the overhead electrical lamps. Loretta loved that earring, although she wasn't sure why: perhaps because it singled Malachai out as different from the general run-of-the-mill gentleman. Not that he needed it. His sheer size and exotic, weatherbeaten demeanor did that even without the earring.

She realized her mother was scurrying after her, trying to catch up with the two of them and she stopped attempting to think. Lately, her thought processes had been muddled anyhow. She tugged at Malachai's arm to get him to slow down. "Mother wants to talk to us," she said, hoping she was wrong.

Without even a groan or a sigh, Malachai stopped walking, turned, and smiled politely at Mrs. Linden, proving to Loretta once again that he could behave like a gentleman when he wanted to, even though he wasn't really one inside. Perhaps that was why she loved him so much. "Beautiful music, Mrs. Linden."

"It was, wasn't it. I particularly asked them to play the last piece." Mrs. Linden, not built for rushing, pressed a hand over her thumping heart. "I thought the title was so appropriate, didn't you?"

"Indeed, it was." Malachai's smile made Loretta's own heart flutter like a hummingbird. She suspected even her mother was affected by all those large white teeth against that swarthy, sun-bronzed face. In an earlier age, Malachai should have been a pirate.

Taking her mother's arm, Loretta leaned into the woman, as if to impart a confidence. Her mother always loved it when Loretta acted like a normal daughter. "Did you know that Captain Quarles' ship is *The Moor's Revenge,* Mother?"

Mrs. Linden gasped. "No! Is it really? I had no idea!"

Loretta was proud of Malachai for not pointing out that his ship's name had been printed in every single newspaper in San Francisco for weeks and weeks and weeks. She didn't do it, either. She knew her mother was adept at avoiding newspapers, except for the society columns. She memorized those, or so it seemed to Loretta.

"I thought that was the reason you'd asked for the Purcell piece," she said.

Her mother blinked at her. "Oh, no, dear. I just saw the word *Moor* in the title and thought it would be nice if they played it."

The corner of Malachai's mouth twitched, but he didn't laugh. "You were correct, Mrs. Linden," was all he said.

"You certainly were," agreed Loretta, not quite as successful as he at repressing her humor.

"I have something that I think will be fun for us as we take our refreshments, dear," Mrs. Linden said with a confidential giggle.

Oh, dear. Loretta didn't quite trust her mother's idea of "fun." "Oh?" she said. "What might that be?"

Her mother glanced around, as if ascertaining that no one else could overhear. "A Ouija Board."

Loretta's mouth fell open. "A *what?*" Never, in all her days, had she envisioned her mother enjoying anything as frivolous as a Ouija Board. Not that her mother wasn't frivolous, because she was; but formerly, Mrs. Linden wouldn't have dared bring such a thing in the house for fear of Mr. Linden's scorn. There wasn't an iota of fancy or imagination in Mr. Linden.

Mrs. Linden patted Loretta's arm frantically. "Don't yell, dear. It's a Ouija Board. Mrs. Phillips brought it over, so your father can't laugh at us. He wouldn't dare be ugly to Mrs. Phillips."

Loretta couldn't help herself. She started to laugh.

"Who's Mrs. Phillips?" Malachai asked, in what passed, from him, as a whisper.

Struggling to control herself—her mother was looking at her in hurt disapproval—Loretta stammered, "M-Mr. Phillips owns th-the b-b-bank!" She hooted and slapped a hand over her mouth.

"Loretta!"

"I'll just take her out here until she stops laughing," Malachai said to Mrs. Linden. He shoved open one of the French windows leading out to a balcony and dragged Loretta outside with him, leaving Mrs. Linden in the hallway, looking after them with a puzzled frown on her vague, pretty face.

Fog curled around the white wrought-iron bars holding the railing up, and the nippy early-December air made Loretta feel slightly less queasy. "Oh, my, I'm sorry. My poor mother."

"She has a lot to put up with," Malachai agreed.

Although her tummy had settled, Loretta's disposition was as volatile as ever. Rubbing her arms, she turned on Malachai. "And exactly what do you mean by that? I know my parents disapprove of—"

He shut her up in the way that had become customary for him in the past several weeks, by grabbing and kissing her. It worked every time, even though Loretta felt as though she'd let her side down from time to time. Still, she leaned into his kiss, knowing as she did so that she loved and adored this man now and would undoubtedly do so forever, thereby ruining her life, because he'd surely tire of her one of these days. But at least he hadn't yet.

When they finally drew apart, both were panting slightly, and Loretta, at least, was happy. "Oh, my," she whispered. "I'm quite warm now."

He chuckled. "Me, too."

She gazed up at him with wonder. Of all the unlikely things to happen, she thought, the notion that Malachai Quarles had become her lover was perhaps the unlikeliest. He looked startlingly handsome this evening, in his black tails and pristine white shirt. He looked like a pirate who'd left the sea in order to toy with society for a little while and who would return to his nefarious activities as soon as he'd had his fill of wine and women. And he was

hers. At least for a little while. She sighed content-
edly.

He took her by the shoulders and looked down
into her eyes. She sighed again, only this sigh
wasn't one of contentment.

"Listen to me, Loretta Linden. We need to get
married. It's no good, just being lovers. You *have* to
marry me."

"I don't want to talk about it, Malachai," she said
wearily. "Not tonight. I don't feel well enough."

She *had* felt well, until he'd brought up the M
word. All of a sudden, her tummy began to feel
funny again. Pooh.

His brows drew down into a deep V. "What do you
mean, you don't feel well? Why the hell didn't you
tell me?" He took her arm and dragged her toward
the French window. "Do you need a coat? What the
devil do you mean, wearing that thing if you don't
feel well? There's nothing to it, for God's sake!"

"It's the height of fashion!" Loretta cried, her
feelings wounded, digging in her heels and clinging to the balcony railing. "I hoped you'd like it."

He pulled on her arm. She clung to the railing.
"I'll like it better when you take it off, but you have
no business being out here in the cold when you're
wearing next to nothing!"

"Stop pulling on me!" Loretta implored. "I'm
fine. Really. I—Oof!" Malachai lifted her in his
strong arms and put her down on the hall carpet as
he kicked the window shut.

Since she found herself looking directly into the
startled face of Joshua Pearlman, she smiled
brightly as she patted her gown, which had become
ruffled as Malachai carried her. "Mr. Pearlman!"

He backed up a pace and tugged at his evening jacket. "Miss Linden."

Having had lots of practice, although not for quite a while, Loretta batted her eyelashes at the musician. "Your music was simply wonderful, Mr. Pearlman. I so enjoyed it." Recalling that she owed him an apology, she opened her mouth, but didn't get to use the air she sucked in.

"Pearlman," said Malachai who, Loretta realized, had loomed up behind her. "Enjoyed the concert. My ship's *The Moor's Revenge,* you know. That's why Miss Linden laughed back there. She didn't know you were going to play that one."

Joshua Pearlman seemed to shrink in front of Loretta's eyes. Odd how that happened so often when her friends met Malachai. The only male friend to whom she'd introduced him who seemed unaffected by his imposing presence was Jason.

"Er . . . thank you," Pearlman stammered. "Er . . . must be getting along now. Refreshments, and all that." He turned, gestured to his musical associates, and they all slunk past Malachai and hurried down the hallway.

A young female violinist peered back over her shoulder. Loretta frowned, knowing the woman was eyeing Malachai. Drat her. Loretta knew from experience with her friends that you couldn't trust musicians, who tended to be eccentric and immoral. Or so she'd been told, although perhaps the commentary had been intended for ragtime musicians and not those of the classical persuasion.

"What the devil's wrong with him?" Malachai demanded, staring after the retreating early-music ensemble.

"You frighten people, Malachai. I think it's your eyebrows. And your size, of course."

His gaze whipped from the musicians to her, and Loretta saw that she'd diverted him from concerns about marriage or her health. She patted his arm and took it in both of her hands. "Come along now, dear. Let's eat something."

The notion of food made her stomach pitch unpleasantly, but she knew that Malachai needed lots of food in order to maintain his magnificent physique.

When they entered the front parlor, Loretta saw that Mrs. Phillips and her mother had already set up the Ouija Board. Jason and Marjorie were looking on, and Loretta noticed that Marjorie didn't appear disapproving for once. She actually seemed interested.

Glancing at the door to the dining room and deciding she didn't want to face all the food laid out in there, she said to Malachai, "Why don't you go fill yourself a plate. I want to see the famous Ouija Board."

"Huh. I've heard of them, but never seen one before."

"Some of my friends enjoy working with them, although I'm not sure I believe that one can actually communicate with the spirits through them."

The look he gave her told Loretta that he didn't believe it, either, and that he harbored no doubts on the matter. "You want something to eat?"

Pressing a hand to her cummerbund, Loretta wrinkled her nose. "Not yet. I picked up a bug at the soup kitchen and haven't felt much like eating lately."

He leaned down and stared directly into her eyes. "Are you telling me the truth?" His voice was gruff.

Startled, she said, "Of course, I'm telling you the truth! Why would I lie about a bug?"

Straightening, he said, "I don't know." He hesitated for a moment, making Loretta wish she hadn't brought up the subject of a bug. "Are you sure you're well enough for this party? I'll take you home right now, if you want me to. I don't give a hang about parties."

How sweet he was sometimes, even though he'd hate it if she told him she thought so. She smiled up at him, glad she'd put on her spectacles since she could see his concerned expression clearly. "Thank you so much, Malachai, but I want to stay here and play with the Ouija Board."

"Well . . . if you're sure."

"I'm sure. Thank you."

For some inexplicable reason, Loretta's eyes filled with tears. Fortunately, Malachai had already turned around and started for the dining room and didn't witness her embarrassingly emotional reaction to his courtesy.

Giving herself a hard mental shake and telling herself to shape up, Loretta went to the group gathered around the Ouija Board. Marjorie looked up from her seat on a nearby chair and smiled at her. Jason, Loretta noticed, was hovering behind Marjorie's chair, looking as if he aimed to fight off any other man who tried to chat with Marjorie. Mrs. Linden nearly upended the board when she spotted Loretta and jumped to her feet.

"Loretta! This is such fun! Come here and try it. Mrs. Phillips is a perfect angel to direct everything for us."

Mrs. Phillips, a plump, gray-haired lady with a wide metaphysical streak, glanced up and said, "I'm not directing it, Dorothea. I'm only channeling the spirit." She spoke as if she meant it, so Loretta didn't giggle or grin.

Clasping her hands to her bosom, Mrs. Linden stepped aside. "Sit on the sofa, dear. Just put your fingers on that little triangular wooden thing—"

"The planchette," said Mrs. Phillips.

"Er . . . yes. The planchette." Mrs. Linden smiled upon Mrs. Phillips. To Loretta she added, "But don't press heavily. The spirit Mrs. Phillips brought up—"

"Princess Azizarozahata," purred Mrs. Phillips.

"Yes," concurred Mrs. Linden, nodding like a bobble-headed doll. "Princess Azizarozahata, who was an Egyptian—"

"Sumerian," muttered Mrs. Phillips.

"Yes. She was a Sumerian princess who had a disastrous love affair and was killed—"

"Thrown to the royal tigers," elucidated Mrs. Phillips. Loretta felt her nose wrinkling and stopped it at once.

"Yes, she was thrown to the royal tigers, and she's telling us all sorts of exciting things."

"It truly is entertaining," murmured Marjorie, whose cheeks had flushed a becoming pink, probably under the influence of Jason's continued presence.

"Come here, dear." Mrs. Linden gestured for Loretta to join her on the sofa, so Loretta humored her. She thought Ouija Boards were entertaining, if one didn't take them seriously. And she didn't, of course.

***

Malachai almost dropped his plate of food when he wandered into the parlor from the dining room and saw his beloved leaning over a table, her cleavage the focus of all masculine eyes. Damn them!

He gave the room a general all-purpose glower that succeeded in averting all gentlemanly eyes except those of Jason Abernathy, who grinned at him like an imp from behind Marjorie's chair. Malachai didn't resent Jason's knowing smirk too much; they were on the same side of the issue of marriage for Loretta and Malachai.

Since he knew better than to bellow at Loretta to sit up straight and stop making an exhibition of herself, he strolled over to the sofa, attempting to act casual. He had to fight the urge to rip his evening coat off and throw it over her shoulders. That outfit she wore was pretty, but it was damned distracting. Malachai didn't approve of it on the grounds that he preferred only himself to be distracted by Loretta's feminine attributes.

She noticed him and cried, "Oh, Malachai, this is such fun! We're just getting started." She sat up straight as she smiled at him, thus accomplishing the purpose Malachai's coat would have served, and without the accompanying hullabaloo.

"Huh," he said, and popped a shrimp into his mouth.

"I want to know if my daughter will ever marry," said Mrs. Linden with a twinkling frown for Loretta and a big grin for Malachai.

He stifled the impulse to roar at her that her damned daughter would be married right this minute if he had anything to say about it. Instead, he bit into a crab cake and smiled at her, hoping his temper didn't show.

"And I want to know if Loretta will e'er be a mother," said Marjorie in a soft voice that didn't sound at all like her usual one. Malachai chalked up the voice and the color in her cheeks to Jason's presence, and decided he wasn't the only one who had woman trouble. At least Loretta was his lover. As often as she could arrange it, bless her. Malachai doubted that Jason would ever succeed with Marjorie in any way whatsoever, the woman was such a stuffy prig. Marjorie went on, "I think she'd be a vurra fine mother."

"Marjorie!" Loretta's cheeks were pink now, too. Malachai looked upon them with interest. For a female who put so much stock in being modern and in casting aside society's rules and regulations, she sure got embarrassed easily.

"Oh, that's a good question, Marjorie," cried Mrs. Linden. "Ask the board if you'll have children, dear."

"Honestly," said Loretta, clearly peeved. But she asked the question. "Princess Azizarozahata, will I ever be a mother?"

The planchette zipped to the word "Yes" printed on the board, and parked itself.

"Oh, my!" Mrs. Linden clasped her hands to her bosom again. Malachai knew her well enough by this time to understand this as a sign of pleasure. He'd often observed that older females doted on their grandchildren. He, of course, had no first-hand experience of the phenomenon.

"A wee bairn," whispered Marjorie. Her hands were clasped at her bosom, too. Malachai guessed it was one of those . . . what did they call 'em . . . ? Universal female characteristics or something like that.

"Will it be a wee lad or a lassie?"

Loretta, her cheeks a deep cherry color now, said, "This is silly." Silly or not, though, she asked the question. "Will I have a girl or a boy, Princess Azizarozahata?"

The planchette seemed to quiver in the middle of the board and didn't move. Plucking a grape and popping it into his mouth, Malachai moved closer, interested in spite of himself. After all, they were talking about his progeny—or they'd better be.

"Choose one or the other," suggested Mrs. Phillips. "Perhaps the princess is confused."

"Good idea," said Loretta. "Princess, will I have a girl?"

The planchette zoomed to the "No."

"Oh." Loretta sounded disappointed, but she didn't have time to say anything, because the planchette then dashed to the "Yes." She was surprised when the planchette zipped again to the "No," then back to the "Yes." It continued to do this for three or four times before Loretta asked another question.

"I'm confused, Princess. Do you mean I'll have a boy?"

As if possessed, the planchette continued to zigzag across the board, hitting the "Yes," then bouncing over to the "No."

"Well then, I guess I'll have a girl?" Loretta sounded puzzled, understandably so, in Malachai's opinion.

The planchette continued its zigzag dance across the Ouija Board, Malachai looking on and nibbling on shrimps and crab cakes, Loretta squinting through her spectacles with a befuddled air.

This state of affairs continued for several seconds

until Marjorie suddenly gasped, clapped her hands to her cheeks, and cried out, "You canna mean you're having *twins!* Oh, my!"

The planchette zoomed to the "Yes," and stopped. Malachai, watching in fascination, fancied the little wooden triangle was panting from its exertion.

Then Marjorie's question and the board's answer struck him, and he dropped his plate. Fortunately, he'd consumed everything that had been resting thereon, and the carpet was a thick Turkish weave, so the plate didn't break. "You're *what?*" he roared.

Loretta gave a start and looked up at him. "Twins?" she whispered.

Mrs. Linden's surprised glance went from Loretta to Malachai and back again. The room went silent.

TWENTY

Without a care to propriety or anything else, Malachai took two long strides toward the Ouija Board, shoved Mrs. Phillips aside, reached across the table, and plucked Loretta up from the sofa. She squeaked in astonishment, but Malachai didn't stop to excuse or explain himself.

Carrying her in his arms, he marched them both through a frozen sea of surprised guests, out of the front parlor, and back to the French windows leading to the balcony. He kicked the windows open, marched outside, and kicked them shut again. Then he tore off his coat, threw it over Loretta's shoulders, and stood her on the balcony squarely in front of himself, his broad back shielding her from any eyes that might attempt to pry into their business.

He didn't let go, but leaned into her, bending down to stare straight into her eyes. Someone rattled the knob on the window, and he kicked back, hitting the door with his heel. Whoever it was went away. "Are you pregnant?"

She blinked up at him, as if he'd asked the question in ancient Sumerian. "Wha—wha—"

So he asked it again, enunciating clearly. "Are you pregnant?"

"P-pregnant? Why, I . . . I don't . . . I . . . don't know."

"You said you picked up a bug. What are your symptoms?"

Stammering, Loretta listed them. "Well . . . I've been very tired. A bit queasy. I feel a little sickish, especially in the morn—Oh, my God!" The light dawned, and her mouth dropped open.

"You are." Malachai turned a full circle, sucking in thick, foggy air, his insides boiling. "You are."

"I . . . I . . ." Loretta looked as though she might faint for the second time in her life if given the least little push to do so. "Maybe I am." Her voice almost wasn't there.

This was it. This was the final blow to Malachai's patience. He couldn't take any more. He stopped pacing in circles and stopped before Loretta. He put both hands on her shoulders. "Now see here, Loretta. I won't take any more nonsense from you. We're going to be married, and we're going to be married *now*."

"I . . . I . . ."

"I don't care if you have to violate every principle in your entire body, you're going to marry me!" He realized he was shouting and endeavored to lower his voice. It wasn't an easy thing to do. He expected an audience was gathering in the hallway.

"But . . ."

"No buts!" He bent down further and said in a harsh voice, "Do you have any idea how I grew up?"

He didn't really expect an answer, but she shook her head. "N-no. You never told me."

"Well, I'll tell you now." He took another deep, foggy breath. "I was a product of your precious damned *free love*, Loretta. I don't know who my mother was, and she probably didn't know who my father was, and I'm pretty damned sure he never even knew he had a son. I grew up in an orphanage, Loretta, succored by a herd of nuns who didn't care if I lived or died. It was hell, but it was better than dying on the streets, which is what would have happened if the nuns didn't run a charity orphanage and hadn't taken me in. I'll be *damned* if I'll allow any child of mine grow up like that."

Her mouth had formed a shocked O. "I didn't know . . ."

"It was *hell*, dammit, and it's the main reason I swore I'd never beget brats all over the world."

She gasped.

"And I won't beget bastards, either. No child of mine is going to grow up unloved and without knowing his parents. My children are going to bear my name, and I'm going to be their father, for as long as they live. And they'll *know* me. And *you*, my dear, are going to be my wife. Whether you want to be or not!" There. He'd said it, and he meant it.

"Oh, Malachai!"

You could have knocked Malachai over with a feather when she threw herself into his arms and burst into tears. Uneasy with this emotional display from a woman whom he knew to disdain such things, he held her closely and patted her shoulder, wondering if he'd been a trifle too harsh with her.

"I didn't know any of that," she sobbed. "You poor little boy. Oh, you poor, *poor* little boy!"

"Well, now, I'm not a little boy any longer," he said, embarrassed.

"No, but you were. I had no idea!"

He shrugged uncomfortably. "I made something

of myself in spite of my beginnings," he pointed out.

"But it must have been so *hard!*"

"Well . . . I guess it was kind of—"

"Oh, Malachai, I love you *so* much!"

She did? Malachai had suspected as much, but she'd never said it out loud before. It gave him a slushy, mushy feeling in his chest.

Before he could stop himself, he whispered, "I love you, too, Loretta." Again before he could stop himself, he added, "God help me."

For some reason, the knowledge that Malachai wanted to marry her because he'd had such a difficult childhood comforted Loretta when she realized she was going to violate her feminist, free-thinking standards. It didn't hurt that he'd admitted that he loved her, either.

There were two frilly white, wrought-iron chairs on the balcony. Malachai had pushed one of them against the French doors. He'd been sitting in that one, so that no one could interrupt their tête-à-tête, for several minutes, Loretta on his lap, before she managed to regain control of herself.

And that was another thing. She didn't mind being so emotional now that she knew it was due to her impending motherhood.

Motherhood! She was going to be a mother!

"Our children aren't going to be forced into specific roles, either, darling," she whispered into Malachai's lapel. She'd abandoned her spectacles, which now resided in Malachai's evening coat's pocket, and she'd probably ruined his clean white handkerchief by crying into it for so long. He didn't seem to care.

Malachai said, "Huh."

"I mean it," she said, trying to sound as if she really did mean it.

He gave her another "Huh." She got the feeling he wasn't quite as ardent about the role issue as she, probably because he was only glad he'd won his point at last and she'd agreed to marry him.

"If we have a little girl and she wants to play baseball and climb trees, we'll allow her to do it."

"That's fine by me." He nuzzled her hair. She had to push her black flower back into place, but she didn't mind.

"And if we have a little boy and he *doesn't* want to play baseball, we won't force him to do so."

He shrugged his large, comforting shoulders, and Loretta sighed. She really didn't feel up to delivering a lecture on the unfairness of stereotypical roles for men and women. It had been a rather trying evening, all things considered, although it looked as if it was going to end happily.

And they were going to be married! And she'd hardly had to sacrifice any of her principles to agree to it. After all, society being what it was, she couldn't honestly expect a child to survive without various hurtful neuroses if it had to fight the label "bastard" all its days, could she? Even Malachai, who was ever so levelheaded and practical, had suffered from having been the product of a mother who wasn't wed to his father. Loretta was as determined as Malachai that no child of hers would suffer unnecessarily.

"Are you fit to go back to the party?" Malachai asked gruffly.

She sighed again. "Do you really want to?"

"No, but I suppose we'd better mend some fences. We left sort of abruptly, and after an announcement that probably shocked your parents."

Loretta's conscience smote her. "Oh, dear. I suppose you're right, although it wasn't my fault that we left—" She couldn't finish blaming him, because he covered her mouth—not with this lips this time, but with his huge hand.

"I don't want to fight right now, Loretta. What I want to do is go back in there and announce to everyone that we're engaged to be married. Do you think you can keep from doing anything militant for ten minutes?"

She knew she should resent his phraseology, but she couldn't make herself do it. She also didn't want to go back to the party. She wanted to stay here, on Malachai's lap, with his strong, warm arms around her, for the rest of her life. Well . . . perhaps not that long.

It was a somewhat chilly but extremely nice night, even if it was foggy. But that was romantic, in an odd way. The outdoor electrical lamps were blurry smudges, and gray tendrils of mist curled around Malachai's feet. When she looked out over the grounds of her parents' estate, she saw what looked like a sea of grayish foam, out of which the tips of fir trees peeked, like the masts of a sunken galleon.

That made her think of her experience aboard the *Titanic*, and suddenly the night didn't seem so dreamy.

"Very well." She sighed yet again. "I suppose we do need to get back to the party. Poor Mother is probably beside herself."

The chair took that opportunity to groan

piteously, and Malachai dumped Loretta off his lap and stood up. He held onto her until she'd gained her balance. "Those chairs are damned uncomfortable." He squinted down at the offending piece of furniture. "I'm going to furnish our home with comfortable chairs."

"Our home," Loretta repeated, a modicum of dreaminess returning. "Do you want to build one? Or stay in my house? It's large enough for us and any number of sets of twins." She shrugged off his coat and handed it to him.

He struggled into it. Loretta noticed the wet spot on his lapel and reached up to brush at it, which didn't help any. "I'm sorry I got your coat wet."

Malachai squinted sideways, trying to see his lapel, then tugged to get the garment to fit properly. It was rather wrinkled. "Doesn't matter," he said. With narrowed eyes, he surveyed his beloved. "I think you'd better wash your face and powder your cheeks. You look like you've been crying."

She smiled. "I have been. But you're right. I'd probably better visit my old room before we brave the parents and guests." She took his arm.

He patted her hand where it rested on his arm and shoved aside the chair, which was listing to port. "As to where we'll live, let's talk about it later. I like your place, but we probably should discuss it. After all, we want to rear our children in the best possible surroundings."

Our children. A thrill went through Loretta. She tried not to let it show. "I think San Francisco is a good place to rear children," she murmured.

"San Francisco's a great place," agreed Malachai. "I don't want to move away from San Francisco."

They continued to discuss San Francisco's many

merits as Malachai opened the French windows, scanned the hall in both directions for interlopers, all of whom seemed to have given up and gone away, then led Loretta to the back staircase.

Fifteen minutes later, with Loretta's cheeks freshly powdered and her hair neatly rearranged, Malachai stepped aside to allow Loretta to precede him into the front parlor. Her eyes were still a little bit puffy, but they didn't look bad. This was especially true since they sparkled so brightly. She'd noticed them in her mirror, and had been pleased. Love truly did do wonders for one's looks. It helped, too, that she'd replaced her spectacles. The puffiness of her eyelids was hidden slightly behind her lenses.

As soon as she swept into the room, movement stopped and chatter ceased. Everyone in the entire parlor and in the dining room beyond stopped what they were doing and turned to stare at her and Malachai. Loretta felt herself heat up from embarrassment. She hesitated at the doorway until the comfort of Malachai's huge presence behind her bucked her up. There was nothing like a large man at one's back to give one courage—although she knew life shouldn't be like that.

At this moment, however, Loretta was willing to allow the world to fend for itself. She and Malachai had an announcement to make.

It was Jason who broke the spell. He'd been standing beside the fireplace with Marjorie, Joshua Pearlman, the lady violinist, and Mrs. Linden, who appeared upset. Almost as soon as the guests froze in shock at the advent of Loretta and Malachai into their midst, he lunged away from the fireplace and strode over to the parlor door. "There you are!" he said heartily, as if everything were normal. Taking their clue from him, most of the guests returned to their conversations.

"Here we are," Loretta said wryly. Her amusement at everyone's confusion was helping boost her self-confidence. "And we have an announcement." Under her breath, she added, "I'm sure you and Marjorie and Mother will be pleased with it, Jason, curse you all." She stuck out her tongue at her stand-in brother, then grinned to let him know she was happy in spite of her words.

Jason's eyes widened. "You mean . . . ?" He looked at Malachai, who nodded.

"She finally gave in," he said in his deep, grumbly, thundery voice. Loretta loved his voice.

"Well, I'll be damned." Jason took Malachai's hand and shook it vigorously. "Congratulations, old man! I'm very happy for both of you."

"Condolences might be more on the money," Malachai growled. Loretta smacked his arm, and he grinned, his white teeth against his tanned skin making her breath catch. She wondered if she'd ever get used to his masculine presence. She hoped not, because it was very exciting.

Before they could plan their announcement, Jason turned around, lifted his head and his arms, and clapped. He wore evening gloves, so the clap wasn't as effective as it might have been, but when he roared out, "Quiet, everyone! We have an announcement!" people paid attention.

Once more, chatter in the room stopped, and everyone turned to stare at Jason, Loretta, and Malachai. Jason stepped aside with a sweeping gesture of his arm. "I'll let these two tell it."

Malachai stepped into the breech as if he'd been born to command. Which, come to think of it, he might well have been. She wouldn't be surprised if he'd been fathered by some adventurous sea captain somewhere.

"Miss Linden and I are engaged to be married," he said without preamble. Their audience gasped.

"He doesn't mince words, does he?" Jason whispered in Loretta's ear.

"No, he doesn't, thank God."

"Engaged?" Loretta's father blinked and peered around the room. Loretta suspected he was trying to find his wife, whom he always expected to handle the family's social emergencies.

"Engaged?" This was a squeal, and it came from Loretta's mother, thereby aiding her father in his quest. She helped him further by breaking away from the group she'd been with and hurrying up to her daughter, her arms held wide. "Oh, Loretta! I'm so *happy!*"

Loretta felt silly when her mother threw herself at her. Fortunately, Malachai still stood at her back, so he could both brace and embrace the both of them.

And then the onslaught began. Loretta's father, elbowing people out of his way, charged at them, removed his wife from where she clung to Loretta, and embraced his daughter in a hug the likes of which Loretta hadn't experienced since she was a little girl. It almost made her cry again to see how happy her parents were. She was glad she'd made them happy, even if it did mean her own marriage.

She had a feeling she wasn't going to mind being married to Malachai, though. Not one little bit.

* * *

Malachai sighed with contentment, cupped his hands behind his head, and sank back against the pillows Loretta had thoughtfully propped up against the headboard. "That didn't turn out as bad as I'd feared it would."

She snuggled against him, running her fingers through his thick chest hairs. "What didn't? The announcement or the lovemaking?"

He peered down at her tousled head and wondered if she was joking. His darling wasn't a very ardent jokesmith, so he presumed she was serious, although he couldn't fathom how there could be any doubt about the lovemaking. "The announcement."

She snuggled closer. "Ah. I thought that's what you meant."

"Your parents aren't going to be disappointed that we won't be having a big wedding, are they?"

"Good heavens, no! They're so happy I'm finally getting married, they wouldn't care if we eloped."

Malachai felt his eyebrows lift. "Now there's a good idea.

Loretta didn't speak for a minute, then said slowly, as if still mulling the matter over, "You know, Malachai, that's not a bad idea."

"Huh?"

"If we eloped, it would save a lot of fuss, wouldn't it? I mean, my parents are socially prominent and you're the famous Captain Quarles of *The Moor's Revenge*. If we got married in the regular way, not only would it take time to arrange, but there would be a lot of publicity, and I know you hate publicity." She smiled sweetly up at him. "I think it would be fun."

He grunted. "You only want to elope so you can

get married without being considered conventional."

"Pooh."

Nevertheless, at noon the next day, Captain Malachai Quarles and Loretta Linden were united in holy matrimony by a justice of the peace at San Francisco's Municipal Courthouse without any fanfare, and with Dr. Jason Abernathy and Miss Marjorie MacTavish in attendance as witnesses.

A month later, Mr. and Mrs. Linden hosted a grand ball in their honor. All the best people came. William Frederick Tillinghurst's name wasn't mentioned once. Malachai thought wryly that it was as if San Francisco society was embarrassed that it had once clasped Tillinghurst to its bosom and now intended to pretend he'd never existed.

September, 1915

"Damn you, Malachai Quarles!" A hideous scream followed this bellowed profanity.

Malachai, who was pacing in the reception hall, directly at the foot of the staircase leading up to the bedrooms in his and Loretta's huge Lombard Street mansion, winced as if he were a cringing coward rather than a rough-and-ready sea captain (retired). Derrick Peavey, Loretta and Malachai Quarles' somewhat vague footman, looking fairly seedy in his brand-new uniform, blinked and stared up the stairs, his mouth agape.

"Dinna worry, Captain Quarles," Marjorie said in a soft, understanding voice. "It's only Loretta."

"But she's in pain," Malachai whimpered.

Marjorie laughed. Malachai didn't appreciate

her laugh one bit. "It's normal, though. Ever since the fall, you know, God decreed that women would give birth in pain."

Still pacing, Malachai grumbled, "Stinking plan, if you ask me."

Given Marjorie's conventional predilections, Malachai wouldn't have been surprised to have received a reprimand from the woman. Instead she laughed again. He'd rather have been scolded.

This was awful. It was nerve-wracking. It was the most God-awful, miserable, frightening, panic-inducing—

"*Owwwwwww!*" came from upstairs.

Malachai clamped his teeth together. His head ached from grinding them so hard for so long. He didn't care. Loretta was in pain. And it was all his fault.

"*Aaaaaaagh!*"

"I can't take too much more of this," Malachai growled.

Loretta shrieked again, and he lost his composure completely. With a bound, he started up the stairs.

Marjorie jumped to her feet. "Captain, please! Leave Dr. Abernathy to contend with her by himself. He canna want another patient to deal with. Loretta's plenty enough all by hersel'." As if inspired, she added the one thing that might have stayed Malachai's progress. "Think of the bairn, Captain."

He paused halfway up the staircase. "The bairn," he whispered. "But it's the bairns. At least, we think it is. Are." He rubbed a hand over his stubbly face. "She was huge. Oh, God."

But he slowly came back downstairs.

Twenty minutes later, when he was on the verge of total nervous collapse, he heard an upstairs door open. Racing to the foot of the staircase, he gazed upward, praying that everything was all right up there. He hadn't heard a scream or a curse word for at least five minutes, and his nerves were jumping like water on a hot skillet.

"I'm sure it's all right, Captain," murmured Marjorie.

Derrick Peavey, for whom all this noise and nervousness had been a trifle too much, cowered in a chair against the far wall of the hall.

The maids, Molly and Li, crept into the room from the kitchen, where they'd been preparing sandwiches and coffee, at Dr. Abernathy's instructions. Malachai glanced at them, but didn't speak. Ever since Loretta informed him that the staff of their house was afraid of him, he'd been trying to be less gruff in his dealings with people. He'd discovered that housemaids and housekeepers, unlike sailors, didn't take it as natural when he hollered at them.

Suddenly, Jason Abernathy appeared at the head of the staircase, grinning down upon the assembly like a mischievous imp, if imps grew to six feet. "Relax, Quarles," he said. "Everything's fine."

Malachai couldn't relax. "What is it? Are they? Loretta?"

Chuckling, Jason said, "Loretta's fine." He started down the staircase. "She's not too happy with you at the moment, but she's fine."

Behind him, Malachai heard Marjorie say, "And the bairn?"

"Make that two bairns," Jason said.

He reached the foot of the stairs and held out his hand for Malachai to shake. Malachai's innards were in too much of a turmoil to respond properly, so Jason grabbed the hand dangling limply at his side and shook it without his help. "Congratulations, Captain, you're now the father of a fine, healthy boy and a fine, healthy girl. And, if I may be allowed an opinion on the matter, both of them are beautiful."

"It *was* twins," whispered Malachai, stunned. "Twins. *Twins!*"

Shoving Jason out of the way, he took the stairs three at a time. Still grinning, Jason gazed after him, then turned and smiled at Marjorie, who was wiping tears away. "Go on up, Miss MacTavish. Mrs. Brandeis is swaddling them, but I'm sure she can use your help."

Without a word, Marjorie rushed up the stairs after Malachai.

Derrick Peavey, still hunched in his chair and obviously disconcerted to have seen the captain whom he had known and revered for more than twenty years in such a state, looked at Jason, his eyes wide. "It was the Moors done it."

Jason only laughed.

Experience the Romance of
Rosanne Bittner